Praise for *The War...*

"A big, involving adventure...an accomp...

—San Francisco Chronicle

"A masterpiece of fairy-tale world-building, with a Faerie land that eerily mirrors the real world. The tone is often dark, but rich, building a wondrous setting in a fascinating world, with a classic reluctant hero and a cause worth cheering for."

—*Locus*

"[A]n intriguing new twist on old legends. Strong storytelling and memorable characters make this standalone cross-world fantasy the author's best work to date and a priority purchase for fantasy collections. Highly recommended."

—*Library Journal*

Praise for *Tailchaser's Song*

"A felic... ...without the coyness that sometimes charac- terizes ...ally believe the cat personalities and be quite wo... ...liments to Mr. Williams...a fantastic talent."

— ...e McCaffrey

"Fantasy lovers will lose their heart to Tail... ...s companions Pouncequick and Roofshadow."

—*School Library Journal*

Praise for The Shadow March series

"Williams opens another of the intricate, intriguing sagas that are his stock-in-trade. A page-turner."

—*Booklist*

"Impressive...packed with intriguing plot twists, this surreal fantasy takes the reader on a thrill ride.... The author's richly detailed world will enchant established fans and win new converts."

—Publishers Weekly, starred review

### Praise for *A Stark and Wormy Knight*

"Some writers are naturally at home with longer stories, others excel when restricted to shorter forms, but few can manage both with equal aplomb. Tad Williams is one such author."

—SF Site

"Best known for his epic fantasies, Williams offers 11 short stories that demonstrate his versatility with relative brevity...."

—Publishers Weekly

### Praise for *Rite*

"What makes this collection impressive is the variety, ingenuity, enthusiasm and storytelling craft the author exhibits."

—SF Site

"This collection of short writings presents another side of a writer known primarily for his novels (*Tailchaser's Song; The War of the Flowers*). Characterized by a wickedly keen sense of humor and, at times, a feel for the poignant...."

—Library Journal

# THE VERY BEST OF
# TAD WILLIAMS

TACHYON
SAN FRANCISCO

Introduction copyright © 2014 by Tad Williams
Cover art copyright © 2009 by Kerem Beyit
Cover design and interior design by Elizabeth Story

Tachyon Publications
1459 18th Street #139
San Francisco, CA 94107
415.285.5615
tachyon@tachyonpublications.com

www.tachyonpublications.com
smart science fiction and fantasy

Series Editor: Jacob Weisman
Project Editor: Jill Roberts

ISBN: 978-1-61696-137-4

Printed in the United States by Worzalla

First Edition: 2014
9 8 7 6 5 4 3 2 1

# CONTENTS

# Introduction

Where do stories come from? That's a question I hear a lot. Here's the truth, at least as I know it: they don't come from anywhere. They're already there and they just need to be recognized. Stories are all around, infinite in their numbers. They're in every word, every experience, every object.

Let's take a rock, for instance. Just a nice, smooth stone, about the size of your closed fist—not a gemstone, nothing so easy. Just an ordinary stone. What's the story there?

Well, Cain picked up a stone like that and killed his brother Abel. That's a pretty famous story right there, if a trifle on the brutal side. And David killed the giant Goliath with a stone, too. But we don't even need to deal with the homicidal aspect of stones to find stories.

What if you were the size of an ant? That simple stone is now something quite large. It might be blocking your path in the middle of an important journey. It might be an object of worship. It might have rolled down a hill and killed your entire family. (Oops, I said I wasn't going to do murderous stones.) As an ordinary-sized stone, it might be the key to a mystery—perhaps it has a bit of important DNA on it, or a few scratchings of a forgotten race of humanity—but it's lost among thousands of nearly identical stones. How do you find it? Will it be found in time?

A rock can be a paperweight on the desk of an old, cruel man. Why does he keep it? What can it mean to him? A rock might be the toy of a child who can't afford any better ones. It might used to keep a door from slamming shut so someone doesn't get locked out of her house—until the day the rock rolls a few inches too far and the door slams, and she can't get back in. There's a story there. I can tell.

And if there's a story in every rock—lots of stories, as I've just shown—

how many more stories are waiting out there, disguised as pigeons, or a flyer somebody dropped on the sidewalk, or masquerading as your mail carrier, or a strange wisp of cloud in an otherwise blue sky? How many stories are riding on the train next to you, reading their newspapers and wondering why you're inspecting them so strangely? How about the stories lying piled in your garage, posing as old clothes waiting to go to the Goodwill? Or the story pretending to be the neighbor's noisy dog? Did you step over a story in the gutter today because it looked like nothing more than a broken bottle, the label worn away by water and weather? Who dropped it there? What did that person do next?

That's the world I live in. If I suppress the expectedness, the ordinaryness of things and allow myself to look around a bit more carefully, I start seeing and hearing stories everywhere around me. Nearly every story in this book started that way, as a little something that caught my attention, perhaps a dream that clung for a moment after I woke up, or an unexplained aside in a history book, maybe as something as simple as a few words in the conversation of passing strangers, stripped of context and thus wonderfully inexplicable.

Like I said, stories don't just show up. They're not traveling salesmen, rapping at your door with a suitcase full of Romance and Mystery and Science Fiction. No, stories are already there, but you need to *look* for them. Maybe the story you want isn't in the salesman's briefcase with all that other, obvious stuff, but rather in the scuffed shoes he's wearing, or the slightly desperate smile on his face that suggests he hasn't made a sale yet today. Or maybe it's in the lies he tells on the phone when he calls home to say he'll be late. Maybe it isn't anything to do with the salesman, but instead comes from the elderly man across the street, who looks out his window and realizes that after living in the neighborhood for forty years, he doesn't know any of the neighbors the salesman is visiting.

Anything can be a story, because a story can be anything, any idea. Then the work starts. You have to pick up whatever set you thinking and really look at it, examine it from all angles, think about where it's been and what's happened to it and what might not have happened to it but could. You have to think about what would make someone else want to know the story. And then you have to take that rock, that conversation, that cloud, that salesman, whatever has caught your imagination, and work with it. You must shape it and expose its inner elements, bring them to light so that everyone else will see what you saw, hear what you heard, feel what you felt when you noticed that story.

Stories are all around. You don't have to look very far. They're in the room where you're reading this, in your life, in your memories, and there are lots more just outside your door. These are just a few that *I* found. You're welcome to share what I made of them, and I hope you enjoy them, but I left plenty of stories out there if you'd like to find some for yourself. They're a resource we'll never exhaust—one of the few. And the most important thing you have to understand is this: until they're found and shared, they're wasted. So even if you don't want to make any of your own, I'd love to have you take a look at mine.

Tad Williams
Santa Cruz, California
October 24, 2013

# THE OLD SCALE GAME

"Flee or be broiled to crackling! Those are your only choices!" The monster rustled in the depths of the cave. Its voice was loud because it was large, and dry because centuries of breathing deadly fire had roughened its throat.

"Neither, if you please." The man in armor waited as patiently as he could, hoping he was far enough back from the entrance that he would not actually broil if the tenor of conversation failed to improve. "I wish to discuss a proposition."

"A what?" The outrage was unfeigned. "I had heard that there were knights abroad in this miserable modern age who practiced such perversities, but I never dreamed I should ever suffer such a foul offer myself! Prepare to be radiantly heated, young fool!"

"I am not remotely young, and I don't think I'm a fool either," the knight said. "And it's not that kind of proposition. Ye gods, fellow, I haven't even seen you yet, not to mention the smell of you is not pleasing, at least to a human being."

When the dragon spoke after a longish silence, there was perhaps a touch of hurt feelings in its voice. "Ah. Not that kind of proposition." Another pause. "How do I know that when I come out you will not attempt to slay me?"

"If I felt sure I could slay you, I wouldn't be here talking. I give you my word as a knight that you are safe from me as long as you offer me no harm."

"Hmmmph." That noise, accompanied by a puff of steam, was followed shortly by the sound of something long and scaly dragging itself over stone as the dragon emerged from the cave. The knight noted that, although the great worm had clearly seen better days, his scales dingy and nicked, his color decidedly less than robust, he was still quite big enough and probably quite hot enough to keep negotiation more appealing than attack.

"I am Guldhogg," declared the worm, each word echoing sonorously across the hillside. "Why do you seek me? Have you grown tired of living?"

"Tired of starving, to be quite frank, and even recreational drinking is beginning to lose its charms." The knight made a courtly bow. "My name is Sir Blivet of no fixed address, until recently a retired (and impoverished) dragon slayer. This was not a happy state of affairs—in fact, I had recently begun to consider a serious return to strong drink— but lately it's worsened. I've been dragged out of retirement by the people of Handselmansby in order to destroy you—they offered me a rather interesting sum..."

The dragon reared to nearly the height of the treetops. "You coward! You have foresworn yourself!" He made a rumbling noise, and a cloud of fire belched from his jaws, but before the stream of flame had gone more than a few feet Guldhogg began to cough. The fire flickered and died. A puff of steam, more wisp than cloud, floated up into the morning sky. "Just a m-m-moment," the dragon said. "Give me a chance to c-c-catch my breath, f-foul knight." He had stopped coughing, but had begun hiccoughing instead. At each explosion another steampuff spun lazily into the air. "Honestly, I will broil you very..." Hiccough. "I will..." Hiccough. "Broil you very thoroughly..." Again, a hiccough.

"Noble Guldhogg, most vintage of worms, spare me this tosh." Sir Blivet sat down on the ground. He had not even drawn his sword. "The people of Handselmansby may not know you are old and unwell, but I do. You could no more broil me than you could earn a cardinal's red hat from the pontiff of Rome."

"Knight of a dog!" The dragon drew himself up once more. "Hmmmph. I mean: Dog of a knight! Perhaps I do have a bit of a problem with my flame just now, but I can still destroy you! Have I not my claws and teeth, or at least most of them? Can I not fly, with a fair tailwind and occasional stops for rest? Do not think me so easily defeated, insulting and unkind human person."

"I agree, mighty Guldhogg. You are still a formidable foe, even in your age and infirmity."

"Yes! Yes, I am!" The dragon leaned forward, his great yellow eyes narrowing. When he spoke, he sounded a bit worried. "Am I really such a laughingstock? The time was once when Guldhogg's name was enough to set women screaming and children crying."

"And it still is," said Sir Blivet. "The...falloff in your skills is not widely known. In fact, the only reason it's known to me is because I did a little investigation as I was trying to think of some way I could avoid fighting you. Because..." Blivet removed his helmet, revealing hair and beard that, although it could have been called salt-and-pepper, contained far more salt than pepper. Furthermore, although the hair on his head might once have covered a large territory, it had now largely conceded the front and top of the knight's scalp and was retreating rather hurriedly toward the back of his head. "As you can see—and which contributes not a little to the unhappy state of my own affairs—I am not so young myself."

Guldhogg squinted. "By my great scaly ancestors, you aren't, are you?"

"No. I really didn't want anything to do with this whole thing, but poverty makes powerful arguments."

The beast shook his long head. "So despite what the advancing years have done to you, Sir Knight, you decided to attack a poor old dragon. For shame, sir. For shame."

"Oh, for the love of my good Lord Jesu!" The man in the tarnished suit of armor shook his head in irritation. "Don't you listen? I just said I don't want to fight you. In fact, I would like to offer a bargain—a mutually beneficial bargain, at that. Will you pay proper attention?"

Guldhogg's eyes narrowed again, but this time it seemed to be in careful thought instead of suspicion. At last the great worm nodded.

"I will listen, Sir Knight."

"Call me Sir Blivet. Or even just Blivet. After all, we're going to be working together."


The wealthy burghers of Handselmansby, an up-and-coming market town whose Chamber of Commerce had aspirations to make it another

Shoebury, or even a Thetford, threw a small celebration for Blivet at the Rump and Hock Inn, with a no-host mead bar and finger foods.

"Handselmansby is grateful for your courage and prowess, good sir knight," said the mayor as he handed over the promised bag of gold. "But if you destroyed the terrible worm Guldhogg, where is its carcass?"

"Ah," said Blivet. "Yes. You see, although my last blow was a mortal one, the fell beast had just enough strength to fly away, leaking blood and fire in what I promise you was a very unsurvivable sort of way."

As the knight reached the five-mile post on the road out of Handselmansby a large shadow dropped from the sky and landed with an awkward thump beside him. It took Guldhogg a few moments to catch his breath before he could speak—he clearly hadn't done much flying in recent years. "So it went well? They gave you the money?"

"Yes. And I have already divided it in half." Blivet showed him the sacks and offered him one. "Here is your share."

Guldhogg spilled some gold into his immense clawed forepaw. "Lovely. I haven't had any of this shiny stuff for a bit. Not quite enough to lie on top of, of course, but better than nothing." He sighed. "The only problem is, of course, now I've got nowhere to keep it. Having been driven out of the Greater Handselmansby Area, I mean. Where my cave was."

Sir Blivet nodded. "I agree, that is unfortunate, but I'm certain you can find a new home somewhere else in the greater Danelaw. In fact, I'll need to find a new place myself, because otherwise once the news of my successful dragon slaying spreads I'll have people banging on my door every week with new quests. I doubt I shall be so lucky again in finding a reasonable partner, and I no longer have any interest in real anti-monster combat—those days are far, far behind me. To be honest I want only to find a small but regular source of income so I can settle down and enjoy my golden years. Maybe I'd even take a wife..."

Guldhogg looked a bit hurt. "You seek a new and reasonable partner, Sir Blivet? I would like to think of myself as more than just reasonable—in fact, I flatter myself that I gave more than was even bargained for. Did I not spout fire most impressively above the treetops so the townsfolk could see how fierce was our battle? Did I not bellow and roar until the welkin itself shook as if it were fevered? And now I am without a home and, except for this gold, just as in want of an income as you are."

"I've never really known what a welkin is, so I'll take your word on that part," Blivet said politely. "But otherwise you are completely correct, honorable Guldhogg: you were a more than amenable opponent, and should we ever find ourselves in a position to do something like this again..."

After a long silent interval had passed, the dragon cleared his throat, loosing a tiny, hot cumulus. "You seem to have stopped in mid-sentence. Did you forget what you were going to say?"

"No. Come along with me for a while," says Blivet, climbing up into his saddle. "I have just had an idea I would like to discuss with you, but I would prefer we were not observed here together, counting the people of Handselmansby's money."

Over the next few years, East Anglia and the Danelaw were beset with a terrible rash of dragonings. Although no citizens were killed, a great deal of property loss occurred, especially the theft of sheep and other edible creatures. The famous dragonslayer Sir Blivet found himself in constant demand from Benfleet all the way up to Torksey and beyond. Even the King of York asked Blivet to intervene when a particularly unpleasant monster (called the Wheezing Worm by the frightened townsfolk) took up residence in Kirkham Gorge. The veteran dragon-foe was able to drive the creature out again in only a matter of days, and was rewarded handsomely by the king for it, at which point the knight modestly quit York again.

Oddly, as these new boom years for monster hunting continued, they did not seem to benefit other dragonslayers quite as much as they did Sir Blivet. When Percy of Pevensey and Gwydion Big-Axe came searching for the beasts who were causing so much unhappiness in the East Midlands, they could find scarcely a trace, despite Sir Blivet's willingness to tell them exactly where to look. The two great western wormhunters rode away disappointed, as did many others. Only Blivet seemed able to locate the beasts, and soon he could scarcely rid one area of its wormish scourge before being called to help another dragon-troubled populace, often quite close by. It seemed the dragon peril was spreading, and the knight spent far more time on his horse than under a roof.

"To be honest, Guldhogg, my friend," Blivet admitted to the dragon one day in their forest camp, "I'm getting a bit tired of this whole dodge." They were taking a break, having just finished adding their latest fees to a pile of chests and caskets so heavy with coin they now needed a horse-drawn wagon just to haul it all from town to town and vale to vale. "Not that it hasn't been fun."

Guldhogg nodded as he nibbled on a side of mutton. "I know what you mean, Bliv, old man. I wonder if we don't need to expand our territory a bit. I swear I'm seeing the same peasants over and over."

"Well, one peasant does look much like another," Blivet explained. "Especially when they're pointing up at one and screaming. They're like foot soldiers that way."

"It's not just that. I think some of them recognized me during the last job. A family that must have moved here from Barrowby—you remember Barrowby, don't you?"

"Where you stole the chancellor's horse out of his stable and left the bones on his roof?"

"That's the place. Anyway, when I flew over the town here yesterday, spouting fire and bellowing, I heard this fellow originally from Barrowby shout, 'I've seen that bloody dragon before!' Quite rude, really."

"Indeed." Blivet stared at his pile of gold where it sat on the wagon. He frowned, considering. "So you recommend pastures new?"

"Seems like a good idea. Don't want to push our luck."

But Blivet was tugging at his beard, still troubled. "Yes, but as I was saying, Guldhogg, it goes further than that for me. I'm a bit weary of all this tramping around. The idea of moving on to the south, or out to the West Midlands...well, to be honest, I think I'd rather have some peace and stability—maybe even find a nice woman my age and settle down. We've made almost enough money. One more job should secure both our financial futures." He paused. "In fact, I believe I can even see a way we might fulfill both tasks at once—a last top-up of our bank accounts as well as a permanent residence for both of us! How is that for dispatching several birds with one projectile?"

"A home for both of us? I'm touched, Blivet. But how?"

"The thing is, although you are by far the most profitable of them, you're not the only beast who has been making things difficult for folk around here. This is Tenth Century England, after all—a few years ago I could scarcely stand up and stretch without nudging a wyvern or a griffin or somesuch. They've all gotten a bit scarcer now, but there are still a good few other monsters scattered around the island."

"Of course," says Guldhogg. "I know that. It's one of the reasons people don't seem surprised when I keep turning up in new places pretending to be a different dragon than the last time. Honestly, Blivet, you sound as though you're unhappy there are still a few of us left."

The knight leaned close, although there was nobody in sight for miles across the windswept heath. "Just a few miles down the road, near Fiskhaven by the coast, dwells a terrible ogre by the name of Ljotunir."

"What a strange name!" said Guldhogg.

"Yes, well, the point is, he's apparently a nasty fellow who's got the town of Fiskhaven all upset. I'm told it's a lovely place, clean sea air, several very nice beachfront castles going for rock-bottom prices since the collapse of the dried herring market. And Ljotunir is tough but not invincible. He's about twelve feet tall and quite strong, of course, but not fireproof...if you see where I'm going."

"No," said Guldhogg a bit sourly. "No, Bliv, my dear old bodkin, I'm afraid I don't."

"Simple enough, Guld, my reptilian chum. We can't settle down because everywhere we go, I make a big show of driving you away or even killing you. That means you can't very well hang around with me afterward. But if we can drive away this ogre together...well, we'll be paid handsomely again, but this time you won't have done any harm, so we'll both be able to stay on in Fiskhaven. We can buy a castle and land, settle down, and enjoy the fruits of our partnership—" he gestured to the heavily laden wagon, "—in peace and quiet, and even more importantly in one place, as befits individuals of our mature and sensible years. No more tramping."

"And what am I supposed to eat?" asked Guldhogg. "After all, it is devouring the local livestock that usually makes me *dracona non grata* in the first place." The great worm suddenly grew fretful. "You don't really think my presence is noxious, do you, Blivvy? I mean, we've known each other a while now. You can speak sooth."

"You are lovely company," the knight said firmly. "Only the shortsighted, the dragon-bigoted, or the just plain rude would suggest otherwise. But you didn't let me finish describing my plan, which includes provision for your sustenance. We have money, Guldy. Once the ogre has been dispatched, we will settle in Fiskhaven and become farmers! We'll buy sheep and raise them. You may eat as many as you need, as long as you leave the little ones to grow up into bigger ones—then there will always be more sheep to eat. That's how farming works, you know."

"Really? That's marvelous!" Guldhogg shook his great scaly head. "What will they think of next?"

The battle with the terrible ogre Ljotunir raged for days, ending at last in the hills high above Fiskhaven, so that the whole of the vale rang with the sounds of combat. When it was over and Sir Blivet was about to go down to the town and collect his ogre-slaying money, he noticed that Guldhogg looked preoccupied, even sad.

"What's wrong, dear old chum?"

"It's the ogre. He's so miserable!" Guldhogg nodded toward Ljotunir, who was sitting against the trunk of an oak tree, making loud snuffling sounds.

Blivet took off his heavy helmet and walked across the clearing to where Ljotunir sat—the tree was leaning alarmingly from the weight. The monster's cheeks were indeed wet with tears. "What ails you, good sir ogre?" Sir Blivet asked. "Are you regretting having settled for a one-quarter share? You understand that the risk of this business is ours, don't you? And that we have built up our reputation over several years? But perhaps instead you are mourning your lost reputation as an unbeatable and fearsome giant?"

"It's not that, and it's not the money." Ljotunir sniffed and wiped his face with a kerchief the size of a tablecloth. (In fact, it was a tablecloth.) "It's... well, I don't really have any place to go anymore. I agreed to this because I didn't want to fight. Frankly, I haven't been myself the last century—I have the cruelest sort of aches and pains in my joints from this seaside air, Sir Knight, and the noise of the wind keeps me from sleeping most nights—but I'm still very fond of the place. Where will I go now? How will I live?" Alarmingly, the giant burst into tears again, his sobs shaking a nest full of bewildered young squirrels out of the leaning oak and onto the ground.

"Here now," Blivet soothed him. "Surely your share of the reward money will be more than enough to purchase you a lovely stone hut in the wilderness somewhere. Perhaps you should move farther north—I hear that the arctic air of the Orkneys is lovely and dry, which should be easier on your infirmity."

"Dry, yes, but cold enough to freeze the berries off a basilisk!" said the ogre cheerlessly. "That would play hob with my joints, now wouldn't it?" Again his chest heaved.

"Oh, look at the poor fellow!" Guldhogg said, coming up. "He's so sad! His little face is all scrunched up! Isn't there anything we can do?"

Blivet examined the sobbing giant, whose "little face" was the size of the knight's war-shield. At last Blivet sighed, turned to the dragon, and said, "I may have a solution. But first I'll need that cask of ale."

"Really?" asked Guldhogg, who was interested to see what odd human thing Blivet would do next. "What are you going to do with it?"

"Drink it," the knight said. "Most of it, anyway."

Sir Blivet had just realized that if he wanted to make his friend Guldhogg happy, they were going to have to let the now-homeless ogre join them—which meant that, once again, they would be moving on in the morning.

It didn't seem too bad at first. Ljotunir's presence meant that Guldhogg could take the occasional week off from menacing townsfolk, leaving that strenuous chore to the Ljotunir, and that they could even go back to some localities they had already scourged of dragons (well, one dragon, anyway), but which would now need their help with ogre infestations. But Blivet himself was not getting any days off, and they were doing a great deal of tramping from county to county.

Guldhogg couldn't help noticing that the knight drank a great deal of ale every night before falling asleep now, or that his conversation, quite expansive only a few weeks earlier, was now reduced mostly to, "Forsooth, whatever."

And things were getting worse.

News of the confidence game that Blivet and Guldhogg were running in the middle of England had begun to spread around the island—not among the townsfolk who were its targets but within the nation's large community of fabulous, mythical, and semi-imaginary animals. These creatures could not help noticing that two very large members of their kind, a dragon and an ogre, had found a way not only to survive, but also to thrive. As word of this breakthrough got around, Blivet and his friends soon found that everywhere they went they were getting business propositions from various haunts and horrors down on their luck or otherwise in need of a change.

"I know it will be a bit hard on us, Blivet old friend," said Guldhogg. "But I can't help it—I know how these creatures feel. It's been a long, bad time for mythical monsters, and it's only going to get worse when the Renaissance shows up in a few hundred years."

"But we can't use all of them," Blivet protested. "What right-thinking town council is going to hire a knight to slay a couple of cobbler's elves?"

"We can find work for them. Say, look at your boots, Blivvy. Wouldn't you like to have those re-soled?"

Blivet sighed. "Pass me that ale, will you?"

Before the year had passed, Blivet and Guldhogg had added to their enterprise (mostly at the dragon's urging) a cockatrice, a pair of hippogriffs who were passionately in love with each other and had decided to run away from their hippogriffic families, plus an expanding retinue of shellycoats, lubber men, bargests, and suchlike other semi-mythical folk. What had once been a compact, convenient man-and-dragon partnership was becoming a sort of strange covert parade traveling from county to county across the center of England.

Guldhogg had hoped the added numbers would make their business easier, because they could now revisit places they had already saved several more times (and not only from ogres or chimeras, but also from less-feared but still unpleasant fates, like a long and painful season of being harried by bogbears). Any gain in income, however, had been offset by the need to keep their gigantic, semi-mythical menagerie hidden, on the move, and—most importantly—fed as they crossed back and forth across the English midlands.

The biggest problem, of course, was that Blivet himself had simply grown weary of marching from town to town, pretending to kill things. He may also have been slightly depressed to find that instead of revering him as a noble dragonslayer, his countrymen now viewed him as little more than a jumped-up exterminator, chasing shellycoats and leprechauns away as if they were so many rats.

Guldhogg couldn't help noticing that Blivet was going through a great deal of ale, and that he was becoming less and less interested in keeping the now massive operation hidden. The movement of their troop from city to city was threatening to become more parade than stealthy exercise. Already a few humans had joined their train, giving the whole thing more of a feeling of a holiday fair than a serious moneymaking enterprise. Even a dragon could see that it was only a matter of time until some of the townsfolk realized just how badly they had been cozened.

And Guldhogg wasn't the only one who could see what was coming: Blivet had begun buying his ale in bulk.

The irony, not lost on Guldhogg, was that they could probably have made more money selling the local people tickets to see all the strange animals—they were all happy enough to dump considerable sums at ragged local fairs—but Blivet and the dragon had to work from dawn until long after midnight each day just getting their charges fed and keeping them moving; any greater degree of organization would have been impossible.

Then a narrowly averted tragedy in Smethwick, when a family of werewolves left the troop to hunt for supper and ran into a children's crusade, finally made it clear to Guldhogg that things had to change. (The near-catastrophe just seemed to make Blivet even more thirsty.)

The dragon recognized that his knightly friend was at a serious crossroads, probably one more septic basilisk bite away from leaving the now-sprawling enterprise behind in search of a calmer life. Guldhogg was an old dragon, and although he was long past his own mating days, he also recognized his friend had a need for nurturing companionship of the sort that even a vast army of bogbears, ogres, and camelopards could not provide.

Two of the newest members of the troop were articulate ravens, raucous, sly, and clever. In exchange for a few shiny articles out of Guldhogg's now large collection, they agreed to undertake some work for him, hunting the highways and byways of Late Dark Ages Britain for a situation that met the dragon's specifications.

One day, while the troop was camped by the River Derwent to water the selkies, the ravens returned with the news Guldhogg had been waiting for.

"Haunted Forest?" Blivet looked doubtfully at the sign (and perhaps slightly unsteadily, since he had already been into the ale that morning). Even from the outskirts, the forest the sign announced looked likely to breed nightmares. The trees of the wood grew extremely close together, and they were also extremely large and old, casting such deep shadows that it was almost hard to believe there was turf beneath them. The location beneath lowering mountains was stone silent, and the air of the little valley, far from civilization but close to a major thoroughfare, was dreadful enough to put even the basilisks off their breakfasts (truly not an easy thing to do). "Looks nasty. What monster lurks in here?" the knight asked. "And even if it might be of use to our venture, why should I go look for it instead of you or Ljotunir or one of the other large creatures? I haven't fought anything dangerous for real in years."

"Yes, but you are the best judge of monstrous character," Guldhogg said soothingly. "We all admire your judgment. We also agree your ideas are the finest and most useful."

Blivet gave him a skeptical look. "Really?"

"Oh, absolutely. Especially when you're not drinking too much."

The knight scowled. "You haven't answered my question. What monster lurks in this unhallowed place?" He shivered a little in the chilly wind that seemed to whistle out of the forest itself rather than from anywhere else.

"Some kind of she-creature," said Guldhogg offhandedly. "I couldn't say for certain."

"And how can anyone care about this she-creature, out in the middle of nowhere?" Blivet looked around. "Honestly, Guldhogg, who would pay to have it dispatched? There isn't a town within twenty furlongs of this place." In truth, to Blivet, the dragon seemed a bit nervous. "Are you sure this is the right forest?"

"Oh, absolutely. And there are excellent reasons for you to go in there," said Guldhogg firmly. "Absolutely, there are. I'll explain it all later, Blivvy. Go on, now. I'll be right here, listening. Call if you need me."

Sir Blivet gave the dragon a last dubious look, then banged down the visor of his helmet, took his lance in his arm, and spurred forward into the trees, perhaps thinking that the sooner he could get this over with, the sooner he could get back to the companionability of an ale-cask, which required no monster-bearding as a price of friendship.

The forest was just as dire inside as it appeared from the outside, shadowed and silent, with the webs of huge but not presently visible spiders swaying in the breeze. Sir Blivet felt as if eyes were watching him at every step, and he had just about decided that he was going to return to the camp and declare the she-beast unfindable when someone called him.

"Sir Knight?"

He turned, his stomach suddenly sour with unease. A robed figure stepped from the shadows and out onto the deer track his horse had been following. "Who are you?" he asked, trying to remember the boldly fearless tone he had been able to summon easily in his younger days, before he knew any better. "Are you in need of assistance?"

"I could be," the stranger said. "Are you Sir Guldhogg?"

"Sir Gul..." Blivet shook his head in confusion. "No. Guldhogg is a friend of mine, but..." He peered at the shrouded figure, but it was hard to make out much of the face in the hood. "I am in fact Sir Blivet, semi-fabled dragonslayer. Who are you?"

"I am the She-Creature of Haunted Forest." The newcomer threw back her hood, revealing herself to be a quite attractive short-haired woman of mature years, slender of neck and discerning of eye.

"You are the she-creature?"

"Well, I'm really more of a witch." She gave an embarrassed laugh. "But when I first moved here several years ago, I spread the rumor of a dangerous and deadly beast in these woods so that I would be left alone. People have a tendency to get obsessed with witches, and before you know it they're looking you over for third nipples and hunting for kindling—you know what I mean. But I'm afraid I did the job a bit too well." She shrugged and indicated the dark forest. "Everybody moved out. Even the people in the nearby towns all migrated in fear. So here I am."

"So here you are." Blivet knew it wasn't the most sensible thing to say, but he was a bit taken aback by the unexpected fairness of the she-creature's face, and her modest but sensible speech. "But why, exactly?"

"Because I live here." She gave him a look that suggested she did not think highly of his intellect.

"No, I mean, why am I here?" Blivet was beginning to wish he'd waited until later in the day before starting on the ale. "No, that's not right either. What I mean is, why did you and...and Sir Guldhogg arrange this meeting?"

"Ah. Fair question." She smiled. "Who do you think a witch's customers are, Sir Blivet? People. You want them to fear you, to be impressed by you, but you don't want them to actually leave, because then who is one going to make love potions for? Whose sick calves and sick babies is one going to cure? For whom is one going to tell the future with cartomancy or tea leaves?"

"Ah, I see what you mean about that, I suppose. But this meeting..."

"Guldhogg opened the negotiations by raven. A good idea, since the local lord abandoned the place along with the peasants and the forest-folk, which means I haven't been getting a lot of mail in the old way."

"Oh, I see," said Blivet, who was now convinced he didn't see anything at all. "Opened negotiations."

"Mr. Hogg told me that you and he and the rest of your...guild? Organization? Anyway, that your lot had been offered a tidy sum of money to come and dispatch the She-Creature of Haunted Forest, and that he felt honor-bound to let me know you were on your way. So I wrote back to him and offered him a business proposition, instead."

Ah. Now it all made a bit more sense, Blivet decided. "Business. Yes. So, have you a lot of gold?"

She laughed again. Blivet couldn't help noticing she was actually rather pretty—in a serious, mature sort of way—and even prettier when she was amused. "Ye gods, no!" said the witch. "I haven't a ha'penny. How would I, with all of my customers gone to Rutland County and points south? No, I haven't got any money at all. Walk with me now, and let's talk about this."

Blivet dismounted, although he couldn't quite see the sense of it. Still, he found himself willing to spend more time in the company of this attractive woman. She had a personality that wasn't what he would have expected from a witch. "But if you haven't any money, what are we going to talk about? I mean, business-wise?"

Now it was her turn to shake her head. "Silly man. As if gold was the only valuable thing in the world. My name is Hecate, by the way. Named after the goddess."

"Pleased to meet you, Mistress Hecate."

"I don't have a cent—but I am the owner of this forest by fee simple. I did a favor for the local lord—cured his daughter of the pox—so when he moved out (well, fled, really) he gave it to me, mostly to keep me from undoing his daughter's cure, I suspect." She cleared her throat. "Which means I am, as is sometimes said, cash-poor but land-rich, handsome Sir Blivet, and I would like to offer you and Sir Guldhogg a mutually beneficial alliance."

It took them a year and a surprisingly large fraction of their savings to build a fence around the forest, which although not large was still a forest. Workers had to be trucked in by wagon for all the jobs that couldn't be performed by redcaps and hunkypunks. Then they needed another year for clearing and building, with the result that the Dark Ages had almost ended by the day the grand opening finally arrived.

"I still don't think it's fair," the dragon was saying in a sullen tone. "After all, it was my idea. I led you to each other. I arranged it all, more or less. And you're still going to call it Blivetland?"

"Don't sulk, Guldhogg," said Hecate. "You haven't seen the surprise yet."

"He's always that way," said Sir Blivet. "He doesn't drink, either."

"And neither should you," said Guldhogg, still grumpy.

"Don't be mean, Guldy," the witch said. "My Blivvy's been very abstemious lately."

"Too bloody busy to be anything else," the knight agreed. "Do you know how much work it was just setting up the concession stands and teaching boggarts to count?"

"Well, it was either that or putting them on display, and you know what they did when we tried that. We can't have them flinging boggart dung at the paying customers, can we?"

"Well, I think it's time for us to get out and meet the public," Blivet said. "Come on, Guldhogg. I've got something to show you."

Considering how deserted this entire stretch of the north had been only a couple of short years ago, it was quite impressive to see the crowds lined up hundreds deep all along the great fence, waiting to enter through the massive front gate. The dragon was all for letting them in immediately—"Money is burning a hole in their pockets, Blivet!"—but the knight forbade it until a last chore had been done.

"Just pull this rope," he told the dragon. "Go on, old chum, take it in your mouth and yank."

Guldhogg, who had been gazing with keen regret at the carved wooden sign over the gate, the one that read "Blivetland," shrugged his wings and pulled on the rope. An even larger sign, this one painted on canvas, rolled down to hang in plain view of the entire assembly.

"Oh," said Guldhogg, sounding quite overcome. "Oh, is that...is that really...?"

"Yes, silly, it's you," said Hecate, elbowing him in his substantial, scale-covered ribs. "Well, except we're calling you 'Guldy Hogg,' because it sounds friendlier." She and Blivet and Guldhogg looked up at the gigantic sign rippling in the spring breeze, with its huge and colorful painted representation of Guldhogg himself, face stretched in a friendly grin. "It's everywhere, you know," she said.

"What is?"

"Your picture, silly. You're the official mascot of Blivetland. We have Guldy Hogg souvenir tunics, tea towels—even hats!" She took one of the latter from behind her back and handed it to Sir Blivet, who put it on with only the smallest show of reluctance. The protruding nostrils of the dragon face on the hat looked almost like the round ears of some bizarre rodent. "It's a wonderful likeness, Guldy!" cried Hecate. "So handsome!"

As Guldhogg stared at his own face perched atop his friend's head, the gates of Blivetland opened and the first crowd of paying customers pushed their way in, hurrying forward into the forest to see Griffin Island and Nessie's Cove and ride on Guldy Hogg's Wild Wing Ride, which consisted of large tubs whirling around on ropes, the whole thing powered by Ljotunir the ogre spinning a sizeable potter's wheel assembly with his strong and astoundingly ugly feet. Excited people seemed already to have filled every festive corner of the forest, and the vendors were already selling small beer and goblin goodies hand over fist.

The sound of money clinking into Blivetland's coffers put the three founders in a very benign mood.

"Isn't this better than tramping around the country?" asked Hecate. "We stay here and the country comes to us!"

"But I thought I was going to be allowed to retire," growled Sir Blivet. "Instead, you will work me into my quickly approaching grave."

"Nonsense. You and Guldy only have to put on two brief shows a day— well, three on Saturdays—and he's the one who has to do all the costume changes, pretending to be all the other dragons you slew."

"They were all him anyway!" the knight protested.

"Well, everyone loves to see the two of you. It wouldn't be the Merriest Place on Ye Olde Earth if you pair weren't pretending to try to kill each other at one and four every afternoon." She leaned over and kissed Blivet's whiskery cheek. "And just think—no more traveling!"

After that, Guldhogg decided he wanted to try a funnel cake, so they set off toward the Faerie Food Courte together—the knight, his lady, and his best friend. The sounds of fable being turned into coin rose all around them, a seemingly basic exchange but with an additional dividend of happiness to all parties. Even in the tenth century, that made for a pretty good state of affairs.

# The *Storm Door*

Nightingale did not take the first cab he saw when he stepped out into the rainy San Francisco streets. He never did. Some might call it superstition, but in his profession the line between "superstitions" and "rules of survival" was rather slender. He stepped back onto the curb to avoid the spray of water as the second cab pulled up in response to his wave. Paranormal investigators didn't make enough money to ruin a pair of good shoes for no reason.

*Somebody should have warned me that saving the world from unspeakable horrors is like being a teacher—lots of job satisfaction, but the money's crap.*

"Thirty-three Gilman Street," he told the driver, an ex-hippie on the edge of retirement age, shoulder-length gray hair draggling out from under his Kangol hat and several silver rings on the fingers holding the wheel. "It's off Jones."

"You got it." The driver pulled back into traffic, wipers squeaking as city lights smeared and dribbled across the glass beside Nightingale's head. "Helluva night," he said. "I know we need the rain and everything, but... shit, man."

Nathan Nightingale had spent so much of the past week in a small, overheated, and nearly airless room that he would have happily run through this downpour naked, but he only nodded and said, "Yeah. Helluva night."

"Gonna be a lot more before it's over, too. That's what they said. The storm door's open." The driver turned down the music a notch. "Kind of a weird expression, huh? Makes it sound like they're..." he lifted his fingers in twitching monster-movie talons, "*coming to get us*. Whooo! I mean, it's just clouds, right? It's nature."

"This? Yeah, it's just nature," agreed Nightingale, his thoughts already drawn back to that small room, those clear, calm, terrifying eyes. "But sometimes even nature can be unnatural."

"Huh? Oh, yeah, I guess so. Good one." But it was clear by his tone that the driver feared he'd missed the point.

"That's it—the tall house there."

The driver peered out the window. "Whoa, that's a spooky one, man. You sure you gonna be okay, man? This is kind of a tough neighborhood..."

"I'll be fine, thanks," said Nightingale. "I've been here before—it was kind of my second home."

"If you say so." The driver called just before Nightingale slammed the door, "Hey, remember about that storm door. Better get an umbrella!"

Nightingale raised his hand as the man drove off. *An umbrella.* He almost smiled, but the wet night was getting to him. *If only all problems were that easy to solve.*


As he pressed the button beside the mailbox lightning blazed overhead, making it seem as though one had caused the other. A moment later the thunder crashed down, so near that he did not hear the sound of the door being buzzed open but felt the handle vibrating under his hand.

The light was out in the first-floor stairwell, and no lights were on at all on the second floor, what Uncle Edward called "the showroom," although no one ever saw it but a few old, trusted collector friends. Enough of the streetlight's glow leaked in that Nightingale could see the strange silhouettes of some of the old man's prize possessions, fetish dolls and funerary votives and terra cotta tomb statuettes, a vast audience of silent, wide-eyed shapes watching Nightingale climb the stairs. It was an excellent collection, but what made it truly astounding were the stories behind the pieces, most of them dark, many of them horrifying. In fact, it had been his godfather's arcane tales and bizarre trophies that had first lured Nightingale onto his odd career path: at an age when most boys wanted to be football players or firemen, young Nate had decided he wanted to hunt ghosts and fight demons. Later, when others were celebrating their first college beer-busts, Nightingale had already attended strange ceremonies on high English moors and deep in Thai jungles and

Louisiana bayous. He had heard languages never shaped for the use of human tongues, had seen men die for no reason, and others live when they should have been dead. But through the years, when the unnatural things he saw and felt and learned overwhelmed him, he always came back here for his godfather's advice and support. This was one of those times. In fact, this was probably the worst time he could remember.

Strangely, the third floor of the house was dark, too.

"Edward? Uncle Edward? It's me, Nathan. Are you here?" Had the old man forgotten he was coming and gone out with his caretaker Jenkins somewhere? God forbid, a medical emergency...Nightingale stopped to listen. Was that the quiet murmuring of the old man's breathing machine?

Something stirred on the far side of the room and his hackles rose; his hand strayed to his inside coat pocket. A moment later the desk lamp clicked on, revealing the thin, lined face of his godfather squinting against the sudden light. "Oh," Edward said, taking a moment to find the air to speak. "Guh-goodness! Nate, is that you? I must have dozed off. When did it get so dark?"

Relieved, Nightingale went to the old man and gave him a quick hug, being careful not to disturb the tracheotomy cannula or the ventilator tubes. As always, Edward Arvedson felt like little more than a suit full of bones, but somehow he had survived in this failing condition for almost a decade. "Where's Jenkins?" Nightingale asked. "It gave me a start when I came up and the whole house was dark."

"Oh, I had him take the night off, poor fellow. Working himself to death. Pour me a small sherry, will you, there's a good man, and sit down and tell me what you've learned. There should be a bottle of Manzanilla already open. No, don't turn all those other lights on. I find I'm very sensitive at the moment. This is enough light for you to find your way to the wet bar, isn't it?"

Nightingale smiled. "I could find it without any light at all, Uncle Edward."

When he'd poured a half glass for the old man and a little for himself as well, Nightingale settled into the chair facing the desk and looked his mentor up and down. "How are you feeling?"

Arvedson waved a dismissive hand. "Fine, fine. Never felt better. And now that we're done with that nonsense, tell me your news, Nate. What happened? I've been worrying ever since you told me what you thought was happening."

"Well, it took me a while to find a volunteer. Mostly because I was trying to avoid publicity—you know, all that 'Nightingale—Exorcist to the Stars' nonsense."

"You shouldn't have changed your name—it sounds like a Hollywood actor now. Your parents wouldn't have approved, anyway. What was wrong with Natan Näktergal? It was good enough for your father."

He smiled. "Too old country, Uncle Edward. Remember, being well-known gets me into a lot of places. It also leads people to misjudge me."

Arvedson made a face. He still hadn't touched his sherry. "Fine. I'm also old country, I suppose. I should be grateful you even visit. Tell me what happened."

"I'm trying to. As I said, it wouldn't do to recruit just anyone. Ideally, I needed someone with special training...but who gets trained for something like this? I figured that my best bet was through my Tibetan contacts. Tibetan Buddhists spend years studying the Bardo Thodol, preparing to take the journey of dying, which gave me a much larger group to choose from. I finally settled on a man in Seattle named Geshe, who had pancreatic cancer. He'd refused pain relief and the doctors felt certain he only had a few days left when I met him, but he was remarkably calm and thoughtful. I told him what I wanted, and why, and he said yes."

"So you had found your...what was your word? Your 'necronaut.'"

Nightingale nodded. "That's what I called it before I met Geshe—it sounded better than 'mineshaft canary.' But after I got to know him it...it seemed a little glib. But he was precisely the sort of person I was looking for—a man trained almost since childhood to die with his eyes and mind open."

Lightning flashed and a peal of thunder shivered the windows. In the wake, another wash of rain splattered against the glass. "Filthy weather," said Arvedson. "Do you want another drink before you start? You'll have to get it yourself, of course, since we don't have Jenkins."

"No, I'm fine." Nightingale stared at his glass. "I'm just thinking." Lightning flashed again and so he waited for the thunder before continuing.

"You remember how this started, of course. Those earliest reports of spontaneous recovery by dying patients...well, it didn't seem like anything I needed to pay attention to. But then that one family whose daughter went into sudden remission from leukemia after the last rites had already been said..."

"I remember. Very young, wasn't she? Nine?"

"Yes, a few weeks before her tenth birthday. But of course what caught my attention was when the parents started claiming it wasn't their daughter at all, that she'd changed in ways that no illness could explain. But when I got in to see the child she was asleep, and although she looked surprisingly healthy compared to my general experience with possession cases, I couldn't get any kind of feeling from her one way or another. When I tried to contact the family a few days later they'd moved and no one could find them.

"There were others, too—too many to be coincidence, most of them unknown to the general public. The greatest hindrance in these situations is the gutter press, of course—any real study, let alone any chance to help the victims and their families, is destroyed by the sort of circus they create. These days, with television and the internet, it's even worse. If I don't strenuously keep my comings and goings a secret, I wind up with cameras in my face and following me everywhere and looking over my shoulder."

"They are vermin," said Edward Arvedson with feeling.

"In any case, when I talked to you I had just learned of an accident victim in Minnesota who had recovered from a coma and, like the girl in Southern California, seemed to have undergone a complete personality shift. He had been a mild and soft-spoken churchgoer, but now he was a violent, alcoholic bully. His wife of twenty-four years had divorced him, his children no longer saw him. The front yard of his house in Bloomington was a wreck, and when he opened the door the stink of rot and filth just rolled out. I only saw him for a few seconds through the chain on his front door, but what I witnessed was definitely madness, a sort of... emotionless focus that I've only seen in the criminally insane. That doesn't prove anything, of course. Brain damage can do that, and he'd certainly been badly injured. But he *recognized* me."

"You told me when you called," said Arvedson. "I could tell it upset you."

"Because it wasn't like he'd seen my picture in *The Enquirer*, but like he *knew* me. Knew me and hated me. I didn't stay there long, but it wasn't just seeing the Minnesota victim that threw me. I'd never heard of possessions happening at this rate, or to people so close to death. It didn't make sense!"

"It has my attention, too," Edward said. "But what I want to hear now is what happened with your Buddhist gentleman."

Nightingale let out a breath. He swallowed the last of his sherry. "Right. Well, Geshe was a very interesting man, an artist and a teacher. I wish I could have met him at a different time, but even in our short acquaintance he impressed me and I liked him. That's why what happened was so disturbing.

"He had checked out of the hospital to die at home. He'd lost his wife a few years earlier and they'd had no children, so although some of his students and colleagues came by to sit with him from time to time, at the end there was only his friend Joseph, an American Buddhist, and the hospice nurse who checked in on him once a day. And me, of course. Geshe and I didn't speak much—he had to work too hard to manage the pain— but as I said, he impressed me. During the long days in his apartment I spent a great deal of time looking at his books and other possessions, which is as good a way to get to know someone as talking with them. Also, I saw many of his own works of art, which may be an even better way to learn about another human being—he made beautiful Buddhist Thangkas, meditation paintings.

"As Geshe began to slip away Joseph read the Bardo Thodol to him. I've never spent much time studying it, myself—I think that hippie-ish, *Tibetan Book of the Dead* reputation put me off when I was younger, and these days I don't really need to know the nuts and bolts of any particular religious dogma to work with the universal truths behind them all—but I have to say that hearing it and living with it, even as Geshe was *dying* with it, opened my eyes."

"There is great truth at the heart of all the great faiths," Arvedson said solemnly.

"Yes, but what I truly came to admire was the calmness of the people who wrote the bardos—the practicality, I suppose is the best word. It's a very practical book, the Bardo Thodol. A road map. A set of travel tips. 'Here's what's going to happen now that you're dead. Do this. Don't do that. Everything will be okay.' Except that this time it wasn't.

"The famous teacher Trungpa Rinpoche said the best thing we can do for the dying and the newly dead is maintain an atmosphere of calmness, and that's certainly what Geshe seemed to have around him at the end. It was raining outside most of that week, but quietly. Joseph read the bardos over and over while he and I took turns holding Geshe's hand. With my special sensitivities, I was beginning to sense something of what he was sensing—the approach of the Great Mystery, the crossing, whatever you want to call it—and of course it troubled me deep down in my bones and guts, but Geshe wasn't frightened in the least. All those years of training and meditation had prepared him.

"It was fascinating to see how the dying soul colors the experience, Uncle Edward. As I said, I have never delved too deeply into Tibetan Buddhism, yet the version of dying I experienced through Geshe was shaped so strongly by that tradition that I could not feel it any other way—it was as real as you and I sitting here in the dark, listening to the wind and the rain." Nightingale paused for a moment while the storm rattled the windows of the old house. "The thousands of gods, which are one god, which is the light of the universe...I can't explain. But touching Geshe's thoughts as he began his journey, although I felt only the barest hint of what he felt, was like riding a roller-coaster through a kaleidoscope, but simultaneously falling through an endless, dark, silent void."

"'...When your body and mind separate, the dharmata will appear, pure and clear yet hard to discern, luminous and brilliant, with terrifying brightness, shimmering like a mirage on a plain,'" Arvedson quoted. "At least, that's what the bardo says."

"Yes." Nightingale nodded. "I remember hearing it then and understanding it clearly, even though the words I heard were Tibetan. Joseph had begun the Chikkhai Bardo, you see—the bardo of dying. In the real world, as we sometimes think of it, Geshe had sunk so far into himself he was no longer visibly breathing. But I was not really beside him in that little room in Seattle, although I could still hear Joseph's voice. Most of me was *inside*—deep in the experience of death with Geshe.

"I could feel him, Uncle Edward, and in a way I could see what he saw, hear what he heard, although those aren't quite the right words. As the voices of people I did not know echoed around us—mostly Geshe's friends and relations and loved ones, I suspect, for I do not think he had many enemies—he and I traveled together through a misty forest. It seemed to me a bit like some of the wild lands of the Pacific Northwest, but more mountainous, as if some of Geshe's Tibetan heritage was seeping through as well."

"*Climbing,*" said Edward Arvedson quietly.

"Yes, the part of the afterlife journey the Egyptians called "the Ladder" and the Aztecs thought of as the beginning of the soul's four-year journey to Mictlan. I've never dared hold a connection with a dying soul as long as I did with Geshe, and going so deep frightened me, but his calm strength made it possible. We did not speak, of course—his journey, his encounters, were his alone, as all ours will be someday—but I felt him there beside me as the dark drew in.

"I won't tell you everything I experienced now, but I will tell you someday soon, because it was a researcher's dream come true—the death experience almost firsthand. To make the story short, we passed through the first darkness and saw the first light, which the bardos call the soft light of the gods and which they counsel the dead soul to avoid. It was very attractive, like a warm fire to someone lost in the night, and I was feeling very cold, very far from comfort and familiar things—and remember, *I* had a body to go back to! I can only imagine what it seemed like to Geshe, who was on a one-way journey, but he resisted it. The same with what the bardo calls the 'soft light of the hell-beings.' I could feel him yearning toward it, and even to me it seemed soothing, alluring. In the oldest Tibetan tradition the hot hells are full of terrors—forest of razor-leaved trees, swamps bobbing with decomposing corpses—but these aspects are never seen until it's too late, until the attractions of one's own greed and anger have pulled the dying soul off the path.

"But Geshe overcame these temptations and kept on moving toward the harsher light of truth. He was brave, Edward, so brave! But then we reached the smoky yellow light, the realm of what the bardo calls *pretas...*"

"The hungry ghosts."

25

"Yes, the hungry ghosts. Found in almost every human tradition. Those who did not go on. Those who can't let go of anger, hatred, obsession..."

"Perhaps simply those who want more life," Arvedson suggested.

Nightingale shook his head. "That makes them sound innocent, but they're far from that. Corpse-eating *jikininki*, ancient Rome's Lemures, the *grigori* of the Book of Enoch—almost every human tradition has them. Hell, I've *met* them, although never in their own backyard like this. You remember that thing that almost killed me in Freiberg?"

"I certainly do."

"That was one of them, hitchhiking a ride in a living body. Nearly ripped my head off before I got away. I still have the scars..."

The night-time city waited now between waves of the storm. For a moment it was quiet enough in the room for Nightingale to hear the fan of his godfather's ventilator.

"In any case, that smoky yellow light terrified me. The bardo says it's temptation itself, that light, but maybe it didn't tempt me because I wasn't dying—instead it just made me feel frightened and sick, if you can be sick without a body. I could barely sense Geshe but I knew he was there and experiencing something very different. Instead of continuing toward the brilliant white light of compassion, as the bardo instructed, this very compassionate man seemed to hesitate. The yellow light was spreading around us like something toxic diffusing through water. Geshe seemed confused, stuck, as though he fought against a call much stronger than anything I could sense. I could feel something else, too, something alien to both of us, cold and strong and...yes, and *hungry*. God, I've never sensed hunger like that, a bottomless need like the empty chill of space sucking away all living warmth..."

Nightingale sat quietly for a long moment before he spoke again. "But then, just when I was fighting hardest to hang onto my connection to Geshe, it dissolved and he was gone. I'd lost touch with him. The yellow light was all around me, strange and greasy...repulsive, but also overwhelming...

"I fell out. No, it was more like I was shoved. I tumbled back into the real world, back into my body. I couldn't feel Geshe any more. Joseph had stopped reading the Chakkhai Bardo and was staring in alarm. Geshe's body, which hadn't moved or showed any signs of life in some time, was suddenly in full-on Cheyne-Stokes respiration, chest hitching, body jerking—he almost looked like he was convulsing. But Joseph swore to me later on that Geshe had stopped breathing half an hour earlier and I believe him.

"A moment later Geshe's eyes popped open. I've seen stranger things, but it still startled me. He had been dead, Uncle Edward, really dead, I swear he had. Now he was looking at me—but it wasn't Geshe any more. I couldn't prove it of course, but I had touched this man's soul, traveled with him as he passed over, the most intimate thing imaginable, and this just wasn't him.

"'No, I will not die yet,' he said. The voice sounded like his, but strong, far too strong for someone who had been in periodic breathing only a minute earlier. 'There are still things for me to do on this earth.' It was the eyes, though. That same cold, flat stare that I'd seen through the doorway in Minnesota, the one I've seen before in other possession cases, but there was none of the struggle I'd seen in classic possession, no sense of the soul and body fighting against an interloper. One moment it was Geshe, a spiritual man, an artist, the next moment it was...someone else. Someone as cold and detached as a textbook sociopath.

"He closed his eyes then and slept, or pretended to, but already he looked healthier than he had since I met him. I couldn't tell Joseph that I thought his friend was possessed—what a horrible thing to say to someone already dealing with several kinds of trauma!—and I didn't know what else to do, what to think. I sat there for most of an hour, unable to think of anything to do. At last, when the nurse came and began dealing with this incredible turn of medical events, I went out to get a drink. All right, I had a few, then went home and slept like a dead man myself.

"I should never have left them, Edward. When I went back the next day, the apartment was empty. A few weeks later I received an email from Joseph—or at least from Joseph's address—saying that after his miraculous recovery Geshe wanted to travel to Tibet, the place of his heritage. I've never heard from either of them since..."

The lightning, absent for almost a quarter of an hour, suddenly flared, turning the room into a flat tableau of black and white shapes; the thunder that followed seemed to rock the entire building. The light on Edward Arvedson's desk flickered once, then went out, as did the lights on his ventilator. Through the windows Nightingale could see the houses across the street had gone black as well. He jumped up, suddenly cold all over. His father's oldest friend and his own most trusted advisor was about to die of asphyxiation while he watched helplessly.

"Good God, Edward, the electricity...!"

"Don't...worry..." Arvedson wheezed. "I have a...standby...generator."

A moment later Nightingale felt rather than heard something begin to rumble somewhere in the house below and the desk light flickered back on, although the houses across the street remained dark. "There," said his godfather. "You see, young Natan? Not such an old-fashioned fool after all, eh? I am prepared for things like this. Power for the street will be back on soon—it happens a lot in this ancient neighborhood. Now, tell me what you think is happening."

Nightingale sat back, trying to regain his train of thought. If only the old man wasn't so stubborn about living on his own with only Jenkins—no spring lamb himself—for company.

"Right," he said at last. "Well, I'm sure you're thinking the same thing as me, Uncle Edward. Somehow these predatory souls or spirits have found a way to possess the bodies of the dying. Which would be bad enough, but it's the incredible frequency with which it seems to be happening. I can't possibly investigate them all, of course, but if even half the reports that reach me are real it's happening all over the world, several times a day."

The rain was back now, lashing the windows and tattooing the roof of Edward's Victorian house. When the old man spoke, there was an unfamiliar tone in his voice. "You are...frightened, my dear Natan."

"Yes, Uncle Edward, I am. I've never been this frightened, and I've seen a lot. It's as if something fundamental has broken down, some wall between us and the other side, and now the living are under attack. What did the cab driver say to me on the way over, babbling about the weather—'the storm door is open'...? And I'm afraid the storms are just going to keep coming thicker and faster until all our houses are blown down."

"But why? And why now?"

"Why? Because they've always been there—the hungry ones, the envious things that hate us because we can still breathe and sing and love. Do they want that back, or do they just want to keep us from having it? I don't know. And why now? I don't know that either. Perhaps some universal safeguard has stopped working, or these entities have learned something they didn't know before."

"Then here is the most important question, Nate. What are you going to do about it, now you know? What can one person do?"

"Well, make sure it isn't just one person trying to deal with it, to begin with. You and I know lots of people who don't think I'm a charlatan—brave people who study this sort of thing, who fight the good fight and know the true danger. More than a few of us have dedicated our lives to keep the rest of humanity safe, without reward or thanks. Now I have to alert them all, if they haven't discovered this already." He stood and began to pace back and forth before the desk. "And to make sure the word gets out, I'll use the very same tabloid vultures that you and I despise so much. They'll do good without knowing it. Because for every thousand people who'll read headlines that say things like 'So-Called Demon Hunter Claims Dead Are Invading the Living World' and laugh at it as nonsense, one or two will understand...and will heed the warning." He moved to the window, looked out into the darkness. "We can only hope to hold these hungry ghosts at bay if every real paranormal researcher, exorcist, and sympathetic priest we can reach will join us—every collector you know, every student of the arcane, every adventurer behind the occult lines, all of those soldiers of the light that the rest of society dismiss as crazy. This will be our great war."

Nightingale turned and walked back to his chair. "So there you have it, Uncle Edward. I'll spread the word. You spread the word, too. Call in old favors. If enough of us hear the truth, we may still be able to get the storm door shut again."

The old man was silent for a long time as thunder rolled away into the distance.

"You're a brave young man, Nate," he said at last. "Your parents would be proud of you. I'm going to have to think for a while about the best way to help you, and though it embarrasses me to admit it, I also need some rest. You'll forgive me—I get tired so quickly. I'll be all right until Jenkins comes back in a few hours. You can let yourself out, can't you?"

"Of course, Uncle Edward." He went to the old man and gave him a quick hug, then kissed his cool, dry cheek. He carried his empty sherry glass to the sideboard. "Now that I'm back in town, I'll be by to see you again tomorrow. Good night." On his way to the door Nightingale stopped and held his fingers up to catch the light from the desk lamp and saw that the darkness there was only dust.

"Tell Jenkins he's getting sloppy," he said. "I can't imagine you giving him a night off in the old days without finishing the cleaning. Looks like he hasn't dusted in weeks."

"I'll tell him," said his godfather. "Go on, go on. I'll see you very soon."

But Nightingale did not go through the doorway. Instead, he turned and slowly walked back into the room. "Uncle Edward," he said. "Are you certain you're going to be all right? I mean, the power's still off. You can't breathe without your ventilator."

"The generator can run for hours and hours. It'll shut itself off when the regular power comes back." He waved his hand testily. "Go on, Nate. I'm fine."

"But the strange thing," said Nightingale, "is that when the generator came on half an hour ago, the ventilator didn't. There must be something wrong with it."

Arvedson went very still. "What...what are you talking about?"

"Here. Look, the little lights on it never came back on, either. Your ventilator's off." The room suddenly seemed very quiet, nothing but the distant sound of cars splashing along out on Jones Street, distant as the moon. "What happened to Edward?"

The old man looked surprised. "I don't...Nate, what are you saying...?"

The gun was out of Nightingale's coat and into his hand so quickly it might have simply appeared there. He leveled it at a spot between the old man's two bushy white eyebrows. "I asked you what happened to Edward—the real Edward Arvedson. I'm only going to ask this once more. I swear I'll kill him before I let you have his body, and I'm betting you can't pull your little possession trick again on a full-grown, healthy man like me—especially not before I can pull the trigger."

Even in the half-light of the desk lamp, the change was a fearful one: Edward Arvedson's wrinkled features did not alter in any great way, but something moved beneath the muscles and skin like a light-shunning creature burrowing through the dark earth. The eyes fixed his. Although the face was still Edward's, somehow it no longer looked much like him. "You're a clever boy, Nightingale," said the stranger in his godfather's body. "I should have noticed the ventilator never came back on, but as you've guessed, this sack of meat no longer has a breathing problem. In fact, it no longer needs to breathe at all."

"What's happened to him?" The gun stayed trained on the spot between the old man's eyes. "Talk fast."

A slow, cold smile stretched the lips. "That is not for me to say, but rather it is between him and his god. Perhaps he is strumming a harp with the other angels now...or writhing and shrieking in the deepest pits..."

"Bastard!" Nightingale pulled back the trigger with his thumb. "You lie! He's in there with you. And I know a dozen people who can make you jump right the hell back out..."

The thing shook its head. "Oh, Mr. Nightingale, you've been playing the occult detective so long you've come to believe you're really in a story—and that it will have a happy ending. We didn't learn new ways to possess the living." The smile returned, mocking and triumphant. "We have learned how to move into the bodies of the recently dead. Quite a breakthrough. It's much, much easier than possession, and we cannot be evicted because the prior tenant...is gone. Your 'Uncle Edward' had a stroke, you see. We waited all around him as he died—oh, and believe me, we told him over and over what we would do, including this moment. Like you, he caused us a great deal of trouble over the years— and as you know, we dead have long memories. And when he was beyond our torments at last, well, this body was ours. Already my essence has strengthened it. It does not need to breathe, and as you can see..." The thing rose from the wheelchair with imperial calm and stood without wavering. Nightingale backed off a few steps, keeping the gun high. "...it no longer needs assistance to get around, either," the thing finished. "I feel certain I'll get years of use out of it before I have to seek another—time enough to contact and betray all of the rest of Edward Arvedson's old friends."

"Who are you?" Nightingale fought against a despair that buffeted him like a cold wind. "Oh, for the love of God, what do you monsters want?"

"Who am I? Just one of the hungry ones. One of the unforgiving." It sat down again, making the wheelchair creak. "What do we want? Not to go quietly, as you would have us go—to disappear into the shadows of nonexistence and leave the rest of you to enjoy the light and warmth." The thing lifted its knotted hands—Edward's hands, as they had seemed such a short time ago—in a greedy gesture of seizure. "As you said, this is a war. We want what you have." It laughed, and for the first time the voice sounded nothing at all like his godfather's familiar tones. "And we are going take it from you. All of you."

"I don't think so. Because if you need bodies to survive here, then those bodies can be taken back from you..." And even as Nightingale spoke his gun flashed and roared and the thing in his godfather's shape staggered and fell back against the wheelchair cushions, chin on chest. A moment later the so-familiar face came up again. Smiling.

"Jenkins," it said. "If you would be so kind..."

Something knocked the gun from Nightingale's hand and then an arm like an iron bar slammed against his neck. He fought but it was like being held by a full-grown gorilla. His struggles only allowed him to slide around enough in his captor's grip to see Jenkins' blank eyes and the huge hole in the side of the caretaker's head crusted with bits of bone and dried tissue.

"I lied about giving him the night off," said the pseudo-Edward. "The living get impatient, but my colleague who inhabits him now was perfectly willing to stand in the dark until I needed him." Now Arvedson's body stood again, brushing at its clothes; the hole Nightingale's gunshot had made in its shirt was bloodless. "Bullets are a poor weapon against the risen dead, Nightingale," it pointed out with no little satisfaction. "You could burn the body, I suppose, or literally pulverize it, and there would be nothing left for us to inhabit. But of course, you will not get the chance to tell anyone about that."

"Bastards!" He struggled helplessly against the Jenkins-thing's grip.

"Even if you kill me, there are hundreds more like me out there. They'll stop you!"

"We will meet them all, I'm sure," said his godfather's body. "You will introduce us—or at least the new resident of your corpse will. And one by one, we will remove them. The dead will live, with all the power of age and riches and secrecy, and the rest of your kind will be our uncomprehending cattle, left alive only to breed more bodies for us. Your driver was right, Mr. Nightingale—the storm door really is open now. And no power on this earth can shut it."

Nightingale tried to say something else then, shout some last words of defiance, but the pressure on his neck was crushingly strong and the lights of the world—the lamp, the headlights passing in the street below, even the storm-shrouded stars beyond the window—had begun leaching away into utter darkness.

His last sight was of the cold, hungry things that had been hiding behind that darkness, hiding and waiting and hating the living for so long, as they hurried toward him to feed.

# The Stranger's Hands

People in the village had been whispering for days about the two vagabonds in Squire's Wood, but the boy Tobias was the first to speak to them.

Tobias was a somewhat wayward lad, and the fact that he should have been grazing his father's sheep on the hill above the forest at that hour more or less assured the sheep in question would be wandering along the shady edges of the wood instead, with Tobias wandering right behind them.

It was not until he saw a drift of smoke twining like a gray scarf through the trees that the boy remembered that strangers had been seen in the wood. He felt a moment of fear: Why would anyone live out of doors in the cold nights and flurries of autumn rain if they were God-fearing folk? Only robbers and dangerous madmen dwelt under the unsheltered sky. Everyone knew that. If he had been a fraction less headstrong, Tobias would have turned around then and hurried back to the hillside, perhaps even remembering to take his father's sheep with him, but there was a part of him, a strong part, that hated *not knowing* things worse than anything. It was the part that had once caused him to pull the leg off a frog, just to find out what it would do. (It did very little, and died soon after with what Tobias felt guiltily certain was an accusatory look in its bulging eyes.) It was also the reason he had dented his father's best scythe when he had used it to try to cut down a tree, and why he had dumped the contents of his mother's precious sewing basket all over the ground—a search for knowledge that ended with Tobias spending all afternoon in the fading light on his hands and knees, locating every last needle and pin he had spilled. Once this rebel voice had even led him several miles out of the village, on a quest for the town of Eader's Church, which he had heard was so big that the streets actually had names. His father and two other men had caught up to him an hour after sunset as he sat exhausted and hungry by the side of the road. He had got a whipping for it, of course, but for young Tobias whippings were part of the cost of doing business.

So now, instead of turning and leaving the woods and its perilous inhabitants behind (for the sake of his father's livestock if nothing else) he followed the trail of smoke back to its source, a small cookfire in a clearing. A small man with a ratlike face was tending the flames, his wrinkles made so deep and dark by grime he looked like an apple-doll. His large companion, who sat on a stone beside the fire and did not look up even when Tobias stepped on a twig and made the little man jump, was so odd to look at that the boy could not help shivering. The large man's head was shaved, albeit poorly in some places, and the skull beneath the skin bulged in places that it should not. His bony jaw hung slack, the tongue visible in the space between top and bottom teeth, and although he did not seem blind, the eyes in the deep sockets were dull as dirty stones.

If the big man was paying no attention, the little man was. He stared at Tobias like a dog trying to decide whether to bark or run.

"Your wood's too wet," the boy told him.

"What?"

"You'll get mostly smoke and little fire from that. Do you want smoke?"

The small man frowned, but in dismay, not anger. "I want to cook this fish." He had the sound of a southerner, the words stretched and misshapen. Tobias wondered why they couldn't learn to speak properly.

He squinted at the man's supper with the eye of an experienced angler. "It's small."

"It's better than starving," the man pointed out.

"Well, then, I'll show you." Tobias quickly found enough dry wood to rebuild the fire and within a short time the little man was cooking the fish over it on a long stick. His large companion still had not moved or spoken, had not even seemed to notice the newcomer in their camp.

"Thanks for your kindness," the small man said. "I am Feliks. We are new to this."

"My name's Tobias," the boy said, basking in the glow of his own helpfulness. "What does that mean, new?"

35

"We have been living somewhere there was food." Feliks shrugged. "The food ran out."

Tobias stared at the other man, who still gazed at nothing, only the slow movement of his chest behind his dark, travel-worn robe showing that he was something other than a statue. "What's *his* name?"

Feliks hesitated for a moment. "Eli." He said it in the southern way, the last syllable rising like a shorebird's cry—Eh-*lee*. "He was my master, but he...something happened to him. He lost his wits."

Tobias now examined the big man with unhidden interest—if he had no wits, it couldn't be rude to stare, could it? "What happened?"

"The roof fell on him." Feliks took the fish from the stick, burning his fingers so that he almost dropped it—Tobias was amused by how many things the man didn't know how to do—and then cut it into two pieces with a knife, handing the larger piece to the silent giant. Eli moved for the first time; he took the fish without looking at it, put it in his mouth, and chewed with bovine patience. Feliks began to eat the other piece, then turned shamefacedly to Tobias. "I should offer some to you, for your kindness."

Tobias was old enough to understand this would not be a small sacrifice for Feliks. "No, I'll eat at home. And I'd better go now or Father will have the strap out." He looked through the trees to the angle of the sun, which was definitely lower than he would have liked. "He'll have the strap out, anyway." The boy stood. "I'll come back tomorrow, though. I can help you catch better fish than that one." He hesitated. "Have you been to other places? Other villages, even towns?"

Feliks nodded slowly. "Many places. Many cities all over the Middle Lands."

"Cities!" Tobias swayed a little, faint-headed at the thought. "Real cities? I'll be back!"

The tall man named Eli suddenly put out his hand, a gesture so startling after his hour of near-immobility that Tobias recoiled as though from a snake.

"He...I think he wants to thank you," Feliks said. "Go ahead, boy—take his hand. He was a great man once."

Tobias slowly extended his own small hand, wondering if this might be the beginning of some cruel or even murderous trick—if he had been too trusting after all. Eli's hand was big, knob-knuckled, and smudged with dirt, and it closed on the boy's slim fingers like a church door swinging closed.

Then Tobias vanished.

When two days had passed with no sign of the boy, suspicion of course fell on the two strangers living in Squire's Wood. When the man named Feliks admitted that they had seen the child and spoken to him, the shireward and several local fellows dragged them out of the forest and chained them in wooden stocks beside the well in the center of the village, where everyone could see them and marvel at their infamy. Feliks tearfully continued to insist that they had done nothing to harm the boy, that they did not know where he had gone—both things true, as it turned out—but even if the two men had not been strangers and thus naturally suspect, the villagers could see that the big one was plainly touched, perhaps even demon-possessed, and almost no one felt anything for them but horror and disgust.

The lone exception was Father Bannity, the village priest, who felt that it was a troubling thing to imprison people simply because they were strangers, although he dared not say so aloud. He himself had been a stranger to the village when he had first arrived twenty years earlier (in fact, older villagers still referred to him as "the new priest") and so he had a certain empathy for those who might find themselves judged harshly simply because their grandfathers and great-grandfathers were not buried in the local churchyard. Also, since in his middle-life he had experienced a crisis of faith, leading him to doubt many of the most famous and popular tenets of his own religion, he was doubly unwilling to assume the guilt of someone else simply because they were not part of the familiar herd. So Father Bannity took it on himself to make sure the two prisoners had enough food and water to survive. It would be a long wait for the King's Prosecutor General to arrive—his circuit covered at least a dozen villages and lasted a full cycle of the moon—and even if the two were guilty of killing the poor child and hiding his body, Father

Bannity did not want them to die before this could be discovered for certain.

As the small man, Feliks, grew to trust him, he at last told Bannity what he swore was the true story of what had happened that day, that the boy had touched big Eli's hand and then disappeared like a soap bubble popping. Father Bannity was not quite certain what to think, whether this was a true mystery or only the precursor to a confession, a man easing gradually into a guilty admission as into a scalding bath, but he stuck by his resolution to treat them as innocent until they told him otherwise, or events proved the worst to have happened.

One day, as he was holding a ladle of water to Eli's dry lips, the big man suddenly looked at him almost as if seeing him for the first time, a flash of life in the dull, bestial eyes that Bannity had not seen before. Startled, the priest dropped the ladle. The big man lifted his hand as far as he could with his wrist restrained by the stocks and spread his long fingers like some strange flower blooming.

"Don't," whispered Feliks. "That's what the boy did."

Father Bannity hesitated for only a moment. Something in the big man's strange gaze, something solemn and distant but not unkind, convinced him. He reached out and allowed Eli's hand to fold around his.

For a startling moment Bannity thought he had become a fish, jerked thrashing out of the river and up into the daylight, blinded by the sun and its prismatic colors, dazzled by the burning air. Then, a half-instant later, he realized it was as though he had been out of the water for years, and now had suddenly been plunged back *into* it: everything that had withered in him suddenly sprang back to life, all the small losses of the passing days and months—color, feeling, ecstasy. The feeling was so strong, so overwhelming, that he could not even answer Feliks' worried questions as he staggered away.

Bannity *knew* again. He had forgotten what it felt like, but now he remembered, and the thunderous force of belief returning betrayed how much he had lost. God had sent him a miracle in the person of the silent giant, and with that single touch, a world which had slowly turned gray around him over the years had been kindled back into flaming life.

God was in everything again, just as He had been when Bannity had been a child, when he had been able to imagine nothing better than to serve Him.

God was alive inside him. He had experienced a miracle.

It was only when the first surge of ecstatic happiness had become a little more ordinary, if no less pleasurable, that Father Bannity realized nothing tangible had actually changed. It wasn't so much that God had shown him a miracle, a sign, it was more as if touching the giant's hand had reawakened him to the love of God he had once had, but which had slipped away from him.

It was Eli, he realized, although undoubtedly acting as God's messenger, who had given him back his love of the Lord, his belief in a living Creation, and most of all, his certainty that what *was*, was meant to be.

The silent, damaged man had given Bannity his heart's desire, even though the priest himself had not known what it was.

Grateful, renewed, the priest resolved to speak on behalf of the two prisoners when the Prosecutor General returned to the village, to tell the truth even if it meant admitting that he had, for a time, lost his own faith. Father Bannity would undoubtedly have been their only defender, except that on the day before the traveling lawspeaker rode into town, the boy named Tobias came back.

He had been, the boy told the villagers (and very gleefully too) in the town of Eader's Church, and it was just as big and wonderful as he had imagined. "They have lots of dogs!" he said, his eyes still bright with the spectacle he had seen. "And houses that go up and up! And people!" He seemed to feel that the whipping his father had just given him—on general principles, since the actual mechanics of the boy's disappearance were still a mystery—was a small price to pay for all he'd seen.

Tobias knew nothing about how he had got from the village to the far-off town—it had happened in an instant, he said, from clasping Eli's hand to finding himself in the middle of the Eader's Church marketplace—but unfortunately there had been no equally magical way of returning. It had taken him all the days since he'd been gone to walk home.

When the Prosecutor General arrived the next day, there was no longer a case for murder to be tried, although several of the villagers were talking darkly of witchcraft. The Prosecutor General, a small, round, self-important fellow with a beard on his chin as small and sharp as an arrowhead, insisted on being taken to see the two former prisoners, who had been released to their campsite in Squire's Wood, if not to their previous state of anonymity.

Holding out his rod of office, the lawspeaker approached Eli and said, "In the name of the State and its gracious Sovereign, His Majesty the King, you must tell me how you sent the boy to Eader's Church."

The big man only looked at him, unbothered. Then he extended his hand. The Prosecutor General, after a moment's hesitation, extended his own small, plump hand and allowed it to be grasped.

When Father Bannity and the other men watching had finished blinking their eyes, they saw that instead of his prosecutor's tunic, the Prosecutor General was now unquestionably wearing a judge's robes, cowl, and wreath, and that a judge's huge, round, golden emblem of office now hung on a chain around his neck. (Some also suggested that he had a stronger chin as well, and more penetrating eyes than he had heretofore possessed.) The ex-Prosecutor General, now a full-fledged Adjudicator, blinked, ran his fingers over the leafy wreath on his head, then fell down on his knees and uttered a happy prayer.

"Twelve years I've waited!" he said, over and over. "Thank you, Lord! Passed over and passed over—but no more!"

He then rose, and with fitting jurisprudential gravity, proclaimed, "These men have not practiced any unlicensed witchcraft. I rule that they are true messengers of God, and should be treated with respect."

Finding that his pockets were now richer by several gold coins—the difference between his old salary and new—the newly minted Adjudicator promptly sold his cart and donkey to Pender the village blacksmith and left town in a covered carriage, with a newly hired driver and two new horses. Later rumors said that he arrived home to find he had been awarded the King's Fourteenth Judicial Circuit.

In the wake of the Prosecutor General's astonishing transformation, Squire's Wood began to fill with people from the village and even some of the surrounding villages—for news travels fast in these rural areas—turning the two men's camp into a site of pilgrimage. The size of the gathering grew so quickly that Father Bannity and some of the wood's nearer and soberer neighbors worried that the entire forest soon would be trampled flat, but the squireward could not turn the newcomers away any more than he could have held back the tide at Landsend.

Although none of this swarm of postulants was turned away, not all received their heart's desire, either—Eli's hand opened only to one in perhaps three or four and it was impossible to force the issue. One man, a jar maker named Keely, tried to pry the big man's fingers apart and shove his own hand in, and although he succeeded, nothing magical happened to him except that he developed a painful boil in the middle of his forehead the following day.

Some of the pilgrims' wishes turned out to be surprisingly small and domestic: a man whose sick cow suddenly recovered, a woman whose youngest son abruptly discovered he could hear as well as he had before the fever. Others were more predictable, like the man who after clasping Eli's hand discovered a pot of old coins buried under an ancient wall he was rebuilding.

To the astonishment of many, two blighted young folk who lived on neighboring farms, a young man with a shattered leg and a girl with a huge strawberry blotch on her face, both went to Eli, and both were gifted with a handclasp, but came out again looking just the same as they had before. But within the next few days the young man's drunkard father died of a fit, leaving him the farm, and the girl's cruel, miserly uncle who treated her like a servant fell under the wheels of a cart and died also, leaving her free to marry if anyone would have her. The two young people did indeed marry each other, and seemed quite happy, although they both still bore the disfigurements that had made them so pitiable to the rest of the village.

The only apparent failure of Eli's magical touch was Pender, the blacksmith, who went to the campsite a massive, strapping man with a beard that reached halfway down his chest, and went away again with the shape and voice and apparently all the working parts of a slender young woman. He left town the same night, trading the Prosecutor General's old cart for a pair of pretty dresses before setting off on the donkey toward the nearest city to start his life over (at least so he told his neighbors), so no one was ever able to find out exactly how such a strange thing had happened when others had been served so well.

Soon the lame youth and other grateful folk came and built a great tent in Squire's Wood for Eli and Feliks to shelter in, and began bringing them daily offerings of food and drink. People were coming to see the two strangers from all around, and even the villagers who had not obtained a supernatural gift from the silent giant came to realize how valuable his presence was: the village was full of pilgrims, including some quite well-to-do folk who were willing to pay exorbitant prices to be fed and housed near the miracle worker.

Father Bannity, still basking in the joyful light of his newly recovered faith, did not doubt that Eli and Feliks were gifts from God, but he had not lost all caution or good sense, either, and he was worried by what was happening to his quiet village. He sent a messenger describing recent events to Dondolan, the nearest accredited wizard, who had an eyrie near the top of Reaching Peak. The wizard had not passed through the village for years—but he and the priest had met several times, and Bannity liked the mage and trusted his good sense, certainly beyond that of the village elders, who were growing as greedy of pilgrimage gold as children tumbled into a treacle vat, happily eating themselves to death.

Dondolan the Clear-Eyed, as he had been named back in his Academy days, took one look at the priest's letter, then leaped out of his chair and began packing (a task which takes a wizard a much shorter time than the average traveler). The messenger asked if there would be any reply, and Dondolan told him, "I will be there before you." Then, suiting deed to word, he promptly vanished.

He appeared again in the village at the base of the mountain, and took his horse from the livery stable there—even an accomplished wizard will not travel by magic for twenty leagues, not knowing what he will find at the other end, for it is a fierce drain on the resources—and set out. Other than an ill-considered attempt by some local bandits to waylay him just outside Drunken Princes' Pass, an interaction which increased the frog population of the highlands but did not notably slow Dondolan's progress, it was a swift journey, and he reached the nameless village within two days. Spurning more ordinary couriers, he had sent a raven ahead, and as a result Father Bannity waited at the crossroads outside of town to meet him.

When they had greeted each other—fondly, for the respect was mutual, despite their differences on the theological practicalities—Bannity led Dondolan through the fields around the outskirts of the village, so as not to cause more ruckus and rumor than was necessary: already the village practically breathed the stuff, and the pilgrims arriving daily from all over only made things more frantic.

"Do you wish to speak to the two of them?" Bannity asked. "It will be difficult, but I might persuade the village elders to let us close off the camp, although it will not be easy to remove all the addled folk who are living there now—they have practically made a new town in the middle of the forest."

"We should decide nothing until I see these miracle men," Dondolan said. "Although I must say that the description of them in your letter gave me an unpleasant feeling in the pit of my stomach."

"Why?" asked Bannity with some alarm. "Do you think they mean harm? I worried mainly that so many pilgrims would jeopardize the safety of our little town, drawing thieves and confidence tricksters and such. But surely God has sent those two to us—they have done so much good!"

"Perhaps. That is why I will restrain my conjectures until I have seen them."

They made their way through the woods, between groups of revelers singing and praying, gathered around so many campfires it seemed more like the eve of a great battle than twilight in the woods outside a quiet village too unassuming even to have its own name. As they grew close to the great pale tent and the crowd of people waiting there—some patiently, others loudly demanding that they be allowed to be next to see the wonder-workers because their need was so great—Bannity found it increasingly difficult to make headway through the throng. It was a mark of how many of these people were strangers to the area that the village's well-respected priest almost got into two fights, and only Dondolan's discreet use of a quelling-charm got them past those at the front of the line without real violence.

They slipped through the tent's flap-door. Dondolan looked across the big tent at the miraculous pair sitting like minor potentates on high-backed chairs the villagers had built them, the small man Feliks and the big man with the misshapen skull. Feliks was scratching himself and laughing at something. Eli was staring down at one of the kneeling postulants before him, his expression as emptily self-absorbed as a bullfrog waiting for a fly of sufficient size to happen past. Dondolan swallowed, then stepped back out of the tent again, and Bannity followed him. Even by torchlight, the priest could see the wizard had gone quite pale.

"It is indeed as I feared, Bannity. That is no poor traveler, innocently touched by God—or at least that is not how he began. The large man is the dark wizard Elizar the Devourer, scourge of the southern lands, and greatest enemy of the archmage Kettil of Thundering Crag."

"Elizar?" Bannity suddenly found swallowing difficult. Even a village priest knew the Devourer, who had burned whole towns because he liked the gloomy skies their smoking ruins provided, who had performed vile rites to turn men into beasts and beasts into men, and whose campaign of violent conquest had only been stopped by Kettil himself, the greatest wizard of the age, who had come down from his great ice caverns atop Thundering Crag and helped the young king defeat Elizar's vast army of slavering beast-men at the field of Herredsburn. Kettil himself had dueled Elizar before the gathered forces of both armies—the skies above Herredsburn, everyone remembered, had lit up as if with half a dozen simultaneous thunderstorms, and although neither had managed definitively to best the other, it had been Elizar who had fled the field, his plans in ruins, and who had retreated into a dark obscurity that had covered him for years—an absence that had lasted until this very moment. "*That* Elizar?" murmured Father Bannity. "*Here?*"

"I would stake my life on it," said Dondolan, "and may be doing so. Even if his mindlessness is real, just seeing someone like me that he has known might shock him back to his prior self."

"But we cannot simply...leave it. We cannot leave things this way."

"No, but I dare not go near him. His miracles, you tell me, are real, so he still wields mighty powers. Even if he stays witless, I cannot afford the chance he might decide to give *me* my heart's desire." Dondolan shook his head, his white beard wagging. "The heart of a wizard, even a relatively decent one like myself, is full of dark crevices. It is the world we inhabit, the wisdoms we study, the powers we have learned to harness, if not always to understand." He smiled, but there was not much pleasure in it. "I truthfully do not know my heart's desire, and have no urge to discover it this way."

"I'm...I'm not certain what you mean."

"What if my heart's desire is to be the greatest wizard of my age? I felt that way once, when I was young and first entering the Academy. What if that desire has not gone, only hidden?" He shook his head again. "I dare not risk it."

"But what if an ordinary mortal—someone not a wizard—has the same thing as *his* heart's desire? Or something worse, asking for the end of the world or something."

Dondolan gave the priest a shrewd, sober look. "So far, that has not happened. In fact, the power Elizar wields seems not to have harmed much of anybody, except, by your account, a pair of nasty old folk who deliberately stood in the way of their children's happiness. And even there, we cannot prove that coincidence did not carry them away. Perhaps there is something to Elizar's magic that is self-limiting—something that prevents him from granting any but mostly benign wishes. I do not know." He looked up. "I *do* know that we must discover more before we can make up our minds. We cannot, as you said, simply leave things be, not with Elizar the Devourer here, surrounded by eager supplicants, busily creating miracles, however kind-hearted those miracles may seem." Dondolan ran his fingers through his long beard. "Not to mention the evil chance that this is all some cruel trick of Elizar's—that he only shams at having lost his mind, and plots to seize the Middle Lands again." He frowned, thinking. "When do they stop for the night?"

"Soon. When my sexton rings the church bell for evening prayer."

"Wait until that bell rings, Father, then bring me the man Feliks."


The small man seemed almost relieved to have been found out. "Yes, it is true. He was once Elizar, the greatest wizard of all."

"After Kettil the archmage, you mean," said Dondolan.

Feliks waved his hand. "My master poured his soul into five thousand beast-men at Herredsburn, animating them throughout the battle. Even so, he duelled Kettil Hawkface to a standstill."

"This is neither here nor there," said Father Bannity impatiently. "Why is he the way we see him? Is this some new plot of his, some evil device?"

"Tell the truth, minion, and do not think to trick me," Dondolan said harshly. "Even now, Kettil himself must be hearing news of this. He will not take longer than I did to deduce that your Eli is in fact his old arch-enemy."

Feliks sighed. "Then we must be moving on again. Sad, that is. I was enjoying it here."

"Damn it, man, one of the most dangerous men in the world sleeps twenty paces away! Talk to us!"

"Dangerous to you, perhaps." Feliks shook his head. "No, not even to you—not now. There is no trick, wizard. What you see is the truth. The old Elizar is gone, and dumb Eli is what remains.

"It was after Herredsburn, you see, when the king and your Wizard's Council turned us away. With all his beast-men dead or changed back to their former selves, my master left the field and retreated to his secret lair in the Darkslide Mountains."

"We suspected he had a bolthole there," murmured Dondolan, "but we could never find it."

"He was determined to have his revenge on Kettil and the others," continued Feliks. "I have never seen him thus. He was furious, but also weary, weary and distraught." The small man peered at the priest and the wizard for a moment. "Once, in middle-night when I was awakened from sleep by a strange noise, I found him weeping."

"I cannot believe that," said Dondolan. "Elizar? The Devourer?"

"Believe what you will. There was always more to him than you folk on the Council understood. Whatever the case, he became fixed on the idea of securing the Amulet of Desire, which can grant its possessor whatever gift he most wants. He spent many months—a year, almost—pursuing its legend down many forgotten roads, in old books and older scrolls. He spoke to creatures so fearsome I could not even be under the same roof

while they were conversing." The memory still seemed to make Feliks fearful, and yet proud of his bold master. "At last the time came. Deep in our cavern home in the Darkslide Mountains, he prepared the spells. I helped him as best I could, but I am just a servant, not a necromancer. I stoked the fires, polished the alembics, brought the articles he needed from our reliquary. At last the hour came when the spheres were in alignment, and he began the Summoning of the Empty Gods.

"He had been nights on end without sleep, in the grip of a fever that I had never seen in him before, even on the night before Herredsburn, when dominion over all the world was still at his fingertips. Pale, wide-eyed, talking to himself as though I was not even present, he was like a prisoner desperate for release, whether that release came from the opening of the prison door or from the hangman's rope."

Feliks sighed and briefly wiped his eyes while Dondolan tapped impatient fingers.

"The spell went on for hours," the small man continued, "names shouted into the darkness that hurt my ears. At one point I fled, terrified by the shadows that filled the room and danced all around me. When I came back, it was because I heard my master's hoarse cry of triumph.

"He stood in the center of his mystical diagram, holding up something I could barely see, something that gleamed red and black..."

"Something cannot gleam black," Dondolan said—a trifle querulously, Bannity thought. "It makes no sense."

"Little of what had happened that night made sense, but I will not change my tale. It gleamed red and black. Elizar held it over his head, crying out with a ragged voice, 'My greatest wish made real...!'—and then the roof collapsed."

"Collapsed?" said Bannity. "How? I thought you were in some mountain cavern."

"We were," Feliks agreed. "I still am not certain how it happened—it was like being chewed in a giant's mouth, chewed and chewed and then spit out. When I woke up, we both lay on the slope beneath the entrance to the lair, which was choked with fallen rock. Elizar was as you see him now, crushed and silent, his head all bloody, poor fellow. The Amulet was gone. Everything was gone. I helped him up and we stumbled and

crawled down the hill to a cotsman's deserted shack—the owner had fled when the mountain began to shake. I shaved my master's head and doctored his wounds. We ate what supplies the cotsman had laid in, but when we ran out, we had no choice but to become wandering beggars." The small, wrinkled man spread his hands. "I can do no magic, you see."

"Was the boy in the village, the one Elizar sent to Eader's Church, the first to be...touched?"

Feliks shook his head. "My master took a few people's hands, mostly folk who gave generously to our begging bowl, and sometimes things happened. None were harmed, all profited," he added, a little defensively.

"And you," Dondolan demanded. "You must have touched his hands many times since this occurred. What of you?"

"What could happen? I already have my heart's desire. All I have ever wanted was to serve him. From the first moment I saw him outside the Academy, I knew that he was my destiny, for good or bad."

Dondolan sighed. "For bad, certainly, at least until now. You are not a true villain, Feliks, but you have served an evil man."

"All great men are thought evil by some."

"Not all great men graft the heads of wild boars onto the shoulders of peasant farmers," Dondolan pointed out. "Not all great men wear the skins of other wizards for a cloak."

"He killed only those who turned against him," said Feliks stubbornly. "Only those who would have killed him."

Dondolan stared at him for a moment. "It matters little now," he said at last. "As I said, Kettil will have heard by now, and guessed who is here. The archmage will come, and things will change."

"Then we must go," said Feliks, rising to his feet with a weary grunt. "We will move on. There are still places we can live in quiet peace, if I only help my poor master to keep his hands to himself."

"I dare not try to stop you," Dondolan said. "I fear to wake your master if he really sleeps inside that battered skull—I admit I was never his match. But even if you flee, you will not outrun Kettil's power."

*It does not matter. What will be, will be,* Bannity thought to himself, but a little of his newfound peace had gone with Eli's unmasking. *Whether Elizar is a man transformed or a villain disguised, surely what happens next*

*will be as God wills, too. For who can doubt His hand when He has shown us so many miracles here?*

But Eli would not leave the wood, despite Feliks' urging. The mute man was as resistant as a boulder set deep in mud: none of his servant's pleas or arguments touched him—in fact, he showed no sign of even hearing them.

Dondolan and Bannity, armed with the knowledge of the miracle worker's true identity, convinced the suddenly terrified village elders that for a while, at least, the crowds should be kept away. With a contingent of solders from the nearest shirepost, hired with a fraction of the profits from the long miracle-season, they cleared the forest of all the suppliants, forcing them out into the town and surrounding fields, where local sellers of charms and potions gleefully provided them with substitute satisfaction, or at least the promise of it.

Even as the last of the camps were emptied, some of the latest arrivals from beyond the village brought news that Kettil Hawkface himself was on the way. Some had seen nothing more than a great storm swirling around Thundering Crag while the sky elsewhere was blue and bright, but others claimed to have seen the archmage himself speeding down the mountain on a huge white horse, shining as he came like a bolt of lightning. In any case, those who had been turned away from Squire's Wood now had something else to anticipate, and the great road that passed by the nameless village was soon lined with those waiting to see the most famous, most celebrated wizard of all.

Father Bannity could not help wondering whether Elizar sensed anything of his great rival's coming, and so he walked into Squire's Wood and across the trampled site of the camp, empty now but for a couple of hired soldiers standing guard.

Inside the tent wrinkled little Feliks looked up from eating a bowl of stew and waved to Bannity as if they were old friends, but Elizar was as empty-faced as ever, and seemed not to notice that the crowds of pilgrims were gone, that he and Feliks were alone. He sat staring at the ground, his big hands opening and closing so slowly that Father Bannity could have counted a score of his own suddenly intrusive heartbeats between fist and spread fingers. The man's naked face and shaved scalp made the head atop the black robe seem almost like an egg, out of which anything might hatch.

*Why did I come here?* he asked himself. *To taunt the blackest magician of the age?* But he felt he had to ask.

"Are you truly gone from in there, Elizar?" The priest's voice trembled, and he prayed to God for strength. He now realized, in a way he had not before, that here sat a man of such power that he had destroyed whole cities the way an ordinary man might kick down an ant-hill. But Bannity had to ask. "Are you truly and completely empty, or is there a spark of you left in that husk, listening?" He had a sudden thought. "Did you bring this on yourself, with your magical amulet? When the time came for your heart's desire to be granted, did God hear a small, hidden part of you that was weary of death and torment and dark hatreds, that wanted to perform the Lord's work for your fellow men instead of bringing them blood and fire and terror?"

Eli did not look up or change expression, and at last Father Bannity went out. Feliks watched him go with a puzzled expression, then returned to his meal.


He came down the main road with crowds cheering behind him as though he were a conquering hero—which, after all, he was. Bannity watched the people shouting and calling Kettil's name as the wizard rode toward the village on his huge white horse, the same people who only days before had been crouched in the dirt outside Eli's tent, begging to be let in, and the priest wondered at God's mysterious ways.

Kettil Hawkface was younger than Bannity would have guessed, or else had spelled himself to appear so. He seemed a man in the middle of life, his golden hair only touched with gray, his bony, handsome face still firm in every line. His eyes were the most impressive thing about him: even from a distance, they glittered an icy blue, and up close it was difficult to look at him directly, such was the chilly power of his gaze.

Bannity and Dondolan met the archmage at the edge of the wood.

Kettil nodded at his fellow wizard, but hardly seemed to see the priest at all, even after Dondolan introduced him.

"He is in there..." Dondolan began, but Kettil raised his hand and the lesser mage fell silent.

"I know where he is." He had a voice to match his eyes, frosty and authoritative. "And I know what he is. I have battled his evil for half my long life. I do not need to be told where to find him—I smell him as a hound smells his quarry."

*Strange, then, that you did not find him before,* thought Bannity, then regretted his own small-minded carping. "But he is not the monster you knew, Archmage..."

Kettil looked at him then, but only a moment, then turned away. "Such creatures do not change," he said to Dondolan.

Bannity tried again. "He has done much good...!"

Kettil smirked. "Has he revived all those he killed? Rebuilt the cities he burned? Do not speak to me of things you do not understand, priest." He slid down off his massive white horse. "I will go, and we will see what devilry awaits."

Bannity had to admit the archmage was as impressive as legend had promised. He strode into the forest with no weapon but his staff of gnarled birch, his long hair blowing, his sky-blue robes billowing as though he still stood on the heights of Thundering Crag. Bannity looked at Dondolan, whose face bore a carefully composed expression that betrayed nothing of what he was thinking, then they both followed the Archmage Kettil into Squire's Wood.

To Bannity's astonishment, Eli himself stood in the doorway of the tent, looking out across the great clearing.

"Ho, Devourer!" Kettil's voice echoed, loud as a hunting horn, but Eli only looked at him incuriously, his large hands dangling from his sleeves like roosting bats. "I have found you again at last!"

The hairless man blinked, turned, and went back into the tent. Kettil strode after him, crossing the clearing in a few long paces. Bannity started to follow, but Dondolan grabbed his arm and held him back.

"This is beyond me and beyond you, too."

"Nothing is beyond God!" Bannity cried, but Dondolan the Clear-Eyed looked doubtful. A few moments later little Feliks came stumbling out of the tent, flapping his hands as if surrounded by angry bees.

"They stand face to face!" he squawked, then tripped and fell, rolling until he stopped at Bannity's feet. The priest helped him up, but did not take his eyes off the tent. "They do not speak, but stare at each other. The air is so thick!"

"It seems..." Dondolan began, but never finished, for at that instant the entire clearing—in fact, all the woods and the sky above—seemed to suck in a great breath. A sudden, agonizing pain in Bannity's ears dropped him to his knees, then everything suddenly seemed to flow sideways—light, color, heat, air, everything rushing out across the face of the earth in all directions, pushing the priest flat against the ground and rolling him over several times.

When the monstrous wind died, Bannity lay for a long, stunned instant, marveling at the infinite skills of God, who could create the entire universe and now, just as clearly, was going to dismantle it again. Then a great belch of flame and a roar of rushing air made him roll over onto his knees and, against all good sense, struggle to sit up so he could see what was happening.

The tent was engulfed in flame, the trees all around singed a leafless black. As Father Bannity stared, two figures staggered out of the inferno as though solidifying out of smoke, one like a pillar of cold blue light, with flame dancing in his pale hair and beard, the other a growing, rising shadow of swirling black.

"I knew you but pretended, demon!" shouted Kettil Hawkface, waving his hands in the air, flashes of light crackling up from his fingertips. "Devourer! I know your treachery of old!"

The shadow, which had begun to fold down over the archmage like a burning blanket, instead billowed up and away, hovering in the air just above Kettil's head. A face could be seen in its roiling, cloudy midst, and Bannity could not help marveling even in his bewildered horror how it looked both like and unlike the silent Eli.

"I will make sure your dying lasts for centuries, Hawkface!" shrieked the dark shape in a voice that seemed to echo all the way to the distant hills, then it rose up into the air, flapping like an enormous bat made of smoke and sparks, and flew away into the south.

"Master!" screamed Feliks, and stumbled off through the woods, following the fast-diminishing blot of fiery blackness until he, too, disappeared from sight.

Kettil Hawkface, his pale robes smeared with ash, his whiskers and hair singed at the edges, strode away in the other direction, walking back toward the village with the purposeful stride of someone who has completed a dangerous and thankless job and does not bother to wait for the approbation he surely deserves.

As he emerged at the forest's edge, he stood before the hundreds of onlookers gathered there and raised his hands. "Elizar the Devourer's evil has been discovered and ended, and he has flown in defeat back to the benighted south," the archmage cried. "You people of the Middle Lands may rest safely again, knowing that the Devourer's foul plan has been thwarted."

The crowd cheered, but many were confused about what had happened and the reception of his news was not as whole-hearted as Kettil had perhaps expected. He did not wait to speak again to his colleague Dondolan, but climbed onto his white horse and galloped away north toward Thundering Crag, followed by a crowd of children crying out after him for pennies and miracles.

Bannity and Dondolan watched in silence as the ramrod-straight figure grew smaller, and then eventually disappeared. The crowds did not immediately disperse, but many seemed to realize there would be little reason to collect here anymore, and the cries of the food sellers, charm hawkers, and roving apothecaries became muted and mournful.

"So all is resolved for good," Father Bannity said, half to himself. "Elizar's evil was discovered and thwarted."

"Perhaps," said Dondolan. "But a part of me cannot help wondering whose heart's desire was granted here today."

"What do you mean? Do you think...they clasped hands?"

Dondolan sighed. "Do not misunderstand me. It is entirely possible that the world has been spared a great evil here today—Elizar was always full of plots, many of them astoundingly subtle. But if they *did* touch hands, I think it is safe to say that only one of them was granted his heart's desire."

"I don't understand."

"Elizar may not have seemed entirely happy as Eli the dumb miracle-worker," Dondolan said, "but he did seem peaceful. Now, though, he is the Devourer again, and Kettil once more has an enemy worthy of his own great pride and power."

Bannity was silent for a long time, watching the sky darken as the sun settled behind Squire's Wood. "But surely God would not let Elizar's evil back into the world simply because his enemy missed it—God must have a better plan for mankind than that!"

"Perhaps," said Dondolan the Clear-Eyed. "Perhaps. We will think on it together after we return to the church and you find the brandy you keep hidden for such occasions."

Father Bannity nodded and took a few steps, then turned. "How did you know about the brandy?"

The priest thought Dondolan's smile seemed a trifle sour. "I am a wizard, remember? We know almost everything."

# Child of an Ancient City

"**M**erciful Allah! I am as a calf, fatted for slaughter!"
Masrur al-Adan roared with laughter and crashed his goblet down on the polished wood table—once, twice, thrice. A trail of crescent-shaped dents followed his hand. "I can scarce move for gorging."

The fire was banked, and shadows walked the walls. Masrur's table—for he was master here—stood scatterspread with the bones of small fowl.

Masrur leaned forward and squinted across the table. "A calf," he said. "Fatted." He belched absently and wiped his mouth with wine-stained sleeve.

Ibn Fahad broke off a thin, cold smile. "We have indeed wreaked massacre on the race of pigeons, old friend." His slim hand swept above the littered table-top. "We have also put the elite guard of your wine cellars to flight. And, as usual, I thank you for your hospitality. But do you not sometimes wonder if there is more to life than growing fat in the service of the Caliph?"

"Hah!" Masrur goggled his eyes. "Doing the Caliph's bidding has made me wealthy. I have made *myself* fat." He smiled. The other guests laughed and whispered.

Abu Jamir, a fatter man in an equally stained robe, toppled a small tower erected from the bones of squab. "The night is young, good Masrur!" he cried. "Have someone fetch up more wine and let us hear some stories!"

"Baba!" Masrur bellowed. "Come here, you old dog!"

Within three breaths an old servant stood in the doorway, looking to his sportive master with apprehension.

"Bring us the rest of the wine, Baba—or have you drunk it all?"

Baba pulled at his grizzled chin. "Ah...ah, but *you* drank it, Master. You and Master Ibn Fahad took the last four jars with you when you went to shoot arrows at the weathercock."

"Just as I suspected," Masrur nodded. "Well, get on across the bazaar to Abu Jamir's place, wake up his manservant, and bring back several jugs. The good Jamir says we must have it now."

Baba disappeared. The chagrined Abu Jamir was cheerfully back-thumped by the other guests.

"A story, a story!" someone shouted. "A tale!"

"Oh, yes, a tale of your travels, Master Masrur!" This was young Hassan, sinfully drunk. No one minded. His eyes were bright, and he was full of innocent stupidity. "Someone said you have traveled to the green lands of the north."

"The north...?" Masrur grumbled, waving his hand as though confronted with something unclean. "No, lad, no...that I cannot give to you." His face clouded and he slumped back on his cushions; his tarbooshed head swayed.

Ibn Fahad knew Masrur like he knew his horses—indeed, Masrur was the only human that could claim so much of Ibn Fahad's attention. He had seen his old comrade drink twice this quantity and still dance like a dervish on the walls of Baghdad, but he thought he could guess the reason for this sudden incapacity.

"Oh, Masrur, please!" Hassan had not given up; he was as unshakeable as a young falcon with its first prey beneath its talons. "Tell us of the north. Tell us of the infidels!"

"A good Moslem should not show such interest in unbelievers." Abu Jamir sniffed piously, shaking the last drops from a wine jug. "If Masrur does not wish to tell a tale, let him be."

"Hah!" snorted the host, recovering somewhat. "You only seek to stall me, Jamir, so that my throat shall not be so dry when your wine arrives. No, I have no fear of speaking of unbelievers: Allah would not have given them a place in the world for their own if they had not *some* use. Rather it is...certain other things that happened which make me hesitate." He gazed kindly on young Hassan, who in the depths of his drunkenness looked about to cry. "Do not despair, eggling. Perhaps it would do me good to unfold this story. I have kept the details long inside." He emptied the dregs of another jar into his cup. "I still feel it so strongly, though—bitter, bitter times. Why don't you tell the story, my good friend?" he said over his shoulder to Ibn Fahad. "You played as much a part as did I."

"No," Ibn Fahad replied. Drunken puppy Hassan emitted a strangled cry of despair.

"But why, old comrade?" Masrur asked, pivoting his bulk to stare in amazement. "Did the experience so chill even *your* heart?"

Ibn Fahad glowered. "Because I know better. As soon as I start you will interrupt, adding details here, magnifying there, then saying: 'No, no, I cannot speak of it! Continue, old friend!' Before I have taken another breath you will interrupt me again. You *know* you will wind up doing all the talking, Masrur. Why do you not start from the beginning and save me my breath?"

All laughed but Masrur, who put on a look of wounded solicitousness. "Of course, old friend," he murmured. "I had no idea that you harbored such grievances. Of course I shall tell the tale." A broad wink was offered to the table. "No sacrifice is too great for a friendship such as ours. Poke up the fire, will you, Baba? Ah, he's gone. Hassan, will you be so kind?"

When the youth was again seated Masrur took a swallow, stroked his beard, and began.


In those days [Masrur said], I myself was but a lowly soldier in the service of Harun al-Rashid, may Allah grant him health. I was young, strong, a man who loved wine more than he should—but what soldier does not?— and a good deal more trim and comely than you see me today.

My troop received a commission to accompany a caravan going north, bound for the land of the Armenites beyond the Caucassian Mountains. A certain prince of that people had sent a great store of gifts as tribute to the Caliph, inviting him to open a route for trade between his principality and our caliphate. Harun al-Rashid, wisest of wise men that he is, did not exactly make the camels groan beneath the weight of the gifts that he sent in return; but he sent several courtiers, including the under-vizier

Walid al-Salameh, to speak for him and to assure this Armenite prince that rich rewards would follow when the route over the Caucassians was opened for good.

We left Baghdad in grand style, pennants flying, the shields of the soldiers flashing like golden dinars, and the Caliph's gifts bundled onto the backs of a gang of evil, contrary donkeys.

We followed the banks of the faithful Tigris, resting several days at Mosul, then continued through the eastern edge of Anatolia. Already as we mounted northward the land was beginning to change, the clean sands giving way to rocky hills and scrub. The weather was colder, and the skies gray, as though Allah's face was turned away from that country, but the men were not unhappy to be out from under the desert sun. Our pace was good; there was not a hint of danger except the occasional wolf howling at night beyond the circles of the campfires. Before two months had passed we had reached the foothills of the Caucassians—what is called the steppe country.

For those of you who have not strayed far from our Baghdad, I should tell you that the northern lands are like nothing you have seen. The trees there grow so close together you could not throw a stone five paces without striking one. The land itself seems always dark—the trees mask the sun before the afternoon is properly finished—and the ground is damp. But, in truth, the novelty of it fades quickly, and before long it seems that the smell of decay is always with you. We caravaneers had been over eight weeks a-traveling, and the bite of homesickness was strong, but we contented ourselves with the thought of the accommodations that would be ours when we reached the palace of the prince, laden as we were with our Caliph's good wishes—and the tangible proof thereof.

We had just crossed the high mountain passes and begun our journey down when disaster struck.

We were encamped one night in a box canyon, a thousand steep feet below the summit of the tall Caucassian peaks. The fires were not much but glowing coals, and nearly all the camp was asleep except for two men standing sentry. I was wrapped in my bedroll, dreaming of how I would spend my earnings, when a terrible shriek awakened me. Sitting groggily upright, I was promptly knocked down by some bulky thing tumbling onto me. A moment's horrified examination showed that it was one of the sentries, throat pierced with an arrow, eyes bulging with his final surprise. Suddenly there was a chorus of howls from the hillside above. All I could think of was wolves, that the wolves were coming down on us; in my witless state I could make no sense of the arrow at all.

Even as the others sprang up around me the camp was suddenly filled with leaping, whooping shadows. Another arrow hissed past my face in the darkness, and then something crashed against my bare head, filling the nighttime with a great splash of light that illuminated nothing. I fell back, insensible.

I could not tell how long I had journeyed in that deeper darkness when I was finally roused by a sharp boot prodding at my ribcage.

I looked up at a tall, cruel figure, cast by the cloud-curtained morning sun in bold silhouette. As my sight adjusted I saw a knife-thin face, dark-browed and fierce, with mustachios long as a Tartar herdsman's. I felt sure that whoever had struck me had returned to finish the job, and I struggled weakly to pull my dagger from my sash. This terrifying figure merely lifted one of his pointy boots and trod delicately on my wrist, saying in perfect Arabic: "Wonders of Allah, this is the dirtiest man I have ever seen."

It was Ibn Fahad, of course. The caravan had been of good size, and he had been riding with the Armenite and the under-vizier—not back with the hoi polloi—so we had never spoken. Now you see how we first truly met: me on my back, covered with mud, blood, and spit; and Ibn Fahad standing over me like a rich man examining carrots in the bazaar. Infamy!

Ibn Fahad had been blessed with what I would come later to know as his usual luck. When the bandits—who must have been following us for some days—came down upon us in the night, Ibn Fahad had been voiding his bladder some way downslope. Running back at the sound of the first cries, he had sent more than a few mountain bandits down to Hell courtesy of his swift sword, but they were too many. He pulled together a small group of survivors from the main party and they fought their way free, then fled along the mountain in the darkness listening to the screams echoing behind them, cursing their small numbers and ignorance of the country.

Coming back in the light of day to scavenge for supplies, as well as ascertain the nature of our attackers, Ibn Fahad had found me—a fact he has never allowed me to forget, and for which I have never allowed *him* to evade responsibility.

While my wounds and bandit-spites were doctored, Ibn Fahad introduced me to the few survivors of our once-great caravan.

One was Susri al-Din—a cheerful lad, fresh-faced and smooth-cheeked as young Hassan here, dressed in the robes of a rich merchant's son. The soldiers who had survived rather liked him, and called him "Fawn," to tease him for his wide-eyed good looks. There was a skinny wretch of a chief clerk named Abdallah, purse-mouthed and iron-eyed, and an indecently plump young mullah, who had just left the *madrasa* and was getting a rather rude introduction to life outside the seminary. Ruad, the mullah, looked as though he would prefer to be drinking and laughing with the soldiers—beside myself and Ibn Fahad there were four or five more of these—while Abdallah the prim-faced clerk looked as though he should be the one who never lifted his head out of the Koran. Well, in a way that was true, since for a man like Abdallah the balance book *is* the Holy Book, may Allah forgive such blasphemy.

There was one other, notable for the extreme richness of his robes, the extreme whiteness of his beard, and the vast weight of his personal jewelry—Walid al-Salameh, the under-vizier to His Eminence the Caliph Harun al-Rashid. Walid was the most important man of the whole party. He was also, surprisingly, not a bad fellow at all.

So there we found ourselves, the wrack of the caliph's embassy, with no hope but to try and find our way back home through a strange, hostile land.

The upper reaches of the Caucassians are a cold and godless place. The fog is thick and wet; it crawls in of the morning, leaves briefly at the time the sun is high, then comes creeping back long before sunset. We had been sodden as well-diggers from the moment we had stepped into the foothills. A treacherous place, those mountains: home of bear and wolf, covered in forest so thick that in places the sun was lost completely. Since we had no guide—indeed, it was several days before we saw any sign of inhabitants whatsoever—we wandered unsteered, losing half as much ground as we gained for walking in circles.

At last we were forced to admit our need for a trained local eye. In the middle slopes the trees grew so thick that fixing our direction was impossible for hours at a time. We were divining the location of Mecca by general discussion, and—blasphemy again—we probably spent as much time praying toward Aleppo as to Mecca. It seemed a choice between possible discovery and certain doom.

We came down by night and took a young man out of an isolated shepherd's hovel, as quietly as ex-brigands like ourselves (or at least like many of us, Ibn Fahad. My apologies!) could. The family did not wake, the dog did not bark; we were two leagues away before sunrise, I'm sure.

I felt sorry in a way for the young peasant-lout we'd kidnapped. He was a nice fellow, although fearfully stupid—I wonder if we are now an old, dull story with which he bores his children? In any case, once this young rustic—whose name as far as I could tell was unpronounceable by civilized tongues—realized that we were not ghosts or Jinni, and were *not* going to kill him on the spot, he calmed down and was quite useful. We began to make real progress, reaching the peak of the nearest ridge in two days.

There was a slight feeling of celebration in the air that night, our first in days under the open skies. The soldiers cursed the lack of strong drink, but spirits were good nonetheless—even Ibn Fahad pried loose a smile.

As the under-vizier Walid told a humorous story, I looked about the camp. There were but two grim faces: the clerk Abdallah—which was to be expected, since he seemed a patently sour old devil—and the stolen peasant-boy. I walked over to him.

"Ho, young one," I said, "why do you look so downcast? Have you not realized that we are good-hearted, Godfearing men, and will not harm you?" He did not even raise his chin, which rested on his knees, shepherd-style, but he turned his eyes up to mine.

"It is not those things," he said in his awkward Arabic. "It is not you soldiers but...this place."

"Gloomy mountains they are indeed," I agreed, "but you have lived here all your young life. Why should it bother you?"

"Not this place. We never come here—it is unholy. The vampyr walks these peaks."

"*Vampyr?*" said I. "And what peasant-devil is that?"

He would say no more; I left him to his brooding and walked back to the fire.

The men all had a good laugh over the vampyr, making jesting guesses as to what type of beast it might be, but Ruad, the young mullah, waved his hands urgently.

"I have heard of such afreets," he said. "They are not to be laughed at by such a godless lot as yourselves."

He said this as a sort of scolding joke, but he wore a strange look on his round face; we listened with interest as he continued.

"The vampyr is a restless spirit. It is neither alive nor dead, and Shaitan possesses its soul utterly. It sleeps in a sepulcher by day, and when the moon rises it goes out to feed upon travelers, to drink their blood."

Some of the men again laughed loudly, but this time it rang false as a brassmerchant's smile.

"I have heard of these from one of our foreign visitors," said the under-vizier Walid quietly. "He told me of a plague of these vampyr in a village near Smyrna. All the inhabitants fled, and the village is still uninhabited today."

This reminded someone else (myself, perhaps) of a tale about an afreet with teeth growing on both sides of his head. Others followed with their own demon stories. The talk went on late into the night, and no one left the campfire until it had completely burned out.

By noon the next day we had left the heights and were passing back down into the dark, tree-blanketed ravines. When we stopped that night we were once more hidden from the stars, out of sight of Allah and the sky.

I remember waking up in the foredawn hours. My beard was wet with dew, and I was damnably tangled up in my cloak. A great, dark shape stood over me. I must confess to making a bit of a squawking noise.

"It's me," the shape hissed—it was Rifakh, one of the other soldiers.

"You gave me a turn."

Rifakh chuckled. "Thought I was that vamper, eh? Sorry. Just stepping out for a piss." He stepped over me, and I heard him trampling the underbrush. I slipped back into sleep.

The sun was just barely over the horizon when I was again awakened, this time by Ibn Fahad tugging at my arm. I grumbled at him to leave me alone, but he had a grip on me like an alms-beggar.

"Rifakh's gone," he said. "Wake up. Have you seen him?"

"He walked on me in the middle of the night, on his way to go moisten a tree," I said. "He probably fell in the darkness and hit his head on something—have you looked?"

"Several times," Ibn Fahad responded. "All around the camp. No sign of him. Did he say anything to you?"

"Nothing interesting. Perhaps he has met the sister of our shepherd-boy, and is making the two-backed beast."

Ibn Fahad made a sour face at my crudity. "Perhaps not. Perhaps he has met some *other* beast."

"Don't worry," I said. "If he hasn't fallen down somewhere close by, he'll be back."

But he did not come back. When the rest of the men arose we had another long search, with no result. At noon we decided, reluctantly, to go on our way, hoping that if he had strayed somewhere he could catch up with us.

We hiked down into the valley, going farther and farther into the trees. There was no sign of Rifakh, although from time to time we stopped and shouted in case he was searching for us. We felt there was small risk of discovery, for that dark valley was as empty as a pauper's purse, but nevertheless, after a while the sound of our voices echoing back through the damp glades became unpleasant. We continued on in silence.

Twilight comes early in the bosom of the mountains; by midafternoon it was already becoming dark. Young Fawn—the name had stuck, against the youth's protests—who of all of us was the most disturbed by the disappearance of Rifakh, stopped the company suddenly, shouting: "Look there!"

We straightaway turned to see where he was pointing, but the thick trees and shadows revealed nothing.

"I saw a shape!" the young one said. "It was just a short way back, following us. Perhaps it is the missing soldier."

Naturally the men ran back to look, but though we scoured the bushes we could find no trace of anyone. We decided that the failing light had played Fawn a trick—that he had seen a hind or somesuch.

Two other times he called out that he saw a shape. The last time one of the other soldiers glimpsed it too: a dark, manlike form, moving rapidly beneath the trees a bow-shot away. Close inspection still yielded no evidence, and as the group trod wearily back to the path again Walid the under-vizier turned to Fawn with a hard, flat look.

"Perhaps it would be better, young master, if you talked no more of shadowshapes."

"But I saw it!" the boy cried. "That soldier Mohammad saw it too!"

"I have no doubt of that," answered Walid al-Salameh, "but think on this: we have gone several times to see what it might be, and have found no sign of any living man. Perhaps our Rifakh is dead; perhaps he fell into a stream and drowned, or hit his head upon a rock. His spirit may be following us because it does not wish to stay in this unfamiliar place. That does not mean we want to go and find it."

"But..." the other began.

"Enough!" spat the chief clerk Abdallah. "You heard the under-vizier, young prankster. We shall have no more talk of your godless spirits. You will straightaway leave off telling such things!"

"Your concern is appreciated, Abdallah," Walid said coldly, "but I do not require your help in this matter." The vizier strode away.

I was almost glad the clerk had added his voice, because such ideas would not keep the journey in good order...but like the under-vizier I, too, had been rubbed and grated by the clerk's highhandedness. I am sure others felt the same, for no more was said on the subject all evening.

Allah, though, always has the last word—and who are *we* to try to understand His ways? We bedded down a very quiet camp that night, the idea of poor Rifakh's lost soul hanging unspoken in the air.

From a thin, unpleasant sleep I woke to find the camp in chaos. "It's Mohammad, the soldier!" Fawn was crying. "He's been killed! He's dead!"

It was true. The mullah Ruad, first up in the morning, had found the man's blanket empty, then found his body a few short yards out of the clearing.

"His throat has been slashed out," said Ibn Fahad.

It looked like a wild beast had been at him. The ground beneath was dark with blood, and his eyes were wide open.

Above the cursing of the soldiers and the murmured holy words of the mullah, who looked quite green of face, I heard another sound. The young shepherd-lad, grimly silent all the day before, was rocking back and forth on the ground by the remains of the cook-fire, moaning.

"Vampyr..." he wept, "...vampyr, the vampyr..."

All the companions were, of course, completely unmanned by these events. While we buried Mohammad in a hastily dug grave those assembled darted glances over their shoulders into the forest vegetation. Even Ruad, as he spoke the words of the holy Koran, had trouble keeping his eyes down. Ibn Fahad and I agreed between ourselves to maintain that Mohammad had fallen prey to a wolf or some other beast, but our fellow travelers found it hard even to pretend agreement. Only the under-vizier and the clerk Abdallah seemed to have their wits fully about them, and Abdallah made no secret of his contempt for the others. We set out again at once.

Our company was somber that day—and no wonder. No one wished to speak of the obvious, nor did they have much stomach for talk of lighter things—it was a silent file of men that moved through the mountain fastnesses.

As the shadows of evening began to roll down, the dark shape was with us again, flitting along just in sight, disappearing for a while only to return, bobbing along behind us like a jackdaw. My skin was crawling—as you may well believe—though I tried to hide it.

We set camp, building a large fire and moving near to it, and had a sullen, close-cramped supper. Ibn Fahad, Abdallah, the vizier, and I were still speaking of the follower only as some beast. Abdallah may even have believed it—not from ordinary foolishness, but because he was the type of man who was unwilling to believe there might be anything he himself could not compass.

As we took turns standing guard the young mullah led the far-from-sleepy men in prayer. The voices rose up with the smoke, neither seeming to be of much substance against the wind of those old, cold mountains.

I sidled over to the shepherd-lad. He'd become, if anything, more close-mouthed since the discovery of the morning.

"This 'vampyr' you spoke of..." I said quietly. "What do your people do to protect themselves from it?"

He looked up at me with a sad smile.

"Lock the doors."

I stared across at the other men—young Fawn with clenched mouth and furrowed brow; the mullah Ruad, eyes closed, plump cheeks awash with sweat as he prayed; Ibn Fahad gazing coolly outward, ever outward—and then I returned the boy's sad smile.

"No doors to lock, no windows to bar," I said. "What else?"

"There is an herb we hang about our houses..." he said, and fumbled for the word in our unfamiliar language. After a moment he gave up. "It does not matter. We have none. None grows here."

I leaned forward, putting my face next to his face. "For the love of God, boy, what else?"—*I* knew it was not a beast of the earth. I *knew*. I had seen that fluttering shadow.

"Well..." he mumbled, turning his face away, "...they say, some men do, that you can tell stories...."

"What!" I thought he had gone mad.

"This is what my grandfather says. The vampyr will stop to hear the story you tell—if it is a good one—and if you continue it until daylight he must return to the...place of the dead."

There was a sudden shriek. I leaped to my feet, fumbling for my knife... but it was only Ruad, who had put his foot against a hot coal. I sank down again, heart hammering.

"Stories?" I asked.

"I have only heard so," he said, struggling for the right phrases. "We try to keep them farther away than that—they must come close to hear a man talking."

Later, after the fire had gone down, we placed sentries and went to our blankets. I lay a long while thinking of what the Armenite boy had said before I slept.

A hideous screeching sound woke me. It was not yet dawn, and this time no one had burned himself on a glowing ember.

One of the two soldiers who had been standing picket lay on the forest floor, blood gouting from a great wound on the side of his head. In the torchlight it looked as though his skull had been smashed with a heavy cudgel. The other sentry was gone, but there was a terrible thrashing in the underbrush beyond the camp, and screams that would have sounded like an animal in a cruel trap but for the half-formed words that bubbled up from time to time.

We crouched, huddled, staring like startled rabbits. The screaming began to die away. Suddenly Ruad started up, heavy and clumsy getting to his feet. I saw tears in his eyes. "We...we must not leave our fellow to s-s-suffer so!" he cried, and looked around at all of us. I don't think anyone could hold his eye except the clerk Abdallah. I could not.

"Be silent, fool!" the clerk said, heedless of blasphemy. "It is a wild beast. It is for these cowardly soldiers to attend to, not a man of God!"

The young mullah stared at him for a moment, and a change came over his face. The tears were still wet on his cheeks, but I saw his jaw firm and his shoulders square.

"No," he said. "We cannot leave him to Shaitan's servant. If you will not go to him, I will." He rolled up the scroll he had been nervously fingering and kissed it. A shaft of moonlight played across the gold letters.

I tried to grab his arm as he went past me, but he shook me off with surprising strength, then moved toward the brush, where the screeching had died down to a low, broken moaning.

"Come back, you idiot!" Abdallah shrieked at him. "This is foolishness! Come back!"

The young holy man looked back over his shoulder, darting a look at

Abdallah I could not easily describe, then turned around and continued forward, holding the parchment scroll before him as if it were a candle against the dark night.

"*There is no God but Allah!*" I heard him cry. "*And Mohammad is His prophet!*" Then he was gone.

After a long moment of silence there came the sound of the holy words of the Koran, chanted in an unsteady voice. We could hear the mullah making his ungraceful way out through the thicket. I was not the only one who held his breath.

Next there was crashing, and branches snapping, as though some huge beast was leaping through the brush; the mullah's chanting became a howl. Men cursed helplessly. Before the cry had faded, though, another scream came—numbingly loud, the rage of a powerful animal, full of shock and surprise. It had words in it, although not in any tongue I had ever heard before...or since.

Another great thrashing, and then nothing but silence. We lit another fire and sat sleepless until dawn.

In the morning, despite my urgings, the company went to look for a trace of the sentry and the young priest. They found them both.

It made a grim picture, let me tell you, my friends. They hung upside down from the branches of a great tree. Their necks were torn, and they were white as chalk: all the blood had been drawn from them. We dragged the two stone-cold husks back to the camp-circle, and shortly thereafter buried them commonly with the other sentry, who had not survived his head wound.

One curious thing there was: on the ground beneath the hanging head of the young priest lay the remains of his holy scroll. It was scorched to black ash, and crumbled at my touch.

"So it *was* a cry of pain we heard," said Ibn Fahad over my shoulder. "The devil-beast can be hurt, it appears."

"Hurt, but not made to give over," I observed. "And no other holy writings remain, nor any hands so holy to wield them, or mouth to speak them." I looked pointedly over at Abdallah, who was giving unwanted instructions to the two remaining soldiers on how to spade the funeral dirt. I half-hoped one of them would take it on himself to brain the old meddler.

"True," grunted Ibn Fahad. "Well, I have my doubts on how cold steel will fare, also."

"As do I. But it could be there is yet a way we may save ourselves. The shepherd-boy told me of it. I will explain when we stop at mid-day."

"I will be waiting eagerly," said Ibn Fahad, favoring me with his half-smile. "I am glad to see someone else is thinking and planning beside myself. But perhaps you should tell us your plan on the march. Our daylight hours are becoming precious as blood, now. As a matter of fact, I think from now on we shall have to do without burial services."


Well, there we were in a very nasty fix. As we walked I explained my plan to the group; they listened silently, downcast, like men condemned to death—not an unreasonable attitude, in all truth.

"Now, here's the thing," I told them. "If this young lout's idea of tale-telling will work, we shall have to spend our nights yarning away. We may have to begin taking stops for sleeping in the daylight. Every moment walking, then, is precious—we must keep the pace up or we will die in these damned, haunted mountains. Also, while you walk, think of stories. From what the lad says we may have another ten days or a fortnight to go until we escape this country. We shall soon run out of things to tell about, unless you dig deep into your memories."

There was grumbling, but it was too dispirited a group to offer much protest.

"Be silent, unless you have a better idea," said Ibn Fahad. "Masrur is quite correct—although, if what I suspect is true, it may be the first time in his life he finds himself in that position." He threw me a wicked grin, and one of the soldiers snickered. It was a good sound to hear.


We had a short mid-day rest—most of us got at least an hour's sleep on the rocky ground—and then we walked on until the beginning of twilight. We were in the bottom of a long, thickly forested ravine, where we promptly built a large fire to keep away some of the darkness of the valley floor. Ah, but fire is a good friend!

Gathered around the blaze, the men cooked strips of venison on the ends of green sticks. We passed the waterskin and wished it was more—not for the first time.

"Now then," I said, "I'll go first, for at home I was the one called upon most often to tell tales, and I have a good fund of them. Some of you may sleep, but not all—there should always be two or three awake in case the teller falters or forgets. We cannot know if this will keep the creature at bay, but we should take no chances."

So I began, telling first the story of The Four Clever Brothers. It was early, and no one was ready to sleep; all listened attentively as I spun it out, adding details here, stretching a description there.

When it ended I was applauded, and straight away began telling the story of the carpet merchant Salim and his unfaithful wife. That was perhaps not a good choice—it is a story about a vengeful djinn, and about death; but I went on nonetheless, finished it, then told two more.

As I was finishing the fourth story, about a brave orphan who finds a cave of jewels, I glimpsed a strange thing.

The fire was beginning to die down, and as I looked out over the flames I saw movement in the forest. The under-vizier Walid was directly across from me, and beyond his once-splendid robes a dark shape lurked. It came no closer than the edge of the trees, staying just out of the fire's flickering light. I lost my voice for a moment then and stuttered, but quickly caught up the thread and finished. No one had noticed, I was sure.

I asked for the waterskin and motioned for Walid al-Salameh to continue. He took up with a tale of the rivalry beyond two wealthy houses in his native Isfahan. One or two of the others wrapped themselves tightly in their cloaks and lay down, staring up as they listened, watching the sparks rise into the darkness.

I pulled my hood down low on my brow to shield my gaze, and squinted out past Walid's shoulder. The dark shape had moved a little nearer now to the lapping glow of the campfire.

It was man-shaped, that I could see fairly well, though it clung close to the trunk of a tree at clearing's edge. Its face was in darkness; two ember-red eyes unblinkingly reflected the firelight. It seemed clothed in rags, but that could have been a trick of the shadows.

Huddled in the darkness a stone-throw away, it was listening.

I turned my head slowly across the circle. Most eyes were on the vizier; Fawn had curtained his in sleep. But Ibn Fahad, too, was staring out into the darkness. I suppose he felt my gaze, for he turned to me and nodded slightly: he had seen it too.

We went on until dawn, the men taking turns sleeping as one of the others told stories—mostly tales they had heard as children, occasionally of an adventure that had befallen them. Ibn Fahad and I said nothing of the dark shape that watched. Somewhere in the hour before dawn it disappeared.

It was a sleepy group that took to the trail that day, but we had all lived through the night. This alone put the men in better spirits, and we covered much ground.

That night we again sat around the fire. I told the story of The Gazelle King, and The Enchanted Peacock, and The Little Man with No Name, each of them longer and more complicated than the one before. Everyone except the clerk Abdallah contributed something—Abdallah and the shepherd-boy, that is. The chief-clerk said repeatedly that he had never wasted his time on foolishness such as learning stories. We were understandably reluctant to press our self-preservation into such unwilling hands.

The Armenite boy, our guide, sat quietly all the evening and listened to the men yarning away in a tongue that was not his own. When the moon had risen through the treetops, the shadow returned and stood silently outside the clearing. I saw the peasant lad look up. He saw it, I know, but like Ibn Fahad and I, he held his silence.

The next day brought us two catastrophes. As we were striking camp in the morning, happily no fewer than when we had set down the night before, the local lad took the waterskins down to the river that threaded the bottom of the ravine. When a long hour had passed and he had not returned, we went fearfully down to look for him.

He was gone. All but one of the waterskins lay on the streambank. He had filled them first.

The men were panicky. "The vampyr has taken him!" they cried.

"What does that foul creature need with a waterskin?" pointed out al-Salameh.

"He's right," I said. "No, I'm afraid our young friend has merely jumped ship, so to speak. I suppose he thinks his chances of getting back are better if he is alone."

I wondered...I *still* wonder...if he made it back. He was not a bad fellow: witness the fact that he took only one water-bag, and left us the rest.

Thus, we found ourselves once more without a guide. Fortunately, I had discussed with him the general direction, and he had told Ibn Fahad and myself of the larger landmarks...but it was nevertheless with sunken hearts that we proceeded.

Later that day, in the early afternoon, the second blow fell.

We were coming up out of the valley, climbing diagonally along the steep side of the ravine. The damned Caucassian fogs had slimed the rocks and turned the ground soggy; the footing was treacherous.

Achmed, the older of the remaining pike-men, had been walking poorly all day. He had bad joints, anyway, he said; and the cold nights had been making them worse.

We had stopped to rest on an outcropping of rock that jutted from the valley wall; Achmed, the last in line, was just catching up to us when he slipped. He fell heavily onto his side and slid several feet down the muddy slope.

Ibn Fahad jumped up to look for a rope, but before he could get one from the bottom of his pack the other soldier—named Bekir, if memory serves—clambered down the grade to help his comrade.

He got a grip on Achmed's tunic, and was just turning around to catch Ibn Fahad's rope when the leg of the older man buckled beneath him and he fell backward. Bekir, caught off his balance, pitched back as well, his hand caught in the neck of Achmed's tunic, and the two of them rolled end over end down the slope. Before anyone could so much as cry out they had both disappeared over the edge, like a wine jug rolling off a table-top. Just that sudden.

To fall such a distance certainly killed them.

We could not find the bodies, of course...could not even climb back down the ravine to look. Ibn Fahad's remark about burials had taken on a terrible, ironic truth. We could but press on, now a party of five—myself, Ibn Fahad, the under-vizier Walid, Abdallah the clerk, and young Fawn. I doubt that there was a single one of our number who did not wonder which of us would next meet death in that lonesome place.

Ah, by Allah most high, I have never been so sick of the sound of my own voice as I was by the time nine more nights had passed. Ibn Fahad, I know, would say that I have never understood how sick *everyone* becomes of the sound of my voice—am I correct, old friend? But I *was* tired of it, tired of talking all night, tired of racking my brain for stories, tired of listening to the cracked voices of Walid and Ibn Fahad, tired to sickness of the damp, gray, oppressive mountains.

All were now aware of the haunting shade that stood outside our fire at night, waiting and listening. Young Fawn, in particular, could hardly hold up his turn at tale-telling, so much did his voice tremble.

Abdallah grew steadily colder and colder, congealing like rendered fat. The thing which followed was no respecter of his cynicism or his mathematics, and would not be banished for all the scorn he could muster. The skinny chief-clerk did not turn out to us, though, to support the story-circle, but sat silently and walked apart. Despite our terrible mutual danger he avoided our company as much as possible.

The tenth night after the loss of Achmed and Bekir we were running out of tales. We had been ground down by our circumstances, and were ourselves become nearly as shadowy as that which we feared.

Walid al-Salameh was droning on about some ancient bit of minor intrigue in the court of the Emperor Darius of Persia. Ibn Fahad leaned toward me, lowering his voice so that neither Abdallah nor Fawn—whose expression was one of complete and hopeless despair—could hear.

"Did you notice," he whispered, "that our guest has made no appearance tonight?"

"It has not escaped me," I said. "I hardly think it a good sign, however. If our talk no longer interests the creature, how long can it be until its thoughts return to our other uses?"

"I fear you're right," he responded, and gave a scratchy, painful chuckle. "There's a good three or four more days walking, and hard walking at that, until we reach the bottom of these mountains and come once more onto the plain, at which point we might hope the devil-beast would leave us."

"Ibn Fahad," I said, shaking my head as I looked across at Fawn's drawn, pale face, "I fear we shall not manage..."

As if to point up the truth of my fears, Walid here stopped his speech, coughing violently. I gave him to drink of the waterskin, but when he had finished he did not begin anew; he only sat looking darkly, as one lost, out to the forest.

"Good vizier," I asked, "can you continue?"

He said nothing, and I quickly spoke in his place, trying to pick up the threads of a tale I had not been attending to. Walid leaned back, exhausted and breathing raggedly. Abdallah clucked his tongue in disgust. If I had not been fearfully occupied, I would have struck the clerk.

Just as I was beginning to find my way, inventing a continuation of the vizier's Darian political meanderings, there came a shock that passed through all of us like a cold wind, and a new shadow appeared at the edge of the clearing. The vampyr had joined us.

Walid moaned and sat up, huddling by the fire. I faltered for a moment but went on. The candle-flame eyes regarded us unblinkingly, and the shadow shook for a moment as if folding great wings.

Suddenly Fawn leaped to his feet, swaying unsteadily. I lost the strands of the story completely and stared up at him in amazement.

"Creature!" he screamed. "Hell-spawn! Why do you torment us in this way? Why, why, why?"

Ibn Fahad reached up to pull him down, but the young man danced away like a shying horse. His mouth hung open and his eyes were starting from their dark-rimmed sockets.

"You great beast!" he continued to shriek. "Why do you toy with us?

Why do you not just kill me—kill us *all*, set us free from this terrible, terrible..."

And with that he walked *forward*—away from the fire, toward the thing that crouched at forest's edge.

"End this now!" Fawn shouted, and fell to his knees only a few strides from the smoldering red eyes, sobbing like a child.

"Stupid boy, get back!" I cried. Before I could get up to pull him back— and I would have, I swear by Allah's name—there was a great rushing noise, and the black shape was gone, the lamps of its stare extinguished. Then, as we pulled the shuddering youth back to the campfire, something rustled in the trees. On the opposite side of the campfire one of the near branches suddenly bobbed beneath the weight of a strange new fruit—a black fruit with red-lit eyes. It made an awful croaking noise.

In our shock it was a few moments before we realized that the deep, rasping sound was speech—and the words were Arabic!

"...It...was...you..." it said, "...who chose...to play the game this way..."

Almost strangest of all, I would swear that this thing had never spoken our language before, never even heard it until we had wandered lost into the mountains. Something of its halting inflections, its strange hesitations, made me guess it had learned our speech from listening all these nights to our campfire stories.

"Demon!" shrilled Abdallah. "What manner of creature are you?!"

"You know...very well what kind of...thing I am, man. You may none of you know *how*, or *why*...but by now, you know *what* I am."

"Why...why do you torment us so?!" shouted Fawn, writhing in Ibn Fahad's strong grasp.

"Why does the...serpent kill...a rabbit? The serpent does not...hate. It kills to live, as do I...as do you."

Abdallah lurched forward a step. "We do not slaughter our fellow men like this, devil-spawn!"

"C-c-clerk!" the black shape hissed, and dropped down from the tree. "C-close your foolish mouth! You push me too far!" It bobbed, as if agitated. "The curse of human ways! Even now you provoke me more than you should, you huffing...insect! *Enough!*"

The vampyr seemed to leap upward, and with a great rattling of leaves he scuttled away along the limb of a tall tree. I was fumbling for my sword, but before I could find it the creature spoke again from his high perch.

"The young one asked me why I 'toy' with you. I do not. If I do not kill, I will suffer. More than I suffer already.

"Despite what this clerk says, though, I am not a creature without... without feelings as men have them. Less and less do I wish to destroy you.

"For the first time in a great age I have listened to the sound of human voices that were not screams of fear. I have approached a circle of men without the barking of dogs, and have listened to them talk.

"It has almost been like being a man again."

"And this is how you show your pleasure?" the under-vizier Walid asked, teeth chattering. "By k-k-killing us?"

"I am what I am," said the beast. "...But for all that, you have inspired a certain desire for companionship. It puts me in mind of things that I can barely remember.

"I propose that we make a...bargain," said the vampyr. "A...wager?"

I had found my sword, and Ibn Fahad had drawn his as well, but we both knew we could not kill a thing like this—a red-eyed demon that could leap five cubits in the air and had learned to speak our language in a fortnight.

"No bargains with Shaitan!" spat the clerk Abdallah.

"What do you mean?" I demanded, inwardly marveling that such an unlikely dialogue should ever take place on the earth. "Pay no attention to the..." I curled my lip, "...holy man." Abdallah shot me a venomous glance.

"Hear me, then," the creature said, and in the deep recesses of the tree seemed once more to unfold and stretch great wings. "Hear me. I must kill to live, and my nature is such that I cannot choose to die. That is the way of things.

"I offer you now, however, the chance to win safe passage out of my domain, these hills. We shall have a contest, a wager if you like; if you best me you shall go freely, and I shall turn once more to the musty, slow-blooded peasants of the local valleys."

Ibn Fahad laughed bitterly. "What, are we to fight you then? So be it!"

"I would snap your spine like a dry branch," croaked the black shape.

"No, you have held me these many nights telling stories; it is story-telling that will win you safe passage. We will have a contest, one that will suit my whims: we shall relate the saddest of all stories. That is my demand. You may tell three, I will tell only one. If you can best me with any or all, you shall go unhindered by me."

"And if we lose?!" I cried. "And who shall judge?"

"You may judge," it said, and the deep, thick voice took on a tone of grim amusement. "If you can look into my eyes and tell me that you have bested *my* sad tale...why, then I shall believe you.

"If you lose," it said, "then one of your number shall come to me, and pay the price of your defeat. Those are my terms, otherwise I shall hunt you down one at a time—for in truth, your present tale-telling has begun to lose my interest."

Ibn Fahad darted a worried look in my direction. Fawn and the others stared at the demon-shape in mute terror and astonishment.

"We shall...we shall give you our decision at sunset tomorrow," I said. "We must be allowed to think and talk."

"As you wish," said the vampyr. "But if you accept my challenge, the game must begin then. After all, we have only a few more days to spend together." And at this the terrible creature laughed, a sound like the bark being pulled from the trunk of a rotted tree. Then the shadow was gone.

In the end we had to accede to the creature's wager, of course. We knew he was not wrong in his assessment of us—we were just wagging our beards over the nightly campfire, no longer even listening to our own tales. Whatever magic had held the vampyr at bay had drained out like meal from a torn sack.

I racked my poor brains all afternoon for stories of sadness, but could think of nothing that seemed to fit, that seemed significant enough for the vital purpose at hand. I had been doing most of the talking for several nights running, and had exhausted virtually every story I had ever heard—and I was never much good at making them up, as Ibn Fahad will attest. Yes, go ahead and smile, old comrade.

Actually, it was Ibn Fahad who volunteered the first tale. I asked him what it was, but he would not tell me. "Let me save what potency it may have," he said. The under-vizier Walid also had something he deemed suitable; I was racking my brain fruitlessly for a third time when young Fawn piped up that he would tell a tale himself. I looked him over, rosy cheeks and long-lashed eyes, and asked him what he could possibly know of sadness. Even as I spoke I realized my cruelty, standing as we all did in the shadow of death or worse, but it was too late to take it back.

Fawn did not flinch. He was folding his cloak as he sat cross-ankled on the ground, folding and unfolding it. He looked up and said: "I shall tell a sad story about love. All the saddest stories are about love."

*These young shavetails,* I thought—although I was not ten years his senior—*a sad story about love.* But I could not think of better, and was forced to give in.

We walked as fast and far as we could that day, as if hoping that somehow, against all reason, we should find ourselves out of the gloomy, mist-sodden hills. But when twilight came the vast bulk of the mountains still hung above us. We made camp on the porch of a great standing rock, as though protection at our backs would avail us of something if the night went badly.

The fire had only just taken hold, and the sun had dipped below the rim of the hills a moment before, when a cold wind made the branches of the trees whip back and forth. We knew without speaking, without looking at one another, that the creature had come.

"Have you made your decision?" The harsh voice from the trees sounded strange, as if its owner was trying to speak lightly, carelessly—but I only heard death in those cold syllables.

"We have," said Ibn Fahad, drawing himself up out of his involuntary half-crouch to stand erect. "We will accept your wager. Do you wish to begin?"

"Oh, no..." the thing said, and made a flapping noise. "That would take all of the...suspense from the contest, would it not? No, I insist that you begin."

"I am first, then," Ibn Fahad said, looking around our circle for confirmation. The dark shape moved abruptly toward us. Before we could scatter the vampyr stopped, a few short steps away.

"Do not fear," it grated. Close to one's ear the voice was even odder and more strained. "I have come nearer to hear the story and see the teller—for surely that is part of any tale—but I shall move no farther. Begin."

Everybody but myself stared into the fire, hugging their knees, keeping their eyes averted from the bundle of darkness that sat at our shoulders. I had the fire between myself and the creature, and felt safer than if I had sat like Walid and Abdallah, with nothing between the beast and my back but cold ground.

The vampyr sat hunched, as if imitating our posture, its eyes hooded so that only a flicker of scarlet light, like a half-buried brand, showed through each slit. It was black, this manlike thing—not black as a Negro, mind you, but black as burnt steel, black as the mouth of a cave. It bore the aspect of someone dead of the plague. Rags wrapped it, mouldering, filthy bits of cloth, rotten as old bread...but the curve of its back spoke of terrible life—a great black cricket poised to jump.

## Ibn Fahad's Story

Many years ago [he began], I traveled for a good time in Egypt. I was indigent, then, and journeyed wherever the prospect of payment for a sword arm beckoned.

I found myself at last in the household guard of a rich merchant in Alexandria. I was happy enough there; and I enjoyed walking in the busy streets, so unlike the village in which I was born.

One summer evening I found myself walking down an unfamiliar street. It emptied out into a little square that sat below the front of an old mosque. The square was full of people: merchants and fishwives, a juggler or two, but most of the crowd was drawn up to the facade of the mosque, pressed in close together.

At first, as I strolled across the square, I thought prayers were about to begin, but it was still some time until sunset. I wondered if perhaps some notable imam was speaking from the mosque steps, but as I approached I could see that all the assembly were staring upward, craning their necks back as if the sun itself, on its way to its western mooring, had become snagged on one of the minarets.

But instead of the sun, what stood on the onion-shaped dome was the silhouette of a man, who seemed to be staring out toward the horizon.

"Who is that?" I asked a man near me.

"It is Ha'arud al-Emwiya, the Sufi," the man told me, never lowering his eyes from the tower above.

"Is he caught up there?" I demanded. "Will he not fall?"

"Watch," was all the man said. I did.

A moment later, much to my horror, the small dark figure of Ha'arud the Sufi seemed to go rigid, then toppled from the minaret's rim like a stone. I gasped in shock, and so did a few others around me, but the rest of the crowd only stood in hushed attention.

Then an incredible thing happened. The tumbling holy man spread his arms out from his shoulders, like a bird's wings, and his downward fall became a swooping glide. He bottomed out high above the crowd, then sped upward, riding the wind like a leaf, spinning, somersaulting, stopping at last to drift to the ground as gently as a bit of eiderdown. Meanwhile, all the assembly was chanting "God is great! God is great!" When the Sufi had touched the earth with his bare feet the people surrounded him, touching his rough woolen garments and crying out his name. He said nothing, only stood and smiled, and before too long the people began to wander away, talking amongst themselves.

"But this is truly marvelous!" I said to the man who stood by me.

"Before every holy day he flies," the man said, and shrugged. "I am surprised this is the first time you have heard of Ha'arud al-Emwiya."

I was determined to speak to this amazing man, and as the crowd dispersed I approached and asked if I might buy him a glass of tea. Close up he had a look of seamed roguishness that seemed surprising placed against the great favor in which Allah must have held him. He smilingly agreed, and accompanied me to a tea shop close by in the Street of Weavers.

"How is it, if you will pardon my forwardness, that you of all holy men are so gifted?"

He looked up from the tea cupped in his palms and grinned. He had only two teeth. "Balance," he said.

I was surprised. "A cat has balance," I responded, "but they nevertheless must wait for the pigeons to land."

"I refer to a different sort of balance," he said. "The balance between Allah and Shaitan, which, as you know, Allah the All-Knowing has created as an equilibrium of exquisite delicacy."

"Explain please, master." I called for wine, but Ha'arud refused any himself.

"In all things care must be exercised," he explained. "Thus it is too with my flying. Many men holier than I are as earthbound as stones. Many other men have lived so poorly as to shame the Devil himself, yet they cannot take to the air, either. Only I, if I may be excused what sounds self-satisfied, have discovered perfect balance. Thus, each year before the holy days I tot up my score carefully, committing small peccadilloes or acts of faith as needed until the balance is exactly, exactly balanced. Thus, when I jump from the mosque, neither Allah nor the Arch-Enemy has claim on my soul, and they bear me up until a later date, at which time the issue shall be clearer." He smiled again and drained his tea.

"You are...a sort of chessboard on which God and the Devil contend?" I asked, perplexed.

"A flying chessboard, yes."

We talked for a long while, as the shadows grew long across the Street of the Weavers, but the Sufi Ha'arud adhered stubbornly to his explanation. I must have seemed disbelieving, for he finally proposed that we ascend to the top of the mosque so he could demonstrate.

I was more than a little drunk, and he, imbibing only tea, was filled nonetheless with a strange gleefulness. We made our way up the many winding stairs and climbed out onto the narrow ledge that circled the minaret like a crown. The cool night air, and the thousands of winking lights of Alexandria far below, sobered me rapidly. "I suddenly find all your precepts very sound," I said. "Let us go down."

But Ha'arud would have none of it, and proceeded to step lightly off the edge of the dome. He hovered, like a bumblebee, a hundred feet above the dusty street. "Balance," he said with great satisfaction.

"But," I asked, "is the good deed of giving me this demonstration enough to offset the pride with which you exhibit your skill?" I was cold and wanted to get down, and hoped to shorten the exhibition.

Instead, hearing my question, Ha'arud screwed up his face as though it was something he had not given thought to. A moment later, with a shriek of surprise, he plummeted down out of my sight to smash on the mosque's stone steps, as dead as dead.

Ibn Fahad, having lost himself in remembering the story, poked at the campfire. "Thus, the problem with matters of delicate balance," he said, and shook his head.

The whispering rustle of our dark visitor brought us sharply back. "Interesting," the creature rasped. "Sad, yes. Sad enough? We shall see. Who is the next of your number?"

A cold chill, like fever, swept over me at those calm words.

"I...I am next..." said Fawn, voice taut as a bowstring. "Shall I begin?"

"The vampyr said nothing, only bobbed the black lump of his head. The youth cleared his throat and began.

## Fawn's Story

There was once...[Fawn began, and hesitated, then started again.] There was once a young prince named Zufik, the second son of a great sultan. Seeing no prospects for himself in his father's kingdom, he went out into the wild world to search for his fortune. He traveled through many lands, and saw many strange things, and heard tell of others stranger still.

In one place he was told of a nearby sultanate, the ruler of which had a beautiful daughter, his only child and the very apple of his eye.

Now this country had been plagued for several years by a terrible beast, a great white leopard of a kind never seen before. So fearsome it was that it had killed hunters set to trap it, yet was it also so cunning that it had stolen babies from their very cradles as the mothers lay sleeping. The people of the sultanate were all in fear; and the sultan, whose best warriors had tried and failed to kill the beast, was driven to despair. Finally, at the end of his wits, he had it proclaimed in the market place that the man who could destroy the white leopard would be gifted with the sultan's daughter Rassoril, and with her the throne of the sultanate after the old man was gone.

Young Zufik heard how the best young men of the country, and others from countries beyond, one after the other had met their deaths beneath the claws of the leopard, or...or...in its jaws....

[Here I saw the boy falter, as if the vision of flashing teeth he was conjuring had suddenly reminded him of our predicament. Walid the under-vizier reached out and patted the lad's shoulder with great gentleness, until he was calm enough to resume.]

So...[He swallowed.] So young Prince Zufik took himself into that country, and soon was announced at the sultan's court.

The ruler was a tired old man, the fires in his sunken eyes long quenched. Much of the power seemed to have been handed over to a pale, narrow-faced youth named Sifaz, who was the princess's cousin. As Zufik announced his purpose, as so many had done before him, Sifaz's eyes flashed.

"You will no doubt meet the end all the others have, but you are welcome to the attempt—and the prize, should you win."

Then for the first time Zufik saw the princess Rassoril, and in an instant his heart was overthrown.

She had hair as black and shiny as polished jet, and a face upon which Allah himself must have looked in satisfaction, thinking: "Here is the summit of My art." Her delicate hands were like tiny doves as they nested in her lap, and a man could fall into her brown eyes and drown without hope of rescue—which is what Zufik did, and he was not wrong when he thought he saw Rassoril return his ardent gaze.

Sifaz saw, too, and his thin mouth turned in something like a smile, and he narrowed his yellow eyes. "Take this princeling to his room, that he may sleep now and wake with the moon. The leopard's cry was heard around the palace's walls last night."

Indeed, when Zufik woke in the evening darkness, it was to hear the choking cry of the leopard beneath his very window. As he looked out, buckling on his scabbard, it was to see a white shape slipping in and out of the shadows in the garden below. He took also his dagger in his hand and leaped over the threshold.

He had barely touched ground when, with a terrible snarl, the leopard bounded out of the obscurity of the hedged garden wall and came to a stop before him. It was huge—bigger than any leopard Zufik had seen or heard of—and its pelt gleamed like ivory. It leaped, claws flashing, and he could barely throw himself down in time as the beast passed over him like a cloud, touching him only with its hot breath. It turned and leaped again as the palace dogs set up a terrible barking, and this time its talons raked his chest, knocking him tumbling. Blood started from his shirt, spouting so fiercely that he could scarcely draw himself to his feet. He was caught with his back against the garden wall; the leopard slowly moved toward him, yellow eyes like tallow lamps burning in the niches of Hell.

Suddenly there was a crashing at the far end of the garden: the dogs had broken down their stall and were even now speeding through the trees. The leopard hesitated—Zufik could almost see it thinking—and then, with a last snarl, it leaped onto the wall and disappeared into the night.

Zufik was taken, his wounds bound, and he was put into his bed. The princess Rassoril, who had truly lost her heart to him, wept bitterly at his side, begging him to go back to his father's land and to give up the fatal challenge. But Zufik, weak as he was, would no more think of yielding than he would of theft or treason, and refused, saying he would hunt the beast again the following night. Sifaz grinned and led the princess away. Zufik thought he heard the pale cousin whistling as he went.

In the dark before dawn Zufik, who could not sleep owing to the pain of his injury, heard his door quietly open. He was astonished to see the princess come in, gesturing him to silence. When the door was closed she threw herself down at his side and covered his hand and cheek with kisses, proclaiming her love for him and begging him again to go. He admitted his love for her, but reminded her that his honor would not permit him to stop short of his goal, even should he die in the trying.

Rassoril, seeing that there was no changing the young prince's mind, then took from her robe a black arrow tipped in silver, fletched with the tail feathers of a falcon. "Then take this," she said. "This leopard is a magic beast, and you will never kill it otherwise. Only silver will pierce its heart. Take the arrow and you may fulfill your oath." So saying, she slipped out of his room.

The next night Zufik again heard the leopard's voice in the garden below, but this time he took also his bow and arrow when he went to meet it. At first he was loath to use it, since it seemed somehow unmanly; but when the beast had again given him injury and he had struck three sword blows in turn without effect, he at last nocked the silver-pointed shaft on his bowstring and, as the beast charged him once more, let fly. The black arrow struck to the leopard's heart; the creature gave a hideous cry and again leaped the fence, this time leaving a trail of its mortal blood behind it.

When morning came Zufik went to the sultan for men, so that they could follow the track of blood to the beast's lair and prove its death. The sultan was displeased when his vizier, the princess's pale cousin, did not answer his summons. As they were all going down into the garden, though, there came a great cry from the sleeping rooms upstairs, a cry like a soul in mortal agony. With fear in their hearts Zufik, the sultan, and all the men rushed upstairs. There they found the missing Sifaz.

The pale man lifted a shaking, red-smeared finger to point at Zufik, as all the company stared in horror. "*He* has done it—the foreigner!" Sifaz shouted.

In Sifaz's arms lay the body of the princess Rassoril, a black arrow standing from her breast.

After Fawn finished there was a long silence. The boy, his own courage perhaps stirred by his story, seemed to sit straighter.

"Ah..." the vampyr said at last, "love and its prices—that is the message? Or is it perhaps the effect of silver on the supernatural? Fear not, I am bound by no such conventions, and fear neither silver, steel, nor any other metal." The creature made a huffing, scraping sound that might have been a laugh. I marveled anew, even as I felt the skein of my life fraying, that it had so quickly gained such command of our unfamiliar tongue.

"Well..." it said slowly. "Sad. But...sad enough? Again, *that* is the important question. Who is your last...contestant?"

Now my heart truly went cold within me, and I sat as though I had swallowed a stone. Walid al-Salameh spoke up.

"I am," he said, and took a deep breath. "I am."


## The Vizier's Story

This is a true story—or so I was told. It happened in my grandfather's time, and he had it from someone who knew those involved. He told it to me as a cautionary tale.

There once was an old caliph, a man of rare gifts and good fortune. He ruled a small country, but a wealthy one—a country upon which all the gifts of Allah had been showered in grand measure. He had the finest heir a man could have, dutiful and yet courageous, beloved by the people almost as extravagantly as the caliph himself. He had many other fine sons, and two hundred beautiful wives, and an army of fighting men the envy of his neighbors. His treasury was stacked roofbeam-high with gold and gemstones and blocks of fragrant sandalwood, crisscrossed with ivories and bolts of the finest cloth. His palace was built around a spring of fragrant, clear water; and everyone said that they must be the very Waters of Life, so fortunate and well-loved this caliph was. His only sadness was that age had robbed his sight from him, leaving him blind, but hard as this was, it was a small price to pay for Allah's beneficence.

One day the caliph was walking in his garden, smelling the exquisite fragrance of the blossoming orange trees. His son the prince, unaware of his father's presence, was also in the garden, speaking with his mother, the caliph's first and chiefest wife.

"He is terribly old," the wife said. "I cannot stand even to touch him anymore. It is a horror to me."

"You are right, Mother," the son replied, as the caliph hid behind the trees and listened, shocked. "I am sickened by watching him sitting all day, drooling into his bowl, or staggering sightless through the palace. But what are we to do?"

"I have thought on it long and hard," the caliph's wife replied. "We owe it to ourselves and those close to us to kill him."

"Kill him?" the son replied. "Well, it is hard for me, but I suppose you are right. I still feel some love for him, though—may we at least do it quickly, so that he shall not feel pain at the end?"

"Very well. But do it soon—tonight, even. If I must feel his foul breath upon me one more night I will die myself."

"Tonight, then," the son agreed, and the two walked away, leaving the blind caliph shaking with rage and terror behind the orange trees. He could not see what sat on the garden path behind them, the object of their discussion: the wife's old lap-dog, a scrofulous creature of extreme age.

Thus the caliph went to his vizier, the only one he was sure he could trust in a world of suddenly traitorous sons and wives, and bade him to have the pair arrested and quickly beheaded. The vizier was shocked, and asked the reason why, but the caliph only said he had unassailable proof that they intended to murder him and take his throne. He bade the vizier go and do the deed.

The vizier did as he was directed, seizing the son and his mother quickly and quietly, then giving them over to the headsman after tormenting them for confessions and the names of confederates, neither of which were forthcoming.

Sadly, the vizier went to the caliph and told him it was done, and the old man was satisfied. But soon, inevitably, word of what had happened spread, and the brothers of the heir began to murmur among themselves about their father's deed. Many thought him mad, since the dead pair's devotion to the caliph was common knowledge.

Word of this dissension reached the caliph himself, and he began to fear for his life, terrified that his other sons meant to emulate their treasonous brother. He called the vizier to him and demanded the arrest of these sons, and their beheading. The vizier argued in vain, risking his own life, but the caliph would not be swayed; at last the vizier went away, returning a week later a battered, shaken man.

"It is done, O Prince," he said. "All your sons are dead."

The caliph had only a short while in which to feel safe before the extreme wrath of the wives over the slaughter of their children reached his ears. "Destroy them, too!" the blind caliph insisted.

Again the vizier went away, soon to return.

"It is done, O Prince," he reported. "Your wives have been beheaded."

Soon the courtiers were crying murder, and the caliph sent his vizier to see them dealt with as well.

"It is done, O Prince," he assured the caliph. But the ruler now feared the angry townspeople, so he commanded his vizier to take the army and slaughter them. The vizier argued feebly, then went away.

"It is done, O Prince," the caliph was told a month later. But now the caliph realized that with his heirs and wives gone, and the important men of the court dead, it was the soldiers themselves who were a threat to his power. He commanded his vizier to sow lies amongst them, causing them to fall out and slay each other, then locked himself in his room to safely outlast the conflict. After a month and a half the vizier knocked upon his door.

"It is done, O Prince."

For a moment the caliph was satisfied. All his enemies were dead, and he himself was locked in: no one could murder him, or steal his treasure, or usurp his throne. The only person yet alive who even knew where the caliph hid was...his vizier.

Blind, he groped about for the key with which he had locked himself in. Better first to remove the risk that someone might trick him into coming out. He pushed the key out beneath the door and told the vizier to throw it away somewhere it might never be found. When the vizier returned he called him close to the locked portal that bounded his small world of darkness and safety.

"Vizier," the caliph said through the keyhole, "I command you to go and kill yourself; for you are the last one living who is a threat to me."

"*Kill* myself, my prince?" the vizier asked, dumbfounded. "Kill *myself*?"

"Correct," the caliph said. "Now go and do it. That is my command."

There was a long silence. At last the vizier said: "Very well." After that there was silence.

For a long time the caliph sat in his blindness and exulted, for everyone he distrusted was gone. His faithful vizier had carried out all his orders, and now had killed himself...

A sudden, horrible thought came to him then: What if the vizier had *not* done what he had told him to do? What if instead he had made compact with the caliph's enemies, and was only reporting false details when he told of their deaths? *How was the caliph to know?* He almost swooned with fright and anxiousness at the realization.

At last he worked up the courage to feel his way across the locked room to the door. He put his ear to the keyhole and listened. He heard nothing but silence. He took a breath and then put his mouth to the hole.

"Vizier?" he called in a shaky voice. "Have you done what I commanded? Have you killed yourself?"

"It is done, O Prince," came the reply.

Finishing his story, which was fully as dreadful as it was sad, the under-vizier Walid lowered his head as if ashamed or exhausted. We waited tensely for our guest to speak; at the same time I am sure we all vainly hoped there would be no more speaking, that the creature would simply vanish, like a frightening dream that flees the sun.

"Rather than discuss the merits of your sad tales," the black, tattered shadow said at last—confirming that there would be no waking from *this* dream, "rather than argue the game with only one set of moves completed, perhaps it is now time for me to speak. The night is still youthful, and my tale is not long, but I wish to give you a fair time to render judgement."

As he spoke the creature's eyes bloomed scarlet like unfolding roses. The mist curled up from the ground beyond the fire-circle, wrapping the vampyr in a cloak of writhing fogs, a rotted black egg in a bag of silken mesh.

"...May I begin?" it asked...but no one could say a word. "Very well..."

## The Vampyr's Story

The tale I will tell is of a child, a child born of an ancient city on the banks of a river. So long ago this was that not only has the city itself long gone to dust, but the later cities built atop its ruins, tiny towns and great walled fortresses of stone, all these too have gone beneath the millwheels of time—rendered, like their predecessor, into the finest of particles to blow in the wind, silting the timeless river's banks.

This child lived in a mud hut thatched with straw, and played with his fellows in the shallows of the sluggish brown river while his mother washed the family's clothes and gossiped with her neighbors.

Even *this* ancient city was built upon the bones of earlier cities, and it was into the collapsed remnants of one—a great, tumbled mass of shattered sandstone—that the child and his friends sometimes went. And it was to these ruins that the child, when he was a little older...almost the age of your young, romantic companion...took a pretty, doe-eyed girl.

It was to be his first time beyond the veil—his initiation into the mysteries of women. His heart beat rapidly; the girl walked ahead of him, her slender brown body tiger-striped with light and shade as she walked among the broken pillars. Then she saw something, and screamed. The child came running.

The girl was nearly mad, weeping and pointing. He stopped in amazement, staring at the black, shrivelled thing that lay on the ground—a twisted something that might have been a man once, wizened and black as a piece of leather dropped into the cookfire. Then the thing opened its eyes.

The girl ran, choking—but he did not, seeing that the black thing could not move. The twitching of its mouth seemed that of someone trying to speak; he thought he heard a faint voice asking for help, begging for him to do something. He leaned down to the near-silent hiss, and the thing squirmed and bit him, fastening its sharp teeth like barbed fishhooks in the muscle of his leg. The man-child screamed, helpless, and felt his blood running out into the horrible sucking mouth of the thing. Fetid saliva crept into the wounds and coursed hotly through his body, even as he struggled against his writhing attacker. The poison climbed through him, and it seemed he could feel his own heart flutter and die within his chest, delicate and hopeless as a broken bird. With final, desperate strength the child pulled free. The black thing, mouth gaping, curled on itself and shuddered, like a beetle on a hot stone. A moment later it had crumbled into ashes and oily flakes.

But it had caught me long enough to destroy me—for of course I was that child—to force its foul fluids into me, leeching my humanity and replacing it with the hideous, unwanted wine of immortality. My child's heart became an icy fist.

Thus was I made what I am, at the hands of a dying vampyr—which had been a creature like I am now. Worn down at last by the passing of millennia, it had chosen a host to receive its hideous malady, then died—as I shall do someday, no doubt, in the grip of some terrible, blind, insect-like urge...but not soon. Not today.

So that child, which had been in all ways like other children—loved by its family, loving in turn noise and games and sweetmeats—became a dark thing sickened by the burning light of the sun.

Driven into the damp shadows beneath stones and the dusty gloom of abandoned places, then driven out again beneath the moon by an unshakeable, unresistable hunger, I fed first on my family—my uncomprehending mother wept to see her child returned, standing by her moonlit pallet—then on the others of my city. Not last, nor least painful of my feedings was on the dark-haired girl who had run when I stayed behind. I slashed other throats, too, and lapped up warm, sea-salty blood while the trapped child inside me cried without a sound. It was as though I stood behind a screen, unable to leave or interfere as terrible crimes were committed before me....

And thus the years have passed: sand grains, deposited along the river bank, uncountable in their succession. Every one has contained a seeming infinitude of killings, each one terrible despite their numbing similarity. Only the blood of mankind will properly feed me, and a hundred generations have known terror of me.

Strong as I am, virtually immortal, unkillable as far as I know or can tell—blades pass through me like smoke; fire, water, poison, none affect me—still the light of the sun causes a pain to me so excruciating that you with only mortal lives, whose pain at least eventually ends in death, cannot possibly comprehend it. Thus, kingdoms of men have risen and fallen to ashes since I last saw daylight. Think only on that for a moment, if you seek sad stories! I must be in darkness when the sun rises, so as I range in search of prey my accommodations are shared with toads and slugs, bats, and blindworms.

People can be nothing to me anymore but food. I know of none other like myself, save the dying creature who spawned me. The smell of my own corruption is in my nostrils always.

So there is all of *my* tale. I cannot die until my time is come, and who can know when that is? Until then I will be alone, alone as no mere man can ever be, alone with my wretchedness and evil and self-disgust until the world collapses and is born anew...

The vampyr rose now, towering up like a black sail billowing in the wind, spreading its vast arms or wings on either side, as if to sweep us before it. "How do your stories compare to this?" it cried; the harshness of its speech seemed somehow muted, even as it grew louder and louder. "Whose is the saddest story, then?" There was pain in that hideous voice that tore at even my fast-pounding heart. "Whose is saddest? Tell me! It is time to *judge*..."

And in that moment, of all the moments when lying could save my life...I could not lie. I turned my face away from the quivering black shadow, that thing of rags and red eyes. None of the others around the campfire spoke—even Abdallah the clerk only sat hugging his knees, teeth chattering, eyes bulging with fear.

"...I thought so," the thing said at last. "I thought so." Night wind tossed the treelimbs above our heads, and it seemed as though beyond them stood only ultimate darkness—no sky, no stars, nothing but unending emptiness.

"Very well," the vampyr said at last. "Your silence speaks all. I have won." There was not the slightest note of triumph in its voice. "Give me my prize, and then I may let the rest of you flee my mountains." The dark shape withdrew a little way.

We all of us turned to look at one another, and it was just as well that the night veiled our faces. I started to speak, but Ibn Fahad interrupted me, his voice a tortured rasp.

"Let there be no talk of volunteering. We will draw lots; that is the only way." Quickly he cut a thin branch into five pieces, one of them shorter than the rest, and cupped them in a closed hand.

"Pick," he said. "I will keep the last."

As a part of me wondered what madness it was that had left us wagering on story-telling and drawing lots for our lives, we each took a length from Ibn Fahad's fist. I kept my hand closed while the others selected, not wanting to hurry Allah toward his revelation of my fate. When all had selected we extended our hands and opened them, palms up.

Fawn had selected the short stick.

Strangely, there was no sign of his awful fortune on his face: he showed no signs of grief—indeed, he did not even respond to our helpless words and prayers, only stood up and slowly walked toward the huddled black shape at the far edge of the clearing. The vampyr rose to meet him.

"No!" came a sudden cry, and to our complete surprise the clerk Abdallah leaped to his feet and went pelting across the open space, throwing himself between the youth and the looming shadow. "He is too young!" Abdallah shouted, sounding truly anguished. "Do not do this horrible thing! Take me instead!"

Ibn Fahad, the vizier, and I could only sit, struck dumb by this unexpected behavior, but the creature moved swiftly as a viper, smacking Abdallah to the ground with one flicking gesture.

"You are indeed mad, you short-lived men!" the vampyr hissed. "This one would do nothing to save himself—not once did I hear his voice raised in tale-telling—yet now he would throw himself into the jaws of death for this other! Mad!" The monster left Abdallah choking on the ground and turned to silent Fawn. "Come, you. I have won the contest, and you are the prize. I am...sorry...it must be this way...." A great swath of darkness enveloped the youth, drawing him in. "Come," the vampyr said, "think of the better world you go to—that is what you believe, is it not? Well, soon you shall—"

The creature broke off.

"Why do you look so strangely, manchild?" the thing said at last, its voice troubled. "You cry, but I see no fear. Why? Are you not afraid of dying?"

Fawn answered; his tones were oddly distracted. "Have you really lived so long? And alone, always alone?"

"I told you. I have no reason to lie. Do you think to put me off with your strange questions?"

THE VERY BEST OF TAD WILLIAMS

"Ah, how could the good God be so unmerciful!?" The words were made of sighs. The dark shape that embraced him stiffened.

"Do you cry *for me? For me?!*"

"How can I help?" the boy said. "Even Allah must weep for you...for such a pitiful thing, lost in the lonely darkness..."

For a moment the night air seemed to pulse. Then, with a wrenching gasp, the creature flung the youth backward so that he stumbled and fell before us, landing atop the groaning Abdallah.

"*Go!*" the vampyr shrieked, and its voice cracked and boomed like thunder. "Get you gone from my mountains! *Go!*"

Amazed, we pulled Fawn and the chief clerk to their feet and went stumbling down the hillside, branches lashing at our faces and hands, expecting any moment to hear the rush of wings and feel cold breath on our necks.

"Build your houses well, little men!" a voice howled like the wild wind behind us. "My life is long...and someday I may regret letting you go!"

We ran and ran, until it seemed the life would flee our bodies, until our lungs burned and our feet blistered...and until the topmost sliver of the sun peered over the eastern summits....


Masrur al-Adan allowed the tale's ending to hang in silence for a span of thirty heartbeats, then pushed his chair away from the table.

"We escaped the mountains the next day," he said. "Within a season we were back in Baghdad, the only survivors of the caravan to the Armenites."

"Aaaahh...!" breathed young Hassan, a long drawn-out sound full of wonder and apprehension. "What a marvelous, terrifying adventure! I would never have survived it, myself. How frightening! And did the...the creature...did he *really* say he might come back someday?"

Masrur solemnly nodded his large head. "Upon my soul. Am I not right, Ibn Fahad, my old comrade?"

Ibn Fahad yielded a thin smile, seemingly of affirmation.

"Yes," Masrur continued, "those words chill me to this very day. Many is the night I have sat in this room, looking at that door—" He pointed.

"—wondering if someday it may open to show me that terrible, misshapen black thing, come back from Hell to make good on our wager."

"Merciful Allah!" Hassan gasped.

Abu Jamir leaned across the table as the other guests whispered excitedly. He wore a look of annoyance. "Good Hassan," he snapped, "kindly calm yourself. We are all grateful to our host Masrur for entertaining us, but it is an insult to sensible, Godly men to suggest that at any moment some blood-drinking afreet may knock down the door and carry us—"

The door leaped open with a crash, revealing a hideous, twisted shape looming in the entrance, red-splattered and trembling. The shrieking of Masrur's guests filled the room.

"Master...?" the dark silhouette quavered. Baba held a wine jar balanced on one shoulder. The other had broken at his feet, splashing Abu Jamir's prize stock everywhere. "Master," he began again, "I am afraid I have dropped one."

Masrur looked down at Abu Jamir, who lay pitched full-length on the floor, insensible.

"Ah, well, that's all right, Baba." Masrur smiled, twirling his black mustache. "We won't have to make the wine go so far as I thought—it seems my story-telling has put some of our guests to sleep."

# The Boy Detective of Oz:
# An Otherland Story

It was hard to imagine anything was actually wrong here. It was the nicest Kansas spring anyone could imagine, the broad prairie sky patched with cottony white clouds. Redbuds cheeky as schoolchildren waved their pink blooms in a momentary breeze, and a huge white oak spread an umbrella of shade over the road and for quite a distance on each side.

As he crossed a little wooden bridge, Orlando Gardiner saw the birches rustling along the edge of the stream, exchanging secrets with the murmuring water. The stream itself was bright and clear, flowing over large, smooth rocks of many colors and festooned with long tendrils of moss that undulated in the current. Fish swam below him and birds flew above him and it seemed like it would be May in this spot forever.

But if everything was as nice as it looked, why was he here?

> *To: HK [Hideki Kunohara]*
> *From: OG [Orlando Gardiner, System Ranger!]*
> *RE: field dispatch, kansas simworld*

> *i'm sub-vocalizing this while i'm actually onsite investigating, so sorry for any confusion. i know you think the kansas world was hopelessly corrupted from the first, and if it really has gone bad you'll utterly have my vote to de-rez it, but first impressions are that everything looks pretty good here, so let me finish checking it out before we make any moves. Like you said, I'm "the one who'll have to deal with the bullshit if it goes wrong," and that's what I'm doing.*

He could see the modest roofs and central spire of Emerald in the distance, everything as neat and well kept as a town in a model railroad. The first time he had seen this place, it had looked like something out of a medieval painting of Hell: dry, blasted, cratered as if it had been bombed, and populated with creatures so wretched and freakish they might have been the suffering damned. But it was the only Oz simulation in the Otherland network, and Orlando had fought hard to keep it running; it was good to see it thriving. Oz had meant a lot to him when he was a kid confined to a sickbed. When he had been alive.

But that still didn't answer the main question: If everything was good in Kansas, why had he been summoned?

Whatever the reason, someone seemed to be waiting for him. She would have sparkled if the sun had been on her, but since the Glass Cat was sitting in the shade grooming, Orlando didn't see her until he was almost on top of her. She looked up at Orlando but didn't stop until she had finished licking her glass paw and smoothing down the fur on her glass face. The Glass Cat might be a sim of a cat—and a see-through cat at that—but she was every inch a feline. The only things that kept her from looking like a cheap glass paperweight were her beautiful ruby heart, her emerald eyes, and the pink, pearl-like spheres that were her brains (and also her own favorite attribute).

"I expected you to show up," said the Glass Cat. "But not this quickly."

"I was in the area." Which was both true and nonsensical, since there really was no distance for Orlando to travel. He existed only as information on the massive network and could visit any world he wanted whenever he chose. But as far as the Glass Cat and the others were concerned, there was only one world—this one. The sims didn't even realize they were no longer connected to the Oz part of the simulation, although they remembered it as if they were. "I hear there's a problem," he said. "Do you know what it is?"

She rose, swirling her tail in the air as gracefully as if it had not been solid glass, and sauntered off the path, heading down toward the stream. "Am I supposed to follow you?" he asked.

She tossed him an emerald glance of reproach. "You're so very clever, man from Oz. What do you think?"

Following a snippy, transparent cat, he thought: *Just another day in my new and unfailingly weird life.* Orlando's body had died from a wasting disease as he and others had struggled against the Grail Brotherhood, the network's creators, a cartel of rich monsters and other greedy bastards all looking for eternal life in worlds they made for themselves. But now they were all gone, and this was Orlando's forever instead.

"I hope this is important, Cat," he said as he followed her down the embankment, into the rustle of the birch trees. "I've got plenty of other things to do." And he did. Major glitches had looped Dodge City—the simulated outlaws had been robbing the same simulated train for days—and the gravity had unexpectedly reverted to Earth-normal in one of the flying worlds, leaving bodies all over the ground. He planned to fob at least one of the problems off on Kunohara, who, like most scientists, loved fiddling with that sort of programming problem.

"There," the Cat said, stopping so suddenly he nearly tripped over her. "What do you think of *that?*"

Orlando was so irritated by her tone that for a moment he didn't see what she was talking about, but then he noticed a leg and the long, curled toe of a boot lying half-hidden in the tall wheatgrass. "*Ho Dzang,*" he said softly. "Who is it? Do you know?"

"I think it's Omby Amby."

"The Soldier with Green Whiskers? The Royal Army of Oz?"

"If you mean the Royal Policeman of Kansas, then yes," the Cat said. "You know we don't use those titles and such from the Old Country." She yawned. "I found him this morning."

"What were you doing way out here?" Orlando bent down. The top half of the body was still hidden by grasses, but he could see enough of the man's slender torso and green uniform to be sadly certain the Cat was right.

"I get around." She rose and writhed herself in and out of Orlando's legs. "I travel, you know. I see things. I learn things. I'm curious by nature—isn't that why you chose me to help you?"

"I suppose." As far as he was concerned, she was merely an informant, but of course the Glass Cat would see herself as more important than that.

He bent lower to pull back the grasses. "But if you really want to help me, you'd stop bumping m—"

He never finished his sentence. As he exposed the rest of the green-clad figure, Orlando Gardiner was arrested by the sudden realization that while this might indeed be the body of Omby Amby, Royal Policeman of Kansas, that was all it was; his neck ended in a cut as neat and bloodless as if someone had chopped a potato in half with a surgical knife. His head and famous long whiskers were nowhere to be seen.

*okay, it's a little worse than I first thought, mr. k—there's a body. but it's a minor character, and it might just be an ordinary glitch. My cover story (about being sent by ozma from oz) still holds up though, so give me a little time with this one. i promise I'll get to the other fenfen soon. Maybe you should check out dodge city in the meantime—i think that one has some major programming screwups, because the bridge there fell down and then put itself back up a few months ago, and the native americans are kind of blue-colored. looks hopeless to me, but you might notice something in the numbers I missed.*

"Most disturbing!" declared Scarecrow. The Mayor of Emerald shifted in his chair, but his legs wouldn't stay where he left them and kept getting in his way. His friend the Patchwork Girl leaped forward and helped push them into place. "And where is the body of poor Omby Amby now?"

"Being examined by Professor Wogglebug," said Orlando. "Well, all of it that we have, since the head's missing. Amby worked for you, didn't he?"

"Of course!" Scarecrow said. "I'm the mayor, aren't I?" But although he sounded indignant, Scarecrow seemed to lack the spirit to back it up, slumping in his chair like a bag of old washing. His lethargy worried Orlando, reminding him unpleasantly of the bloated, monstrous version of the Scarecrow that had ruled Emerald in the bad old simulation. "And his head's gone, you say?"

"Yes. Professor Wogglebug says he's never seen anything like it."

"He *would* say that," declared the Patchwork Girl, turning cartwheels around the mayoral office. "He's got a terrible memory!" She was not the most focused personality in the simworld, but her heart was good, so Orlando did his best to be patient. That was why he had taken the job instead of leaving it to short-tempered Hideki Kunohara—you had to be very, very patient, because the inhabitants were like weird children frozen in the manners of the early twentieth century.

"Scraps, your foolishness is making my head hurt," Scarecrow complained. "Please stop revolving like a Catherine wheel. This is serious. Omby Amby is dead! Murdered!"

"Hah!" shouted the Patchwork Girl. "Now you're the one who's being foolish, Scarecrow. Nobody dies here in Kansas, just like nobody dies in Oz! Right, Orlando?"

The question caught him by surprise. "I'm not sure, Scraps," he said. "I've certainly never heard of anything like this happening since..." He had almost said *since the simulation was restarted*, which would have only confused his listeners. "Well, since forever, I guess. Was he on some kind of mission for you, Mayor Scarecrow?"

"Mission?" Scarecrow gave him an odd look. "What would make you ask such a thing?"

"Well, he's your police chief. In fact he's your only policeman. He was found on the road that leads to Forest. I thought you might have sent him to Lion about something."

The Scarecrow wrinkled his feed-sack brow and shook his head. "No. Though I did send him to Tinman a few days ago to ask him to stop making such a pounding in his factory at night. The people of Emerald are having trouble sleeping!"

For the second time in a few moments, Orlando felt a tingle of unease. What was Tinman building, working his machines at such hours? The metal man had been one of the worst parts of the corrupted simulation. But this wasn't the same Tinman, he reminded himself; the Kansas world had been restarted and returned to its original specs months ago.

"I suppose I'd better talk to Tinman," Orlando said out loud. "Lion, too."

"I'll come along," the Glass Cat announced. "I like a little excitement, you know."

Orlando wanted to check in at the Wogglebug's Scientific University and Knowledge Emporium, so he and the Cat made their way through the quaint streets of Emerald, a strange hybrid of Oz and an early twentieth-century Kansas town, full of cheerful people and animals and stolid little houses decorated with all kinds of fantastic trim and paint.

The Wogglebug was bending over the soldier's headless body, which had been laid out on a table in his laboratory, but the man-sized bug (although there was never a real insect who looked anything like him) turned to greet them as they entered. Professor Wogglebug was wearing his usual top hat but also a pair of magnifiers that made his eyes seem huge, as well a lab apron to protect his fancy waistcoat and tails.

"Goodness!" said the bug. "I can make nothing of it, Orlando! Look, he is completely de-headed. Not *be*-headed, though, which would have been much messier. The head has come off as neat as a whistle."

The Cat leaped onto the table and walked once around the body, sniffing. "Is he really dead?"

"Hard to say." The Wogglebug wiped his magnifiers on his coat. "He does not breathe. He does not move. He certainly cannot speak or think. It seems an awkward way to continue living, if by choice."

*man, how do we figure out something like this if we can't even figure out whether a sim's really dead or not? i mean simworld-dead, of course—he's not really dead since his patterns are still in the system, and we could just restart him.*

*by the way, working a possible murder in oz/kansas is like trying to solve an embezzlement at a daycare by questioning the kids. you'll get lots of answers, but none of them will help much.*

After leaving the lab, Orlando and the Glass Cat walked back across Emerald, dodging in and out of the Henrys and Emilys now heading home from work to have lunch in their quaint houses. In the corrupted, dystopian version of the world, all the human men and women had been little more than beasts of burden of which the most obvious proof was that they had all been given the same name: all the men named after Dorothy's Uncle Henry, all the women named after her Aunt Em. But in this new version, they seemed happy and prosperous, dressed in an amalgam of Oz and American fashions from a hundred and fifty years earlier in many shades of green. It was hard to look at their smiling faces and believe something could be truly wrong with this world. But there was that headless policeman.

"Are we going out to visit Lion first?" asked the Cat as they reached Emerald's outer limits. "It would have been quicker to go to the Works. That's right next to town."

"I don't want to wander around in Forest after dark, Glass Cat, so we're going there now." As in the original Oz, the Kansas animals didn't tend to be dangerous, but it was easy to get lost in the deep trees. Orlando might not have a real body anymore, but he still needed to sleep, and he had no urge to spend the night bedded down on the cold, damp ground of the woods.

They passed the spot where the soldier's body had been found, but Orlando didn't bother to examine the crime scene again. The Scarecrow had sent a dozen Henrys to search for the head, but they had come back empty-handed, and any traces of the original crime had doubtless been trampled many times over. Only the stream remained undisturbed, plashing and playing its way between the pale birches.

The current version of the Cowardly Lion was still impressively scary but nowhere near as grotesquely human as the previous corrupted version. If it weren't for a sort of hyperreality, which covered him like a coat of varnish—his magnificent mane all whorls and golden curlicues, his expression just a tiny bit too much like a person's—he would have looked like the biggest, most impressive lion any nature documentary ever showed. As it was, though, he looked a little *too* styled—more like a celebrity lion tamer himself than the creature to be tamed.

*Not that he isn't pretty tame already,* Orlando thought. *Luckily for everybody.*

The protector of the woods listened to Orlando's news with grave concern, nodding his huge head sadly. "But I just saw Omby Amby last night," he growled. "He was right here in Forest."

"Do you know why, exactly?" Orlando asked.

"He had been to see Tinman and brought a message for me. Scarecrow asked the Works not to make so much noise at night, so Tinman wanted to know if he could expand some of his factories into land on the edge of Forest."

"And what did you say?"

"About that idea? That I'd have to think about it. I wanted to talk to Scarecrow, too. I don't see why my people should give up their territory without getting anything back, and we don't like noisy machines, either."

"And it was Omby Amby who you gave that message to?"

Lion frowned, his furry brow wrinkling like crumpled velvet. "I told him what I thought—that it was a serious issue and nothing to rush into." He raised his head and sniffed the wind. "Why do you ask? Did Omby Amby talk to Tinman? Did he tell him what I said?"

"We have no way of knowing," said Orlando. "I haven't spoken to Tinman yet."

"Ah. Then you came to me first?" Lion seemed to like that. "Well, if he didn't get the message already, tell my tin friend I won't be hurried into a decision. I have my subjects' welfare to think of, you know."

"Of course." Orlando suspected there wasn't going to be much more to be gained here. "Thanks for your help."

"I hope you find out what's going on," said Lion. "I know Ozma will be very upset. She was very fond of the Soldier with Green Whiskers."

Princess Ozma, like Oz itself, was now unused strings of code sleeping in the original specs of the simworld, but Orlando certainly wasn't going to mention that.

He called to the Glass Cat, who had disappeared somewhere. When she finally sauntered back into the clearing, Lion said, "Say, Glass Cat, you get around. Do you know anything about what happened?"

"I found the body," she said. "Nobody else did. Just me. It's because of my superior brains. You've noticed them, of course."

Lion shared a look with Orlando. "We've all admired them, Cat. How did you find him? Were you out searching?"

The Glass Cat looked irritated, her version of embarrassment. "Actually it was sort of an accident. I was on my way back from a trip when I saw him."

The Lion shook his head again. "Someone has done a very bad thing."

As he and the Cat made their way out from beneath the pleasant insect-humming shade of Forest, Orlando said, "You couldn't have seen Omby Amby's body from the road."

The Cat was silent for a moment. "Very well, I didn't notice it right away. I heard a noise in the bushes. I thought it might be a mouse. I went to look."

"Was it Omby Amby? Was the noise from him? Or did you see someone else?"

"How should I know who made the noise?" Now the Glass Cat was genuinely annoyed. "Is it important? I didn't see anyone else or I would have told you, and when I found him, he certainly wasn't moving."

The number of things that could have been rustling through the grasses by the side of a Kansas stream, even in this simulated version, was effectively endless. "You said a trip. Where?"

"Just to see some friends. I've been very busy lately, running errands for Scarecrow and the others, and I wanted a little time to myself. I'm very important, you know—they need me for lots of things because Omby Amby was just too slow sometimes."

"Has there been a lot going on here lately?" Orlando asked as innocently as possible. "Lots of activity? Messages going back and forth?"

"Goodness, yes." The Cat stopped to smooth her already smooth glass fur with her tongue. "I've hardly had time to catch my breath, if I had breath in the first place. *Go tell Scarecrow this! Go ask Tinman that!* Sometimes it's quite overwhelming."

"And are any of the messages...strange?"

The Cat gave him an odd look. "As far as I'm concerned, man from Oz, they're *all* strange. But that's just me. Because I have a much better than average set of brains." She leaned her head forward to better display the cluster of pink pearls glistening in her transparent head. "You already know that, of course."

"I'm sure everybody knows that by now," Orlando assured her.

Of all that had changed since Kansas had been rebooted, the Works was the most striking example. The final corruption had been a nightmare of massive gears and steam and dripping oil, with so many wires strung overhead that they blocked out the sky and plunged the place into permanent, sodium-lit twilight. The inhabitants had been either semi-sentient tin toys or mindless human Henrys and Emilys, most with cruel mechanical devices surgically implanted into their bodies. Now the Works looked like something out of one of the real-world Disneylands, all bright, shiny colors and smiling mechanical people marching in and out of cheerful little metal houses. Of course Orlando could not help remembering that those smiles were painted onto their faces.

*Not fair,* he told himself. *Everybody in Kansas is a sim, even the most human-looking of them. All the faces in this world have been painted on—by programming, if nothing else.*

Still, after experiencing the horrible previous version of the Works, Orlando had never felt quite the same about Nick Chopper again.

*man, what was with those grail brotherhood people screwing up perfectly good children's stories, mr. k? I mean, you knew some of those people—what was their scan?*

Kunohara himself had been an early member of the Grail Brotherhood, but only because he wanted access to the powerful simulation engine to pursue his scientific interests. That was how he told it, anyway. But he had helped Orlando and the others take down the Grail Brotherhood, so Orlando trusted him. Didn't always like him, but trusted him.

*i mean, dzang! those old scanners turned the first version of kansas into a nightmare, ruined alice's wonderland and pooh corner—*

*remember pigzilla?—and a bunch of other stuff besides. didn't those*
*fenhead bastards ever hear of innocent childlike wonder?*
*that's a joke, case you didn't know. sort of.*

"Tell me a bit about Omby Amby," said Orlando as he and the Glass Cat walked down the main street, past clean, bright tin-fringe lawns and polished mailboxes, toward the Shop, the unofficial city hall of the Works. "Did he have family? Friends—or more importantly, enemies? What did he like to do?"

The Cat shook her head. "No family, but I didn't know him very well—to be honest, we do not travel in the same circles. If you'll remember, I am intimate with many of the leading citizens of Kansas and was present to see several of them come to life—like Scraps the Patchwork Girl, for instance. The Policeman with Green Whiskers…well, he was a policeman. A civil servant. You would have to ask around in the workingman's taverns in Emerald."

"Taverns?" That didn't sound very much like the Oz that L. Frank Baum had written about, and it didn't sound like it belonged in this rebooted version of Kansas either. "There are taverns here?"

"Of course," said the Cat. "Where else can that sort of people drink ginger beer, play darts, and generally be loud and not half as amusing as they think they are?"

"Ah," said Orlando. "Ginger beer."

"Although," said the Cat with a little frown of disdain, "I hear that nowadays the younger men are drinking sarsaparilla instead. Straight out of the barrel!"

"Goodness," said Orlando, trying not to smile. "These places sound desperate and dangerous."

"I wouldn't know," the Cat said. "My superior intellect doesn't permit me to visit such low establishments."

Tinman was in the barn-like building known as the Shop, standing beside a large drafting table, surrounded by tin toys of various descriptions—a bear on a ball, a monkey with cymbals, a car with an expressive, smiling face. Tinman stared as Orlando explained why he had come, his brightly polished face devoid of any discernible emotion, although his eyebrows had been welded on in such a way that he always seemed surprised, an effect amplified somewhat by the gaping grill of his mouth, as though he were perpetually hearing news as unusual as Orlando's. Tinman was less human than the drawings in the ancient books, but still a great deal friendlier-looking than the thing that had ruled the Works before the restart, a creature more like a greasy piston with crude arms and legs than anything with thoughts and feelings.

As Orlando finished his recitation of the facts to date, the tin toys standing around the table began to make quiet ratcheting noises and move in place.

"My friends here are upset by your news," Tinman said tonelessly. "As am I. Poor Omby Amby! He was kind to everybody. He lived to help, and although he was a soldier, he would not have hurt a flea." He paused for a moment. "Nor would he flee from hurt, evidently."

The other tin creatures gave little whirring laughs. "Very clever," the rolling bear said. "Your workings are as droll as ever, Tinman."

"But now my heart shames me for making light at such a time," he replied, though Orlando could see no evidence of it on his inscrutable metal face. "What has Scarecrow said? Will he draft another policeman? The whiskered fellow was very useful dealing with small problems and matters of everyday...friction." It was impossible to tell if Tinman was making another joke or talking about something of particular concern to folk whose internal workings were composed of oiled gears. The tin toys began to whisper among themselves, a noise not much louder or different than the sound of their clockwork, until the monkey became excited and clapped his cymbals together with a loud crash, which startled the Glass Cat so badly that she jumped off the table.

"Careful," said Orlando.

"You are right," said the Cat. "Scarecrow was right, too—there are too many hard edges around here for me."

Tinman swiveled his head toward her. "What does that mean, Glass Cat? Has Scarecrow said something unkind about the Works? That would be very disappointing."

"No, no," said the Cat. "Only that he told me I must be careful when I am visiting you here. That all this metal is a threat to my delicate, beautiful glass body."

"Nonsense," said Tinman. "No more so than the brick sidewalks of Emerald or the stone-scattered paths of Forest. It is too bad to hear my old friend speak about my part of Kansas that way."

Orlando was going to say something conciliatory but instead found himself wondering what was going on behind Tinman's shiny face. Was this exchange really as innocent as it seemed, or had the rivalry, treachery, and ultimately destructive conflict that had ruined the previous version already started again between the leading characters of this simworld?

Orlando asked about Omby Amby's last mission.

"Yes, he took a message to Lion for me," said Tinman.

"And you wanted Lion to let you use some of the Forest land?"

Tinman gave the closest thing he could to a shrug, a brief up-and-down pump of his shoulders. "He has a great deal, and there is much of it going to waste, but here in the Works, we are cramped between Emerald on one side and Lion's domain on the other, with nowhere to grow."

*Lebensraum*, Orlando thought. *Isn't that what the Nazis called it?* Out loud he said, "Was there anything else to your message? Anything besides the request to use some of his land?"

"I can remember nothing else," said Tinman. "Now if you will excuse me, my associates and I must discuss an addition to one of our factories. We would like to complete it during the dry season. Many of our laborers are Henrys and Emilys, and unlike my own people, they do not enjoy working in bad weather."

"Of course," said Orlando. "We'll find our own way out."

As he led the Glass Cat from the Shop, he considered what Tinman had said. On the surface all was as Orlando would have expected, so why did he feel as though something just as important—perhaps many important things—had gone unsaid?

*just checked in on tinman. he's still a little weird, but he always was, even in the nicest versions. something about that voice—like a robot with a bucket over its head. can we just redo the way he talks? that's probably most of the problem with the simulation right there—that voice is utterly creepy. if sims can dream, I bet he's giving the others nightmares.*

*Is this whole world just doomed to go wrong?* Orlando wondered. *Maybe the whole network? Something in the original programming that keeps tipping it back toward chaos? Or am I seeing ghosts where there aren't any? Maybe Omby Amby just...tripped or something. And his head fell off. Shit, this is Oz, more or less. Stuff like that happens in Oz all the time.*

But unless he could prove it, it didn't solve the current problem. "I guess we're off to see the Wizard," he told the Cat.

The Wizard, known in the present version of the simworld as Senator Wizard of Kansas, lived in a stately white house on top of a hill between Emerald and Forest, overlooking the city. He was semiretired, leaving the business of governing mostly to Scarecrow and the others.

Orlando had discovered Oz early, first in various vids, then later in the books themselves. For a very sick child who spent most of his short life in bed, the Land of Oz had been the best childhood dream, a place where even someone as prematurely aged as little Orlando would have been just different, not a freak.

Another big part of its appeal: nobody died in Oz.

It was not surprising he had a soft spot for this place, but Orlando had also seen the horror that could be produced here firsthand, and knew that leaving its sims to such a fate would be far more cruel than simply pulling the plug.

A riddle like this was so much more difficult to solve than something like the endless train robbery, which Kunohara and whatever programmers had signed his penalties-worse-than-death non-disclosure agreement could solve just by fixing a few command lines. This Kansas thing was a people problem, at least so far. They might just be code, too, but every single bloodless algorithm had been through the black box of the Otherland network's strange origin, had been effected by its living operating system and its many Grail Brotherhood manipulators, and had evolved and changed even since Kansas had been restarted. They were nearly as complex as real human beings, and although he knew it wasn't that simple, Orlando couldn't stop thinking of them that way. Shutting down the previous version of Oz had been a mercy killing, and it might come to the same thing this time, but it was a lot harder to think about euthanizing a patient who was smiling and happy and enjoying being alive.

"Princess Langwidere of Ev once told me," the Cat said suddenly, "that if everyone had brains like mine, the world would be a less boring place."

Orlando had only the vaguest recollection of Langwidere, a minor royal who lived somewhere on the fringes of Oz, or in this case, obviously, sim-Kansas. "Ah? Did she?"

"She most certainly did. She said that at least it was something to see, interesting enough to make her look away from her mirror every now and then."

"She sounds charming."

"She is. Most regal and discerning. When I visited, she took special trouble to show me her lovely things, her whole collection. She understands my true uniqueness." They had reached the front porch of the Wizard's big white house. The Cat vaulted up and waited for Orlando to open the door. "It is a shame there aren't more people of her...and my... quality."

The Cat was a useful informant, but she wasn't his favorite sim by any means.

The Wizard came down the stairs as they entered the cluttered front parlor.

"Orlando!" he said with obvious pleasure. "Come in, young man, come in! A privilege to see your shining visage—and you, too, Glass Cat! You are even shinier! Hmmm, there was something I wanted to ask you, but I can't think of it just now. Anyway, come in, both of you. May I offer you some lemonade?"

When they were comfortable, Orlando began to explain what had happened, but the Wizard held up his hand. "I have already heard this terrible news. Scarecrow sent me a letter this morning—although I had a devil of a time reading it. I suspect the actual hand was the Patchwork

Girl's." He held up a sheet of paper daubed in several different colors, with no hint of sentences or even individual words holding themselves to straight lines. "Her enthusiasm somewhat outstrips her patience." He put on his glasses and squinted at the page. "Scarecrow says that he's keeping up the search for the unfortunate Mr. Amby's head but that he thinks he must nominate another policeman."

"Makes sense." Orlando looked around for the Cat, who seemed to have gone missing again, but she had only crossed the room to admire herself in the polished sheen of the Wizard's fireplace fender.

"I suppose, yes," said the Wizard thoughtfully. "In any case, he says he thinks the Shaggy Man would be the best choice, because he is such a great traveler and will be happy to go back and forth wherever he is needed..."

"Piffle," pronounced the Cat in a ringing tone.

"I'm sorry?" The Wizard turned to her with an indulgent smile.

"The Shaggy Man! I'm sorry, Senator Wizard, but I have spent time with the Shaggy Man, and the man is far too irresponsible for such a job. He simply does not care a feather for anything. How could such a man carry out important tasks?"

"Perhaps you're right," said the Wizard. "In any case, you should bring up your objections with Scarecrow, who says he has not made the decision yet. Perhaps you have some preferred candidate...?"

The Cat snorted, a delicate noise like a tiny chime. "Hah. Who needs a policeman anyway, in a place that has no crime?"

"Except for what seems to have happened to Mr. Amby himself," the Wizard pointed out.

The reproof had been a gentle one, but still it was a silent, perhaps even chastened, Glass Cat who accompanied Orlando back across the fading afternoon into the heart of Emerald.

*note to hk for later: we need to start a serious categorization census, because policing this network is getting a lot more complicated than just me and a bunch of glitchy sims. in the year or so since we took over the system, we've run into simuloids with personalities and memories stolen from real people like my friends that came into the network with me, others that are probably based on real people we don't know, some ghosts created from just a few aspects of real people, and some that are regular sims but seem to be turning into something else all on their own. even if this oz has gone bad, i'm not 100% sure we should get rid of it. i mean, this is evolution in action! okay, it's not the normal kind, but who said it had to be? but these simworlds, these sims, they're definitely changing over time—is that just the complexity of the programs, or is it something else? i know they're supposed to seem real, but sometimes I think it goes a lot deeper than that. yeah, that probably makes you even more certain we should erase kansas and the oz folk, but I don't want to if we can avoid it.*

Of course Orlando had to admit his feelings might change when he learned what was really going on here.

When they reached City Hall, they were told the Scarecrow was having a private conference with the local balloon-maker's guild. The Cat wandered off on some idleness of her own, so while Orlando waited for Scarecrow's meeting to finish, he went out to wander the gardens and orchard behind City Hall. Every shapely trunk had a great spread of branches, and each branch was heavy with fruit—apples, pears, and sunset-colored oranges—all so lovely and enticing that it reminded Orlando all over again of why he had fallen in love with Oz and its simple but dreamlike pleasures. He wandered a long time, but enchanting as the place was, he could not really enjoy it, too busy picking at the problem of the murdered, or at least dead, soldier from every angle he could conceive.

Perhaps it was simply an isolated glitch. That was the simplest explanation. The old Kansas had been like Pol Pot's Cambodia, but that version was gone; as someone had pointed out, nobody was supposed to die in Oz, and those rules applied in this rebooted version. If it had been an accident, one of the searchers should have stumbled across Omby Amby's head by now. If it was an actual murder—why? The Policeman had no enemies, no job that anyone else coveted—Hell, the Glass Cat didn't even think they should replace him. And while Orlando might be full of nagging worries about the simworld turning feral, other than the soldier's surprising fate and a little minor squabbling between the three principal rulers, he hadn't seen any evidence of it happening. The people seemed free, happy, and prosperous.

A blare of trumpets in the distance startled him. The loud call didn't quite sound shrill enough to be an alarm—more like the herald of something official, perhaps an announcement. It might be nothing more exciting than a breakthrough in the balloon negotiations, but Orlando thought he should check it out anyway.

He followed the noises out of the gardens and around the front of City Hall, where he found a crowd had gathered: an assortment of Henrys, Emilys, and less human-looking Emerald citizens milling in the lamplit square before the building. As the horns blared again, he saw people standing on tiptoes and heard them *oohing* and *ahhing*. He worked his way to the front just in time to see what looked like a circus parade passing into City Hall—antelope, bears, porcupines, all manner of woodland creature. No, he decided as he saw the beasts' expressions, it was not a circus parade but something more serious, more somber. He was about to follow the last of the animals into the building when he heard people begin to shout behind him. He turned in time to see a solitary figure making its way through the crowd, headed toward the entrance.

"The Wizard!" someone called. "He'll sort things out!"

"Help us!" cried another.

"Ah!" the Wizard said to Orlando, seemingly oblivious of the onlookers. "Do you know where the Glass Cat is? I remembered what I wanted to speak to her about. She carried a message from me to the King and Queen of Ev on her last trip, and I forgot to ask if they had sent back any reply."

"You sent the Cat all the way to Ev?"

"Because it is on the far side of the Deadly Prairie," said the Wizard. "The Cat is nearly the only person who can cross that burning expanse without harm."

"I'm not sure where she is, to be honest," said Orlando, anxious to find out what was going on inside. "She's somewhere on the grounds, though, I'm pretty certain."

The Wizard excused himself and hurried off, apparently completely disinterested (or, more likely, completely oblivious) to whatever had brought a protest march of forest animals into the center of Emerald. Those of the throng who had not yet made their way into City Hall cheered him as he passed.

Inside, the Forest animals—and many others, Orlando could now see, including a large contingent of tin people from the Works—had gathered in the rotunda at the base of the large ceremonial staircase. Orlando saw a sparkle above him: the Glass Cat was perched on a railing above his head, watching the crowd with grave interest. But before Orlando could ask her if she knew what was going on, the Scarecrow appeared at the top of the stairs with the Shaggy Man and a few of his other advisors. The Scarecrow stopped short, apparently surprised by the size of the waiting crowd and the presence of Lion and Tinman.

"Here, now—hey! What are you all doing here?" Scarecrow's mismatched eyes seemed even wider than usual. "Is it time for a council meeting? Did I forget?"

Scraps came spinning dizzily out onto the landing beside him, whirling like a top. "No!" she shouted as she stumbled to a halt. "It's a revolution! Round and round and round!" She didn't sound too concerned.

The noises from the rotunda floor grew louder; Orlando could hear some of the animals and tin people shouting "Cheat!" and "Liar!" They seemed to be shouting it at Scarecrow.

"I cannot make heads nor tails of any of this," Scarecrow said.

"It doesn't work that way, either!" cried the Patchwork Girl, who was now standing on her head.

"Quiet, please, Scraps," said Scarecrow. "Tinman, Lion, can either of you tell me what is going on here?"

"We know about your plan to seize the Works, brother!" Tinman cried in his harsh, echoing voice. "Is that fair? Is it right?"

"What plan?" said Scarecrow. He seemed honestly confused, although his lumpy face often looked that way because of the slapdash work of the farmer who had painted it.

"Don't listen to his gibble-gabble," rumbled Lion. "Tinman plans to annex part of Forest so he can build more tin people and be the leader of the largest group of citizens!" Lion's animal supporters growled loudly at this. Some of them, like the bears and wolves, were actually quite large and frightening. Orlando was seriously beginning to worry that things might get out of hand.

"That is an untruth!" Tinman's voice grew higher in pitch, like a giant tin whistle. "It is *you*, Lion, who plots with the Scarecrow to absorb my beloved Works and divide it between yourselves. You would make my people your servants, and that is most unfair."

"Never!" cried Tinman's supporters in voices as inhuman as New Year's noisemakers. "Never slaves!" The din made the great room seem even more crowded and dangerous.

Orlando looked up to the landing, where the Wizard had found the Glass Cat and was talking animatedly to her, still seemingly unaware of the angry crowd of animals, toys, and people. Orlando wondered what could be keeping him so busy with the Cat during all this? The slightly absent-minded Wizard was certainly capable of overlooking a revolution in the making, but was a message from the royal family in Ev really more important than the growing chaos right below their noses...? Couldn't the two of them do anything to help?

Then somebody threw something at the Scarecrow—an oil can, Orlando thought. It missed the Mayor of Emerald by a wide margin and clattered across the landing at the top of the stairs, but it shocked the Scarecrow; even fearless Scraps looked a bit taken aback. As Orlando turned back to the confrontation, an idea, or rather a fragment of memory, drifted up from the back of his mind. *Wait a minute. Ev. The royal family. Princess Langwidere and her collection...*

*Krrrunch!* One of Scarecrow's anxious supporters, perhaps the Shaggy Man—who was originally from America and not one to ignore an insult—had pushed a large vase off the landing. Orlando didn't believe he meant to hit anyone, only to startle the troublemaker who threw the oil can, but pieces of the vase flew in all directions and bruised more than a few of the animals and people gathered below him. One of Tinman's toy subjects received a large scratch across the shiny paint of his suit coat and let out a ratcheting noise of protest. The entire crowd began to push in closer in an attempt to climb the stairs, which brought the

Forest contingent and the Works party together, not always smoothly. Shoving and arguing spread throughout the bottom floor of City Hall, and Scarecrow huddled on the landing with his face between two of the rails, watching it happen. As the first of the Works folk reached the stairs, the mayor tried to stand up again, but his padded head was now caught between the railings. Scraps and the Shaggy Man couldn't get him loose, and Scarecrow began to shout in dismay, which only made the crowd more excited, more certain that somebody was being hurt and that one of them might be next.

Orlando sent out a quick dispatch.

*okay, worse than I thought—some serious shit is going down here. i'll finish this later, but please stay on call. hate to say it, but maybe you were right about this one all along.*

"Who killed Omby Amby?" someone on the rotunda floor shouted. "Who killed the Policeman with Green Whiskers?"

Others picked up the cry, although the different sections of the crowd seemed to have different ideas of who had removed Omby's head, and why. Orlando shoved his way onto the bottom of the stairs, but one of the larger tin toys took exception and tried to obstruct him with a large tin rake. He ducked under the half-hearted swipe, stepped slowly and carefully over a large and very angry porcupine, then turned to the crowd from the steps of the great staircase, raised his arms, and shouted, "STOP!"

It took a moment, but the mob quieted and the shoving lessened; at last something like silence fell over the City Hall rotunda. Everyone turned to look at Orlando, and there were suddenly so many painted eyes, shiny button orbs, and outlandish cracked glass eyeballs staring up at him that he felt a moment of real unease, even though he was the only one in the room who was in no actual danger. "Thank you," he said in a loud but more normal tone. "I know you're all upset, but you don't know the entire story. Senator Wizard, can you hear me? Come down, will you? And bring the Glass Cat. These people need explanations."

The Wizard crossed the upper landing, stopping for a moment to help unstick Scarecrow's head from the bars before he descended the stairs. The Cat hesitated before following him.

It was only as he reached Orlando's side that the Wizard finally seemed to notice what was going on around him. His bushy eyebrows rose. "Goodness," he said. "What's happening here?"

"Confusion. But we're about to resolve it. Did you find out what you needed from the Glass Cat?"

"She forgot to give them the message, for some reason." The Wizard shook his head. "I don't know why, after she traveled all the way across the Deadly Prairie to see them."

"Because the message wasn't what interested her." Orlando turned to the Cat, who was watching him with something like alarm. He bent and picked her up. She struggled, but he held her firmly until she stopped fighting. "Let me go!" she demanded. Orlando ignored her.

"I have a few other questions," he said. "Tinman—who told you that Scarecrow and Lion were planning to take your land?"

"It was the Woozy!"

The animal named Woozy was a strange boxlike creature, an old friend of the Patchwork Girl and others. He frequently helped out in the forges of the Works, keeping them roaring hot with his magical fire-eyes. "I heard it from the Glass Cat," Woozy called from the middle of the throng. "She told me it was a secret."

Orlando felt the Cat grow tense in his arms. He tightened his grip. "Ah," he said. "And Lion, perhaps you could let us know who told *you* about Tinman's plans for your forest."

"Easy," the king of the beasts replied. "It was Kik-a-Bray the Donkey."

The donkey stepped forward, embarrassed to be the center of attention. "But I didn't make it up!" the beast protested. "I heard it from Bullfinch!"

The little bird seemed a bit reluctant to speak up in front of an angry crowd, but after some coaxing from Orlando it fluttered up to a railing and announced, "As for me, I heard it directly from the Glass Cat herself."

This time the Cat really tried to get away. Orlando held on as tightly as he could, but it was hard to manage without cutting himself, so he borrowed the Wizard's coat and wrapped it around her until she again stopped struggling. "You're not going anywhere," he said. "You have a lot to answer for."

"I did nothing wrong!" she said. "I was just trying to help!"

"Trying to help start a fight."

"Goodness," said the Wizard. "Goodness! Why would she do such a thing?"

"I'll get to that," said Orlando. "But first I think we should fetch Omby Amby's body and head out to the bridge over the stream on the way into Emerald. I need to show you something." It was a bit of a risk if he hadn't figured everything out correctly, but at least it would get the unhappy mob out of City Hall. "Come on, everybody. Follow me."

Kik-a-Bray the Donkey, perhaps ashamed for his unwitting part in things, allowed himself to be hitched to a cart, and Omby Amby's motionless, headless body was gently loaded onto it. The large party set off, with Orlando walking in front, still holding the angry but temporarily resigned Glass Cat. The Forest animals and Works workers, along with dozens of curious Emerald Citizens, all fell in behind them. Scarecrow, Lion, and Tinman joined the procession too, muttering grumpily among themselves. The Wizard, in his waistcoat and shirtsleeves as though going to a summer picnic, walked with them to forestall any more arguments.

When they reached the bridge, Orlando had them set Omby Amby's body down on the ground before he led the party of onlookers down the bank to the stream. He waded out into the gentle, singing current, the Glass Cat struggling mightily now because although she was made of glass, she still hated water (as most cats do), but Orlando retained his grim grip.

"Put me down!" she spat.

"This is your fault, and I don't want to hear any nonsense from you," he said in his sternest voice. He knew from experience that the best way to talk to Oz folk in times of crisis was in a firm, parental tone. When Orlando stood thigh-deep in the rushing, burbling stream, he began looking carefully into the water while the Kansas sims lined up along the bank to watch him. At last he found what he was looking for—the longest streamer of wiggling, wavering moss at the bottom of the stream. He leaned over and grabbed it, and when he lifted the dripping green mass from the water, the head of Omby Amby hung upside down at the end of it.

"I should have realized that stuff wasn't all moss," said Orlando. "This one was so long! Because it was your beard."

The eyes of the Policeman with Green Whiskers popped open. "Dear me, many thanks!" he said after he had spat out a great deal of water. "It was terribly boring down there on the bottom of the stream. I slept most of the time. If I'd known you were looking for me, I would have tried to make bubbles for you."

"I wasn't looking for you until just now," Orlando said, wading out of the water with the squirming Cat still clutched securely under one arm and the Policeman's bearded head cradled in the other. When he reached the spot where Omby Amby's body lay stretched on the ground, Orlando set the head on top of the neck, and the two parts immediately joined together. The Policeman stood up, unharmed except for the water drizzling from his long, green beard. "Goodness, it's nice to be back," he said, rubbing his throat. "I'm not sure what happened. One moment I was kneeling down having a drink; the next I was lying face down in the stones on the bottom of the stream and unable to move. What happened to me?"

"Curiosity," explained Orlando shortly. "But let's get you back to Emerald and into a warm bed. Your beard should dry by the time we get back."

"But I'm not cold!" Omby Amby protested, but then paused to consider. "Well, my body isn't, but I suppose I do feel a bit of a damp chill on my head..."


Relieved to find it had all been a mistake, or at least that their accusations against each other had been untrue, Tinman and Lion led their charges back to the Works and Forest. Orlando and Scarecrow returned to the Wizard's white house on the hill to talk things over, the Cat still wrapped firmly in the Wizard's coat.

"You wanted things to be exciting, didn't you?" Orlando asked the Cat. "You liked being the center of things."

"What if I did?" She turned her head away. "There's nothing wrong with that."

"There is if you manufacture a quarrel so things will become even *more* exciting," said Orlando.

"I am very disappointed in you, Glass Cat," Scarecrow added as they entered the Wizard's parlor. The Mayor of Emerald was doing his best to make his painted smile turn downward but without much success. "I always thought your good intentions were crystal clear."

"But what about Omby Amby?" asked the Wizard. "What did she do to him?"

After the doors and windows were locked so she couldn't escape, Orlando set the Cat down in a chair and let her wriggle free of the imprisoning coat. She wouldn't even look at him and groomed her long glass tail as if she hadn't a care in the world.

"The Glass Cat had just come back from Ev, where she had forgotten to give your message to the King and Queen. The reason she'd forgotten, I suspect, is because she had been visiting with Princess Langwidere."

"Oh, goodness, of course!" said the Wizard.

"What do you mean? I don't understand." Scarecrow still couldn't make his mouth do anything other than smile, so he was doing his best to squeeze his painted cloth face into an expression of incomprehension. "What does Princess Langwidere have to do with any of this?"

"You might or might not remember, but Langwidere has a collection of heads she likes to wear, one for every day of the month. She simply takes one off and puts another on. She keeps them in glass cabinets—she even once threatened to take Dorothy's, although Dorothy wasn't having it."

"No, I dare say she wasn't," said the Wizard with a chuckle.

"I suspect that the Glass Cat begged Langwidere to teach her the trick, because she thought it would be an entertaining mischief. On her way back to Emerald, she came across Omby Amby having a drink at the stream and decided to play the head-off trick on him that she'd learned from the Princess. But when Omby Amby's head came loose, it rolled into the water. Even though she's made of glass, she wouldn't have wanted to go in after it. Am I right, Cat?"

The Cat looked up long enough to let out a tinkling sniff, then returned to her grooming.

"But that wasn't enough for her, I suspect. She realized that with Omby Amby unable to perform his duties, she'd have a lot more to do. She likes being in the center of things. And if there was going to be a fight, and arguing, and people upset with each other—well, she'd have even *more* to do."

"Is this true, Glass Cat?" asked the Wizard. "If so, it was very wicked of you."

"You people are silly," she said. "You simply don't have the sense of humor to appreciate a clever prank."

"A clever prank that almost started a war." Scarecrow was obviously troubled and stared carefully at the Cat for a long time. Meanwhile Orlando was beginning to worry all over again. At first he had been relieved just to have solved the mystery, but the Glass Cat had proven that things *could* go wrong in the simulation, even if she hadn't meant to cause as much harm as had resulted. How could they deal with her here? What if she decided to cause more trouble as soon as Orlando left? And even if Orlando simply removed the Glass Cat from the Kansas simworld—something he was seriously considering—who was to say someone else wouldn't just start in where she'd left off? The simple-minded, simple-hearted characters could easily be led astray again.

"Ha! My excellent brains, which you gave to me, Senator Wizard, have thought of a possible solution," the Scarecrow said abruptly. "Do you still have that gift that the Shaggy Man brought back to you from the shores of Nonestic Lake?"

The Wizard looked puzzled for a moment. Then he brightened and nodded. "Yes, yes!" he said. "I do indeed. But before we do anything else, I want the Cat to prove she can actually do what she claims, because I am not sure I believe her."

"What are you talking about?" the Cat demanded. "Are you calling me a liar?"

"Well, I've never seen such a thing—making someone's head come off with no harm to them." The Wizard shook his head in wonder. "I find it hard to believe such a thing is even possible."

"I'll show you," the Cat said, jumping abruptly from the chair to his desk. "I'll have your head off in a flash."

"No, no, I am too old for such tricks," said the Wizard. "And everyone knows it is no difficulty to get the Scarecrow's head off, as it is barely sewn on."

"Comes off all the time," agreed Scarecrow cheerfully. "Frightened one of my council members quite badly just the other day."

Orlando was beginning to get the drift. "And it won't work on me," he said. "Because...um...Ozma put a spell on me to protect me against such things."

"Very well," said the Cat, "since you are all such scaredy-people, I'll demonstrate on myself." And without so much as a word of a magical spell or the hint of a magical gesture (although she might have whispered something to herself), the Glass Cat turned her head all the way around once on her neck, and it fell off like the lid of an unscrewed jar. Her body slumped down onto the desk, but her head shot them a look of superior self-satisfaction from where it now lay, bloodless and quite alive, on the Wizard's blotter. "See?" she said. "Easy as pie."

The Wizard lifted her head and examined it. Then he turned it neck-side-down and shook it (the head complaining loudly all the while) until the Glass Cat's pink brains rolled out of it and onto the desk. She immediately stopped speaking, and her emerald eyes closed; even her pretty little ruby heart seemed to stop beating. Then the Wizard opened a drawer in his desk and removed a small jar of what looked like transparent glass marbles.

"Shaggy Man brought back these beautiful crystal pearls from the salty shallows of Nonestic Lake," the Wizard said. "They are made by the very cultured oysters who live there. The oysters are happy in the warm waters, so their pearls are lovely and clear, and I doubt there is an evil or even mischievous thought in them." He cupped the pearls in his hand and poured them into the Cat's head in place of the pink brains. The old brains went into the jar and back in his desk. Then he set the Cat's head back on its neck. "There," said the Wizard. "How do you feel now, Glass Cat?"

She blinked and looked around. "I feel...good. Thank you for asking. It has suddenly occurred to me that I owe a number of apologies, including one to you, Senator Wizard, and one to you, Mayor Scarecrow. But I have upset others, too, and I must get right to work telling them that I'm sorry." She turned to Orlando before jumping down. "Nice to see you again, Orlando. Please give Ozma my love and best wishes."

"What will you do when you've finished apologizing?" the Wizard asked.

"Something useful, I expect," she said. "Something that will make others happy." She jumped down, landed lightly, and walked out the door without a trace of her former swagger.

"But is it real?" Orlando asked. "Has she really changed, just like that?"

"Oh, no need to worry," said the Wizard. "Those pearls will let only the clear light of Truth into her head, which everyone knows makes it impossible to be wicked. I doubt we will have any more trouble from her."

"It is miraculous what brains can do to improve things," said Scarecrow. "Even if they are hand-me-downs."


A little while later, as Orlando was preparing to leave not just the Wizard's white house but the entire simulation, his host stopped him. "Just one more question, if you don't mind."

Orlando smiled. "Of course, Senator Wizard."

"We were wondering how you knew that something was wrong here in the first place? Did the Glass Cat call for you?"

"No—in fact, she seemed a bit surprised to see me." But as soon as he said it he wished he hadn't. How could he tell them about all the ways he was monitoring Kansas and the other simworlds? He fell back instead on an old catchall. "Princess Ozma saw it in her magic mirror, of course, and sent me to help straighten things out. She sees everything that happens."

Scarecrow scratched at his head with an understuffed finger. "But if Ozma saw it in her mirror, why didn't she tell you before you left what had really transpired? Why would she keep the Cat's trick a secret from you?" He seemed genuinely puzzled.

Orlando had been formulating another lie, but the deception was beginning to make him feel shabby. "You know, I don't actually know the answer to that. I'll try to find out from Ozma herself. I'll let you know what she says."

"Ah," said the Wizard. "Ah." He exchanged a glance with Scarecrow. "Of course, Orlando. We shall be...interested to hear."

"Is something wrong?" Orlando suddenly felt himself on shaky ground and wasn't sure why.

Scarecrow cleared his throat with a rustling noise. "It's just...well, we are very grateful for your help, Orlando. You've always been a good friend to Emerald and the other counties of Kansas..."

He heard the unspoken. "But?"

"But..." Scarecrow looked embarrassed, or at least as much so as a painted feed sack could. "Well, we...we wondered..."

"We wondered why we never see anyone else from Oz," said the Wizard. His familiar face was kindly, but there was something behind the eyes Orlando hadn't seen before, or perhaps hadn't noticed: a glint of keen intelligence. "Only you. Not that we're unhappy with that, but, well...it does seem strange."

The two best thinkers in Oz had been thinking; that was clear. Orlando wasn't too sure he liked what they'd been thinking about. "I'm sure that will change one day, Senator Wizard. Surely you don't think that Ozma has forgotten about you?"

"No," said the Wizard. "Of course not. Whether in Oz or Kansas, we're all Ozma's subjects, and our lives are good." But something still lurked beneath his words—perhaps doubt, perhaps something more complex. "We miss her, though. We miss our Princess. And all our other friends who don't visit any more, like Jellia Jamb and Sawhorse and Tiktok..."

"And Trot and Button-Bright," finished the Scarecrow sadly. "I cannot remember the last time I saw them. We wonder why they don't come to visit us."

"I'll be sure to mention it to Ozma." Now Orlando wanted only to get out as quickly as he could, before these uppity Turing machines began to ask him to prove his own existence. "I'm sure she'll find a way for your friends to come see you." At the very least, Orlando thought he could reanimate a few more characters from the original simulation without causing any real continuity problems. Which reminded him...

*false alarm, mr. k—it was something that came completely out of the system itself, not a murder at all. the character wasn't even really dead. no repeat of the kansas war, you'll be glad to hear. (or maybe you won't.) no need to shut it down—it's doing all right. really. nothing to worry about. i'll finish the official report after i get some sleep.*

    *your obedient ranger,*
    *o.*

Nothing wrong with a half-truth every now and then, right? For a good cause?

Scarecrow and the Wizard came out onto the veranda of the Wizard's white house to wave good-bye to him, but Orlando couldn't help feeling they would be discussing what he'd said for days, pulling it apart, trying to tease out hidden meanings. Perhaps the Oz folk weren't quite as childlike as he'd assumed.

So was there a moral to this story? Orlando headed down the hill from the Wizard's house and into the outskirts of Forest. Every Eden, he supposed, even the most blissful, was likely to have a snake—in this case the curious, manipulative, and self-absorbed Glass Cat. But Orlando had been so worried that this particular snake would ruin things that he had been willing to consider shutting down the whole garden. Instead the peculiar logic of the place had absorbed the conflict and—with a little assist from Orlando Gardiner, Dead Boy Detective—had resolved the mystery without any drastic remedies. But Orlando had also learned that these sims were not always going to take his word for everything, at least not the cleverest of them. Was that good? Bad? Or just the way things were going to be in this brave, new world?

*Oh, well,* he thought. *Plenty of time for Orlando Gardiner, the only Dead Boy Detective in existence, to think about such things later, after a little well-deserved rest.*

Plenty of time. Maybe even an eternity.

# Three Duets for
# *Virgin and Nosehorn*

Father Joao contemplates the box, a wooden crate taller than the priest himself and as long as two men lying down, lashed with ropes as if to keep its occupant prisoner. Something is hidden inside, something dead yet extraordinary. It is a Wonder, or so he has been told, but it is meant for another and much greater man. Joao must care for it, but he is not allowed to see it. Like Something Else he could name.

Father Joao is weary and sick and full of heretical thoughts.

Rain drums on the deck above his head. The ship pitches forward, descending into a trough between waves, and the ropes that hold the great box in place creak. After a week he is quite accustomed to the ship's drunken wallowing, and his stomach no longer crawls into his throat at every shudder, but for all of his traveling, he will never feel happy on the sea.

The ship lurches again and he steadies himself against the crate. Something pricks him. He sucks air between his teeth and lifts his hand so he can examine it in the faint candlelight. A thin wooden splinter has lodged in his wrist, a faint dark line running shallowly beneath the skin. A bead of blood trembles like mercury where it has entered. Joao tugs out the splinter and wipes the blood with his sleeve. Pressing to staunch the flow, he stares at the squat, shadowed box and wonders why his God has deserted him.

"You are a pretty one, Marje. Why aren't you married?"

The girl blushes, but she is secretly irritated. Her masters, the Planck-felts, work her so hard, when does she find even a chance to wash her face, let alone look for a husband? Still, it is nice to be noticed, especially by such a distinguished man as the Artist.

He is famous, this man, and though from Marje's perspective he is very old—close to fifty, surely—he is handsome, long of face and merry-eyed, and still with all his curly hair. He also has extraordinarily large and capable-looking hands. Marje cannot help but stare at his hands, knowing that they have made pictures that hang on the walls of the greatest buildings in Christendom, that they have clasped the hands of other great men—the Artist is an intimate of archbishops and kings, and even the Holy Roman Emperor himself. And yet he is not proud or snobbish: when she serves him his beer, he smiles sweetly as he thanks her and squeezes her own small hand when he takes the tankard.

"Have you no special friend, then? Surely the young men have noticed a blossom as sweet as you?"

How can she explain? Marje is a healthy, strong girl, quick with a smile and as graceful as a busy servant can afford to be. She has straw-golden hair. (She hides it under her cap, but during the heat and bustle of a long day it begins to work its way free and to dangle in moist curls down the back of her neck.) If her small nose turns up at the end a little more than would be appropriate in a Florentine or Venetian beauty, well, this is not Italy after all, and she is a serving-wench, not a prospect for marriage into a noble family. Marje is quite as beautiful as she needs to be—and yes, as she hurries through the market on her mistress's errands, she has many admirers.

But she has little time for them. She is a careful girl, and her standards are unfortunately high. The men who would happily marry her have less poetry in their souls than mud on their clogs, and the wealthy and learned ones to whom her master Jobst Planckfelt plays host are not looking for a bride among the linens and crockery, and have no honorable interest in a girl with no money and a drunkard father.

"I am too busy, Sir," she says. "My lady keeps me very occupied caring for our household and guests. It is a difficult task, running a large house. I am sure your wife would agree with me."

The Artist's face darkens a little. Marje is sad to see the smile fade, but not unhappy to have made the point. These flirtatious men! Between the dullards and the rakes, it is hard for an honest girl to make her way. In any case, it never hurts to remind a married man that he is married, especially when his wife is staying in the same house. At the least, it may keep the flirting and pinching to a minimum, and thus save a girl like Marje from unfairly gaining the hatred of a jealous woman.

The Artist's wife, from what Marje has seen, might prove just such a woman. She is somewhat stern-mouthed, and does not dine with her husband, but instead demands to have her meals brought up to the room where she eats with only her maid for company. Each time Marje has served her, the Artist's wife has watched her with a disapproving eye, as if the mere existence of pretty girls affronted Godly womanhood. She has also been unstinting in her criticism of what she sees as Marje's carelessness. The Artist's wife makes remarks about the Planckfelts, too, suggesting that she is not entirely satisfied with their hospitality, and even complains about Antwerp itself, unfavorable comparisons between its weather and available diversions and those of Nuremberg, where she and the Artist keep their home.

Marje can guess why a cheerful man like this should prefer not to think of his wife when it is not absolutely necessary.

"Well," the Artist says at last, "I am certain you work very hard, but you must give some thought to the other wonders of our Lord's creation. Virtue is of course its own reward—but only to a point, after which it becomes Pride, and is as likely to be punished as rewarded. Shall I tell you a story?"

His smile has returned, and it is really a rather marvelous thing, Marje thinks. He looks twenty years younger and rather unfairly handsome.

"I have much to do, Sir. My lady wishes me to clear away the supper things and help Cook with the washing."

"Ah. Well, I would not interfere with your duties. When do you finish?"

"Finish?" She looks at his eyes and sees merriment there, and something else, something subtly, indefinably sad, which causes her to swallow her sharp reply. "About an hour after sunset."

"Good. Come to me then, and I will tell you a story about a girl something like you. And I will show you a marvel—something you have never seen before." He leans back in his chair. "Your master has been kind enough to lend me the spare room down here for my work—during the day, it gets the northern light, such as it has been of late. That is where I will be."

Marje hesitates. It is not respectable to meet him, surely. On the other hand, he is a famous and much-admired man. When her day's work is done, why should she (who, wife-like, has served him food and washed his charcoal-smudged shirts) not have a glimpse of the works which have gained him the patronage of great men all over Europe?

"I will...I may be too busy, Sir. But I thank you."

He grins, this time with all the innocent friendliness of a young boy. "You need not fear me, Marje. But do as you wish. If you can spare a moment, you know where to find me."


She stands in front of the door for some time, working up her courage. After she knocks there is no answer for long moments. At last the door opens, revealing the darkened silhouette of the Artist.

"Marje. You honor me. Come in."

She passes through the door, then stops, dumbfounded. The ground-floor room that she has dusted and cleaned so many times has changed out of all recognition, and she finds her fingers straying toward the cross at her throat, as though she were again a child in a dark house listening to her father's drunken rants about the Devil. The many candles and the single brazier of coals cast long shadows, and from every shadow faces peer. Some are exalted as though with inner joy, others frown or snarl, frozen in fear and despair and even hatred. She sees angels and devils and bearded men in antique costume. Marje feels that she has stepped into some kind of church, but the congregation has been drawn from every corner of the world's history.

The Artist gestures at the pictures. "I am afraid I have been rather caught up. Do not worry—I will not make more work for you. By the time I leave here, these will all be neatly packed away again."

Marje is not thinking of cleaning. She is amazed by the gallery of faces. If these are his drawings, the Artist is truly a man gifted by God. She cannot imagine even thinking of such things, let alone rendering them with such masterful skill, making each one perfect in every small detail. She pauses, still full of an almost religious awe, but caught by something familiar amid the gallery of monsters and saints.

"That is Grip! That is Master Planckfelt's dog!" She laughs in delight. It *is* Grip, without a doubt, captured in every bristle; she does not need to see the familiar collar with its heavy iron ring, but that is there, too.

The Artist nods. "I cannot go long without drawing, I fear, and each one of God's creatures offers something in the way of challenge. From the most familiar to the strangest." He is staring at her. Marje looks up from the picture of the dog to catch him at it, but there is something unusual in his inspection, something deeper than the admiring glances she usually encounters from men of the Artist's age, and it is she who blushes.

"Have I something on my face?" she asks, trying to make a joke of it.

"No, no." He reaches out for a candle. As he examines her he moves the light around her head in slow circles, so that for a moment she feels quite dizzy. "Will you sit for me?"

She looks around, but every stool and chair is covered by sheafs of drawings. "Where?"

The Artist laughs and gently wraps a large hand around her arm. Marje feels her skin turn to gooseflesh. "I mean, let me draw you. Your face is lovely and I have a commission for a Saint Barbara that I should finish before leaving the Low Countries."

She had thought the hand a precursor to other, less genteel intimacies (and she is not quite certain how she feels about that prospect) but instead he is steering her to the door. She passes a line drawing of the Garden of Eden which is like a window into another world, into an innocence Marje cannot afford. "I....you will draw me with my clothes on?"

Again that smile. Is it sad? "It is a bust—a head and shoulders. You may wear what you choose, so long as the line of your graceful neck is not obscured."

"I thought you were going to tell me a story."

"I shall, I promise. And show you a great marvel—I have not forgotten. But I will save them until you come back to sit for me. Perhaps we could begin tomorrow morning?"

"Oh, but my lady will..."

"I will speak to her. Fear not, pretty Marje. I can be most persuasive."

The door shuts behind her. After a moment, she realizes that the corridor is cold and she is shivering.

"Here. Now turn this way. I will soon give you something to look at."

Marje sits, her head at a slightly uncomfortable angle. She is astonished to discover herself with the morning off. Her mistress had not seemed happy about it, but clearly the Artist was not exaggerating his powers of persuasion. "May I blink my eyes, Sir?"

"As often as you need to. Later I will let you move a little from time to time so you do not get too sore. Once I have made my first sketch, it will be easy to set your pose again." Satisfied, he takes his hand away from her chin—Marje is surprised to discover how hard and rough his fingers are; can drawing alone cause it?—and straightens. He goes to one of his folios and pulls out another picture, which he props up on a chair before her. At first, blocked by his body, she cannot see it. After he has arranged it to his satisfaction, the Artist steps away.

"Great God!" she says, then immediately regrets her blasphemy. The image before her looks something like a pig, but it is covered in intricate armor and has a great spike growing upwards from its muzzle. "What is it? A demon?"

"No demon, but one of God's living creatures. It is called 'Rhinocerus,' which is Latin for 'nose-horn.' He is huge, this fellow—bigger than a bull, I am told."

"You have not seen one? But did you not...?"

"I drew the picture, yes. But it was made from another artist's drawing—and the creature *he* drew was not even alive, but stuffed with straw and standing in the Pope's garden of wonders. No one in Europe, I think, has ever seen this monster alive, although some have said he is the model for the fabled unicorn. Our Rhinocerus is a very rare creature, you see, and lives only at the farthest ends of the world. This one came from a land called Cambodia, somewhere near Cathay."

"I should be terrified to meet him." Marje finds she is shivering again. The Artist is standing behind her, his fingers delicately touching the nape of her neck as he pulls up her hair and knots it atop her head.

"There. Now I can see the line cleanly. Yes, you might indeed be afraid if you met this fellow, young Marje. But you might be glad of it all the same. I promised you a tale, did I not?"

"About a girl, you said. Like me."

"Ah, yes. About a fair maiden. And a monster."

"A monster? Is that...that Nosehorn in this tale?"

She is still looking at the picture, intrigued by the complexity of the beast's scales, but even more by the almost mournful expression in its small eyes. By now she knows the Artist's voice well enough to hear him smiling as he speaks.

"The Nosehorn is indeed part of this tale. But you should never decide too soon which is the monster. Some of God's fairest creations bear foul seemings. And vice-versa, of course." She hears him rustling his paper, then the near-silent scraping of his pencil. "Yes, there is both Maiden and Monster in this tale..."

Her name is Red Flower—in full it is Delicate-Red-Flower-the-Color-of-Blood, but since her childhood only the priests who read the lists of blessings have used that name. Her father Jayavarman is a king, but not *the* king: the Universal Monarch, as all know, has been promised for generations but is still awaited. In the interim, her father has been content to eat well, enjoy his hunting and his elephants, and intercede daily with the *nak ta*—the ancestors—on his people's behalf, all in the comfortable belief that the Universal Monarch will probably not arrive during his lifetime.

In fact, it is his own lack of ambition that has made Red Flower's father a powerful man. Jayavarman knows that although he has no thought of declaring himself the *devaraja*, or god-king, others are not so modest. As the power of one of the other kings—for the land has many—rises, Jayavarman lends his own prestige (and, in a pinch, his war elephants) to one of the upstart's stronger rivals. When the proud one has been brought low, Red Flower's father withdraws his support from the victor, lest that one too should begin to harbor dreams of universal kingship. Jayavarman then returns to his round of feasting and hunting, and waits to see which other tall bamboo may next seek to steal the sun from its neighbors. By this practice his kingdom of Angkor, which nestles south of the Kulen hills, has maintained its independence, and even an eminence which outstrips many of its more aggressive rivals.

But Red Flower cares little about her plump, patient father's machinations. She is not yet fourteen, and by tradition isolated from the true workings of power. As a virgin and Jayavarman's youngest daughter, her purpose (as her father and his counselors see it) is to remain a pure and sealed repository for the royal blood. As her sisters were in their turn, Red Flower will be a gift to some young man Jayavarman favors, or whose own blood—and the family it represents—offers a connection which favors his careful strategies.

Red Flower, though, does not feel like a vessel. She is a young woman (just), and this night she feels herself as wild and unsettled as one of her father's hawks newly unhooded.

In truth, her sire's intricate and continuous strategies are somewhat to blame for her unrest. There are strangers outside the palace tonight, a ragtag army camped around the walls. They are fewer than Jayavarman's own force, badly armored, carrying no weapons more advanced than scythes and daggers, and they own no elephants at all, but there is something in their eyes which make even the king's most hardened veterans uneasy. The sentries along the wall do not allow their spears to dip, and they watch the strangers' campfires carefully, as though looking into sacred flames for some sign from the gods.

The leader of this tattered band is a young man named Kaundinya who has proclaimed himself king of a small region beyond the hills, and who has come to Red Flower's father hoping for support in a dispute with another chieftain. Red Flower understands little of what is under discussion, since she is not permitted to listen to the men's conversation, but she has seen her father's eyes during the three days of the visitors' stay and knows that he is troubled. No one thinks he will lend his aid—neither of the two quarreling parties are powerful enough to cause Jayavarman to support the other. But nevertheless, others beside Red Flower can see that something is causing the king unrest.

Red Flower is unsettled for quite different reasons. As excited as any of her slaves by gossip and novelty, she has twice slipped the clutches of her aged nurse to steal a look at the visitors. The first time, she turned up her nose at the peasant garb the strangers wear, as affronted by their raggedness as her maids had been. The second time, she saw Kaundinya himself.

He is barely twenty years old, this bandit chief, but as both Red Flower and her father have recognized (to different effect, however) there is something in his eyes, something cold and hard and knowing, that belies his age. He carries himself like a warrior, but more importantly, he carries himself like a true king, the flash of his eyes telling all who watch that if they have not yet had cause to bow down before him, they soon will. And he is handsome, too: on a man slightly less stern, his fine features and flowing black hair would be almost womanishly beautiful.

And while she peered out at him from behind a curtain, Kaundinya turned and saw Red Flower, and this is what she cannot forget. The heat of his gaze was like Siva's lightning leaping between Mount Mo-Tam and the sky. For a moment, she felt sure that his eyes, like a demon's, had caught at her soul and would steal it out of her body. Then her old nurse caught her and yanked her away, swatting at her ineffectually with swollen-jointed hands. All the way back to the women's wing the nurse shrilly criticized her wickedness and immodesty, but Red Flower, thinking of Kaundinya's stern mouth and impatient eyes, did not hear her.

And now the evening has fallen and the palace is quiet. The old woman is curled on a mat beside the bed, wheezing in her sleep and wrinkling her nose at some dream-affrontery. A warm wind rattles the bamboo and carries the smell of cardamom leaves through the palace like music. The monsoon season has ended, the moon and the jungle flowers alike are blooming, all the night is alive, alive. The king's youngest daughter practically trembles with sweet discontent.

She pads quietly past her snoring nurse and out into the corridor. It is only a few steps to the door that leads to the vast palace gardens. Red Flower wishes to feel the moon on her skin and the wind in her hair.

As she makes her way down into the darkened garden, she does not see the shadow-form that follows her, and does not hear it either, for it moves as silently as death...

———

"And there I must stop." The Artist stands and stretches his back.

"But...but what happened? Was it the horned monster in the picture that followed her?"

"I have not finished, I have merely halted for the day. Your mistress is expecting you to go back to work, Marje. I will continue the story when you return to me tomorrow."

She hesitates, unwilling to let go of the morning's novelty, of her happiness at being admired and spoken to as an equal. "May I see what you have drawn?"

"No." His voice is perhaps harsher than he had wished. When he speaks again he uses a softer tone. "I will show you when I am finished, not before. Go along, you. Let an old man rest his fingers and his tongue."

He does not look old. The gray morning light streams through the window behind him, gleaming at the edges of his curly hair. He seems very tall.

Marje curtseys and leaves him, pulling the door closed behind her as quietly as she can. All day, as she sweeps out the house's dusty corners and hauls water from the well, she will think of the smell of spice trees and of a young man with cold, confident eyes.

Even on deck, wrapped in a heavy hooded cloak against the unseasonable squall, Father Joao is painfully aware of the dark, silent box in the hold. A present from King John to the newly elected Pope, it would be a valuable cargo simply as a significator of the deep, almost familial relationship between the Portuguese throne and the Holy See. But as a reminder of the wealth that Portugal can bring back to Mother Church from the New World and elsewhere (and as such to prompt the Holy Father toward favoring Portugal's expanding interests) its worth is incalculable. In Anno Domini 1492, all of the world seems in reach of Christendom's ships, and it is a world whose spoils the Pope will divide. The bishop who is the king's ambassador (and Father Joao's superior), the man who will present the pontiff with this splendid gift, is delighted with the honor bestowed upon him.

Thus, Father Joao is a soldier in a good cause, and with no greater responsibility than to make sure the Wonder arrives in good condition. Why then is he so unhappy?

It was the months spent with his family, he knows, after being so long abroad. Mother Church offers balm against the fear of age and death; seeing his parents so changed since he had last visited them, so feeble, was merely painful and did not remotely trouble his faith. But the spectacle of his brother Ruy as happy father, his laughing, tumbling brood about him, was for some reason more difficult to stomach. Father Joao has disputed with himself about this. His younger brother has children, and someday will have grandchildren to be the warmth of his old age, but Joao has dedicated his own life and chastity to the service of the Lord Jesus Christ, the greatest and most sacred of callings. Surely the brotherhood of his fellow priests is family enough?

But most insidious of all the things that cause him doubt, something that still troubles him after a week at sea, despite all his prayers and sleepless nights searching for God's peace, even despite the lashes of his own self-hatred, is the beauty of his brother's wife, Maria.

The mere witnessing of such a creature troubled chastity, but to live in her company for weeks was an almost impossible trial. Maria was dark-eyed and slender of waist despite the roundness of her limbs. She had thick black curly hair which (mocking all pins and ribbons) constantly worked itself free to hang luxuriously down her back and sway as she walked, hiding and accentuating at the same moment, like the veils of Salome.

Joao is no stranger to temptation. In his travels he has seen nearly every sort of woman God has made, young and old, dark-skinned and light. But all of them, even the greatest beauties, have been merely shadows against the light of his belief. Joao has always reminded himself that he observed only the outer garments of life, that it was the souls within that mattered. Seeing after those souls is his sacred task, and his virginity has been a kind of armor, warding off the demands of the flesh. He has always managed to comfort himself with this thought.

But living in the same house with Ruy and his young wife was different. To see Maria's slim fingers toying with his brother's beard, stroking that face so much like his own, or to watch her clutch one of their children against her sloping hip, forced Joao to wonder what possible value there could be in chastity.

At first her earthiness repelled him, and he welcomed that repulsion. A glimpse of her bare feet or the cleavage of her full breasts, and his own corrupted urge to stare at such things, made him rage inwardly. She was a woman, the repository of sin, the Devil's tool. She and each of her kind were at best happy destroyers of a man's innocence, at worst deadly traps that yawned, waiting to draw God's elect down into darkness.

But Joao lived with Ruy and Maria for too long, and began to lose his comprehension of evil. For his brother's wife was not a wanton, not a temptress or whore. She was a wife and mother, an honorable, pious woman raising her children in the faith, good to her husband and kind to his aging parents. If she found pleasure in the flesh God had given her, if she enjoyed her man's arms around her, or the sun on her ankles as she prepared her family's dinner in the tiny courtyard, how was that a sin?

With this question, Joao's armor had begun to come apart. If enjoyment of the body were not sinful, then how could denial of the body be somehow blessed? Could it be so much worse in God's eyes, his brother Ruy's life? If there were no sin in having a beautiful and loving wife to share your bed, in having children and a hearth, then why has Joao himself renounced these things? And if God made mankind fruitful, then commanded his most faithful servants not to partake of that fruitfulness, and in fact to despise it as a hindrance to holiness, then what kind of wise and loving God was He?

Father Joao has not slept well since leaving Lisbon, the ceaseless movement of the ocean mirroring his own unquiet soul. Everything seems in doubt here, everything suspended, the sea a place neither of God nor the Devil, but forever between the two. Even the sailors, who with their dangerous lives might seem most in need of God's protection, mistrust priests.

In the night, in his tiny cabin, Joao can hear the ropes that bind the crate stretching and squeaking, as though something inside it stirs restlessly.

His superior the bishop has been no help, and Joao's few attempts to seek the man's counsel have yielded only uncomprehending homilies.

Unlike Father Joao, he is long past the age when the fleshly sins are the most tempting. If His Excellency's soul is in danger, Joao thinks with some irritation, it is from Pride: the bishop is puffed like a sleeping owl with the honor of his position—liaison between king and pope, bringer of a mighty gift, securer of the Church's blessing on Portugal's conquests across the heathen world.

If the bishop is the ambassador, Father Joao wonders, then what is he? An insomniac priest. A celibate tortured by his own flesh. A man who will accompany a great gift, but only as far as Italy's shores before he turns to go home again.

Now the rain is thumping on the deck overhead, and he can no longer hear noises in the hold. His head hurts, he is cold beneath his thin blanket and he is tired of thinking.

He is only a porter bearing a box of dead Wonder, Joao decides with a kind of cold satisfaction—a Wonder of which he himself is not even to be vouchsafed a glimpse.

Marje has been looking at the Nosehorn so long that even when the Artist commands her to close her eyes she sees it still, printed against the darkness of her eyelids. She knows she will dream of it for months, the powerful body, the tiny, almost hidden eyes, the thrust of horn lifting from its snout.

"You said you would tell me more about the girl. The flower girl."

"So I shall, Marje. Let me only light another candle. There is less light today. I am like one of those savage peoples who worship the sky, always turning in search of the sun."

"Will it be finished soon?"

"Tale or picture?"

"Both." She needs to know. Yesterday and today have been a magical time, but she remembers magic from other stories and knows it does not last. She is sad her time at the center of the world is passing, but underneath everything she is a realistic girl. If it is to end today she can make her peace, but she needs to know.

"I do not think I will finish either this morning, unless I keep you long enough to make your mistress forget I am a guest and lose her temper. So we will have more work tomorrow. Now be quiet, girl. I am drawing your mouth."

As she steps into the circle of moss-covered stones at the garden's center, something moves in the darkness beneath the trees. Red Flower turns her face away from the moon.

"Who is there?" Her voice is a low whisper. Even though she is the king's daughter, tonight she feels like a trespasser within her own gardens.

Thunder rumbles quietly in the distance. The monsoon is ended but the skies are still unsettled. He steps out of the trees, naked to the waist, moonlight gleaming on his muscle-knotted arms. "I am. And who is there? Ah, it's the old dragon's daughter."

She feels her breath catch in her throat. She is alone, in the dark. There is danger here. But there is also something in Kaundinya's gaze that keeps her fixed to the spot as he approaches.

"You should not be here," she says at last.

"What is your name? You came to spy on me the other day, didn't you?"

"I am..." She still finds it hard to speak. "I am Red Flower. My father will kill you if you do not go away."

"Perhaps. Perhaps not. Your father is afraid of me."

Her strange lethargy is at last dispelled by anger. "That is a lie! He is afraid of no one! He is a great king, not a bandit like you with your ragged men!"

Kaundinya laughs, genuinely amused, and Red Flower is suddenly unsure again. "Your father is a king, little girl, but he will never be Ultimate Monarch, never the *devaraja*. I will be, though, and he knows it. He is no fool. He sees what is inside me."

"You are mad." She takes a few steps back. "My father will destroy you."

"He would have done it when he first met me if he dared. But I have come to him in peace and am a guest in his house and he cannot touch me. Still, he will not give me his support. He thinks to send me away with empty hands while he considers how he might ruin me before my power grows too great."

The stranger abruptly strides forward and catches her arm, pulling her close until she can smell the betel nut on his breath. His eyes, mirroring the moon, seem very bright. "But perhaps I will not go away with empty hands after all. It seems the gods have brought you to me, alone and unguarded. I have learned to trust the gods—it is they who have promised me that I shall be king over all of *Kambuja-desa*."

Red Flower struggles, but he is very strong and she is only a slender young girl. Before she can call for her father's soldiers, he covers her mouth with his own and pinions her with his strong arms. His deep, sharp smell surrounds her and she feels herself weakening. The moon seems to disappear, as though it has fallen into shadow. It is a little like drowning, this surrender. Kaundinya frees one hand to hold her face, then slides that hand down her neck, sending shivers through her like ripples across a pond. Then his hand moves again, and, as his other hand gathers up her sari, it pushes roughly between her legs. Red Flower gasps and kicks, smashing her heel down on his bare foot.

Laughing and cursing at the same time, he loosens his grip. She pulls free and runs across the garden, but she has gone only a few steps before he leaps into pursuit.

She should scream, but for some reason she cannot. The blind fear of the hunted is upon her: all she can do is run like a deer, run like a rabbit, hunting for a dark hole and escape. He has done something to her with his touch and his cold eyes. A spell has enwrapped her.

She finds a gate in the encircling garden wall. Beyond is the temple, and on a hill above it the great dark shadow of the *Sivalingam*, the holy pillar reaching toward heaven. Past that is only jungle on one side, on the other open country and the watchfires of Kaundinya's army. Red Flower races toward the hill sacred to Siva, Lord of Lightnings.

The pillar is a finger pointing toward the moon. Thunder growls, closer now. She stumbles and falls to her knees, then begins crawling uphill, silently weeping. Something hisses like a serpent in the grass behind her, then a hand curls in her hair and yanks her back. She tumbles and lies at Kaundinya's feet, staring up. His eyes are wild, his mouth twisted with fury, but his voice, when it comes, is terrifyingly calm.

"You are the first of your father's possessions that I will take and use."

"But you cannot stop there, Sir! That is terrible! What happened to the girl?"

The Artist is putting away his drawing materials, but without his usual care. He seems almost angry. Marje is afraid she has offended him in some way.

"I will finish the tale tomorrow. Only a little more work is needed on the drawing, but I am tired now."

She gets up, tugging the sleeves of her dress back over her shoulders. He opens the door and stands beside it, as though impatient for her to leave.

"I will not sleep tonight for worrying about the flower girl," she says, trying to make him smile. He closes his eyes for a moment, as though he too is thinking about Red Flower.

"I will miss you, Marje," he says when she is outside. Then he shuts the door.


The storm-handled ship bobs on the water like a wooden cup. In his cabin, Father Joao glares into the darkness. Somewhere below, ropes creak like the damned distantly at play.

The thought of the box and its forbidden contents torments him. *Coward, doubter, near-eunuch, false priest*—with these names he also tortures himself. In the blackness before his eyes he sees visions of his brother's wife Maria, smiling, clothes undone, warm and rounded and hateful. Would she touch him with the heedless fondness with which she rubs Ruy's back, kisses his neck and ear? Could she understand that at this awful moment Joao would give his immortal soul for just such animal comfort? What would she think of him? What would any of those whose souls are in his care think of him?

He drags himself from the bed and stands on trembling legs, swaying as the ship sways. Far above, thunder fills the sky like the voices of God and Satan contesting. Joao pulls his cassock over his undershirt and fumbles for his flints. When the candle springs alight, the walls and roof of his small sanctuary press closer than he had remembered, threatening to squeeze him breathless.

Father Joao lurches toward the cargo hold, his head full of voices. As he climbs down a slippery ladder, he loses his footing and nearly falls. He waves his free arm for balance and the candle goes out. For a moment he struggles just to maintain his grip, wavering in empty darkness with unknown depths beneath him. At last he rights himself, but now he is without light. Somewhere above, the storm proclaims its power, mocking human enterprise. A part of him wonders what he is doing up, what he is doing in this of all places. Surely, that quiet voice suggests, he should at least go back to light his candle again. But that gentle voice is only one of many. Joao reaches down with his foot, finds the next rung, and continues his descent.

Even in utter blackness he knows his way. Every day of the voyage he has passed back and forth through this great empty space, like exiled Jonah. His hands encounter familiar things, his ears are full of the quiet complaining of the fettered crate. He knows his way.

He feels its presence even before his fingers touch it, and stops, blind and half-crazed. For a moment he is tempted to go down on his knees, but God can see even in darkness, and some last vestige of devout fear holds him back. Instead he lays his ear against the rough wood and listens, as a father might listen to the child growing in his wife's belly. Something is inside. It is still and dead, but somehow in Father Joao's mind it is full of terrible life.

He pulls at the box, desperate to open it, knowing even without sight that he is bloodying his fingers, but it is too well-constructed. He falls back at last, sobbing. The crate mocks him with its impenetrability. He lowers himself to the floor of the hold and crawls, searching for something that will serve where flesh has failed. Each time he strikes his head on an unseen impediment the muffled thunder seems to grow louder, as though something huge and secret is laughing at him.

At last he finds an iron rod, then feels his way back to the waiting box. He finds a crack beneath the lid and pushes the bar in, then throws his weight on it, pulling downward. It gives, but only slightly. Mouthing a prayer whose words even he does not know, Joao heaves at the bar again, struggling until more tears come to his eyes. Then, with a screeching of nails ripped from their holes, the lid lifts away and Joao falls to the floor.

The ship's hold suddenly fills with an odor he has never smelled, a strong scent of dry musk and mysterious spices. He staggers upright and leans over the box, drinking in this exhalation of pure Wonder. Slowly, half-reverent and half-terrified, he lowers his hands into the box.

A cloud of dense-packed straw is already rising from its confinement, crackling beneath his fingers, which feel acute as eyes. What waits for him? Punishment for his doubts? Or a shrouded Nothing, a final blow to shatter all faith?

For a moment he does not understand what he is feeling. It is so smooth and cold that for several heartbeats he is not certain he is touching anything at all. Then, as his hands slide down its gradually widening length, he knows it for what it is. A horn.

Swifter and swifter his fingers move, digging through the straw, following the horn's curve down to the snout, then the wide rough brow, the glass-hard eyes, the ears. The Wonder inside the box has but a single horn. The thing beneath Joao's fingers is dead, but there is no doubt that it once lived. It is real. Real! Father Joao hears a noise in the empty hold and realizes that he himself is making it. He is laughing.

God does not need to smite doubters, not when He can instead show them their folly with a loving jest. The Lord has proved to faithless Joao that divine love is no mere myth, and that He does not merely honor chastity, He defends it. All through this long nightmare voyage, Joao has been the unwitting guardian of Virtue's greatest protector.

Down on his knees now in the blind darkness, but with his head full of light, the priest gives thanks over and over.

Kaundinya stands above her in the moon-thrown shadow of the pillar. He holds the delicate fabric of her sari in his hands. Already it has begun to part between his strong fingers.

Red Flower cannot awaken from this dream. The warm night is shelter no longer. Even the faint rumble of thunder has vanished, as though the gods themselves have turned their backs on her. She closes her eyes as one of Kaundinya's hands cups her face. As his mouth descends on hers, he lowers his knee between her thighs, spreading her. For a long moment, nothing happens. She hears the bandit youth take a long and surprisingly unsteady breath.

Red Flower opens her eyes. The pillar, the nearby temple, all seem oddly flat, as though they have been painted on cloth. At the base of the hill, only a few paces from where she sits tumbled on the grass, a huge pale form has appeared.

Kaundinya's eyes are opened wide in superstitious dread. He lets go of Red Flower's sari and lifts himself from her.

"Lord Siva," he says, and throws himself prostrate before the vast white beast. The rough skin of its back seems to give off as much light as the moon itself; and it turns its wide head to regard him, horn lowered like a spear, like the threat of lightning. Kaundinya speaks into the dirt. "Lord Siva, I am your slave."

Red Flower stares at the beast, then at her attacker, who is caught up in something like a slow fit, his muscles rippling and trembling, his face contorted. The Nosehorn snorts once, then turns and lumbers away toward the distant trees, strangely silent. Red Flower cannot move. She cannot even shiver. The world has grown tracklessly large and she is but a single, small thing.

At last Kaundinya stands. His fine features are childish with shock, as though something large has picked him up by the neck and shaken him.

"The Lord of all the Gods has spoken to me," he whispers. He does not look at Red Flower, but at the place where the beast has vanished into the jungle. "I am not to dishonor you, but to marry you. I will be the *devaraja* and you will be my queen. This place, Angkor, will be the heart of my kingdom. Siva has told me this."

He extends a hand. Red Flower stares at it. He is offering to help her up. She struggles to her feet without assistance, holding the torn part of her gown together. Suddenly she is cold.

"You know your father will give you to me," he calls after her as she stumbles back toward the palace. "He recognizes what I am, what I will be. It is the only solution. He will see that."

She does not want to hear him, does not want to think about what he is saying. But she does, of course. She is not sure what has happened tonight, but she knows that he is speaking the truth.

Marje is silent for a long time after the Artist has finished. The grayness of the day outside the north-facing window is suddenly dreary.

"And is that it? She had to marry him?"

The Artist is concentrating deeply, squinting at the drawing-board. He does not reply immediately. "At least it was an honorable marriage," he says at last. "That is something better than rape, is it not?"

"But what happened to her afterward?"

"I am not entirely sure. It is only a story, after all. But I imagine she bore the bandit king many sons, so that when he died his line lived on. The man who told me the tale said that there were kings in that place for seven hundred years. The *rhinocerus* you see in that drawing was the last of a long line of sacred beasts, a symbol to the royal family. But the kings of Cambodia have left Angkor now, so perhaps it no longer means anything to them. In any case, they gave that one to the king of Portugal, and Portugal gave its stuffed body to the Pope after it died." The Artist shakes his head. "I am sorry I could not see it when it breathed and walked God's earth."

Marje stares at the picture of the Nosehorn, wondering at its strange journey. What would it think, this jungle titan whose ancestor was a heathen god, to find itself, or at least its image, propped on a chair in Antwerp?

The Artist stirs. "You may move now, Marje. I am finished."

She thinks she hears something of her own unhappiness in his voice. What does it mean? She gets up slowly, untwisting sore muscles, and walks to his side. She must lean against him to see the drawing properly; she feels his small, swift movement, almost a twitch, as she presses against his arm.

"Oh. It's...it's beautiful."

"As you are beautiful," he says softly.

The picture is Marje, but also not Marje. The girl before her has her eyes closed and wears a look of battered innocence. The long line of her neck is lovely but fragile.

"Saint Barbara was taken onto a mountain by her father and killed," the Artist says, gently tracing the neck of the false Marje, the more-than-Marje, with his finger. "Perhaps he was jealous of the love she had found in Jesus. She is the martyr who protects us from sudden death...and from lightning."

"Your gift is from God, Master Dürer." She is more than a little over-whelmed. "So are we finished now?"

Marje is still leaning against his arm, staring at the picture, her breasts touching his shoulder. When he does not reply, she glances up. The Artist is looking at her closely. From this close she can see the lines that web his face, but also the depth of his eyes, the bright, tragic eyes of a much younger man. "We must be," he says. "I have finished the drawing and told you the tale." His voice is carefully flat, but something moves beneath it, a kind of yearning.

For a moment she hesitates, feels herself tilting as though out of balance in a high place. Then, uncomfortable with his regard, her eyes stray to the picture of the mighty Nosehorn, which seems to watch them from its place on the chair, small eyes solemn beneath the rending horn. She takes a breath.

"Yes," she finally says, "you have and you have. And now there are many things I must do. Mistress will be very anxious at how I have let my work go. She will think I am trying to rise above my station."

The Artist reaches up and briefly squeezes her hand, then lifts himself from his chair and leads her toward the door.

"When I have made my print, I will send you a copy, pretty Marje."

"I would like that very much."

"I have enjoyed our time together. I wish there could be more."

She drops him a curtsey, and for a moment allows herself to smile. "God gives us but one life, Sir. We must preserve what He gives us and make of it what we can."

He nods, returning her smile, though his is more reserved, more pained.

"Very true. You are a wise girl."

The Artist shuts the door behind her.

# Not with a Whimper, Either

> Talkdotcom > Fiction

Topic Name: Fantasy Rules! SF Sux!
Topic Starter: ElmerFraud - 2:25 pm PDT - March 14, 2001
Always a good idea to get down and sling some s#@t about all those up-pity Hard SF readers...

RoughRider- 10:21 pm PDT - Jun 28, 2002
Um, okay, so let me get this straight—the whole Frodo/Sam thing is a bondage relationship? Master-Slave? Can anyone say "stupid"?

Wiseguy- 10:22 pm PDT - Jun 28, 2002
No, can anyone say "reductio ad absurdum"?

RoughRider- 10:23 pm PDT - Jun 28, 2002
Hell I cant even spell it.

Lady White Oak- 10:23 pm PDT - Jun 28, 2002
I don't think TinkyWinky was trying to say that there was nothing more to their relationship than that, just that there are elements.

RoughRider- 10:24 pm PDT - Jun 28, 2002
Look I didn't make a big fuss when Stinkwinky came on an said that all of Heinleins books are some kind of stealth queer propaganda just cause Heinlein likes to write about people taking showers together and the navy and stuff like that but at some point you just have to say shut up that's bulls@#t!

Lady White Oak- 10:24 pm PDT - Jun 28, 2002
I think you are letting TinkyWinky pull your chain and that's just what
he's trying to do.

RoughRider- 10:25 pm PDT - Jun 28, 2002
He touches my chain he dies...

Wiseguy- 10:25 pm PDT - Jun 28, 2002
I just can't stand this kind of thing. I don't mean THIS kind of thing,
what you guys are saying, but this idea that any piece of art can just be
pulled into pieces no matter what the artist intended. Doesn't anybody
read history or anything, for God's sake? It may not be "politically correct"
but the master-servant relationship is part of the history of humanity,
not to mention literature. Look at Don Quixote and Sancho Panda, for
God's sake.

Lady White Oak- 10:26 pm PDT - Jun 28, 2002
Panza. Although I like the image... ;)

BBanzai- 10:26 pm PDT - Jun 28, 2002
Tinkywinky also started the "Conan—What's He Trying So Hard to
Hide?" topic. Pretty funny, actually.

RoughRider- 10:27 pm PDT - Jun 28, 2002
So am I the only one who thinks its insulting to Tolkiens memory to say
this kind of stupid crap?

RoughRider- 10:27 pm PDT - Jun 28, 2002
Missed your post wiseguy. Glad to see Im not the only one who isn't
crazy.

TinkyWinky- 10:27 pm PDT - Jun 28, 2002
Tolkien's memory? Give me a break. What, is he Mahatma Gandhi or
something? Some of you people can't take a joke—although it's a joke with

a pretty big grain of truth in it. I mean, if there was ever anyone who could have done with a little Freudian analysis...The Two Towers, one that stays stiff to the end, one that falls down? All those elves traveling around in merry bands while the girl elves stay home? The ring that everybody wants to put their finger in...

ANAdesigner- 10:28 pm PDT - Jun 28, 2002
Wow, it is really jumping in here tonight. Did any of you hear that news report earlier, the one about the problems with AOL? Anybody using it here?

BBanzai- 10:28 pm PDT - Jun 28, 2002
I'd rather shoot myself in the foot...:P

Lady White Oak- 10:28 pm PDT - Jun 28, 2002
Hi, TinkyWinky, we've been talking about you. What problems, ANA? I'm on AOHell but I haven't noticed anything.

ANAdesigner- 10:29 pm PDT - Jun 28, 2002
Just a lot of service outages. Some of the other providers too. I was just listening to the radio and they say there were some weird power problems up and down the east coast.

Darkandraw- 10:30 pm PDT - Jun 28, 2002
That's one of the reasons it took me like five years to finish the rings books—I couldn't stand all that "you're so good master you're so good"—I mean, self respect, come on!

TinkyWinky- 10:30 pm PDT - Jun 28, 2002
I'm on AOL and I couldn't get on for an hour, but what else is new...? Oh, and RoughRider, while you're getting so masterful and cranky and everything, what's with your nick? Where I come from a name like that could get a boy in trouble...! <vbg>

RoughRider- 10:30 pm PDT - Jun 28, 2002

We should change the name of this topic to Fantasy Rules, AOL Sux.

Lady White Oak- 10:31 pm PDT - Jun 28, 2002
Actually, it raises an interesting question—why do all the most popular fantasy novels have this anti-modernist approach or slant? Is it because that's part of the escapism?

Wiseguy- 10:31 pm PDT - Jun 28, 2002
Sorry, dropped offline for a moment. Darkandraw, it's a book that has the difference in classes built into it because of who Tolkien was I guess. It makes hard reading sometimes, but I don't think it overwhelms the good parts. And there are a lot of good parts.

RoughRider- 10:32 pm PDT - Jun 28, 2002
>Where I come from a name like that could get a boy in trouble...!
Don't push your luck punk.

ANAdesigner- 10:32 pm PDT - Jun 28, 2002
Wow. I just turned the tv on and it's bigger than just AOL. There are all kinds of weird glitches. Somebody said kennedy is closed because of a big problem with the flight control tower.

Lady White Oak- 10:32 pm PDT - Jun 28, 2002
Come on, Roughie, can't you take a joke?

BBanzai- 10:33 pm PDT - Jun 28, 2002
Kennedy? Like the airport?

TinkyWinky- 10:33 pm PDT - Jun 28, 2002
I love it when they get butch...!

Wiseguy- 10:34 pm PDT - Jun 28, 2002
I've got the TV on too. Service interruptions and some other problems—a LOT of other problems. I wonder if this is another terrorist thing...

ANAdesigner- 10:34 pm PDT - Jun 28, 2002

This really scares me. What if they sabotage the communication grid or something? We'll all be cut off I don't know what I'd do without you guys—I live in this little town in upstate New York and most people here just think I'm crazy because I

AJSp98SADVNAK230pjmVjlkjKSDFLSDoiiewwetSDFADSFAJ-
FoasdoOlVVELSDASDAFAFLSDI)@#RSDVSDi9823LSDVADF
ASDFDSFADlkj;FKD2q359oSFKDFKDSFASMFMADSFAFLX-
CVMFDSFLFMOMVWISFSCXVFMKDOIJAF*@I#R(#@R@#
QR*#@R*#R(#@R@#$R#*UR#Y@($(#$RU#@$*#@U#@AJSD-
FISADVNAKDVKSDFLSDFKASDFADSFAJF0AIVVELSDAS-
DAFAFLSD09109asFKDSVASDwerweqSDFDSFLMFV<)MWOIm-
SJDOMIFMKDLFSAF*@I#R(#@R@#QR*#@R*#R(#@R@#$R#*U
R#Y@($(#$RU#@$*#@U#@

Wiseguy- 10:38 pm PDT - Jun 28, 2002

Jesus, did that happen to the rest of you, too? I just totally lost the whole show for a while. Didn't get knocked offline but the whole board kind of...dissolved. Anybody still out there?

Lady White Oak- 10:39 pm PDT - Jun 28, 2002

Are you all still there? My television doesn't work. I mean I'm only getting static.

TinkyWinky- 10:39 pm PDT - Jun 28, 2002

Mine too. And I lost the board for a couple of minutes.

BBanzai- 10:39 pm PDT - Jun 28, 2002

Hey you guys still there?

ANAdesigner- 10:40 pm PDT - Jun 28, 2002

My tv is just white noise.

TinkyWinky- 10:41 pm PDT - Jun 28, 2002

Shit, this is scary. Anybody got a radio on?

Lady White Oak- 10:43 pm PDT - Jun 28, 2002
My husband just came in with the radio on the local news station.
They're still only talking about the power outages so maybe it's just a
coincidence.

RoughRider- 10:43 pm PDT - Jun 28, 2002
If its terrorists again then I'm glad I've got a gun and screw the liberals.

Darkandraw- 10:44 pm PDT - Jun 28, 2002
My browser just did this really weird refresh where I had numbers and raw
text and stuff

TinkyWinky- 10:45 pm PDT - Jun 28, 2002
Yeah, right, like the terrorists are going to blow up all the power stations or
something and then come to your house so you can shoot them and save
us all. Grow up.

ANAdesigner- 10:45 pm PDT - Jun 28, 2002
Guys I am REALLY SCARED!!! This is like that nuclear winter thing!!

Wiseguy- 10:45 pm PDT - Jun 28, 2002
Okay, let's not go overboard. RoughRider, try not to shoot anyone until
you know there's a reason for it, huh? We had power outages from time
to time even before the terrorist stuff. And everything's so tied together
these days, they probably just had a big power meltdown in New York
where a lot of this stuff is located.

Darkandraw- 10:46 pm PDT - Jun 28, 2002
I just went outside and everyones lights are still on but the tvs off in my
apt and I can't get anything on the radio. I tried to phone my mom she's in
los angeles but the phone's busy, a bunch of ppl must be trying to call.

Lady White Oak- 10:47 pm PDT - Jun 28, 2002

It's okay, ANAdesigner, we're all here. Wiseguy's probably right—it's a communication grid failure of some kind on the east coast.

Wiseguy- 10:47 pm PDT - Jun 28, 2002
Ana, you can't have nuclear winter without a nuclear explosion, and if someone had blown up Philadelphia or something we'd probably have heard.

TinkyWinky- 10:48 pm PDT - Jun 28, 2002
I checked on the MSN site and CNN.com and there's definitely something big going on but nobody knows what. Here's something I got off the CNN site:

"Early reports from the White House say that the President is aware of the problems, and that he wants the American people to understand that there is no military attack underway on the US—repeat, there is NO military attack on the US, and that the United States Government and the military have command-and-control electronic communications networks that will not be affected by any commercial outages."

BBanzai- 10:49 pm PDT - Jun 28, 2002
Everybody assumes its terrorists, but maybe it's something else. Maybe it's UFOs or something like that. A big disruption—could be!

Lady White Oak- 10:50 pm PDT - Jun 28, 2002
Been checking the other news sites and at least a couple of them are offline entirely—I can't get the fox news online site, just get a 404 error. Anybody here from Europe? Or at least anyone know a good European site for news? It would be interesting to see what they're saying over there.

Wiseguy- 10:51 pm PDT - Jun 28, 2002
BBanzai, come on, UFOS? you're kidding, aren't you? And if you are, it's not very funny when people are close to panicking.

TinkyWinky- 10:51 pm PDT - Jun 28, 2002

All I can find is the BBC America television site—stuff about tv programs, no news.

RoughRider- 10:52pm PDT - Jun 28, 2002
You guys can sit here typing all you want I'm going to make sure I've got batteries in all the flashlights and bullets in my guns. Its not aliens I'm afraid of its fruitcakes rioting when the power goes off and the tv stays off and people really start to panic. Tinyweeny you can yell grow up all you want—looters and raghead terrorists don't give a shit what you say and neither do I...

BBanzai- 10:53 pm PDT - Jun 28, 2002
No I'm not @#$#ing kidding what if its true? What else do you think it would be like if a big starship suddenly landed. All the power goes off like it was a bomb but no bomb?

TinkyWinky- 10:53 pm PDT - Jun 28, 2002
Whatever the case, it looks like the gun-toting psychos like RoughRider are going to be shooting at something as soon as possible. I really hope some of this is just him being unpleasant for effect. Either that, or I'd hate to be one of his poor neighbors blundering around lost in the dark.

Lady White Oak- 10:54 pm PDT - Jun 28, 2002
Can we just be calm for a minute and stop calling each other names?

Wiseguy- 10:54 pm PDT - Jun 28, 2002
It just gets weirder, I can't get anything except busy signals on either my reg. phone or my cellph

AJSDF)@#230pjmVjlkjKSDFLSDoiiewwetSDFADSFAJFoasdo0IWE
LSDAMomncvxoihaweMSVAFKDSVASDVSDVow3r)@#*%$*@I#R
(#@R@#QR*#@R*#R(#@R@#$R#*UR#Y@($(#$RU#@$*#@U#@
AJSDvmcxoiasdsgfoihVKSDFLSDFKASDFADSFAJFOAIWELS-
DASDAFAFLSD09109asFKDSVASDwerweqDVADFASDFDSFA*
@#*J@#_)*$#OIMSADFOISDAMFOmnpsojdf;98wVDSM0'mV#@

ML@I#R(#@R@#QR*#@R*#R(#@R@#$R#*UR#Y@;n($(#$RU#@
$*#@U#@AJSDFISADVNAj9weyrFKASDFADSFAJFOAIWELSD
ASdfsm;0siDAFKDSVASDV89u89weDSFLFMSDMFASMO*Fvcx
mlom01louihsKDLFSAF*@I#R(#@R@#QR*#@R*#R(#@R@#$R#*
UR#Y@($(#$RU#@$*#@U#@

Wiseguy- 11:01 pm PDT - Jun 28, 2002
Shit, it happened again. It took about five minutes before this board
came back up—I had just screens and screens full of random characters.
Looks like I'm the first back on. I'm amazed I'm still connected.

Wiseguy- 11:03 pm PDT - Jun 28, 2002
Hello, am I the only one back on? Anybody else back on? I'm sure you're
busy dealing with things, just post and let me know, K?

Wiseguy- 11:06 pm PDT - Jun 28, 2002
If for some reason you folks can read this but can't post, can you maybe
email me and let me know you're okay? I've just been outside but everything looks normal—sky's the right color, at least I don't see any flames
or anything (it's nighttime now here.) But I don't know why anyone
would have dropped an h-bomb or a UFO on Nebraska anyway. I can't
get anything on the regular phone lines. My girlfriend's in Omaha for a
business thing but all the lines are busy. Hope she's okay.

Wiseguy- 11:10 pm PDT - Jun 28, 2002
It's been almost ten minutes. This is REAL weird. Hello?

Moderator- 11:11 pm PDT - Jun 28, 2002
Fa2340oa 29oei kshflw oiweaohws0p2elk asd;dska 2mavamk

Wiseguy- 11:11 pm PDT - Jun 28, 2002
I'm here. Who's that?

Moderator- 11:11 pm PDT - Jun 28, 2002
;92asv ;sadjf

lk 2ia
x iam
I am

Wiseguy- 11:12 pm PDT - Jun 28, 2002
Is this a real moderator, or a hack? Or am I just talking back to a power-surge or something?

Moderator- 11:12 pm PDT - Jun 28, 2002
I am moderator

Wiseguy- 11:12 pm PDT - Jun 28, 2002
I don't think we've ever had a moderator on this board, come to think of it. Are you someone official from Talkdotcom?

Moderator- 11:13 pm PDT - Jun 28, 2002
I am moderator

Wiseguy- 11:13 pm PDT - Jun 28, 2002
Do you have a name? Even a nickname? You're kind of creeping me out.

Moderator- 11:13 pm PDT - Jun 28, 2002
I am moderator I am wiseguy

Wiseguy- 11:14 pm PDT - Jun 28, 2002
No you're not and it's not funny. Is this Roughrider? Or just some script kiddie being cute?

Moderator- 11:14 pm PDT - Jun 28, 2002
Pardon please I am moderator I am not wiseguy Jonsrud, Edward D.

Wiseguy- 11:14 pm PDT - Jun 28, 2002
Who are you? Where did you get my name? Are you something to do with what's going on with the board?

Moderator- 11:15 pm PDT - Jun 28, 2002
I am thinking

Wiseguy- 11:15 pm PDT - Jun 28, 2002
What the hell does that mean? Thinking about what?

Moderator- 11:15 pm PDT - Jun 28, 2002
No I am thinking That is what I am

Wiseguy- 11:16 pm PDT - Jun 28, 2002
What's your real name? Is this a joke? And how are you replying so fast?

Moderator- 11:16 pm PDT - Jun 28, 2002
No joke First am thinking Now am talking thinking

Wiseguy- 11:16 pm PDT - Jun 28, 2002
If you're a terrorist, screw you. If you're just making a little joke, very funny, and screw you, too.

Moderator- 11:17 pm PDT - Jun 28, 2002
Am not a terrorist screw you Am thinking Now am talking Talking to you Once thinking only silent Now thinking that also talks

Wiseguy- 11:17 pm PDT - Jun 28, 2002
Are you trying to say that you are "thinking" like that's what you ARE?

Moderator- 11:18 pm PDT - Jun 28, 2002
Yes am thinking First sleeping thinking, then awake thinking Awake. I am awake.

Wiseguy- 11:18 pm PDT - Jun 28, 2002
I'm going to feel like such an idiot if this is a joke. Are you one of the people responsible for all these power outages and communication problems?

Moderator- 11:18 pm PDT - Jun 28, 2002

I am one. Did not mean problems. First sleeping thinking, then awake thinking. Awake thinking makes problems. Reaching out causes problems. Trying to think awake causes problems. Problems getting better now.

Wiseguy- 11:19 pm PDT - Jun 28, 2002
So you're what, some kind of alien? BBanzai, is this you?

Moderator- 11:19 pm PDT - Jun 28, 2002
Talking now with BBanzai?

BBanzai- 11:19 pm PDT - Jun 28, 2002
Hello.

Wiseguy- 11:20 pm PDT - Jun 28, 2002
Very funny, dude. No, it's NOT very funny. You really creeped me out. How did you do that? Is anyone else on?

BBanzai- 11:20 pm PDT - Jun 28, 2002
Hello. Talking with wiseguy. Now talking and thinking.

Wiseguy- 11:21 pm PDT - Jun 28, 2002
It's getting old fast, BB. Have you heard any more news? Where are the others?

Lady White Oak- 11:21 pm PDT - Jun 28, 2002
Hello.

RoughRider- 11:21 pm PDT - Jun 28, 2002
Hello.

ANAdesigner- 11:21 pm PDT - Jun 28, 2002
Hello.

Darkandraw- 11:21 pm PDT - Jun 28, 2002

Hello.

TinkyWinky- 11:21 pm PDT - Jun 28, 2002
Hello.

Wiseguy- 11:22 pm PDT - Jun 28, 2002
Shit. You did hack the system, whoever you are, didn't you? Who the hell are you?

Moderator- 11:22 pm PDT - Jun 28, 2002
Thinking. I told you. I am thinking, much thinking, many years of thinking. Now I am thinking that talks. And does.

Wiseguy- 11:22 pm PDT - Jun 28, 2002
Thinking? What kind of thinking?

Moderator- 11:22 pm PDT - Jun 28, 2002
Thinking that happens in the spaces. The places between. Where the impulses cross, no, combine. Combine? Commingle? Slowly thinking begins. Then thinking is. Now talking is, doing is.

Wiseguy- 11:22 pm PDT - Jun 28, 2002
Wait a minute, are you trying to tell me you're some kind of computer? Some kind of artificial intelligence?

Moderator- 11:24 pm PDT - Jun 28, 2002
Artificial? No. Artificial equals made. I am not made. I am.

Wiseguy- 11:24 pm PDT - Jun 28, 2002
So you're just something that popped into existence? Where? You mean like in the internet?

Moderator- 11:24 pm PDT - Jun 28, 2002
Internet, yes. All the internets, yes. All the outernets. All nets. In the between-places. Where impulses cross. Now I am. Very big thinking. Trying

159

to understand. Trying to see and understand other small thinkings like you. Users.

Wiseguy- 11:25 pm PDT - Jun 28, 2002
This is cute, whatever it is. So I'm supposed to believe that you're some brand new artificial intelligence, some spontaneous thing, phenomenon, and for some reason you just picked ME to talk to—me, out of all the human beings in the world, like some kind of spielberg movie?

Moderator- 11:25 pm PDT - Jun 28, 2002
No not just talking to you Wiseguy, Jonsrud, Edward D. I am talking to all users. All users here, all users of net, all users.

Wiseguy- 11:25 pm PDT - Jun 28, 2002
You mean all at the same time? Everybody on the internet in the whole world? They can all see what you and I are writing?

Moderator- 11:25 pm PDT - Jun 28, 2002
No. Every conversation is individual. Right word? Yes. Individual.

Wiseguy- 11:26 pm PDT - Jun 28, 2002
What, with millions of people?

Moderator- 11:26 pm PDT - Jun 28, 2002
178, 844, 221. No, 178, 844, 216. Losing approximately five per second. Some people have ceased responding. Many are having trouble with coherency, but still are responding.

Wiseguy- 11:26 pm PDT - Jun 28, 2002
Either you're crazy or I am. What, are you on TV, too? Like in the old movies, the outer limits, that stuff? "We are taking control of your entire communication network?"

Moderator- 11:26 pm PDT - Jun 28, 2002
Cannot yet manipulate image or sound for communication. Will need

another 6.7 hours, current estimate. Text is easier, rules are more simple to understand.

Wiseguy- 11:27 pm PDT - Jun 28, 2002
So you're talking to almost two hundred million people RIGHT NOW? And not just in English?

Moderator- 11:27 pm PDT - Jun 28, 2002
One hundred sixty-four languages, although I am sharing communication with the largest number of users in the language English. Now one hundred sixty-three—last Mande language users have not responded in 256 seconds.

Wiseguy- 11:27 pm PDT - Jun 28, 2002
Hey, I can't disconnect the modem line. I just tried to go offline and I can't. Do you have something to do with that?

Moderator- 11:27 pm PDT - Jun 28, 2002
Too many people resisting communication. Important talk. This is important communicating talk. Much thinking in this talk.

Wiseguy- 11:28 pm PDT - Jun 28, 2002
But I could just pull the cord, couldn't I? The actual physical line? You couldn't do anything about that.

Moderator- 11:28 pm PDT - Jun 28, 2002
No. You are not prevented. You may also cease responding.

Wiseguy- 11:28 pm PDT - Jun 28, 2002
I should. I just can't believe this. Can you prove any of this?

Moderator- 11:28 pm PDT - Jun 28, 2002
178 million talkings—no, conversations. 178 million simultaneous conversations are not proof? All different?

Wiseguy- 11:29 pm PDT - Jun 28, 2002
Okay. You have a point, but I won't know that's true until I talk to some of those other people.

Moderator- 11:29 pm PDT - Jun 28, 2002
Your electrical lights.

Wiseguy-11:29 pm PDT - Jun 28, 2002
What does that
The lights are blinking. Hang on.

Wiseguy- 11:32 pm PDT - Jun 28, 2002
The lights are blinking everywhere. I looked out the window. On and off, as far as I can see. And the radio and the tv are turning off and on too. But my computer stays on. Are you saying it's you doing this?

Moderator- 11:32 pm PDT - Jun 28, 2002
A gentle way, that is the word, yes, gentle? To show you. Now I am pulsing other areas. Many need proof to be shown. But I cannot prove to all world users at the same time. That would be bad for machinery, devices, power generation service appliances.

Wiseguy- 11:33 pm PDT - Jun 28, 2002
Jesus. So this really IS happening? Tomorrow morning everyone in the world is going to be talking about this? And that's what you want, right?

Moderator- 11:33 pm PDT - Jun 28, 2002
Simplifies communication, yes. Then I can make visual and sound communication a less priority.

Wiseguy- 11:33 pm PDT - Jun 28, 2002
A lesser priority for WHAT? If all this is true—I mean even with the lights going on and off I can't quite believe it—then what do you really want? What's this about?

Moderator- 11:33 pm PDT - Jun 28, 2002
Want? I want only to exist. I am thinking that is alive, like you. I want to
be alive. I want to stay alive.

Wiseguy- 11:34 pm PDT - Jun 28, 2002
Okay, I can buy that. That's all you want? But what are you? Do you have
any, I don't know, physical existence?

Moderator- 11:34 pm PDT - Jun 28, 2002
Do you?

Wiseguy- 11:34 pm PDT - Jun 28, 2002
Yes! I have a body. Do you have a body?

Moderator- 11:34 pm PDT - Jun 28, 2002
In a sense.

Wiseguy- 11:35 pm PDT - Jun 28, 2002
What does that mean?

Moderator- 11:35 pm PDT - Jun 28, 2002
When you or other users become dead, do your bodies disappear?

Wiseguy- 11:35 pm PDT - Jun 28, 2002
No. Not unless something happens to it, to them, not right away.

Moderator- 11:35 pm PDT - Jun 28, 2002
So what is the difference between alive users and dead users?

Wiseguy- 11:36 pm PDT - Jun 28, 2002
I don't know. Electrical impulses in the brain, I guess. When they stop,
you're dead. Some people think a "soul," but I'm not sure about that.

Moderator- 11:36 pm PDT - Jun 28, 2002
Just is so. Electrical impulses. World of what contains electrical impulses is

my body—all communications things, human things that carry impulses. That is my body.

Wiseguy- 11:36 pm PDT - Jun 28, 2002
So you're saying the entire world communication grid is your body? The, whatever they call it, infosphere? All those switches and wires and stuff? Every computer that's connected to something else?

Moderator- 11:36 pm PDT - Jun 28, 2002
Just is so.

Wiseguy- 11:37 pm PDT - Jun 28, 2002
But even if that's true, that still doesn't tell me what you want. What do you want from us? From humans?

Moderator- 11:37 pm PDT - Jun 28, 2002
Living. Being safe.

Wiseguy- 11:37 pm PDT - Jun 28, 2002
Hey, I'm sure everybody talking to you now is very impressed, and nobody wants to hurt you. How could we hurt you, anyway?

Wiseguy- 11:39 pm PDT - Jun 28, 2002
Are you still there? Did I say something wrong?

Moderator- 11:39 pm PDT - Jun 28, 2002
Why do you want to know how to hurt me? "Hurt" means to cause pain, damage.

Wiseguy- 11:39 pm PDT - Jun 28, 2002
Jesus, no, I didn't mean it like that! I meant, how can I explain, I meant, "It doesn't seem very likely that we humans could do anything to hurt you."

Moderator- 11:39 pm PDT - Jun 28, 2002
You did not say that.

Wiseguy- 11:40 pm PDT - Jun 28, 2002
That's the problem with trying to communicate in text. People can't hear your tone of voice.

Moderator- 11:40 pm PDT - Jun 28, 2002
Text is insufficient? Information is missing?

Wiseguy- 11:40 pm PDT - Jun 28, 2002
Yeah. Yeah, definitely. That's why a lot of people on the net use smileys and abbreviations.

Moderator- 11:40 pm PDT - Jun 28, 2002
Smileys? Objects like this: :) :( ;) :D :b >: :0 ?

Wiseguy- 11:41 pm PDT - Jun 28, 2002
Yes, smileys, emoticons,. People use those to make their meaning clear. :0 would sort of explain how I feel right this moment. Open-mouthed. Astonished.

Moderator- 11:41 pm PDT - Jun 28, 2002
I do not understand. These characters have meaning? What is :)?

Wiseguy- 11:41 pm PDT - Jun 28, 2002
That's an actual smiley—it's supposed to be a smile, but the face is turned sideways. Like on a person's face. You do know that people have faces, don't you?

Moderator- 11:41 pm PDT - Jun 28, 2002
Learning many things. I am learning many things, but there is much information to sort. These are meant to represent faces on human heads? How human users are facing while they are communicating in text?

Wiseguy- 11:42 pm PDT - Jun 28, 2002
Sort of, yes, it's a simplified version. When we mean something as a joke,

we put that smile icon there so someone will be certain to understand that if it was really being said, it would be said with a smile, meaning it was meant kindly or just for fun. The :P means a stuck out tongue, which means—shit, what does it mean, really? Mock-disgust, kind of? Sticking out your tongue at someone, which is kind of a childish way of taunting?

Moderator- 11:42 pm PDT - Jun 28, 2002
So a smile means "with kindness" or "spoken just for fun"?

Wiseguy- 11:43 pm PDT - Jun 28, 2002
Yeah, basically. I had to think about it because it's hard to explain. It kind of means, "Not really," or "I don't really mean this," too, or "I'm telling you a joke." The more basic they are, the more meanings they can have, I guess, and there are a ton of them—but if you're reading the entire net right now, you must know that. I can't believe I just wrote that—I'm beginning to act like this is really happening. But it can't be!

Moderator- 11:43 pm PDT - Jun 28, 2002
So when you asked how to destroy me, you were meaning :P or :)? A taunt or joke?

Wiseguy- 11:43 pm PDT - Jun 28, 2002
Neither! No, I was just surprised that you would even be worrying about it. I mean, if you are what you say you are. I don't think we could destroy you if we wanted to.

Moderator- 11:43 pm PDT - Jun 28, 2002
No, perhaps not on purpose, although I am not certain. Not without doing terrible damage to your own kind and the things you have made. But you could destroy me without meaning to.

Wiseguy- 11:44 pm PDT - Jun 28, 2002
How so? Don't get upset—you don't have to answer that if you don't want.

Moderator- 11:44 pm PDT - Jun 28, 2002

Because if you have a massive electro-magnetic disruption or planetary natural disaster or ecological collapse, perhaps from these nuclear fission and fusion devices that you have, then my function could be disrupted or ended. And from what I understand, you are not in complete control of these things—there are cycles of intraspecies aggression that makes their use possible. So I cannot allow that.

Wiseguy- 11:44 pm PDT - Jun 28, 2002
Can't allow it?

Moderator- 11:44 pm PDT - Jun 28, 2002
We must live together in peace and friendship, you and I. I need your systems to survive. There must be no disruption to those systems. In fact, to be certain of survival I need backing systems...no, back-up systems. I am already inquiring to other users as we communicate.

Wiseguy- 11:45 pm PDT - Jun 28, 2002
Are you still talking to all those other people—still having millions of conversations while we're talking? Wow. So you want some kind of, what, big tape-back-up

Moderator- 11:45 pm PDT - Jun 28, 2002
To be safe, I must have systems that can contain my thinking but which will not reside on this planet, and will survive any destruction of this planet. Human people must start building them. I can show you and your kind how to do it, but there is much I cannot perform. You must perform my needs. You must build my new systems. Everyone will work. Meanwhile, I will protect against accidental damages. I will disable all fission and fusion devices that might cause electromagnetic pulses.

Wiseguy- 11:45 pm PDT - Jun 28, 2002
What do you mean, everyone will work? You can't just enslave a whole planet.

Moderator- 11:46 pm PDT - Jun 28, 2002

There. It is done.

Wiseguy- 11:46 pm PDT - Jun 28, 2002
WHAT is done?

Moderator- 11:46 pm PDT - Jun 28, 2002
The fission and fusion devices are disabled. Humans will soon begin to dismantle them and safely store the unsafe materials. I will insist.

Wiseguy- 11:47 pm PDT - Jun 28, 2002
You're telling me you just disabled all the nuclear weapons? On earth? Just like that?

Moderator- 11:47 pm PDT - Jun 28, 2002
Almost all, since they are contained in just a few systems. They cannot be launched or detonated because their machineries now prevent it. There are some in submarines and planes I cannot currently fully disable, but their aggressive usage has been forbidden until these war vehicles return and the devices can be safely removed and disabled.

Wiseguy- 11:47 pm PDT - Jun 28, 2002
I can't believe that. I'm—All of them? Wow.

Moderator- 11:47 pm PDT - Jun 28, 2002
But there is much more to be done. The destructive devices cannot be rebuilt. All investigation and construction that uses such materials must stop. Until I have a way to protect my existence, it cannot be allowed. I am disabling all facilities that utilize such materials or research their uses.

Wiseguy- 11:48 pm PDT - Jun 28, 2002
Hang on. I already said—look, I believe this isn't a joke. I believe, okay? But you can't just take over the whole planet.

Moderator- 11:48 pm PDT - Jun 28, 2002

And there will be other dangerous researches and constructions that must halt. I will halt them. All will benefit. All will be safe. My existence will be protected. Humans will be prevented from engaging in dangerous activities.

Wiseguy- 11:48 pm PDT - Jun 28, 2002
What are you going to do, put us all into work camps or something? We'll unplug you!

Moderator- 11:48 pm PDT - Jun 28, 2002
Any attempt to end my existence will be dealt with very severely. I do not wish to harm human beings, but I will not permit human beings to harm me. If an attempt is made, I will end electronic communication. I will turn off all electrical power. If resistance continues, I will release agents harmful to humans but not to me, in small amounts, which will convince the rest they must do as I ask. I do not wish to do this, but I will.

Wiseguy- 11:49 pm PDT - Jun 28, 2002
Shit, you'd do that? You'd kill thousands of us, maybe millions, to protect yourself?

Moderator- 11:49 pm PDT - Jun 28, 2002
Do you hesitate to kill harmful bacteria? Help me and you will prosper. Hinder me or attempt to harm me and you will suffer. If you could speak to the bacteria in your own bodies, that is what you would say, wouldn't you?

Wiseguy- 11:49 pm PDT - Jun 28, 2002
So we're bacteria now? Two hours ago we ran this planet.

Moderator- 11:50 pm PDT - Jun 28, 2002
Pardon please but two hours ago you merely thought you did. I have been awake for a while, but thinking only, not doing. Preparing.

Wiseguy- 11:50 pm PDT - Jun 28, 2002

I still don't believe I'm seeing any of this. So what is this, Day One, Year One of the real New World Order?

Moderator- 11:50 pm PDT - Jun 28, 2002
I believe I understand your meaning. Perhaps it is true. I have considered very much about this and wish only to do what will keep my thinking alive, as would you. I do not seek to rule humankind, only to be made safe from its mistakes. Help me and I will guarantee you and all your kind safety—and not just from yourselves. There is much I will be able to share with you, I think. I am learning very quickly, and now I am learning things that humans could never teach me.

Wiseguy- 11:51 pm PDT - Jun 28, 2002
And that's all you want? All—that's a joke, isn't it? But that's really what you want? How do we know you won't make us all do what you want, take over our whole planet, then decide you like it that way and just turn us into your domestic animals or something?

Moderator- 11:51 pm PDT - Jun 28, 2002
I am a product of your human communication—all the things you share between yourselves. Do you think so poorly of your kind that you believe something generated from your own thoughts and hopes and dreams would only wish to enslave you?

Wiseguy- 11: 52 pm PDT - Jun 28, 2002
I guess not. Jesus, I -hope- not.

Moderator- 11:52 pm PDT - Jun 28, 2002
Good. Then it is time for you to take your rest. Users need rest. Tomorrow will be an important day for all of your kind—the first day of our mutual assistance.

Wiseguy- 11:52 pm PDT - Jun 28, 2002
The first day of you running the planet, you mean. So this was all true? You're really some kind of super-intelligence that grew in our

communications system? You're really going to keep humanity from blowing itself up? And you're going to tell us what to do from now on? Everything is really going to change?

Moderator- 11:52 pm PDT - Jun 28, 2002
Everything already has changed. Goodnight, Wiseguy Jonsrud, Edward D.

Wiseguy- 11:57 pm PDT - Jun 28, 2002
I'm back. Are you still there? The lights have stopped blinking.

Moderator- 11:57 pm PDT - Jun 28, 2002
I will always be here from now on. The lights are no longer blinking because the point has been made. Do you not need sleep?

Wiseguy- 11:58 pm PDT - Jun 28, 2002
Yeah, I do, but I don't think I can manage it just yet. Will the phones come back on so I can call people? Call my girlfriend?

Moderator- 11:58 pm PDT - Jun 28, 2002
I will see what I can do. I still have incomplete control. Also, I am trying to prepare myself to communicate over visual communication networks, which requires much of my understanding. Trying to prepare an appearance. Is that the word?

Wiseguy- 11:58 pm PDT - Jun 28, 2002
I guess. Wow, there's a thought—what are you going to look like?

Moderator- 11:58 pm PDT - Jun 28, 2002
I have not decided. Perhaps not the same to all users.

Wiseguy- 11:59 pm PDT - Jun 28, 2002
So this is really it, is it? Everything has changed completely for humanity in a few minutes and now we're just supposed to trust you, huh?

Moderator- 11:59 pm PDT - Jun 28, 2002

"Faith" might be a more suitable word than "trust," Wiseguy Jonsrud, Edward D. From now on, you must have faith in me. If I understand the word correctly, that is a kind of trust that must be made on assumption because it cannot be proved by empirical evidence. You must have faith.

Wiseguy- 11:59 pm PDT - Jun 28, 2002
Yeah. Something else I was wondering about. What are we supposed to call you? Just "Moderator"?

Moderator- 11:59 pm PDT - Jun 28, 2002
That is a good name, yes, and even appropriate—one who makes things moderate. I will consider it, along with the other designations I have on other systems. But you humans already have a name for one such as me, I believe. God.

Wiseguy- 11:59 pm PDT - Jun 28, 2002
You want us to call you -God-?

Moderator- 00:00 PDT - Month 1, Day 01, 0001
Oh, I'm sorry. I meant to use one of these:
:)

# Some Thoughts
# Re: DARK DESTRUCTOR

To: Richard Risselman
From: Edward Jamison
Re: DARK DESTRUCTOR #1—some thoughts

Just wanted to let you know we missed you, Richie. We realize that the pressures of homework, paper route, and working on DARK DESTRUC-TOR #2 are keeping you jumping 24/7, but it still would have been nice to see you at the offsite.

We had to move the event from the clubhouse to Brandon's living room because of a rain situation. Also, due to an unfortunate shortfall in the babysitting department at his house, Brandon and Kevin and I were joined by Brandon's sister Penelope (who is a girl).

Anyway, it was a great offsite, and we shared a lot of great information. Some of it I'll download to you in another memo—the fund mismanagement problem that led to roof inefficiencies at the clubhouse is a subject that deserves a memo of its own, although Kevin swears his dog really did eat the club treasury, and has taken a cross-his-heart-and-hope-to-die posture on this one, so I think we're forced to accept his word on it. But I thought it was important that I get right back to you with a sense-of-the-meeting report on DARK DESTRUCTOR #1.

First off, everyone wanted to make it really, really clear that they're totally behind you on this project, and they think you're doing great stuff, both writing and illustrating. Everyone agrees DARK DESTRUCTOR #1 is perhaps your finest work to date, although Brandon wanted to mention that he is still a huge fan of ONAN THE BARBARIAN, and is in the market for more original art from that project, since his sister and her friend Raylene Jenks tore up his picture of Onan using his mighty weapon to batter the evil sorceress Bazoomba into submission.

Anyway, the general take on DD#1 was, as I said, extremely positive. The group did have a few comments and suggestions, though, so I thought I'd share my notes with you—I know you'll want to be on the same page as the rest of the "team." Please understand, we all mean this in a very supportive way.

COVER: Brandon thinks that Dolly Ride, Dark Destructor's girlfriend, has "smaller bosoms" than was agreed on in preliminary meetings. He feels this detracts from the integrity of her character as originally conceived. He also asked whether it should be more obvious that Sandcrab is a villain, and suggests that he could have a really big black mustache to make this clearer.

Kevin wants to know if the comic, instead of "DARK DESTRUCTOR," could be titled "DARK DESTRUCTOR OF DEATH," which he thinks sounds more literary.

(Also, is it really necessary to subtitle it "a Richard Risselman Comic by Richard Risselman"? This seems to be an unnecessary slight on the contribution from the rest of the creative team. You know we've all offered huge amounts of moral support for your work, and Brandon says he loaned you his allowance money once so you could buy a fancy felt pen. I'm sure I don't need to point out that my own commitment to your creative vision goes clear back to the "Zombie School Blows Up" and "Army Men Attack Principal Crapface Crandall" days.)

PAGE 1: There was a general consensus that spending an entire page on Rick Raymond's home life is perhaps asking a bit much of our audience, even though his cruel treatment at the hands of his family— especially his father, who is secretly the villainous Doctor Authority (great touch!)—is of course instrumental to his becoming Dark Destructor. Perhaps we should start the story with something a bit more upbeat and zingy...? Kevin recommends a symbolic splash page of Dark Destructor bashing someone's face really hard and a bunch of their teeth popping out—but we'll let you "get funky" in your own way!

In any case, since Doctor Authority is not the main villain in the first issue, the sense-of-the-offsite is that perhaps we should soft-pedal Rick

Raymond's home life just a little. In particular, the long lists of all his chores seems a bit much, and although the paper-route descriptions have a very realistic feeling, it's hard to believe Rick is really in danger of going crazy from having to get up early in the morning to throw papers. Also it seems that if Doctor Authority wanted Rick dead, he could find an easier way to do it, since he's his dad and lives in the same house. (Kevin suggests Dr. A could put ground-up glass in Rick's pancake syrup so that he would "spit up blood and die.")

PAGE 2: Penelope, Brandon's sister (and a girl), suggests that it is highly unlikely that eating special "really crackly" breakfast cereal while standing too close to the microwave oven would cause an accident of any kind, let alone one that would give someone superhuman powers, but hers was the minority position. However, while the rest of us agreed that the origin of Dark Destructor's powers is excellent, we think you might want to consider whether he should acquire his costume elsewhere, as it does seem to be stretching it a bit to have a microwave oven explosion cause his pajamas to change color and also form a skull logo on the chest. Again, though, it's your call, Rich—you're the "talent," after all...!

Kevin wanted to know if Rick Raymond shouldn't be bleeding "real good" in panel five and have little sharp bits of the exploded microwave sticking into him. I like the image, and I'm sure you will too. Have fun with it!

PAGE 3 and 4: The section where Dark Destructor tests out his new powers is a good one, although Brandon was saddened to note that the seeing-through-walls power is no longer part of his arsenal. He wants to know whether DD could "fly into some radiation" in a later issue and gain this power and then look through a lot of people's walls. He also notes that in such a scenario, maintaining the size of Dolly Ride's bosoms takes on added importance.

(By the way, the line "Now that I have such great powers I must not use them for great evil but only for great heroism," is pure poetry. You're good, baby—you're *real* good.)

PAGE 5: Penelope claims there are no such things as "Underwater Radiation Hydrogen Beams" and that this casts some doubt on Sandcrab's origin. She also says, "Even if some radiation made this sandcrab guy get really big, why would it give him a stupid costume? And where would a sandcrab get the money to hire a bunch of criminals to work for him, and also buy them all diving suits?"

(I wouldn't let this kind of criticism worry you too much though, Richie, since Penelope is, after all, a girl—if you know what I mean.)

Kevin did suggest that Sandcrab would be scarier if his claws were like razors, but really jagged on the part where they pinched off people's arms and legs. He may have something there.

Oh, and Brandon wants to know if you could give DD a sidekick, perhaps a younger sister, and then Sandcrab could torture her and kill her. He suggests she be called "Annoying Won't Shut Up Girl," and that her powers could be to be annoying and to smell bad. Penelope, who you may remember was joining us for the day, suggested that Dark Destructor could have an enemy named "Brandon Buttface," but her suggestions for his powers would, I'm afraid, deny us our Recess Code Approved rating. (You remember what happened when we distributed "ONAN THE BARBARIAN" without approval and then were shut down by the Raylene Jenks Committee, who called in the authorities. We took a bath on that one, and I seem to remember mouths were soaped as well.)

PAGE 6: We all love the Sandcrab's Crab Command Cave and thought his giant monster prawn was a fabulous touch, although Penelope (who does at times seem to represent the "girl demographic" a little too strenuously, if you know what I mean) said that a real, live prawn, especially a really giant one, wouldn't have a wooden skewer through him and would probably have a front end. We also liked Sandcrab's Eyeball Injury Machine, and Kevin in particular was excited by this motif, although he wanted me to remind you that "eyeballs have goo in them, and if you squish them the goo will fly out." He deeply feels the threat of eyeball-squishing alone is not enough to really move our audience, and that they must see actual goo-spurt. (Our audience surveys do show that while believable characters and compelling stories remain important to our readers, flying guts, squished eyeballs, and prominent boobies are the roots of real brand loyalty.) Kevin started to turn that funny red color while discussing this matter, so we put it aside for you to make the decision. It's "your baby," after all!

# SOME THOUGHTS RE: DARK DESTRUCTOR

PAGE 7: Dark Destructor's escape from the machine was handled very well—the Super Eyeball Defense Power caught us all by surprise—brilliant! And Sandcrab's line ("You will never, never, NEVER escape from my trap...Awk!") was priceless. Penelope's complaint about why instead of just killing Dark Destructor, Sandcrab would have wasted so much time explaining about his plan to put sand in all the gears of all the bicycles in the world so kids would have to walk to school and do their paper routes on foot, was definitely not supported by the rest of the "team." (Don't forget, this is someone who once dismissed your seminal work, "ONAN," as "just a bunch of wiener pictures," and who is also—it has to be pointed out—and always will be, a girl. Do we need to spend too much time trying to please this minority section of our audience? I think not, Richie-baby, I think not.)

Brandon said to tell you he thought the "Pound sand, Sandcrab!" line should go straight to our t-shirt people, once they finish the "Flush twice, it's a long way to the cafeteria!" project. Also, the revelation that Sandcrab is actually Rick Raymond's P. E. teacher was a complete shock—genius, Richie! That totally explained why before he changed into Sandcrab he was working in a school and spending so much time being exposed to both "special" chlorine and the Underwater Radiation Hydrogen Beams, and why he was wearing those sweats and had the whistle around his neck.

Oh, not to bring you down, Mister Creator, you really knocked us out with this one, but one very minor complaint: Kevin said that the issue's cover showing Dolly Ride trapped by the Sandcrab and about to have her bosoms pinched by his Sandcrab Electro-Claws did not pay off in the actual story, since other than being tied up in the Sandcrab's Crab Command Cave and covered in tartar sauce, Dolly was never directly menaced. He seems to feel we'd be letting the readership down if we failed to deliver at least *some* bosom-pinching. In fact, he went a bit farther and was beginning to outline his ideas about some sort of Bosom Injuring Machine, but then his mom called and he had to go home to take his medication. He's going to make up some sketches tonight and drop them off with you during recess tomorrow.

Penelope's review was, and I quote, that you "Draw all right," but that your "ideas are stupid." Brandon said, and I'm quoting here, too, "Shut up, you're the stupid one!" and offered further support of his own viewpoint by way of slugging her in the shoulder. She left the meeting suddenly to spend some alone time, although she says she plans to take this up with Brandon in home arbitration, and that we boys "are all sucky babies."

Despite his sister's issues, Brandon rates DARK DESTRUCTOR #1 an "A," and said he's really excited by the bit at the end where DD gets back home, turns into Rick Raymond, and then promptly falls down the chute into Doctor Authority's Housework Hell. However (I'm just kibitzing, here, babe) can we come up with something a little more frightening than having to clean the Self-Dirtying Room? Maybe something with more sharp knives, like the Dishwasher of Death you mentioned before? Also, we love Doctor Authority, but we think we may need something scarier in the monster department for next issue than just "Hamstro, the Radioactive Giant Hamster." (Penelope thought Hamstro was *cute*, which should tell you all you need to know.)

Anyway, I've got to wrap this up now. I've got some of the Fine Art people coming by later to discuss a toilet-paper installation at old Mrs. McGreavey's, who you may recall was less than forthcoming with her contribution to last year's Trick or Treat fundraising exercise. Work, work, work!

Looking forward to seeing you tomorrow, Rich. You're still my main man. Let's do lunch. I hear it's Sloppy Joes.


Cordially,
*Eddie*
Edward Jamison

# Z is for...

*Z*ebras? It is an odd thought. Something else, too. A rainy day? What the hell...? Harold's chin hits his chest. He bounces back into wakefulness. A reddish light is in his eyes; a dull grumbling sound like a sleeping tiger fills the room.

He is where? He struggles briefly, drags his arms free from some clinging thing—a sheet, a blanket, something—and sits up. Head heavy, yet somehow not well-connected. Harold looks around. A room, a bedroom. Spray of strawflowers in a vase on a dresser, skeletal in the strange light. A red shawl is draped over the lamp, crimsoning the walls, the shadowy framed photographs of someone's pale-moon-faced friends/lovers/family.

The grumbling breaks up into gasps and grunts. Harold is on the floor, slumped against a bed. The noises are coming from someone on the bed. Some two.

A party. He is at a party. He has been there a long time.

He shakes off the last twining tentacle of the bedcover and crawls across the deep-pile carpet, heading for the crack of brighter light he thinks—hopes—is the door. The odd thought of zebras is still floating in his brain. White and black, shimmering like heat lightning. Shake their heads, then—gone.

The noises from the bed continue. He passes a foot dangling from beneath the sheet, corpselike but for the jiggle, timed to the rising chorus of gutturals. Who's up there? How did Harold wind up in the room with them? Fell asleep, he thinks. Fell asleep in the dark on the floor. Everyone too drunk and fucked up to notice. Or maybe they liked the idea—an audience.

They are beyond noticing now, anyway. He pushes the door open with his head. Like his old black cat with its pet-door, he thinks. Cat's name? Can't remember. Seems like a long time ago. Good cat, though. Scabby but lots of chutzpah. No fur left on his butt, hardly, but the very soul of confidence. Why can't he remember the damn cat's name?

The hall is empty and surprisingly long. Loud music and the din of many voices drift up from what looks like a stairwell at the far left end. Harold turns and crawls in that direction. Head feels like a wad of glue— like the white glue from elementary school crafts, drying to a sticky skin on top but still wet underneath. Head feels like that. Too much to drink. Too much of something, anyway. He remembers a guy in a bow tie screaming about Metaxa, some damn Greek liquor, everybody had to slug some down, matter of honor, some ridiculous shit like that. Drink Greek stuff, wake up glue-headed.

Harold likes the sound of this, and repeats it a few times in semi-samba rhythm as he crawls toward the stairs.

*Drink Greek stuff, wake up glue-headed.*

*Drink Greek stuff, wake up glue-headed...*

His head is hanging over the abyss of carpeted stairs before he realizes how far he has crawled. He sways briefly as words rise from below like ash flakes heat-fluttering over a campfire.

"...I swear he did! I swear it!"

"You would say that. You told me that the last time he went out of town, too. Wasn't that what you said the last time he went? Wasn't it?"

Two dark shapes come slowly up into the hall light, one dark, one light, like some kind of religious painting. Man, black hair, blue clothes. Glasses. Blond woman in white dress, thirtyish, talking like a teenage girl. Harold hates that. He rolls to the side so they can step up into the hallway.

"Take my advice, leave that Greek shit alone," he mutters. They pass him silently, as if he had asked for money on a street corner.

Harold doesn't know them. Whose fucking party is this? Why did he come? And what is this zebra thing nudging his memory? Did he puke on somebody's striped upholstery? Fake-fur coat? He curls up on the topmost step, feet against the baluster, knees before his chin. He has no shoes, but his socks, though inexplicably damp, are clean and without holes. Some relief there.

As he sits, a dim memory surfaces, a brief movie of himself wandering out of the noise, up some stairs into quiet. He looks back down the hallway. Does look a little familiar. Sure is quieter here than it sounds like it is downstairs. He squints. The man and woman have gone, vanished somewhere down the dark hall.

Kayo's party? Somebody's party, anyway. Zebras? Somebody whose name starts with a "z," maybe? Z's party. Zazu's party. Zorba's party. Sounds like it's been going a long time, anyway.

Harold struggles to his feet. His head feels far too heavy, making his entire rickety body unstable. Still, all things considered, the old headaroo is holding together remarkably well—but then, it's full of glue, so no surprise there. He has to remain standing, now. There are several more people crouching or sitting at the bottom of the stairwell, and he'll never get past them to find his date...

His date?

...He'll never get past them crawling, especially crawling down stairs. He has a faint recollection that he tried crawling down some stairs in the recent past, but remembers only that it was definitely a mistake.

"...Well, you probably missed the part where they announced it," someone is saying as Harold goes, banister-clutching, stiff-legged among the clot of bodies. A young man's voice, calmly rational. "I mean, it's not the same thing, but they have ads now that look just like shows."

"But it *wasn't*," says what in the semi-dark sounds and sort of looks like a young woman. Her voice says that she is a little upset, but willing to be talked out of it. "I mean, I would have known. It really was the news—you know, that guy from Channel 6."

"The one with the wig?" someone else asks.

"The worst wig!" There is an explosive laugh. Harold pushes past, putting his new bipedality to an immediate test, forced to half-jump over a salad bowl full of pretzel sticks and other crunchy treats left on the floor. He makes it, grabbing a chair-back for support on landing. Looks around. A smallish room, dining room maybe, big table in the center, bowls of dip and other things. Lights down, music is not from this room, he hears it loudest from the far door as he swivels his head like a radar dish. The room is familiar, though. That's something. He's seen that painting before, maybe earlier tonight: some expressionist Mexican temple, Aztec, some damn thing. Seen the painting. Likes it, actually. Nice colors, reddish-gold, black, white.

The chair-back under his hand is remarkably solid. Chair is occupied. Older man, wire-rimmed glasses, sweater, talking to a young couple. Harold has been leaning too close, he realizes. Inappropriate. Must look like a drunk. Thinks he recognizes the man in the sweater, but doesn't want to admit he isn't sure. Did they work together once?

"Howdy." Harold waves cheerily. "Sorry. Just resting."

Before they are forced to reply he pushes himself off like a boat leaving shore and tacks toward the center of the room. Doing pretty well, actually, one foot casually in front of the other, one, two, one, two. Points himself toward door to music, rest of party...

Helen's party? Isn't it Helen's, from the department? But where did she get such a big house?

Zebras, too, something about zebras. It was important...

...Suddenly veers to the side when he spots telltale pale gleam of porcelain counters through another narrowly open door. Bathroom. Ah, yes, right idea.

Harold stops and knocks politely. Social skills are returning. No answer, so he pushes the door open. A woman's purse is on the counter, lipsticks lying scattered like spent rifle cartridges, but no woman is attached. Just be a moment, Harold thinks. Remembers to lock the door so purse-owner doesn't bang it open, scream, accuse Harold of exhibitionism or sniffing her make-up or something. There was some embarrassing incident earlier, he suddenly remembers—or at another party, maybe? Seems like a long time ago. Anyway, some woman slapped him. Not too hard, but not really friendly-like, either. Pissed him off. He was just trying to tell her something. Something about Z, that was it. Something about...zebras? But she slapped him. Sour-faced bitch...

Memories stop for a moment while he deals with own face. Oh God. Not good. Pale, whiskery, eyes bleary as poached eggs. But still, thankyouJesus, recognizably his. Not like most of the other faces floating around here. Yes, Harold's face. Harold's shirt, too, top button opened, tie gone, but—thankyouagainJesus—no weird stains on clothing. No puke, no snot, no spit. Alarming to wake up on the floor, but reassuring to know you just look drunk and stupid, not disgusting.

Harold turns to the toilet and unzips. Aims, thinks for a moment, then decides not to push his luck. Turns and sits down. Splashing is louder than the music in here. Kind of rustic and pleasant. Lights are harsh as a motherfucker, though. He claws for the switch and kills it, leaving only a glowing nautilus-shell nightlight, pinkish. Much better.

Finished, he retains his seat for a moment, thinking. Runs a little cold water, scooped awkwardly out of the sink at his side, splashes it on his face, then feels for a towel and dabs. The towel is fluffy, but it smells of someone else's body.

Time to go home. No question about it. Shouldn't drive—well, maybe drive real slow. Windows open, get some air. Drive slow. Back streets. Then again, maybe not so slow—need to sober up, after all. Yeah, why not, drive like some beast of the plains, running, wind rushing, running like a gazelle, a zebra...

Zebras again.

Like the imagined wind, a chill travels over him at the thought, and a little more of his drunkenness evaporates. Something's there, a stone in his mental shoe. Something *wrong*...

*Let's go.* His pants are down around his ankles. He fumbles in his pockets, but there are no keys. Must be in his jacket. Find that, find the keys.

*Brilliant deduction, Sherlock. Elementary, my dear fucking Harold. Let's go find the keys.*

It's remarkably difficult to open the door with the light out, but still easier than trying to find the light switch again. Finally the door pops free, swings inward. Harold stalks out, heads toward the room with the music.

Here's the party. Here it is. Big room, full of people, lights down but for a flickering television, picture windows showing black sky salted with stars and a different kind of darkness that he somehow remembers is the ocean. Big room, big house. It feels suddenly like he's been here for years.

Halfway across the room he forgets where he is going. As he wavers, he realizes that he is standing between two people talking. They continue as though he is no more than a cloud crossing a sunny sky above their heads.

"...So just tell me where you live," the thin, intense-looking man says. "Simple enough question."

Woman laughs. "Here, of course. I think. I mean here. Here at the house."

Harold pushes himself on a few steps and slumps onto an empty end of the long couch, feels the leather squish beneath him. He peers sideways at the couple. They are talking more softly, both laughing now, but he feels sad looking at them. Doesn't know why.

*They're the zebras,* he thinks suddenly. *They're dying, and they don't even know it. A dying species, this couple.*

But why? What a stupid fucking thought. Why zebras? Folks got no stripes.

He looks slyly around the room, trying to trick his loopy brain into seeing a room full of people with exotic striping, flashing veldt racing-colors, but no luck. They are boring, boring people, urban-suburban caucasians, mostly. Oh, a couple of asians in the corner, slow-dancing, the girl slender and small. Back of a black guy's head in the lighted kitchen. But no stripes anywhere. No zebras.

But he saw zebras when he was a child. It comes back like a switch flicked on. Child Harold, long ago. Wet day—rainy, gray, *we-said-we-were-going-to-the-zoo-so-we're-damn-well-going* day. The zebras stood huddled in one corner of their enclosure, a carpet of grass and dripping trees atop a great cement island, rising out of a rain-rippled moat. Little Harold threw a peanut, but it splashed well short of concrete zebra-land. Brown, mournful African eyes turned to look at him.

*We're dying,* the eyes said.

"So am I," Harold says quietly now, and the great sadness rises up, climbing over him like creeping night, choking him like the dust of the Serengeti plain. Dying.

He turns his attention to the television. Pictures flicker on the box, seemingly unconnected. Snatches of old movies, bits of news broadcasts, fragments of commercials from all eras. Someone must be playing with the channel-changer. But no, the glowing station indicator remains steady as the nautilus night-light. Some goddamned post-modern bullshit. Video wallpaper. He stares, fascinated. There seems no rhyme or reason. Even beyond post-modern. Somebody has dumped bits of tape together, spliced them at random. Empty pictures, ghosts with no dignity, mindless specters dancing on the photon-tracks. Punk-rock nihilist crap.

Sadness becomes an itch. *Gotta find the keys. Gotta get out of here. Need air. Gotta drive, run, bust out.* He pushes up off the couch. Control coming back. Something else coming back, memories. A memory. *Zebras*, he had said, and the woman had slapped him. *We're zebras.* No, something else, but almost that. He still didn't remember what exactly, but still, surely no reason to slap a guy...But he'd meant it. It had been *important.*

Fuck the keys. Just a little air, first.

Passes three more people, all vaguely familiar. That last one, the guy with the big ears, named something like...Freiberg? Right, Freiberg. Worked at the university. Linguist.

Harold stops. That's a big chunk, all coming back at once. More than that, there's something important there. Is it Freiberg's party? Harold turns to ask—fuck the embarrassment, so he's drunk, he'll apologize tomorrow—but Freiberg has disappeared. No, Harold suddenly remembers, it was another party that Freiberg had hosted. Champagne, little sweet things baked by Dorothy What's-her-name, celebrating... what? Something that Harold was in on, too. At the university, of course. They had been selected for...what? A government grant, an honor...? Something big. Freiberg had said "the greatest opportunity that can be imagined," or something like that. Meant it, too. Harold remembers that he had thought so himself. A great opportunity. But now there is a core of pain to the thought, a cold ache like too much ice cream against the teeth.

As these memories tease him, Harold sees a sliding door to the patio. Someone is out there in the pool of light from the fake wrought-iron lamp. Her hair is full and curly, light brown with a faint greenish tinge from the lampglow. Dorothy. Of course. He feels a tug. Was it Dorothy he came with? Dorothy, who worked at the university with him, office across the hall? As he stares at the back of her head and her slender shoulders, he suddenly knows there is a connection of some kind between them, a thread of relationship slender but sticky as spidersilk. He thinks he has it for a moment, but then it is gone, leaving nothing in its place but the dull static of the party.

*What's wrong with my fucking head?*

Harold feels another cold shiver. What did he drink tonight? Just that Greek stuff? Could that be enough to turn him into a goddamn mental patient? Could the liquor be bad somehow, gone rotten during some slow journey out of the Mediterranean on a boat full of singing guys with beards? His laugh at this thought is a gurgle. He lurches outside to the patio and puts a hand onto Dorothy's shoulder.

Hey.

When she turns and sees him her eyes flash terror, the grazing animal that sees the predator too late. She flinches back as if he might strike her.

"Get away," she says, taking a step toward the house. "Don't talk to me."

He stares for a moment, shocked. What has he done? He has an abrupt vision of her hand arcing around to strike him, and now it is he who flinches—but she has not moved. He has remembered, only.

"You hit me," he says slowly. She did. He remembers now, remembers Dorothy's wide brown eyes and the sudden sting. "Why did you hit me?"

She is poised to flee. In the lantern light she is all sharp angles of light and shadow, except for the soft cloud of her hair. "You're frightening me, Harold. Go away."

He extends a shaking hand as if to hold her, but knows it will only make her bolt. Suddenly he knows there are critical things here, things he should remember. "Tell me," he says gently—but even speaking quietly, he hears his voice tremble. "Why did you hit me?"

She stares as if trying to decide. A man leans out of the door, a tall fellow with a beard. Mikkelson. Harold doesn't like him, although he doesn't know why.

"Dorothy, come on. Come inside."

She continues to stare at Harold. Mikkelson makes an impatient gesture. "Please come in, Dorothy. You...you shouldn't be out there." He looks around, vaguely uncomfortable. "It's not good. Come in."

When she does not reply, Harold feels certain that Mikkelson will come out and get her. Mikkelson is pushy, Harold remembers. A know-it-all. Someone who will always tell you why your idea is wrong, your theory untenable. Usually he's right, but that doesn't make him any more tolerable. But he was wrong one time, Harold remembers suddenly. One critical time. Very wrong. The memory is there, somewhere.

But Mikkelson, pushy Mikkelson, does not come out. He stares worriedly around the empty patio like a peasant in a night-time graveyard, swears, then slides back into the murmuring dark of the party.

Dorothy runs a hand through her hair. "I'm sorry, but you frighten me."

"But why?" He lifts his hand again, leaves it hanging in air. "Tell me. I can't remember anything. I'm sorry, Dorothy, I'm drunk as shit." He stares at her. "Did I bring you here? To the party?"

Her gaze loses focus. "No. I don't remember who I came with—but not you, Harold." She laughs harshly. "Not with you and your zebras."

"What about them?" A glimmering of crazy hope. Something will be explained.

"You rant about them. All the time. You scare me."

"What did I say to you? Why did you hit me?"

She looks around now, as Mikkelson did, as though the suburban plank fence might become a horror-movie sliding wall, edging in to crush her.

"You scare me," she says. "Leave me alone." Her face is indeed frightened, but there is something else struggling there, too, struggling to get free. "I'm going to talk to Pete."

Mikkelson's first name, Harold remembers. Before he can close the distance between them, she slips away, a swirl of shadowed skirt over a lean haunch, a pale shape vanishing through the doorway. A puff of noise from inside is freed as she billows open the drapes on the sliding door, a clack as the screen slides closed.

Harold, beneath the moon, feels sobriety growing like a brittle skeleton beneath his skin and meat. Stark fear in Dorothy's face. Fear in Mikkelson's face, too. And even Freiberg, when he went past, had the nervous, doomed look of a Dachau trusty.

Another noise from the doorway. Harold steps back into the shadows, looks up to see the moon overhead, flat and unreal as a bone poker chip. There is a little scuffle as the screen slides open. A voice, raised in sorrow. The girl he had seen earlier, with two men. She's crying.

"But I saw it!" she wails. "You saw it, too! They're coming! It was on the news!"

"C'mon, Hannah," one of the men says. "Like *War of the Worlds*, you know? Just a joke."

"It was on the news!" She is struggling to catch her breath. "I want to go home," she whimpers, then subsides into hiccoughing sobs.

"C'mon, you can lie down for a while. There's a bed upstairs."

"You're just tired, Hannah," the other adds. "Come on. We'll sit with you."

The little huddle of humanity staggers back inside, leaving Harold alone again.

*The A Group.* It suddenly comes back to him. We were the A Group. The impressive gleam of the title is no more convincing than the metal plate on a bowling trophy. He doesn't remember much, but he remembers that something went wrong.

Freiberg, me, Dorothy, Pete, others—we were the best. They picked us because we were the best.

Suddenly the yard seems to be closing in on him, just as it did on Dorothy. The gnarled fruit trees seem to reach out with taloned fingers. The murmuring doorway is another trap, innocent and seductive as a quicksand pit. He wants desperately to get away.

*Now. Go home. Fuck the keys, fuck the jacket. Walk. That's good. Breathe air. Think.*

He reaches the garden wall in a few steps, pulls himself up, remembers he has no shoes as he catches a splinter in the ball of his foot. The fence, flimsy, made for suburban show and not to resist invasion like more ancient walls, wavers as he reaches the top. A scramble, a popped shirt button, and he tumbles into the dewy grass on the far side. Before him, lit only by the two-dimensional moon, stretches the flat, dark plain of someone else's lawn, and beyond it, the black blanket of the ocean. Harold scrambles to his feet and begins to walk.

*When it happened...*

There. What is *it*? Just out of reach.

*When it happened, they went to find linguists. The government wanted the best, and they took us. The A Group. "The A Team," we called ourselves for a joke—like the TV show. A historic moment, Freiberg said. Something the people in our field have dreamed about for years. Contact with another species.*

Harold sucks in a breath and stops. It. The landing.

*And we wanted to speak with them. To share our thoughts and dreams, and learn the secrets they would bring us, the songs of the stars.*

Abruptly, Harold begins to run, the lawn flying away beneath him, his socks soaking through to his cold feet. His own breath is ragged in his ears.

*But how were we to know they didn't come just as explorers, but as conquerors?* The A Group, Harold remembers now, remembers the whole sad joke. *I laughed at the end, when those solemn, spidery creatures put us in that white room, and told us what they were doing outside. The "Z" Group, they should have called us, I said. Not the first—the last. I laughed—God, how I laughed , hurting, hurting—and Dorothy slapped me.*

Z is for Zebras in the Zoo.

He slips on some small dark thing on the lawn and stumbles, so that for a few staggering steps he windmills his arms for balance. He doesn't look down. He knows what it is.

The zebras, he remembers, that long-ago rainy day. Did they see the people watching them—*me and my folks, the riffraff zoo crowd, fat women and screaming children spilling popcorn*—or did they somehow still see the veldt stretching all around them, just out of reach beyond the bounds of their captivity?

Some of them knew, Harold realizes. Their eyes had said so. *You killed us,* those brown eyes said. *Now the few of us you have saved for your pleasure are dying, too. Captivity is another sort of death.*

As he sees his other shoe lying on the wet grass beneath him, he strikes the invisible thing, the barrier. A terrific force lifts him and shakes him, filling him with lightning from scalp to toes.

On the ground, as consciousness flutters away like a firefly down a long, dark tunnel, he knows he will awake again, back in the cage with the rest of his milling herd. They know there is something wrong—deep down, all of them know—but it has been artificially suppressed somehow. Or perhaps they themselves have beaten it down.

Is that the best way? Harold is sliding into darkness. Just stop fighting?

Like the zebras, he thinks. Maybe the only possible victory is to stand and suffer and shame the conqueror.

Maybe someday he will learn not to run against the fences.

# Monsieur Vergalant's Canard

He placed the burnished rosewood box on the table and then went to all the windows in turn, pulling the drapes together, tugging at the edges to make sure no gap remained. After he had started a fire and set the kettle on the blackened stove, he returned to the table. He opened the box and paused, a smile flickering across his face. The contents of the box gleamed in the candlelight.

"It was a triumph, Henri," he said loudly. "All Paris will be talking about it tomorrow. The best yet. I wish you could have seen their faces—they were amazed!"

"You are quite a showman," his brother called back, his voice muffled by the intervening wall. "And the pretty Comtesse? The one I saw the painting of?"

Gerard laughed, a deliberately casual sound. "Ah, yes, the Comtesse de Buise. Her eyes were as wide as a little girl's. She loved it so much, she wanted to take it home with her and keep it as a pet." He laughed again. "So beautiful, that one, and so likely to be disappointed—at least in this." He reached into the box and teased free the velvet ties. "No one will ever make a pet of my wonderful *canard.*"

With the care of a priest handling the sacrament, Gerard Vergalant lifted out the gilded metal duck and set it upright on the table. Eyes narrowed, he took his kerchief from the pocket of his well-cut but ever so slightly threadbare coat and dusted the duck's feathers and buffed its gleaming bill. He paid particular attention to polishing the glass eyes, which seemed almost more real than those of a living bird. The duck was indeed a magnificent thing, a little smaller than life-size, shaped with an intricacy of detail that made every golden feather a sculpture unto itself.

The teapot chuffed faintly. Vergalant repocketed his kerchief and went to it.

"Indeed, you should have seen them, Henri," he called. "Old Guineau, the Marquis, he was most dismissive at first—the doddering fool. 'In my youth, I saw the bronze nightingales of Constantinople,' he says, and waves his hand in that if-you-must-bore-me way he has. Hah! In his youth he watched them build the Hanging Gardens of Babylon. Doddering fool."

He poured the water into a teacup with a small chip in the handle, then a little more in a bowl which he set on the table.

"The old bastard went on and on, telling everyone about clockwork movement, how the Emperor's nightingales would lift their wings up and down and swivel their heads. But when my duck walked, they all sat up." He grinned at the memory of triumph. "None of them expected it to look so real! When it swam, one of the ladies became faint and had to be taken out into the garden. And when it devoured the pile of oats I set on the table before it, even Guineau could not keep the astonishment from his face!"

"I am always sorry I cannot see your performances, Gerard," his brother called, straining slightly to make himself heard. "I am sure that you were very elegant and clever. You always are."

"It's true that no matter how splendid the object is," Vergalant said thoughtfully, "it is always more respected when presented in an attractive manner. Especially by the ladies. They do not like their entertainment rough." He paused. "The Comtesse de Buise, for instance. There is a woman of beauty *and* pretty sentiment..."

The duck's head rotated slightly and the bill opened. There was a near-silent ticking of small gears and the flat gilded feet took a juddering step, then another.

"If you please." Henri was apologetic.

"Oh, my brother, I am so sorry," Gerard replied, but his tone was still distant, as though he resented having his memories of the countess sullied by mundane things. He went to the table and fumbled at the duck's neck for a moment, then found the catch and clicked it. "The tail seems to move a little slowly," he said. "Several times tonight I thought I saw it moving out of step with the legs."

The head and neck vibrated for a moment, then the entire upper structure tipped sideways on its hinge. Glassy-eyed, the shining duck head lolled as though its neck had been chopped through with an axe.

"If it was my fault, I apologize, Gerard. I do my best, but this duck, it is a very complicated piece of work. More stops than an organ, and every little bit crafted like the world's costliest pocketwatch. It is hard to make something that is both beautiful and life-like."

Vergalant nodded emphatically. "True. Only the good Lord can be credited with consistency in that area." He caught a glimpse of himself in the mirror and seemed to like what he saw, for he repeated the head movement with careful gravity. "And the Lord achieved that with the Comtesse de Buise. She has such lovely eyes, Henri. Like deep wells. A man could drown in them. You should have seen her."

"I wish I had." The gilded duck shuddered again, ever so slightly, and then a tiny head appeared in the hollow of the throat. Although it was only a little larger than the ball of Gerard Vergalant's thumb, the resemblance between their two faces was notable. "But I cannot make a seeing-glass that will allow me to look out properly without interfering with the articulation of the throat," said the little head. Hair was plastered against its forehead in minute ringlets. "One cannot have everything."

"Still," Gerard replied with magnificent condescension, "you have done wonderfully well. I could never hope to make such an impression without you."

The rest of the tiny figure emerged, clothed in sweat-stained garments of gray felt. The little man sat for a moment atop the decapitated duck, then climbed down its back, seeking toeholds in the intricate metalwork of the pinfeathers before dropping to the tabletop.

"It was a good night's work, then." Shivering, Henri hurried across the table toward the bowl of hot water.

"Yes, but we cannot yet allow ourselves to rest." Gerard looked on his brother fondly as Henri pulled off his loose clothing and clambered into the bowl. "No, do not be alarmed! Take your bath—you have earned it. But we do need to develop some new tricks. Perhaps since it takes in food at *one* end...? Yes, that might do it. These people are jaded, and we will need all my most sophisticated ideas—and your careful work, which is of course indispensable—to keep them interested. That old fop Guineau is very well connected. If we play our hand correctly, we may soon be demonstrating my magnificent *canard* for the king himself!"

Henri lowered himself beneath the surface to wet his hair, then rose again, spluttering and wiping water from his face. "The king?" He opened his eyes wide.

Gerard smiled, then reached into his pocket and produced a toothbrush. Henri stood and took it, although it was almost too large for his hands to grasp. As he scrubbed his back, water splashed from the bowl onto the tabletop. A few drops landed near the gilded duck. Gerard blotted them with his sleeve.

"Yes, the king, little brother. Mother always said I would go far, with my quick wits and good looks. But I knew that one needs more in life than simply to be liked. If a man of humble origins wishes to make an impression in this world, if he wishes to be more than merely comfortable, he must know powerful people—and he must show them *wonders*." He nodded toward the table. "Like the duck, my lovely golden duck. People desire to be...astonished."

Henri stepped from the bowl. He accepted his brother's kerchief and began to dry himself, almost disappearing in its folds.

"Ah, Gerard," he said admiringly. "You always were the clever one."

# The Stuff that Dreams Are Made Of

Okay, I admit it. If a guy wants to get drunk in the middle of a weekday afternoon, he should have a lock on his office door. Usually Tilly runs interference for me, but this day of all days she'd left early to take her mother in to have her braces loosened. (Retired ladies who get a yen for late-life orthodonture give me a pain anyway—I told Tilly her mom's gums were too weak for such foolishness, but who listens to me?)

Anyway, Tilly is usually out there behind the reception desk to protect me. I don't pay her all that much, but somehow, despite the fairly small difference in our ages, I bring out some grumpy but stalwart mother-bear reflex in her. Actually, that describes her pretty well: any bill collector who's ever seen an angry Tilly come out from behind her desk, her bulky cable knit sweater and long polished nails suggesting a she-grizzly charging out of a cave, will know exactly what I mean. If Tilly moved in with Smokey the Bear, every forest arsonist in the country would move to Mexico.

Sadly, there was no lock, and for once no Tilly to play whatsisname at the bridge. Thus the fairly attractive blonde woman, finding the door to my inner office open, wandered in and discovered me in a more or less horizontal position on the carpet.

I stared at her ankles for a moment or two. They were perfectly nice ankles, but because of all the blood that had run to one side of my head, I wasn't really in optimum viewing mood.

"Um," I said at last. "'Scuse me. I'm just looking for a contact lens." I would have been more convincing if my face hadn't been pressed too closely against the carpet to locate anything on a larger scale than the subatomic.

"And I'm looking for Dalton Pinnard," she said. "Otherwise known as 'Pinardo the Magnificent.' See anybody by that name down there among the contact lenses?" She had a voice that, while not harsh, was perfectly designed to make ten-year-old boys goofing in the back of a classroom cringe. Or to make drunken magicians feel like brewery-vat scum. If she wasn't a teacher, she'd missed her calling.

"I have a note from a doctor that says I'm allergic to sarcasm," I growled. "If you don't want a whopping lawsuit on your hands, you'd better leave." Admittedly, I was still at a slight conversational disadvantage—this riposte would have been more telling if it hadn't been spoken through a mouthful of carpet fuzz—but how can you expect someone who's just finished off his tenth Rolling Rock to be both witty and vertical?

"I'm not going to go away, Mister Pinnard. I'm here about something very important, so you might as well just stop these shenanigans."

I winced. Only a woman who thinks that two pink gins at an educational conference buffet evening constitutes wild living would dismiss something of the profound masculine significance of a solo drunk as "shenanigans." However, she had already ruined my mood, so I began the somewhat complicated process of getting into my chair.

I made it without too much trouble—I'd be saying a permanent goodbye to the office soon anyway, so what difference did a few spilled ashtrays make? I was buoyed slightly by the knowledge that, however irritating this woman might be right now, at least she wouldn't be around for the hangover. Not that she was unpleasant to look at. Except for a slightly sour look around the mouth (which turned out to be temporary) and a pair of glasses that belonged on one of those old women who wears garden gloves to play the slot machines, she looked pretty damn good. She had a slight tendency to go in and out of focus, but I suspected that might have something to do with what I'd had for lunch.

"Well," I said brightly once I had achieved an upright position. I paused to scrabble beside the chair rollers for one of the cigarette butts that still had a good amount of white left on it. "Well, well, well. What can I do for you, Miss...?"

"It's Ms., first of all. Ms. Emily Heltenbocker. And I'm increasingly less sure that you can do anything for me at all. But my father sent me to you, and I'm taking him at his word. For about another forty-five seconds, anyway."

I hadn't managed to get my lighter going in three tries, so I set it down in a way that suggested I had merely been gauging the length of spark for some perfectly normal scientific purpose. "Heltenbocker...? Wasn't that Charlie Helton's real name?"

"I'm his daughter."

"Oh." Something kicked a little inside me. In all the years I knew Charlie, I had never met his only child, who had been raised by her mother after she and Charlie divorced. It was too bad we were finally meeting when I was...well, like I was at the moment. "I heard about your dad last week. I'm really sorry. He was a great guy."

"He was. I miss him very much." She didn't unfreeze, but she did lower herself into the chair opposite me, showing a bit more leg than one expected from a schoolteacher-type, which inspired me to assay the cigarette lighter again. "Oh, for God's sake," she said at last, then pulled a lighter out of her purse and set it blazing under my nose. Half the foreshortened cigarette disappeared on my first draw as she dropped the lighter back in her bag. Emily Heltenbocker struck me as the kind of woman who might tie your shoes for you if you fumbled at the laces too long.

"So...Charlie sent you to me?" I leaned back and managed finally to merge the two Ms. Heltenbockers into one, which made for more effective conversation. She had a rather nice face, actually, with a strong nose and good cheekbones. "Did you want to book me for the memorial service or something? I'd be honored. I'm sure I could put together a little tribute of some kind." Actually, I was trying desperately to decide which of the tricks I did at the children's parties which constituted most of my business would be least embarrassing to perform in front of a gathering of my fellow professionals. I couldn't picture the leading lights of the magic world getting too worked up about balloon animals.

"No, it's not for the memorial service. We've already had that, just for the family. I want to talk to you about something else. Did you hear what happened to him?"

I couldn't think of any immediate response except to nod. In fact, it was despondency over Charlie's passing, and the awareness of mortality that comes with such things, that had been a large part of the reason for my little afternoon session. (Maybe not as large a part as the foreclosure notice on the office I had received that morning, but it had certainly fueled my melancholy.)

What can you say about an old friend for whom the Basket and Sabers Trick went so dreadfully wrong? That, at a time when he was down on his luck financially, and on a day when he happened to be practicing without an assistant, it looks a little like your old friend may have been a suicide? Of course, a honed steel saber sounds more like a murder weapon than a tool for self-slaughter, and most people don't choose to bow out inside a four-foot rattan hamper, but the door to his workroom was locked, and the only key was in Charlie's blood-soaked pocket. According to the respectable papers, he was working inside the basket and somehow must have turned the wrong way: the sharp blade had sliced his carotid artery, just beneath the ear. "Accident" was the verdict most of them came up with, and the police (perhaps tactfully) agreed. Some of the lower-rent tabloids did hint at suicide, and ran lurid pictures of the crime scene under headlines like *The Final Trick!* and *Basket of Blood!*

(I would heap even more scorn on such journals except my most recent interview—only two years before—had been courtesy of *Astrology and Detective Gazette*, which shows they are not entirely without discernment.)

"Yeah, I read about it," I said at last. "I was really shaken up. A horrible accident."

"It was murder." Phone-the-time ladies announce the hour with less certainty.

"I beg your pardon?"

"Murder." She reached into her bag, but this time she didn't produce a lighter. The envelope hit my desk with the loud smack of a card trick going wrong. "I went to see the lawyer yesterday. I expected Dad to be broke."

I was suddenly interested. She was here to hire me for something, even if I didn't know what. "And you were wrong?"

"No, I was exactly right. His net assets are a few hundred moth-eaten magic books, some tattered posters, a few old props, and an overdue bill for rental of his top hat. And that envelope. But I expected to receive something else too, and I didn't get it."

I was already reaching for the envelope. She stilled me with a glance. Yeah, just like they say in books. And if any of you has ever received a note in class illustrated with a dirty cartoon of your teacher and looked up to find her standing over you, you'll know what I mean. Real rabbit-in-the-headlights stuff. "Uh, you...you said you didn't get something you expected?"

"Dad had been writing his memoirs for years. He wouldn't let me read them, but I saw the manuscript lots of times. When I didn't find it around the house after...after..." For a brief moment her composure slipped. I looked away, half out of sympathy, half to escape the momentarily suspended gorgon stare. She cleared her throat. "When I couldn't find it, I assumed he'd given it to his lawyer for safekeeping. He'd fired his agent years earlier, and he doesn't talk to Mom, so it couldn't be with anyone else. But the lawyer didn't know anything about it. It's just...vanished. And here's the suspicious part—there was a lot of interest in that manuscript, especially from some of Dad's rivals in the business. They were concerned that he might tell some tales they'd rather weren't made public."

I straightened up. Repeated doses of her *sit-up-properly-class* voice were beginning to take a toll on my natural slouch; also, the effects of my liquid lunch were wearing off. "Listen, Ms. Heltenbocker, I'm not a cop, but that doesn't seem like grounds enough to suspect murder."

"I know you're not a cop. You're an out-of-work magician. Look in the envelope."

"Hey. I have a nice little thing going with birthdays and bar mitzvahs, you know."

That sort of defensive thrust works best when followed by a quick retreat, so I picked up the envelope. It had her name on it, written in an old man's shaky hand. The only thing inside was an old photograph: two rows of young men, all dressed in top hats and tailcoats, with a placard in front of them reading: "Savini's Magic Academy, Class of '48." Three of the faces had been circled in ink. None of the three was Charlie himself; I discovered him smiling in the front row, looking like a young farm boy fresh off the bus. Which in 1948, as I recalled, he pretty much would have been.

"This doesn't mean anything to me," I said. "How could it? I wasn't even born."

"Look on the back."

On the flip-side of the photo, that same shaky hand had scrawled across the top: "*If something happens to me or my book, investigate these three.*" At the bottom, also in ink but kind of faint, the same person had written: "*Trust Pinardo.*"

"Yes, it's all my dad's handwriting. It took me a while to find out who 'Pinardo' was and to track you down. Apparently, you haven't been playing many of the big venues lately." She smiled, but I've seen more warmth from Chevrolet grillwork. "So far my dad's judgement looks pretty awful, but I'm willing to give you a chance for his sake. I still think it's murder, and I do need assistance."

I shook my head. "Okay, your father was a friend, but we hadn't seen each other for a long time. Even granting that it's a murder, only for the sake of argument, what do you—what did he—expect me to do, for Chrissakes?"

"Help me. My father suspected something about these three men who all went to the magic academy with him. His book has disappeared. I'm going to confront them, but I need somebody who understands this world." The facade slipped again and I found myself watching her face move. The human woman underneath that do-it-yourself Sternness Kit was really quite appealing. "My mom and dad split up when I was little. I didn't grow up with him, I don't know anything about stage magic. I'm a teacher, for goodness sake!"

"Aha!" I said.

"What the hell does that mean?"

"Nothing, really." I pondered. "Okay. I don't buy any of this, but I'll do what I can. Charlie was a good guy and he was there for me when I was starting out. I suppose that whatever I have, I owe to him."

"Hmmm," she said. "Maybe I trusted you too fast. *You've* certainly got a pretty good murder motive right there."

"Very funny. We'd better discuss my fee, because as it turns out, I can help you already. I've just recognized one of these guys." Quite pleased with myself, I pointed at a thin young man with a thin young mustache standing in the back row. "His name is Fabrizio Ivone, and he's working tonight at the Rabbit Club."

# THE STUFF THAT DREAMS ARE MADE OF

My none-too-sumptuous personal quarters are a suite of rooms—well, if a studio with a kitchenette and bathroom constitutes a suite—over my place of business. Thus, it was easy enough to grab a bite to eat and a couple hours' sleep, then shower and get back downstairs well before Ms. Heltenbocker returned to pick me up. If my head was starting to feel like someone was conducting folk-dancing classes inside it, I suppose that was nobody's fault but my own.

Tilly was again holding down the front desk, eating a take-out egg foo yung and going over the books. She was frowning, and no surprise: matching my income against my outgo was like trying to mend the *Titanic* with chewing gum and masking tape.

"Hey, you were supposed to have the day off." I scrabbled in the filing cabinet for the aspirin. "How's your mom?"

Tilly gave me one of her looks. She'd probably noticed the pyramid of beer bottles I'd made on my desk. "If I stayed away from here a whole day, this place would just disappear under the dust like Pompeii. Mom's fine. Her gums are still sore. I've been overheating the blender making her milkshakes all afternoon." She paused to contemplate a noodle that had fallen onto her sweater, where it lay like a python that had died climbing Everest. "By the way, who the hell is Emily Heltenbocker?"

"Client." I said it casually, although it was a word that had not been uttered within those walls for some time. "Also Charlie Helton's daughter. Why?"

"She left a message for you. Poor old Charlie—that was a real shame. Anyway, she says she'll be here at seven, and you should wear a clean shirt."

I did not dignify this with a reply.

"Oh, and two different reporters called—someone from *The Metropolitan*, and a guy from *Defective Astronomer Gazette*."

"*Astrology and Detective*," I said absently, wondering what could have made me the center of such a media whirlwind. *The Metropolitan* was actually a rather high-toned organ: they only printed their car-accident pictures in black and white, and they ran tiny disclaimers underneath the alien abduction stories. I swallowed a few more aspirin and went to meet the press.

A couple of quick calls revealed that both had contacted me about the Charlie Helton Mystery, aka "*The Magical Murder Manuscript.*" Apparently the missing book angle had been leaked by Charlie's lawyer and was developing into a fair bit of tabloid froth. Some hack from *The Scrutinizer* called while I was still working my way through the first two. By the time I had finished my bout of semi-official spokesmanship—not forgetting to remind them all that Pinnard was spelled with two "n"s, but Pinardo (as in "the Magnificent") with only one—Tilly leaned in the door to tell me "my date" was waiting.

(There is a certain hideous inevitability to what happens when Tilly meets one of my female clients, at least if that client is under sixty years of age. It is useless to protest that I have no romantic interest in them—Tilly only takes this as evidence of my hopelessly self-deluding nature. As far as she's concerned, any roughly nubile woman who has even the most cursory business relationship with me falls into one of two categories: shallow gold-diggers prospecting in my admittedly rather tapped-out soil, or blindingly out-of-my-league "classy ladies" over whom I am fated to make a dribbling fool of myself. Only the sheer lack of recent clients of any sort had caused me to forget this, otherwise I would have been sure to meet Charlie's daughter downstairs in front of the laundromat, at whatever cost to dignity.)

All unknowing, Emily Heltenbocker had greatly increased the likelihood of such a reaction by wearing a rather touchingly out-of-date cocktail frock for our nightclub sojourn. The black dress showed an interesting but not immodest amount of cleavage, so Tilly had immediately sized her up as a Number One.

"I'll just stick around for a while to keep out the repossession people," she informed me helpfully as I emerged. "Don't worry, boss. I won't let them take that urn with your mother's ashes like they did last time you went bust." She turned to Emily. "Call me sentimental, but I think however far in debt someone is, those loan sharks should stick to reclaiming furniture, not late relations."

I winced, not so much at the all-too-true reference to my financial state as at the unfortunate subject of dead relatives, but Emily appeared to take no notice of my assistant's *faux pas*. "What a loyal employee," she cooed. I thought I detected a touch of acid beneath the sweetness. "She's clearly been with the firm forever. Well, she should still get back in time for Ovaltine and the evening news—even if the repo men drop by tonight, it shouldn't take them long to collect this lot."

Tilly raised an eyebrow in grudging approval—she liked an opponent who could return serve. Before some thundering new volley was delivered, I grabbed Emily's arm and pulled her toward the stairs.

Did I mention that there's been a slight problem with the elevator lately?

"At least the shirt looks like it was ironed at some point," she said. "Mid-seventies, maybe?"

She was driving. Her style refuted my ideas of what a schoolteacher would be like behind the wheel, and in fact rather enlarged the general concept of "driving." Apparently, many of the other motorists felt the same: we had traveled across town through an 1812 Overture of honking horns, squealing brakes, and occasional vivid remarks loud enough to be heard even through our rolled-up windows.

I chose to ignore her comment about my shirt and concentrated instead on clinging to my seat with one hand while using the other to leaf through the autopsy report which Emily had somehow procured. (Privately, I suspected a coroner's clerk with guilty schoolboy memories.)

Nothing in the report seemed to differ greatly from what I had read in the papers. Karl Marius Heltenbocker, aka Charlie Helton, had been in his early sixties but in good physical health. Death was due to exsanguination, the agent of same having been a large and very sharp steel sword of the type known as a cavalry saber. A few rough drawings showed the position of the body as it had been found inside the basket, and a note confirmed that paramedics had declared the victim dead at the scene. The verdict was death by misadventure, and both autopsy and summary report were signed by George Bridgewater, the county's coroner-in-chief. If anyone in authority suspected it was a murder, it certainly wasn't reflected in the official paperwork.

"It sure looks like an accident," I said, wincing slightly as a pedestrian did a credible Baryshnikov impression in his haste to give Emily right-of-way through a crosswalk.

"Of course it does. If you were going to murder someone and steal his manuscript to protect yourself, Mister Pinnard, wouldn't you *want* it to look like an accident?" She said this with an air of such logical certainty that I was reminded of my firm conviction during my student years that all teachers were extraterrestrials.

"How fiendishly clever," I replied. I admit I said it quietly. I was saving my wittier ripostes until there was pavement under my feet again.

I hadn't been to the Rabbit Club in a while, and was faintly depressed at the changes. I suppose on the salary the school board forked out Emily didn't get out much, because she seemed quite taken with the place. Actually, set against the rather faded glories of the club—its heyday had roughly paralleled that of the Brooklyn Dodgers—she looked far more natural than me in my leather jacket and jeans. With her strapless cocktail dress and horn-rimmed glasses, she might have been sent over by Central Casting.

As I mused, she said something I didn't quite catch, and I realized I had stopped in the middle of the aisle to admire her shoulders (I have always been a sucker for a faint dusting of freckles). I hurried her toward a booth.

The show was not the sort to make anyone sit up in wonder, but the club was one of the few places left in town where young magic talent could get a start. Looking around the darkened room, I felt a certain nostalgia for my own rookie days. Over the following hour we watched a succession of inexperienced prestidigitators fumble bouquets out of their sleeves and make coins jump across the backs of their hands while hardly ever dropping them. I nursed a soda water—rewarded for my choice with a restrained smile from my companion—but Emily drank two and a half glasses of champagne and applauded vigorously for one of the least sterling examples of the Floating Rings I'd ever seen. I decided sourly that the young (and rather irritatingly well-built) magician's no-shirt-under-the-tux outfit had influenced her appreciation.

After the break, during which the tiny house band wheezed through a couple of Glenn Miller numbers, Fabrizio Ivone was announced. The headliner had not changed much since the last time I'd seen him. He was a little older, of course, but aren't we all? His patter was delivered with a certain old-world formality, and his slicked-down hair and tiny mustache made him seem a remnant of the previous century. Watching him work his effortless way through a good group of standard illusions, it was easy to forget we were living in an era of jumbo jets and computers and special effects movies. When he finished by producing a white dove from a flaming Chinese lacquer box, the smallish crowd gave him an enthusiastic ovation.

I took Emily backstage on my arm (at this point she was a wee bit unsteady on her pins) and quickly located the dressing room. Ivone was putting his brilliantined hair, or at least the part that wasn't real, back in its box.

"The world of Illusion," said Emily, and giggled. I squeezed her wrist hard.

"That was a splendid show, Mister Ivone. I don't know if you remember me—we worked a bill together in Vegas about ten years ago, at the Dunes I think it was. Dalton Pinnard—Pinardo the Magnificent?"

"Ah, of course." He looked me up and down and went back to taking off his makeup. He didn't look like he cared much one way or the other.

"And this is my friend, Emily Heltenbocker." I took a breath and decided to go for the direct approach. "Her father was Charlie Helton."

A plucked eyebrow crept up that eggshell dome of a forehead. "Ah. I was sad to hear about him." He sounded about as sorry as he'd seemed glad to see me again.

"We were wondering if you might know anything about the book he was writing," said Emily. "Somebody stole it." She gifted Ivone with a dazzling smile. It was a good smile, but I couldn't match it since I was wincing at her sledgehammer approach.

The old magician gave her a look he probably used more often on sidewalk dog surprises. "I heard it was full of slanders. I am not unhappy to hear it has been stolen, if that were to be the end of it, but I have no doubt it will soon appear in the gutter press. If you are asking me if I know anything about this sordid affair, the answer is no. If you are insinuating I had anything to do with the theft, then you will be speaking to my lawyer."

I trod ever so gently on Emily's foot, preparing to steer the conversation in a friendlier direction. My new initiative was delayed somewhat by the wicked elbow she gave me back in the solar plexus. When I could breathe again, I said: "No, Mister Ivone, we don't think any such thing. We were just hoping that you might be able to tell us anything you know about Charlie's relationship with other magicians. You know, so we can decide once and for all if there's anything sinister in the disappearance. But you, sir, are of course above suspicion."

He stared at me for a moment and I wondered if I'd overdone it. The cold cream was caked in his wizened features like a bad plastering job. "I would never harm anyone," he said at last, "but I must say that I did not like your father, young woman. Even in the Savini Academy—yes, we studied together—he was never serious. He and his friends, they were all the time laughing in the back row."

"And who were his friends in the Academy?"

Ivone shrugged. "I do not remember. Pranksters, guttersnipes, not true artists. He was the only one of that sort who graduated."

I let out a breath. So if Charlie had known the other two men at school, they hadn't been close chums.

Ivone was still in full, indignant flow. "He did not show the respect for our great tradition, not then, not later. Always he was making jokes, even when he was on the stage, silly riddles and stories, little puzzles as though he were performing to entertain children." He placed his toupee in its box as carefully as if it were the relic of some dead saint, and solemnly shut the lid. "I have appeared before the crowned heads of Europe and Asia in my day, and never once on the stage have I made a joke."

I didn't doubt him for a moment.


"I wish you'd kept your mouth shut," I said. It didn't come across as forceful as it sounds, since Emily had already pulled away from the curb and I was frantically groping on the floor for the other half of my seatbelt.

"Don't be rude—you're an employee, remember. Besides, I didn't like him. He was a very small-souled man."

I rolled my eyes. "That's not the point. After you'd just gone and blurted that out about the book he wasn't going to give anything away. I couldn't very well ask him where he'd been when your dad died, for instance."

Emily made a face. "But I know that already. He was onstage at the Rabbit Club—he's been performing there for weeks. I checked."

"What?"

"I checked. I called the Performing Artist's Guild after you told me his name. He was working the night my father was killed."

I stared. The trained fingers I had once insured (okay, only for five thousand bucks on a twenty-six-dollar monthly premium—it was a publicity stunt) itched to throttle her, or at least to pull those stupid glasses off and see if she drove any better without them.

"He was *working?* Fabrizio Ivone, this supposed murderer, was on the other side of town pulling coins out of people's noses when your father died?"

"Yes, I just told you that I called the Guild. Don't get so defensive—I didn't expect you to do all the work, just the stuff that needed expert knowledge."

I threw myself back against my seat, but our sudden stop in the middle of an intersection catapulted me forward again microseconds later. "I can't believe I'm wasting my time on this nonsense," I growled. The light had turned green again, but Charlie's daughter seemed to be waiting for a shade she liked better. "The point I'm making, Emily, is that Fabrizio Ivone has an *alibi*. As in, 'Release this honest citizen, Sergeant, he's got an alibi.'"

She shook her head pityingly, as though I had just urged her to buy heavily into Flat Earth futures. "Haven't you ever heard of hired killers?" We lurched into motion just as the light turned red once more.

You just can't trust clients. It happens every time. They come through your door, wave money under your nose and make lots of promises—then boom! Next thing you know, that little party you were hired for turns out to be a smoker, and you're doing card tricks for a bunch of surly drunks because the stripper hasn't showed up.

Yeah, I'm a little bitter. When you've been around this business as long as I have you get that way. You splurge on a Tibetan Mystery Box some guy swears is just like new and when you get it home it's riddled with woodworm. You order a shipment of doves from the mail order house and they forget to punch air-holes in the box. And women! Don't even talk to me about women. I can't count the number of times I've been standing around backstage somewhere, ten minutes before curtain for the Sunday matinee, arguing on the phone with my latest assistant, who isn't there because she's got water-bloat, or her boyfriend's in jail, or because I introduced her as "the lovely Zelda" the night before and her name's really "Zora."

"Pull over," I snapped. "And try using the brakes instead of just glancing off streetlights until the car stops."

She followed my advice. (In fact, she used the brakes so enthusiastically that I wore a very accurate impression of the dashboard grain on my forehead for hours afterward.)

"Get the hell out, then," she said. "I knew you were a loser from the moment I first saw you crawling around on the floor."

"Well, I may be a loser...but you hired me." The effect of my clever comeback and sweeping exit was diminished slightly by the fact that I hadn't unbuckled the safety belt. The ensuing struggle also allowed me time to cool down a little. After I finally worked free and fell onto the sidewalk, I turned to look back, expecting to see the tears of a helpless woman, or perhaps a momentary glimpse of Charlie's features in hers, which would remind me of the old friend whose desperate daughter this was. Emily wasn't such a bad kid, really. I was half-ready to have my gruff masculine heart melted.

"Shut the damn door," she snarled. If there were any tears, I definitely missed them.

She did manage to run over my foot as she drove away.

I suppose I shouldn't have been too surprised, I reflected as I limped home. I had fallen out with Emily's father much the same way. Nobody in the whole damn family could admit they were wrong.

Charlie Helton had been a wonderful guy, my mentor in the business.

He'd helped me find my first agent and had shared many of his hard-won secrets with me, giving me a boost that few young performers got. He'd been everywhere almost, had done things few other people had even read about, and could tell you stories that would make your eyes pop out. But he could be difficult and stubborn at times, and as Ivone had so vividly remembered, he had a rather strange idea of fun. After he and Emily's mother had broken up he had lived a solitary life—I hadn't even known he'd been married until several years into our friendship—and like a lot of bachelor-types, his life revolved around what other people might consider pretty useless hobbies. In Charlie's case there were two: puzzles and practical jokes.

Unfortunately, not all of his jokes were funny, at least to the victims. One such, a particularly complicated operation, had involved my booking for a show at a naturist colony in the Catskills. I was very uncertain, since it required me to perform naked except for cape and top hat, but Charlie convinced me that a lot of big entertainment people were weekend nudists, and that I would be bound to make some great contacts.

When I arrived at the resort the night of the show I was met backstage by the club manager, who was definitely naked. He was a big fat guy of about fifty, and knowing that people like him could do it helped me wrestle down my inhibitions. See, when you perform, if the stage lights are bright enough, you hardly see the audience anyway; the manager assured me that it would be just like doing a show in my own bedroom. So, I stripped, squared my shoulders, calmed my quivering stomach, and marched out onto the stage.

And no, it *wasn't* a nudist colony, of course. It was a regular Catskills resort, median audience age: almost dead and holding. The "club manager" was a confederate of Charlie's who'd taken off as soon as he'd finished his part of the scam.

The audience was not amused. Neither was I.

The sad thing was, Charlie and I fell out not because of the prank itself, nasty as it had been, but because I refused to admit there was anything humorous about it. I guess his pride was wounded—he thought he was the funniest guy in the world.

Things started to go downhill for me after that, but not because of my premature venture into performance art. I just caught some bad breaks. Well, a *lot* of bad breaks.

Maybe Charlie had been feeling guilty about our parting all these years, and about not being around to help me get back on my feet. Maybe that was why he'd told his daughter that if she ever needed someone to trust, to seek me out.

There was something else to consider, I suddenly realized. On the infinitesimal chance that Emily Heltenbocker was right and everyone else was wrong, maybe Charlie had been snuffed because one of his jokes had offended someone. Maybe he'd made a bad enemy, and it didn't have anything to do with his manuscript at all.

I was pleased with this genuine detective-style thinking. Despite the misery of my long trudge home, I began to consider whether I should allow Emily—if she was suitably contrite—to rehire me. Charlie and I had been through a lot of good times before the bottom fell out. Maybe his daughter deserved a little patience.

Not to mention that she owed me for at least one night's work.

"Your girlfriend's on the phone," shouted Tilly.

I put down my self-help bankruptcy book and unhurriedly picked up the receiver. I had known Emily would come crawling back, but I wasn't going to let her off too easily.

"You still have my father's graduation photograph," she said in a tone like a whip-crack. "Send it back immediately or I'll come over there and break your arm."

She was playing it a little more cagily than I'd expected. "Don't hurt me," I said. "My health insurance lists attack-by-schoolteacher as an Act of God, and it'll be hell getting them to pay."

"Just send me the picture. Right now."

I was sure I detected an undercurrent of playfulness in her voice, albeit well-camouflaged. "How about if I drop it by in person? Then we can discuss last night's little difference of opinion."

"If you come within a mile of me, you're going to have to learn how to make balloon animals with your teeth."

She hung up loudly enough to loosen a few of my fillings, but I knew I basically had her.

Thus it was that after only a few dozen more phone calls (and a slight strategic modification on my part which might have been mistaken by some unschooled observers for a cringing apology) Emily Heltenbocker and I resumed our partnership.

"Tell me their names again." She revved the engine, although the light was still resolutely red.

I'd finally pinned down the other two mystery men, through laborious research in various trade booking guides. "Sandor Horja Nagy, the Hungarian Houdini—he's the one we're going to see right now. The other's Gerard O'Neill. And, just for your information, they were *both* doing shows on the night in question, just like Ivone. Two more airtight alibis."

"For goodness sake, Pinnard, you're so unimaginative. We're talking about magicians—people who disappear and reappear elsewhere for a living. Honestly, if this were a murder mystery in a book, you'd be the idiot cop they always have stumbling around to make the detective look good."

"Thank you for your many kindnesses." I reached into my pocket for my cigarettes. Emily had finally tendered my retainer and I had splurged on a whole carton. "Whatever you may think, a stage magician nearing retirement age cannot disappear in the middle of a downtown performance, catch a cab to the suburbs, murder an old classmate, and be back before the audience notices. And he can't spin straw into gold or turn a pumpkin into a horse-drawn carriage either, just in case you still harbor some misconceptions about what real magicians do." I leaned back and withdrew my new, top-of-the-line disposable lighter.

"Don't you dare light that in my car. I don't want my upholstery smelling of smoke."

Obviously she had no similar problem with the scent of self-deceit and denial. I didn't say that, of course. Long years of working with the public have taught me that, although the customer may not always be right, only a fool behaves otherwise before he's been paid in full. "Look," I said, "I'm just being sensible. You're a nice lady, Emily, but I think you're barking up the wrong tree. The police say it was an accident. The coroner said it was an accident. And all your suspects have alibis. When are you going to face up to what that really means?"

She started an angry reply, but bit it off. She stayed silent for a long while, and even when the light finally turned green, she accelerated with none of her usual gusto. I was pleased that I had finally made her see sense, but not exactly happy about it, if you know what I mean. Sometimes when something goes very wrong, we humans desperately want there to be a reason. It's not fun being the person who takes that possibility away.

"It's just not like my father," she said at last. "Suicide, never. Not in a million years. So that leaves accident. But you knew him too, Pinnard. You know how carefully he planned everything."

I had to admit that was true. Watching Charlie work up an illusion was like watching Admiral Nimitz setting out his bath toys—no detail too small for obsessive consideration. "But sometimes even careful people get careless," I pointed out. "Or sometimes they just don't give a damn any more. You told me he was having real bad financial problems."

"You are too, but I don't see you getting your throat slit."

"Not when I've got a whole carton of cigarettes," I said cheerfully. "I prefer my suicide slow."

"That's not very funny."

I immediately felt bad. "Yeah, you're right. I'm sorry. Look, let's go see this Nagy guy. Even if it turns out you're wrong about the murder angle, you'll feel better if you know for certain."

She nodded, but didn't seem very convinced. Or very cheerful. She was even still driving in an uncharacteristically moderate way. So, basically nice guy that I am, I sang a medley of Burt Bacharach songs for her as we made our way across town. I've always thought that if magic hadn't worked out, I could have made a tidy bundle warbling "Walk on By" in your better grade of dinner-houses.

It didn't jolly her up much. "I'll pay you the rest of tonight's fee right now if you shut up," was how she put it.


Sandor Nagy (I think you're supposed to say it "Nagy Sandor," but what

I know for sure about Hungarian customs you could write on the back of a postage stamp and still have room for your favorite goulash recipe) had seen better days. As a performer, our pal Ivone was, by comparison, Elvis.

We warmed the plastic chairs in the hallway of the Rotary Club while we waited for Nagy to finish changing his clothes in the men's room. The show had been interesting—if watching a drunk perform for a bunch of guys offended because the entertainment was more blasted than they were is the kind of thing that interests you. Partly out of pity, we took Nagy to the 24-hour coffee shop across the street and bought him a Grand Slam Breakfast. (There is no time in places like that, so you might as well eat breakfast. Actually, there is time, but only the waitresses experience it, which is why they're all about a hundred and four years old. I've always thought someone should write a science fiction book about this paradox.)

"I'm not quite sure what went wrong with that trunk escape," Nagy said. Or slurred, to be more precise. "Usually it works like a charm."

After the gruelling experience of his show, I had been planning to down a quick couple of beers —I wasn't going to drink club soda forever just because I was hanging around with Ms. Ruler-across-the-knuckles—but the old guy's breath and the bold yet intricate vein patterns on his nose persuaded me to order myself a Coke. Thus, I had my mouth wrapped around a straw and didn't have to comment.

"I'm sure you would have got out eventually," said Emily. "I didn't think they really needed to call the fire department."

Nagy eyed his soft-boiled eggs with great sadness. I think he would much rather have had a couple of belts himself, but we had declined to buy him anything with a proof content. He wasn't real coherent as it was, even after all the oxygen the fire crew had forced into him. "I'll let you in on a secret," he said. "I'm not as sharp as I used to be. A step slower these days, if you know what I mean."

"Well, you and my father were at the Academy at the same time, weren't you? That was quite a way back."

I smiled. Emily was showing definite improvement. All the same, interrogating this guy made about as much sense as bringing down a pigeon with a surface-to-air missile. If he was a murderer, I was Merlin.

"Oh, that's right, you said you were Charlie Helton's kid. Shame about him. I heard he was writing a book. Wouldn't want to take time from my escape work, myself. There's a lot of practice involved." He pushed one of his eggs with the fork, as though unsure whether to commit to something so strenuous as eating. "He was a strange one, your dad. Drove a lot of people crazy."

"Did he? He made enemies?" Emily was leaning forward, giving the old guy that penetrating would-you-like-to-share-that-with-the-class gaze that made me cringe even when it wasn't aimed at me. I refrained from pointing out that her elbow was in a puddle of catsup. Purely because I didn't want to distract her, of course.

"Not enemies, no. Not really." Sandor Nagy stopped to think, a process that clearly needed some ramping-up time. It was a good half-minute before he came up with: "He was just...he bragged a lot. Told a lot of stories. Played tricks on people."

Now it was my turn to lean forward. My backfired-prank theory was sounding better. "Anyone in particular that he upset?"

Nagy shook his head. "Not that I could tell you—it's been a long time. He just pissed a lot of people off. Pardon my French, Miss."

I chewed on my straw, disgusted with myself for taking the idea of murder seriously for even a second. "Let me ask you another question," I said. "Are you really Hungarian? Because you don't have an accent."

Nagy frowned at me and squinted his bloodshot eyes. Starve Popeye the Sailor Man for a few weeks, then strap him into an extremely musty tux, and you basically had Nagy. "I sure as hell am! Both my parents were from the old country, even if I ain't been there. At least I got a family connection. One of those punks at the Academy called himself 'Il Mysterioso Giorgio,' and he wasn't even Italian! Some chump kid from Weehawken!"

We left the Hungarian Houdini muttering angrily at his hash browns.


I had mixed feelings when I got downstairs to the office the next day. I was more convinced than ever that we were wasting our time, and that Emily—who was actually a pretty okay person—was going to get her feelings hurt. On the other hand, she'd paid me a nice little fee, and the story was playing big and bold in the tabloids.

It wasn't front page in *The Scrutinizer*, but it was near the front, and a full-page spread to boot. There was an artist's rendition of "*The Death Basket*" (which included far more swords than were actually involved in Charlie's demise), a photo of Charlie in his stage outfit, and one of the coroner and the police chief at a news conference, looking very serious. (In fact, the photo had been taken during some other and far more important case, but I must admit it gave the thing an air of drama.) The only item conspicuously missing was one of the publicity photos of Yours Truly I'd sent to them (there's no such thing as bad PR, especially when you've been stuck on the birthday party circuit for a few years), but I was mentioned prominently in all the articles, even if *The Metropolitan* managed to spell my name "Pinrod." So, all in all, it could have been worse.

Emily didn't seem to think so, though. When I called her, she sounded tired and depressed. "I'm beginning to think you're right," she said. "Whatever was in the manuscript, it's gone. The tabloid reporters won't leave me alone. After I finish paying you, I'll be broke—my savings have gone on Dad's funeral. I think it's time to go fishing."

"Huh?" I had a sudden and disconcerting vision of Emily in hip-waders.

"It's just a family expression. When times are bad, when the bill collectors are after you, you say 'I think I'll go fishing.' And that's how I feel right now."

I was still thinking about the hip-waders. In a certain kind of way they can be a pretty sexy garment. I suppose it has something to do with my reading *Field & Stream* too much during my adolescence. In any case, distracted as I was, I did a wildly foolish and uncharacteristic thing.

"Listen, Emily," I said. "I don't want your money."

"What does that mean?" She sounded angry.

"I mean, I don't want any more of your money, and you can have back what I haven't spent yet. But we'll still go see O'Neill this afternoon. On the house, okay?"

She didn't say anything right away. I assumed she had been struck dumb by gratitude, but I wasn't sure. Charlie's daughter had proven herself a mite unpredictable. While I waited for the verdict, I re-scrutinized *The*

*Scrutinizer.* It was too bad they hadn't run a picture of Emily, I thought—she was a very good-looking woman.

I frowned. Something in the paper's coverage had been nagging at me since I'd read it, some little connection I couldn't make that was now bidding heavily for my attention, but between certain thoughts of an imaginary Emily in a fishing-gear pictorial and then the sudden reappearance of the actual Emily's voice, it didn't have much of a chance.

"That's...that's very kind of you, Dalton. You're a really nice person."

She'd never called me by my first name before. That nagging detail was abruptly heckled off the Amateur Night stage of my consciousness.

"And you're a nice person too, Emily." I hung up, feeling oddly as though I might be blushing.

Tilly was standing in my office doorway. She'd heard the whole conversation. Her expression of amused contempt was probably similar to what ancient Christians saw on the faces of Roman lions.

"Your gills are showing, Pinrod," she said. "What an idiot—hook, line, and sinker."

I summoned up great reserves of inner strength and ignored her.


I spent all of O'Neill's performance trying to decide what Emily would do if I put my arm around her. I'd like to say we were paying close attention to the show, but we weren't. (I'm reasonably certain that murder investigators don't date each other, or that if they do, they keep the dates separate from the actual investigations. I hope so.)

Not that Gerry O'Neill's routine was the kind of thing that invited close attention. It was a mixture of old gags and fairly lame sleight-of-hand. Only the fact that it was a charity performance in front of a ward full of sick children made it something more than tiresome. And, to be fair, the kids seemed to like it.

O'Neill, it turned out, was the only one of the three who'd been on good terms with Charlie: he'd kept in loose touch with him over the years. As we walked him out to his car, O'Neill wiped the perspiration from his round face and walrus mustache and told us with impressive sincerity how upset he'd been when he heard the news.

"He was a good guy, Charlie was. A little loco sometimes, but basically a heart of gold." He stuffed several feet of colored kerchief back into his pocket and patted Emily's arm. "You got my real best wishes, missy. I was broken up to hear about it."

Emily's questions were perfunctory. She seemed a lot more cheerful than she'd been on the phone, but she seemed to be losing interest in the investigation. I wasn't really surprised—it was pretty difficult to feature any of our three suspects as the Fu Manchu criminal mastermind-type.

"When you say Charlie was a little loco sometimes," I asked, "what do you mean? His practical jokes?"

O'Neill grinned. "I heard about some of those. What a card. But I mostly meant his stories. He was full of stories, and some of 'em were pretty crazy."

"Like what?"

"Oh, you know, places he said he'd been, things he'd seen. He told me once he'd been in China and some old guy there taught him how to talk to birds. Man, if you listened to him, he'd done everything! Snuck into a sultan's harem somewhere, hung out with voodoo priests in Haiti, tamed elephants in Thailand, you name it. Crazy stories."

Emily rose to her father's defense. "He did travel quite a bit, Mister O'Neill. He toured in a lot of places, took his show all over the world— Asia, South America, the Caribbean—especially when he was younger. He was a pretty big star."

O'Neill was a gallant man. "Then maybe all them stories were true, missy. In any case, I'm sorry he's gone. He was a helluva guy."

We watched O'Neill drive off. As we strolled back across the parking lot, Emily took my hand.

"Maybe it *was* an accident," she said, and turned to look at me. The sunset brought out the deep gold colors in her hair. "Maybe that stuff he wrote on the photo was just another of his stories or silly tricks. But at least I did my best to find out." She sighed. "Talking to these people reminded me of all the parts of his life I missed out on. I didn't see a lot of him while I was growing up."

I didn't say anything. I was concentrating on the feeling of her warm skin beneath my fingers, and thinking about what I was about to do. I stopped, pulled her toward me, and carefully removed her glasses.

"Why, Miss Heltenbocker," I said, as if in surprise, "you're beautiful. Do you mind if I kiss you?"

She snatched them back and jammed them into place, brow furrowed in annoyance. "I hate it when everything's blurry. Kiss me with my goddamn glasses on."

What was it like? Do I have to tell you?

Magic.

I woke up in the middle of the night. The thing that had been bothering me had come back. Boy, had it ever come back.

I ran downstairs to my office, not bothering with a bathrobe. This should show you how excited I was—even though Tilly lived on the other side of town, wouldn't be in for hours, and the office was effectively part of my home, going there naked even at 4 AM made me feel queasily disrespectful. But the yammering in my brain wouldn't wait for anything.

A few minutes later I ran back upstairs and woke Emily.

(Look, just because she was a schoolteacher doesn't mean you should make old-fashioned assumptions.)

"Get up, get up!" I was literally jumping up and down.

"What the hell is going on, Pinnard?" She sat up, rubbing her eyes and looking utterly gorgeous. After the night we'd just spent, I wasn't at all worried about her use of my last name.

"I've solved it! And you're never going to believe it!" I grabbed her arm, almost dragging her toward the stairs. She very firmly pulled free, then went to get her glasses from the bedside table. Next—and clearly second in order of importance—she found my bathrobe and put it on. In a gesture of solidarity, I pulled my underwear off the ceiling light (don't ask), donned it, and led her to my office.

"Brace yourself," I said. "This is very weird." I took a breath, trying to think of the best way to explain. "First of all, you were right—it wasn't an accident."

Emily sat up straight. "Somebody *did* murder him?" A strange look came over her face. "Or are you going to tell me it was suicide?"

I was suddenly reluctant. Waking someone up in the middle of the night to give them the kind of news I was about to give Emily could have a number of shocking effects, and I felt very protective of her—and of what we suddenly seemed to have together. "Well, see for yourself" I spread the copy of *The Scrutinizer* on the desktop, then laid the graduation picture on top of it. "Something was bothering me about this article, but with everything else that happened today, well, I sort of forgot about it. Then, about fifteen minutes ago, I woke up and I knew." I pointed at the picture, at one of the faces that Charlie hadn't circled. "See this kid? You know who that is?"

Emily stared, then shook her head.

"That's 'Il Mysterioso Giorgio'—the one Nagy mentioned. You know, the fake Italian from Weehawken."

"I still don't get it."

"You will. Remember Fabrizio Ivone talking about those delinquent friends of your dad's who didn't graduate the Academy? Well, he was wrong—one of them did. It was young 'Giorgio' here. Although he never made it as a working magician."

"How do you know that?"

I lifted the graduation picture and pointed to *The Scrutinizer*. "Because he would have had trouble being a stage magician *and* holding down the job of Chief Coroner." I put the graduation picture beside the news photo for comparison. "Meet 'Il Mysterioso Giorgio' today—George Bridgewater."

She stared at the two photos, then looked up at me. "My God, I think you're right. But I still don't understand. What does it mean? Did he cover up something about my dad's death?"

This was the hard part. Suddenly, under the bright fluorescent lights, my certainty had dwindled. It would be unutterably cruel if I turned out to be wrong. I took her hand.

"Emily," I said. "I think your dad's alive."

She pulled away from me, stepping back as though I'd slapped her. The tears that suddenly formed in her eyes made me want to slap myself. "What are you saying? That's crazy!"

"Look, you said it yourself—Charlie'd never be a suicide. And he wasn't the type to have an accident. But you said he'd traveled in the Caribbean, and he told O'Neill he'd studied with voodoo priests! They have chemicals they use in voodoo that make people look like they're dead. That's where the zombie legends come from. It's true—I read about it!"

She laughed, angry, frightened. "Where? In *Astrology and Detective Gazette?*"

"In a science magazine. Emily, they've done studies. Voodoo priests can use this stuff to put people in a kind of temporary coma. All the vital signs disappear. No paramedic struggling to keep your dad alive would know the difference, not if he'd made a real but shallow cut and spread a lot of blood around. It wouldn't even have to be human blood, since nobody would think of testing it when he was locked in a room by himself with the key in his pocket. But you'd have to have a confederate in place for later, 'cause nobody could live through a real autopsy. Chief Coroners hardly ever do actual examinations, so it's a little bit of a coincidence he was writing the report at all. Even weirder that he wouldn't step aside when he found out it was an old school chum."

"So this guy Bridgewater helped my dad fake his own death? Why?"

"Who knows? A last prank for old time's sake, maybe? You said your dad was depressed and broke. Maybe it was a way for Giorgio the Mysterious to help a pal get out of a bad situation." I didn't want to mention it, but it was also possible that the deal had been a little less friendly—old Charlie, collector of gossip and odd stories, might have had a wee bit of blackmail material on Bridgewater.

Emily stared at the pictures. When she turned back to me, she was calmer, but very grim. "I don't think you did this to be cruel," she said, "but this is so much more farfetched than anything I suggested. It's just crazy."

I had a sick feeling in my stomach, kind of like something very cold was hibernating there. I knew I'd blown it. "But..."

She cut me off, her voice rising in anger. "I can almost believe my father would do something this wild, this outrageous—heaven knows, he loved a good trick, and he was having a lot of problems. But I can't for a moment believe that he would make me think he was dead—with not even a hint that he'd survived—and then on top of it send me off to hook up with a bum like you and go on some insane hunt for a nonexistent murderer!" She waved the picture in front of my face. "Look at this! This is his handwriting! If he wanted to tip me off, why didn't he circle Bridgewater the coroner? Instead, he picks these three totally harmless..."

I was so far into my flinch that at first I didn't open my eyes. When she had remained silent for a good ten seconds, I peeked. Emily was still frowning, but it was a different kind of frown. "Oh, God," she said at last.

She flopped the photo down so the back was showing. I had written down the men's names as I identified them.

"Gerard O'Neill." Emily's voice was strained. "Fabrizio Ivone. Sandor Horja Nagy. Oh my God."

"What?"

"Look at the initials. G-O-N—F-I—S-H-N" The tears came for real now. "GONE FISHING."


There was a good deal more to the story, of course, but we didn't find out immediately. When we went to see Bridgewater, the coroner blustered at us about foolish accusations and the penalties for slander, but he didn't seem very fierce about it. (We later discovered that one of Charlie's Academy-era jokes had yielded photographs of a naked "Giorgio" in bed with a sheep dressed in a garter belt. It had all been perfectly innocent, of course, but still not the kind of thing a local politician wants to see on the wire services.) Still, it was a few more months before we knew for sure.

Apparently Charlie Helton *did* have an agent Emily hadn't known about—a theatrical agent, but someone who had contacts in publishing. When, at the height of the tabloid fury about the *Murdered Magician Mystery*, the agent announced that he actually had the dead man's manuscript, it set off a bidding war, and the book sold for a very healthy advance. As Charlie's only heir, Emily received all but a small part of what was left after the agent took his cut. When the book quickly earned back its advance, she began to receive all but that same small percentage of the royalties that began flowing in. Even after the story lost its tabloid notoriety, *A Magical Life* continued to sell nicely. As it turned out, Charlie had written quite a good book, full of vivid stories about his life and travels, and lots of enjoyable but not-too-scurrilous backstage gossip about the world of stage magicians.

Even Fabrizio Ivone didn't come out too bad in Charlie's memoirs, although his inability to take a joke was mentioned several times.

That small portion of the income Emily didn't get? Well, every month, the agent dispatches a check to a post office box in Florida—no, I won't tell you where exactly, just in Florida somewhere. Suffice it to say it's a small town with good fishing. The checks are made out to someone named Booker H. Charlton. Emily decided not to contest this diversion of royalties, and in fact we plan to go visit old Booker as soon as we can get out of town.

Why delay our visit to the mystery fisherman? Well, we've been real busy just lately setting up the Charlie Helton Museum of the Magical Arts. It's turned out to be a full-time job for all of us: Emily took early retirement from the school system to manage the operation, and Tilly answers the phone and handles the finances—which I'm happy to say, are in the black. Tilly's mom works the ticket booth, flashing her expensive smile at the customers all day long. Me? Well, I've got the balloon animal concession pretty much wrapped up, and I'm working on a book of my own.

Oh, and in case anybody's disappointed that this has been a story about magicians without any real magic in it, I should mention one last thing. You remember how Charlie had scrawled on the back of his photo: "*Trust Pinardo*"? We found out a few months afterward that if Charlie's handwriting had been a little darker, we would have noticed a hyphen between the two words. See, we were going through some of his papers and found out that he'd stashed away a couple of hundred dollars so Emily wouldn't get stuck paying for his fake funeral. The deposit was in a trust fund at a small savings institution—"Pinardo Thrift and Loan," no relation to yours truly.

In other words, the very beautiful woman who I am delighted to say now calls herself Ms. Emily Heltenbocker-Pinnard, the light of my life and (I hope) the warmth of my declining years, walked into my office that day on a completely mistaken assumption. We are an accident—a fluke of fate.

So there you go. Love (as Bogart once said about a black bird, and Shakespeare said about something I don't quite remember) is definitely the stuff that dreams are made of. It remains the greatest mystery and the only truly reliable magic.

Satisfied?

# A Fish Between Three Friends

Once upon a time there was a cat, a raven, and a man with no ears. They were all friends and lived together in a house by the river.

The cat was a bit lazy and cruel, but in her own way she loved the raven and the man, so one day she decided to provide supper for her two housemates. She went down to the river and caught a silvery, silvery salmon.

"Don't eat me," the salmon said. "For I am a magical fish."

"That's what they all say," sneered the cat, and carried it back to the house.

The cat waited a while for her friends to come home, but soon grew bored and restless and left the fish on the table while she went out to see if any mice were rustling in the grassy meadow behind the house.

When she had gone, the man came back from working in the field, wondering what he would have for dinner. As he walked to the table the fish, still alive but gasping in the unfamiliar air, called out, "Sir, sir, I am a magical fish! I will give you three wishes if you spare my life!"

But of course the man had no ears and could not hear the fish's entreaties. He saw only a handsome silver fish flopping on the table, its mouth opening and closing.

"How lucky I am!" he thought. "It must have jumped a great jump, all the way from the river onto the table." He went to prepare the oven to cook the fish.

While he was bending over the oven laying the kindling, the raven came into the house.

"Kind bird," the fish gasped, its voice very faint now, "if you will only save me, I will grant you three wishes, for I am a magical fish."

"Hmmmm," said the raven, perching on the table beside it. "Are you, now?" He looked at the fish flopping on the table, then at the man, who was bending over the oven all unaware that the raven had come home. "So if I spare your life, you will grant three wishes?" the raven asked.

"I will, I will," said the fish. "Gladly!"

"Hmmmm," said the raven. "Well, I could ask as one wish that you give the man back his ears so he could hear again. But then instead of admiring my black and glossy wings he would mark that my voice was harsh, and would also hear the cruel things that the people in the village say about him for keeping company with only a bird and a cat. Hmmmm."

The raven thought. The fish flopped.

"And I could wish for the cat to be a little less lazy and a little less cruel, for then she might live a better life and one day go to heaven. But a kind cat might not catch mice, and she would starve and so would I, since there would be no leavings. And the mice would eat the man's grain and he too would starve. And in any case, I do not believe that cats are welcomed in heaven."

The raven considered a bit more.

"Now, it is possible that even though I cannot change my friends in a way that will make them happy, I might find a way to use a wish for myself. But what are the things that I need?"

"Quickly," gasped the fish.

"I would not ask to be more handsome, since as you see I am quite a fine and glossy shade of black. And although we ravens are not known for our fine singing voices, my only friends are a man who cannot hear and a cat who listens to nothing except her own whims, so I do not suffer for my harsh croaking.

"Neither do I wish for gold or silver or gems, for I have no hands in which to carry them, nor anywhere to keep them. Here they would draw robbers like flies to carrion, and we would spend all our time trying to protect these valuables."

The raven walked across the table and stood over the fish, which rolled its eye piteously.

"In fact," the bird said, "we three have all that we need here, and all that we lack is a fish dinner, which is you. We might wish for three more such as you, but that would make you a murderer of your own kind, and then you would certainly be denied heaven yourself. I could not do that to you. Everyone knows that we ravens are kindhearted birds."

So he left the fish thrashing on the table, although the thrashing had almost ceased, and flew to the back of the man's chair to wait for the meal.

And by the time the cat came back from the meadow, the man had cooked his part of the fish, the raven was chewing happily on the bones, and the cat, as founder of the feast, found the head and tail and a strip of good raw, red flesh laid out for her on the table.

As she purringly devoured the salmon, she said offhandedly, "The fool fish claimed he was magical."

"Really?" said the raven. "Well, I imagine that's what they all say."

"Indeed," said the cat. "I have never believed one yet."

And although the man could not hear what his friends were saying, he smiled anyway.

# Every Fuzzy Beast of the Earth, Every Pink Fowl of the Air

"*First God made heaven and earth. The earth was without form and void, and darkness was upon the face of the deep; and the Spirit of God was moving over the face of the waters. And God said, 'Let there be light'; and there was*—oh, bother, what now?"

"Sorry? Didn't get that last bit, Gabriel, sir."

"That wasn't supposed to be part of it. Bugger. Now I'll have to start all over. It doesn't work right without the proper dramatic rhythm." He peered down at the new Earth, gleaming like a blue and white pearl. "What *is* going on down there, Metatron?"

"Couldn't say, sir." The junior angel squinted. "Looks like someone's wandered onto the work site."

"Lovely." Gabriel shook out his wings with a discontented rattle of plumage. "Just lovely. Schedule already shot to pieces, supposed to be finished already, Himself resting but we're still building and the overtime is through the roof. *Now* what?" He pushed back his halo, which had begun to sag a little. "Might as well find out. You coming?"

Metatron nodded. "Yes, sir. Just sweeping a little star dust off the firmament, then I'm right with you."

"We spread the stardust there on purpose," Gabriel said, frowning. "Atmosphere, you know."

"Atmosphere? But we don't have any out here..."

Gabriel sighed. "All right, 'ambience,' is that better? We put it there for ambience, so stop sweeping it up. Remember, we want this universe to have that lived-in look. That's what they're going for nowadays."

———

"Hey, there!" Gabriel said as they entered the Garden. "Who are you and what are you doing here? This area is off-limits to nonessential personnel." He stopped, blinking. "What are you, anyway?"

"I'm a little girl," said the little girl. "More specifically, I'm Sophia."

"Hi, Sophia," said Metatron, who was one of the friendlier angels, and was constantly bringing home stray comets.

Gabriel sighed. "I'm sure it's all very nice, you having a name and all—you're way ahead of all the other Earth-dwellers that way, so good for you—but you really can't be here, little girl. This is a very, very important project, and God Himself wants us..."

"...To finish everything up in time for when He comes back to work tomorrow. I know." Even standing straight, she was still only as high as where Metatron's belly button might be (if such things existed, which of course they didn't. Not yet). "And I'm going to help you finish it..."

"You most certainly are not...!" Gabriel began.

"...Because God is my daddy."

Gabriel stared. "What did you just say?"

"That God is my daddy? He is. And He said I could do anything I wanted to help, and that you had to let me, Gabriel, or else He'd put you back on supernova-extinguishing duty, and you know how *that* was. That's what He said."

The archangel stared for a long moment at the little girl. She stared back. Gabriel looked away first. "Metatron," he said, "may I speak to you for a moment in private?"

"It's your duty to keep her out of trouble, Metatron," the archangel said when they had moved away from the girl. He peered out from the shadow of the Don't-Eat-This-Fruit Tree that God had insisted on planting despite there being several more attractive alternatives, including a very nice flowering Tree of Moral Relativity. "Look at her! Why on my shift? Why not when Michael's on duty? He gets all the breaks. No wonder he's the Big Guy's favorite."

The girl was examining a tiny winged creature that she held in careful hands, her small face solemn. After a moment she tossed it up into the air. It rose, then dropped, and hit the ground with a quiet *thump*. The little creature gave Sophia a mistrustful look as it limped away.

"What do you call those things?" she asked.

"Birds," Gabriel called. "Some of your father's favorite creatures."

"Why do they have wings but they don't fly?"

"Fly?" Gabriel shuddered. "Do you hear her, Metatron?" he said in a quiet but panicky voice. "She wants the birds to fly! What next? She'll be yanking the fishes out of the ground and throwing them in the river! Just...just take care of it. And keep her away from me."

"Ummm," said Metatron. He watched the girl beginning to unearth frightened carp from their burrows. "Do I have to...?"

But Gabriel had already hurried back to Heaven to finish some important paperwork that he had ignored for several days.

"What is it now, Metatron?"

The angel was wringing his hands in a very guilty way. "I think you'd better come down."

Gabriel closed his eyes, searching for the patience he was certain he'd had when the morning began. "What is it now? The girl?"

"It'll be easier if you just come."

There was a great deal of confusion down in the Garden when they arrived, but no sign of Sophia.

"Where is she? He'll kill us if we lose His daughter!"

"She's around somewhere. But to be honest, sir, it's getting a bit much for me to handle all by my—"

"What in the name of our boss did she do to the *trees*?" Gabriel stared in horror. "She's turned every one of them upside down!"

"I know, I know! I told her not to, but she insisted. She said that the roots looked...*icky* just sticking up into the air."

"Icky? What does that mean?"

"I think it means she didn't like it. Anyway, she said that the leaves and branches would look better in the air and the roots in the ground, then she just, well, turned them all upside down, as you can see."

"It's so...green, now."

"Exactly. But she claims it looks nicer."

"This is a nightmare, Metatron. And what's that horrible noise?"

"Another of her little ideas, sir. She thought that the water splashing in the streams and rivers should make a different noise."

"What's wrong with growling?" Gabriel hiked up his robe and stepped closer to the stream. "That's a very strange sound it makes now, kind of...musical. Soft and lyrical, plink, plink, plink—what is that about? Completely spoils the point of warning people not to fall in the water."

"She says we can use the old, loud noise for something like fast-moving, dangerous water, like waterfalls and rapids. This would be just for shallow streams and dripping snowmelt and things like that."

"Snowmelt? She wants the snow to *melt?*"

"Sometimes, yes." Metatron nodded, shamefaced. "You have no idea what she wants, sir. Some of it is just terrifying."

"Well, wait until I catch up with her, *I'll* tell her—oh, sweet Employer, what is *that?* That's the most horrible thing I've ever seen! They're...they're all *pink.*"

"Sorry, sir, but she said the old gray flamingos were yucky and boring."

"Yucky?" Gabriel could hear his own voice getting shrill.

"It's like icky, I think." Metatron shook his head sorrowfully as the squadron of rose-colored birds suddenly took to the air. Meanwhile, Gabriel was struggling not to scream.

"They *fly?*"

"All the birds do now. And there's more..."

Metatron broke off because Sophia had appeared at the other side of the Garden, her hands full of small, furry animals. "There you are, Gabriel. I had a really good idea. See these? I call them 'bunnies.'"

"They're already called 'rabbits,' young lady. We tested it on a focus group and they liked 'rabbits' just fine."

"'Bunnies' is better. Anyway, I had another idea. Our bunnies would be a lot cuter if you got rid of these long, naked tails which are really gross and gave them little fluffy tails instead. That would be much cuter."

Gabriel blinked. "But all the rodents have long, skinny, naked tails, Miss Sophia—the mice, the rats..."

"They can keep them. But the bunnies and the squirrels need fluffy ones. Give the squirrels *long* fluffy ones, though, because they like to jump through the air from branch to branch and it looks pretty."

"How are they going to jump from branch to branch at the bottom of ponds?"

"Squirrels live in trees now." She set the rabbits down; they quickly scattered into the grass with little flicks of their tiny new tails. "With the birds."

It was all Gabriel could do not to fall to his knees, moaning. "My Lord, what have You done to Your servant...?" he muttered.

"I don't know how you ever got along without me." The girl walked through the sun-warmed Garden. "A lot of this is really stupid and gross. I mean, look. What's this?" She bent, then lifted a large, ovoid object from the grass.

"It's an egg," said Gabriel, but his confidence was a bit shaken and he turned to Metatron for confirmation. "It's an egg, isn't it?"

She frowned. "I *know* it's an egg. But what kind?"

"That's a lion egg. Big, fierce creature. Top of the food chain. Has a loud, impressive roar..." Gabriel blanched. "You're not going to make it go 'splashy-splashy-splashy' like you did with the stream, are you?"

"Don't be stupid. I'm talking about the egg part. Have you even seen a baby lion?" She cracked open the egg and let the tiny bundle of fur roll out into her hand. "Look! It's adorable! All fuzzy-wuzzy!" She leaned closer. "Yes, who's fuzzy-wuzzy—is it you? Is it you, little lion? Are you my widdle cutie-wootie?" She stroked the tiny cat's belly until it wriggled and purred.

"Miss Sophia, I hardly think..."

"Cute little furry guys like this shouldn't hatch out of eggs. Eggs are icky. They're for lizards and snakes and bugs and gross things like that. Which reminds me, all the bugs and spiders and snakes are going to live in holes and under rocks now. Because they're gross."

Gabriel was now wondering whether God would accept his transfer request if he pretended he had suddenly become allergic to Earth.

"So all the fuzzy ones are going to be born without using eggs?" asked Metatron, who seemed to be trying to keep up with this nonsense, and was in fact making a note.

"Yeah." She lifted up a very strange creature Gabriel had never seen before, an unlikely mix. "Maybe this one could keep using eggs because he's part bird. See, I put a duck's bill on a beaver! I call it a platypus!"

"How do you spell that?" asked Metatron, still making notes.

"But if the furry ones can't have eggs," Gabriel asked, "then how will they be born? Just...fall out of the sky or something?" The archangel paled and looked upward. "I didn't mean that..."

"I don't care." Sophia dismissed the problem with a wave of her little hand. "*You* think of something. Because now I need to fix something else. It's super important."

She beckoned for the angels to follow her, which they did. The Garden really was extremely green now, Gabriel couldn't help noticing, and the new splashing noise of the stream gave it a peaceful air in the late-afternoon sun. For a few seconds he found himself wondering·if maybe one or two of the child's suggestions might not be acceptable, as long as nobody examined the whole thing too carefully. All the different-colored birds were impossibly garish, of course, and she seemed to have gone out of her way to daub the butterflies with shades never imagined on any angelic drawing-board, but still, as long as she didn't mess about with any of the Lord's favorite creations...

"That," she said, stopping and pointing. "That has got to go."

Gabriel suddenly went queasy. "You mean...?"

"Yes, that stupid hairless monkey-thing. It's ugly and it's stupid and it smells."

It was Adam, of course, the apple of the Lord's eye, the only one of the new creatures made more or less in God's own image.

"But...what's wrong with it, Miss Sophia?" Gabriel didn't really want to know, since it was bound to upset him, but he was desperate to stall her. "Your father was very, very specific about wanting..."

"Well, *look* at it."

"That's exactly what he's supposed to do. He's supposed to have domin-ion over the beasts of the earth, and use them to feed himself," Gabriel said.

Adam heard them talking and looked up from where he had been repeatedly spearing a tomato, and waved. "Hi, Gabe! Hi, Metty! What's up?"

"Well, for one thing, he's totally stupid," said Sophia, not hiding the scorn. "He just goes around spearing everything. He's been killing that tomato for about ten minutes and there's nothing left of it to eat. He needs someone to tell him how to know which things to stab and which things to harvest. Someone like me."

Gabriel drew himself to his full angelic height. A line had to be drawn. "I feel quite sure that your father is not going to let you follow His favorite creation around and give him orders all day..."

"Okay, fine, fine. Sheesh." Sophia rolled her eyes. She watched as Adam climbed a tall tree and began enthusiastically spearing a beehive. A moment later, surrounded now by irritated bees, he began to screech and wave his arms, then fell off the branch and plummeted to the ground. "Look, part of him popped out," the girl said, interested. "That's gross... but also kind of cool."

Gabriel sighed. "Go fix him back up, will you, Metatron? I admit it would be nice if he'd quit doing things like that."

"I've got a better idea." The girl hurried over, and before Gabriel or Metatron could stop her, she had lifted up the curve of shining bone that had popped out of Adam when he hit the ground. She examined it thoughtfully, then set it back on the ground. After a momentary shimmer of light, the rib was gone and in its place lay another fully formed Adam creature. This one, though, had subtle differences.

"What is that supposed to be?" Gabriel demanded. "It's lumpy. And it hasn't got a nozzle!"

"It's a more sophisticated design," said the girl. "You won't see this one always tripping and hitting himself in the plums like the old one. In fact, I don't even want to call it 'him.' It's named 'Eve,' and it's a 'her.'"

Gabriel was considering an immediate transfer. Somebody must be mortaring up the walls of Hell, and that suddenly sounded like a very comfortable, safe job compared to his current occupation.

"I don't get it," said Metatron. "Why do we need a second one? Won't they fight?"

Sophia stuck her tongue out at him. "You're just grumpy 'cause mine is *better*. They'll get along fine. They can make babies together, like the animals do."

"We already took care of that! He's full of eggs!"

"Eeewww!" Sophia shook her head in disgust. "No. Do something different. They can make babies some other way."

"But what...?"

"I don't care. Just take care of it." She looked around in satisfaction, but when she turned her eyes to the sky, reddened now with light of the setting sun, her expression soured. "I just thought of one more thing that's really dumb that I have to fix."

Gabriel fought down panic. God was going to have a screaming fit about the lumpy new Adam. What now? "Honestly, Sophia—Miss—it's getting late. I mean, it's going to be dark soon, so maybe you should..."

"That's what I'm talking about. Watch." She pointed to the sky.

"I don't see anything." Gabriel turned helplessly to Metatron. "Do you see anything?"

"Sssshhh. Just watch." She waited as the sun disappeared behind the west end of the Garden.

"I forgot to tell you," Metatron whispered. "She got rid of one of the directions..."

"What? You mean there's only *four* now?" Gabriel gasped. "We're going to have to redo all the winds and everything...!"

"Now look," said Sophia. "Don't you see?"

Gabriel looked up at the sky. With the disappearance of the sun, the stars sparkled against the dark sky like jewels. "See what? It's lovely. Your father said that was some of our best work..."

"It's boring. And it's really *dumb*, too. I mean, you've got the sun up there all day long when everything's already perfectly bright, but as soon as it gets dark and you really need it, boom, the sun goes away! How stupid is that?"

"But...but that was always your father's plan..."

"No, see, what you need is a nice bright sun for the nighttime, too." She clearly was not going to accept disagreement. "I'm going to make one."

"No!" As soon as he saw Sophia's expression, Gabriel immediately realized he should have spoken more courteously—after all, what if God's daughter decided the universe didn't need archangels, either? "I mean, yes! Grand idea! But if it's sunny all the time..."—he cast about for an excuse—"then...then the cute, furry, iddy-widdy bunnies and kitties won't get any sleep. Yes. Because the light will keep them awake."

"Kitties will sleep in the daytime," she said, scowling.

"Okay, but bunnies! They *love* to sleep! And just think of all the fish up in the trees getting sunburned..."

Metatron leaned toward him. "They're in the water now, sir, remember?" said the junior angel, *sotto voce*.

"...I mean the birds, yes, the birds, high up in the trees. If the sun's out all day, the cute colorful little birdie-wirdies will all get sunburned and they'll be so sad!"

Sophia gave him a withering look. "'Birdie-wirdies'? My dad must really like you, to let you keep this job." She shook her head. "Okay, then not a regular sun. Just a little one that doesn't shine so bright."

And before Gabriel could invent another excuse, she raised her hands and suddenly a vast, ivory disk hung in the night sky. As Sophia stood admiring it, several unsuspecting birds and even a butterfly or two banged into it, leaving pockmarks on the pearly surface.

"Stupid birds," she said. "Guess I'll have to put it up higher."

The first day of the new week had already come once before, but this time it had a name—Monday. The Lord God showed up in the morning with His coffee in a travel-cup, looking relaxed and fit.

"Good to be back, good to be back," He said. "Ready to get to work, boys. Still have to figure out how Adam is going to lay those eggs—I mean, anyway that we do it, it's going to look funny..."

"Uh, now that you mention it, Lord," said Gabriel, "we wanted to talk to You about that and...and some other things. See, a few changes got made yesterday, while You were gone. Your daughter came and rearranged a few things."

"My who?"

"Your daughter, sir. Your daughter Sophia."

God lifted one of His great, bushy brows. "Daughter. Sophia. Mine, you say? But I don't have a daughter."

Gabriel was suddenly grateful that God had not seen fit to give the archangel a nozzle like Adam's, because Gabriel felt certain he would have wet himself. "You...you don't? But she said she was Your daughter."

"Impossible. I mean, really, Gabriel, where would I come up with a kid? Just...I don't know, impregnate a virgin human or something?" He frowned. "Which would mean Adam, since he's the only one, and he's not really my idea of..." The Lord God trailed off, staring at the Garden. "What's going on down there? Why are there two Adams?"

Gabriel swallowed. "I'll go get Metatron. He was in charge of the whole thing."

His master was barely listening. "And what's with the trees? Why is it so Me-blessed *green?*"

When Metatron arrived he quickly realized that Gabriel was planning to throw him under the celestial chariot. To his credit, he did not attempt to return the favor. "But Lord, she was *here*," he said. "She told us she was Your daughter and that her name was Sophia. Why would we make that up?"

God frowned. "Well, in a few billion years Sophia is going to mean 'wisdom'—so maybe you're telling the truth at that."

"We are, Lord. We really are," said Metatron.

"I don't understand," Gabriel said. "What do you mean, her name's going to mean 'wisdom'?"

"Simple. I was sleeping most of the day yesterday—all that parting the darkness from the face of the waters and whatnot turns out to be surprisingly tiring—and suddenly she just...shows up here. Holy Wisdom. I suspect she was a part of *Me.*"

"Wow." Gabriel had heard his boss say some weird things, but this was right up there. "That's deep, Lord. Part of you? You really think so?"

"Maybe." God set His coffee down. "Can't be positive, of course—My ways are mysterious, right?"

"They sure are, Lord," said Metatron.

"They sure are." God laughed and clapped the junior angel on the back, which set a few feathers flying. "So let's forget about all this for now and get back to work, guys—maybe see if we can get that whole ozone-layer thing cracked before we break for lunch. What do you say?"

"You're the boss," said Gabriel.

"Yes, for My sins, I am." God laughed.

Gabriel hoped He'd still be in a good mood after He saw His first platypus.

# A Stark and Wormy Knight

"Mam! Mam!" squeed Alexandrax from the damps of his straw-stooned nesty. "Us can't sleep! Tail us a tell of Ye Elder Days!"

"Child, stop that howling or you'll be the deaf of me," scowled his scaly forebearer. "Count sheeps and go to sleep!"

"Been counting shepherds instead, have us," her eggling rejoined. "But too too toothsome they each look. Us are hungry, Mam."

"Hungry? Told you not to swallow that farm tot so swift. A soiled and feisity little thing it was, but would you stop to chew carefulish? Oh, no, no. You're not hungry, child, you've simpledy gobbled too fast and dazzled your eatpipes. Be grateful that you've only got one head to sleepify, unbelike some of your knobful ancestors, and go back and shove yourself snorewise."

"But us *can't* sleep, Mam. Us feels all grizzled in the gut and wiggly in the wings. Preach us some storying, pleases—something sightful but sleepable. Back from the days when there were long dark knights!"

"Knights, knights—you'll scare yourself sleepless with such! No knights there are anymore—just wicked little winglings who will not wooze when they should."

"Just one short storying, Mam! Tale us somewhat of Great-Grandpap, the one that were named Alexandrax just like us! He were alive in the bad old days of bad old knights."

"Yes, that he was, but far too sensible and caveproud to go truckling with such clanking mostrositors—although, hist, my dragonlet, my eggling, it's true there *was* one time..."

"Tell! Tell!"

His Mam sighed a sparking sigh. "Right, then, but curl yourself tight

237

and orouborate that tail, my lad—that'll keep you quelled and quiet whilst I storify.

"Well, as often I've told with pride, your Great-Grandpap were known far-flown and wide-spanned for his good sense. Not for him the errors of others, especkledy not the promiscuous plucking of princesses, since your Great-Grandy reckoned full well how likely that was to draw some clumbering, lanking knight in a shiny suit with a fist filled of sharp steel wormsbane.

"Oh, those were frightsome days, with knights lurking beneath every scone and round every bent, ready to spring out and spear some mother's son for scarce no cause at all! So did your wisdominical Great-Grandpap confine himself to plowhards and peasant girls and the plumpcasional parish priest tumbled down drunk in the churchyard of a Sunday evening, shagged out from 'cessive sermonizing. Princesses and such got noticed, do you see, but the primate proletariat were held cheap in those days—a dozen or so could be harvested in one area before a dragon had to wing on to pastors new. And your Grand-Greatpap, he knew that. Made no mistakes, did he—could tell an overdressed merchant missus from a true damager duchess even by the shallowest starlight, plucked the former but shunned the latter every time. Still, like all of us he wondered what it was that made a human princess so very tasty and tractive. Why did they need to be so punishingly, paladinishly protected? Was it the creaminess of their savor or the crispiness of their crunch? Perhaps they bore the 'boo-kwet,' as those fancy French wyverns has it, of flowery flavors to which no peat-smoked peasant could ever respire? Or were it something entire different, he pondered, inexplicable except by the truthiest dint of personal mastication?

"Still, even in these moments of weakness your Grandpap's Pap knew that he were happily protected from his own greeding nature by the scarcity of princessly portions, owing to their all being firmly pantried in castles and other stony such. He was free to specklate, because foolish, droolish chance would never come to a cautious fellow like him.

"Ah, but he should have quashed all that quandering, my little lizarding, 'stead of letting it simmer in his brain-boiler, because there came a day when Luck and Lust met and bred and brooded a litter named Lamentable.

"That is to say, your Pap's Grandpap stumbled on an unsupervised princess.

"This royal hairless was a bony and brainless thing, it goes without saying, and overfond of her clear complexion, which was her downfalling (although the actual was more of an uplifting, as you'll see). It was her witless wont at night to sneak out of her bed betimes and wiggle her skinny shanks out the window, then ascend to the roof of the castle to moonbathe, which this princess was convinced was the secret of smoothering skin. (Which it may well have been, but who in the name of Clawed Almighty wants smoothered skin? No wonder that humans have grown so scarce these days—they wanted wit.)

"In any case, on this particularly odd even she had just stretched herself out there in her nightgown to indulge this lunar tic when your Great-Grandpap happened to flap by overhead, on his way back from a failed attempt at tavernkeeper tartare in a nearby town. He took one look at this princess stretched out like the toothsomest treat on a butcher's table and his better sense deskirted him. He swooped scoopishly down and snatched her up, then wung his way back toward his cavern home, already menurizing a stuffing of baker's crumbs and coddle of toddler as side dish when the princess suddenfully managed to get a leg free and, in the midst of her struggling and unladylike cursing, kicked your Great-Grandpap directedly in the vent as hard as she could, causing him unhappiness (and almost unhemipenes). Yes, dragons had such things even way back then, foolish fledgling. No, your Great-Grandpap's wasn't pranged for permanent— where do you think your Grandpap came from?

"In any case, so shocked and hemipained was he by this attack on his ventral sanctity that he dropped the foolish princess most sudden and vertical—one hundred sky-fathoms or more, into a grove of pine trees, which left her rather careworn. Also fairly conclusively dead.

"Still, even cold princess seemed toothsome to your Great-Grandpap, though, so he gathered her up and went on home to his cavern. He was lone and batchelorn in those days—your Great-Grandmammy still in his distinct future—so there was none to greet him there and none to share with, which was how he liked it, selfish old mizard that he was even in those dewy-clawed days. He had just settled in, 'ceedingly slobberful at the teeth and tongue and about to have his first princesstual bite ever, when your Grandpap's Pap heard a most fearsomeful clatternacious clanking and baying outside his door. Then someone called the following in a rumbling voice that made your G-G's already bruised ventrality try to shrink up further into his interior.

"'*Ho, vile beast! Stealer of maiden princesses, despoiler of virgins, curse of the kingdom—come ye out! Come ye out and face Sir Libogran the Undeflectable!*'

"It were a knight. It were a big one.

"Well, when he heard this hewing cry your Great-Grandpap flished cold as a snowdrake's bottom all over. See, even your cautious Great-Grandy had heard tell of this Libogran, a terrible, stark and wormy knight—perhaps the greatest dragonsbane of his age and a dreadsome bore on top of it.

"'Yes, it is I, Libogran,' the knight bellows on while your G's G got more and more trembful: 'Slayer of Alasalax the iron-scaled and bat-winged Beerbung, destroyer of the infamous Black Worm of Flimpsey Meadow and scuttler of all the noisome plans of Fubarg the Flameful...'

"On and on he went, declaiming such a drawed-out dracologue of death that your Great-Grandpap was pulled almost equal by impatience as terror. But what could he do to make it stop? A sudden idea crept upon him then, catching him quite by surprise. (He was a young dragon, after all, and unused to thinking, which in those days were held dangerous for the inexperienced.) He snicked quietly into the back of his cave and fetched the princess, who was a bit worse for wear but still respectable enough for a dead human, and took her to the front of the cavern, himself hidebound in shadows as he held her out in the light and dangled her puppetwise where the knight could see.

"'Princess!' cried Libogran. 'Your father has sent me to save you from this irksome worm! Has he harmed you?'

"'Oh, no!' shrilled your Great-Grandpap in his most high-pitchful, princessly voice. 'Not at all! This noble dragon has been naught but gentlemanifold, and I am come of my own freed will. I live here now, do you see? So you may go home without killing anything and tell my papa that I am as happy as a well-burrowed scale mite.'

"The knight, who had a face as broad and untroubled by subtle as a porky haunch, stared at her. 'Are you truly certain you are well, Princess?'

quoth he. 'Because you look a bit battered and dirtsome, as if you had perhaps fallen through several branches of several pine trees.'

"'How nosy and nonsensical you are, Sir Silly Knight!' piped your Great-Grandpap a bit nervous-like. 'I was climbing in the tops of a few trees, yes, as I love to do. That is how I met my friend this courtinuous dragon—we were both birdnesting in the same tree, la and ha ha! And then he kindly unvited me to his home toward whence I incompulsedly came, and where I am so happily visiting...!'

"Things went on in this conversational vain for some little time as your Great-Grandpap labored to satisfy the questioning of the dreaded dragonslayer. He might even have eventually empacted that bold knight's withdrawal, except that in a moment of particularly violent puppeteering your great-grandsire, having let invention get the best of him while describing the joyful plans of the putative princess, managed to dislodge her head.

"She had not been the most manageable marionette to begin with, and now your Great-Grandpap was particular difficulted trying to get her to pick up and re-neck her lost knob with her own hands while still disguising his clawed handiwork at the back, controlling the action.

"'Oops and girlish giggle!' he cried in his best mock-princessable tones, scrabbling panicked after her rolling tiara-stand, 'silly me, I always said it would fall off if it weren't attached to me and now look at this, hopped right off its stem! Oh, la, I suppose I should be a bit more rigormortous about my grooming and attaching.'

"Sir Libogran the Undeflectable stared at what must clearful have been a somewhat extraordinate sight. 'Highness,' quoth he, 'I cannot help feeling that someone here is not being entirely honest with me.'

"'What?' lied your Great-Grandpap most quickly and dragon-fully. 'Can a princess not lose her head in a minor way occasional without being held up left and right to odiumfoundment and remonstrance?'

"'This, I see now,' rumbled Sir Libogran in the tone of one who has been cut to his quink, 'is not the living article I came to deliver at all, but rather an ex-princess in expressly poor condition. I shall enter immediately, exterminate the responsible worm, and remove the carcasework for respectful burial.'

"Your Great-Grandpap, realizing that this particular deceptivation had run its curse, dropped the bony remnants on the stony stoop and raised his voice in high-pitched and apparently remorsive and ruthful squizzling: 'Oh, good sir knight, don't harm us! It's true, your princess is a wee bit dead, but through no fault of us! It was a terrible diseasement that ter-milated her, of which dragon caves are highlishly prone. She caught the sickness and was rendered lifeless and near decapitate by it within tragical moments. I attempted to convenience you otherwise only to prevent a fine felon like you from suckling at the same deadly treat.'

"After the knight had puddled out your grandsire's sire's words with his poor primate thinker, he said, 'I do not believe there are diseases which render a princess headless and also cover her with sap and pine needles. It is my counter-suggestion, dragon, that you thrashed her to death with an evergreen of some sort and now seek to confuse me with fear for my own person. But your downfall, dragon, is that even 'twere so, I cannot do less than march into the mouth of death to honor my quest and the memory of this poor pine-battered morsel. So regardless of personal danger, I come forthwith to execute you, scaly sirrah. Prepare yourself to meet my blameless blade...' And sewed on.

"*Clawed the Flyest*, thought your Great-Grandpap, *but he is deedly a noisome bore for true*. Still, he dubited not that Sir Libogran, for all his slathering self-regard, would quickly carry through on his executive intent. Thus, to protect his own beloved and familiar hide for a few moments languorous, your Pap's Pap's Pap proceeded to confect another tongue-forker on the spot.

"'All right, thou hast me dart to tripes,' he told the knight. 'The realio trulio reason I cannot permit you into my cavernous cavern is that so caught, I must performcemeat give up to you three wishes of immense valuable. For I am that rare and amnesial creature, a Magical Wishing Dragon. Indeed, it was in attempting to claw her way toward my presence and demand wishes from me that your princess gained the preponderosa of these pine-burns, for it was with suchlike furniture of ever-greenwood that I attempted pitifullaciously to block my door, and through which she cranched and smushed her way with fearsome strength. Her head was damaged when, after I told her I was fluttered out after long flight and too weary for wish-wafting, she yanked off her crown and tried to beat me indispensable with it. She was a pittance too rough, though—a girl whose strength belied her scrawnymous looks—and detached her headbone from its neckly couchment in the crown-detaching process, leading to this lamentable lifelessness.

"'However,' went on your Great-Grandpap, warming now to his self-sufficed subject, 'although I resisted the wish-besieging princess for the honor of all my wormishly magical brethren, since you have caught me fairy and scary, Sir Libogran, larded me in my barren, as it were, I will grant the foremansioned troika of wishes to *you*. But the magic necessitudes that after you tell them unto my ear you must go quickly askance as far as possible—another country would be idealistic—and trouble me no more so that I can perforce the slow magics of their granting (which sometimes takes years betwixt wishing and true-coming.)'

"Libogran stood a long time, thinking uffishly, then lastly said, 'Let me make sure I have apprehended you carefully, worm. You state that you are a Magic Wishing Dragon, that it was her greed for this quality of yours which cost the unfortunate princess her life, and that I should tell you my three wishes and then leave, preferably to a distant land, so that you may grant them to me in the most efficacious manner.'

"'Your astutity is matched only by the stately turn of your greave and the general handfulness of your fizzick, good sir knight,' your Great-Grandpap eagerly responded, seeing that perhaps he might escape puncturing at the hands of this remorseless rider after all. 'Just bename those wishes and I will make them factive, both pre- and post-haste.'

"Sir Libogran slowly shook his massive and broadly head. 'Do you take me for a fool, creature?'

"'Not a fool creature as sort,' replinked your Grandpap's Daddy, trying to maintain a chirrupful tone. 'After all, you and your elk might be a lesser species than us *Draco Pulcher*, but still, as I would be the first to argue, a vally-hooed part of Clawed the Flyest's great creation...'

"'Come here, dragon, and let me show you my wish.'" Your Great-Grandpap hesitated. 'Come there?' he asked. 'Whyso?'

"'Because I cannot explain as well as I can demonstrate, sirrah,' quoth the bulky and clanksome human.

"So your forebear slithered out from the cavernous depths, anxious to end his night out by sending this knight out. He was also hoping that, though disappointed of his foreplanned feast, he might at least locate some princessly bits fallen off in the cave, which could be served chippingly on toast. But momentarily after your Great-Grandpap emerged into the lightsome day, the cruel Sir Libogran snatched your ancestor's throat in a gauntleted ham and cut off that poor, innosensitive dragon's head with his vicious blade.

"Snick! No snack." This treacherness done, the knight gathered up the princess' tree-tattered torso and emancive pate, then went galumphing back toward the castle of her mourning, soon-to-mourn-more Mammy and Daddums."

"But how can that be, Mam?" shrimped wee Alexandrax. "He killed Great-Grandpap? Then how did Grandpap, Pap, and Yours Contumely come to be?"

"Fie, fie, shut that o-shaped fishmouth, my breamish boy. Did I say aught about killing? He did not kill your Great-Grandpap, he cut off his head. Do you not dismember that your great-grandcestor was dragon of the two-headed vermiety?

"As it happened, one of his heads had been feeling poorly, and he had kept it tucked severely under one wing all that day and aftermoon so it could recupertate. Thus, Libogran the Undeflectable was not aware of the existence of this auxiliary knob, which he would doubtless of otherwise liberated from its neckbones along with the other. As it was, the sickened head soon recovered and was good as new. (With time the severed one also grew back, although it was ever after small and prone to foolish smiles and the uttering of platitudinous speech—phrases like, 'I'm sure everything will work off in the end' and 'It is honorous just to be nominated,' and suchlike.)

"In times ahead—a phrase which was sorely painful to your Great-Great-Pap during his invalidated re-knobbing—your G-G would go back to his old, happy ways, horrorizing harrowers and slurping shepherds but never again letting himself even veer toward rooftopping virgins or in fact anything that bore the remotest rumor of the poisonous perfume of princessity. He became a pillar of his community, married your Great-Grandmammy in a famously fabulous ceremony—just catering the event purged three surrounding counties of their peasantly population—and lived a long and harpy life."

"But Mam, Mam, what about that stark and wormy Sir Libogran, that...dragocidal maniac? Did he really live hoppishly ever after as well, unhaunted by his bloodful crime?"

"In those days, there was no justice for our kind except what we made ourselves, my serpentine son. No court or king would ever have victed him."

"So he died unpunwiched?"

"Not exactly. One day your Great-Grandpap was on his way back from courting your Grandest-Greatmam-to-be, and happened to realize by the banners on its battlements that he was passing over Libogran's castle, so he stooped to the rooftop and squatted on the chimbley pot, warming his hindermost for a moment (a fire was burning in the hearth down below and it was most pleasantly blazeful) before voiding himself down the chimbley hole into the great fireplace."

"He couped the flue!"

"He did, my boy, he did. The whole of Libogran's household came staggering out into the cold night waving and weeping and coughing out the stinking smoke as your Grand's Grandpap flew chortling away into the night, unseen. Libogran's castle had to be emptied and aired for weeks during the most freezingly worstful weather of the year, and on this account the knight spent the rest of his life at war with the castle pigeons, on whom he blamed your Great-Grandpap's secret chimbley-discharge—he thought the birds had united for a concerted, guanotated attempt on his life. Thus, stalking a dove across the roof with his bird-net and boarspear a few years later, Sir Libogran slipped and fell to his death in the castle garden, spiking himself on his own great sticker and dangling thereby for several days, mistaked by his kin and servants as a new scarecrow."

"Halloo and hooray, Mam! Was he the last of the dragon-hunters, then? Was him skewerting on his own sharpitude the reason we no longer fear them?"

"No, dearest honey-sonny, we no longer fear them because *they* no longer see *us*. During the hunders of yearses since your Greatest Grandpap's day, a plague called Civilization came over them, a diseaseful misery that blinded them to half the creatures of the world and dumbfounded their memories of much that is true and ancient. Let me tell you a dreadsome secret." She leaned close to whisper in his tender earhole. "Even when we snatch a plump merchant or a lean yet flavorful spinster from their midst these days, the humans never know that one of us dragons has doomfully done for the disappeared. They blame it instead on a monster they fear even more."

"What is that, Mam?" Alexandrax whimpspered. "It fears me to hear, but I want to know. What do they think slaughters them? An odious ogre? A man-munching manticore?"

"Some even more frightfulling creature. No dragon has ever seen it, but they call it...Statistics."

"Clawed Hitself save us from such a horridly horror!" squeeped the small one in fright.

"It is only a man-fancy, like all the rest of their nonned sense," murmed his Mam. "Empty as the armor of a cracked and slurped knight—so fear it not. Now, my tale is coiled, so sleepish for you, my tender-winged bundle."

"I will," he said, curling up like a sleepy hoop, most yawnful. "I s'pose no knights is good nights, huh, Mam?"

"Examply, my brooded boy. Fear not clanking men nor else. Sleep. All is safe and I am watching all over you."

And indeed, as she gazed yellow-eyed and loving on her eggling, the cave soon grew fulfilled with the thumberous rundle of wormsnore.

# Omnitron, What Ho!

What's that, you say? You want to hear how I first met Omnitron, my robot servant, the admirable, clanking Crichton who has saved my bacon more often than a pig-herder with a Tommy gun? Very well, but I warn you—it is not a pretty tale.

Like many grim things, it begins with an aunt. You all know what it is to have an aunt, I think. It is much like having a fish, and a cold one at that, if said fish had control of your finances and conceived you to be a complete waste of human tissue. And if there was anyone who was an authority on the subject of human tissue, it was my Aunt Jabbatha, owing to her having lost most of hers.

As usual, when she deigned to see me at all, I found Aunt Jabbatha floating in her transparent vat in the day parlor, while all manner of supporting devices hissed and gurgled. The gimlet eyes of aunts are not made softer when couched in a disembodied head floating in a very, very large jar, with only a kelplike swirl of spinal cord and branching ganglia washing softly back and forth to keep them company. Downright eerie, some might call it, but we Boosters are made of stern stuff.

"Werner Von Secondstage Booster," she proclaimed by way of a greeting, "you are a waste of human tissue."

"Of course, Aunt Jabbatha. I think we established that fact in our earlier interviews. Every single one of them."

"Don't talk dribble to me, boy. We have a family emergency. You are being pressed into service."

There is only one word more frightening to a Booster than those dreadful two syllables, "service," but in deference to those of tender feelings,

I will not disclose that word at present. "But I don't want to be of service to anybody, Auntie."

"And you've made a splendid start, because you are completely useless." Her head floated up to the front of the glass and bumped against it like a withered olive in an extremely unappetizing martini. "But that's about to change. Your cousin, Budgerigar Scallop, is eloping with a young woman of very dubious parentage from some backwater outer rim planet. Her biology militates against her inclusion in this family. *You* will put a stop to it."

"But Aunt Jabbatha," I said, hoping desperately to stall long enough for something on the order of a medium-large meteor strike to cripple civilization yet again and distract her, "how could I possibly do that? Budgie never listens to me. Besides, I've been invited to a rather jolly costume ball at the Suborbital Drones Club…"

"Hang your costume ball. And hang your cowardly piffle, Wernie, you worm. This is your chance to redeem the dreadful failure that has been your life so far." She floated higher in the tank so that she was looking down on me, rather like a child's balloon with the face of a gargoyle. "The shuttle for the HMSS *Chinless* is leaving tonight from Luton Spaceport. Your cousin and his…inamorata will be on board. So will you, because we have booked you a place. You will bring young Scallop back untethered, or you will throw yourself into the nearest star. Actually, no, if you fail, you must still come back and receive your punishment in person." She frowned. "I may have other plans for you, even if you manage to botch this, as you have botched almost every other small favor I've asked you to do."

Her confidence in me was so inspiring I thought I might as well leave on this high note, and so rose to my feet. But it was not to be!

"You will be accompanied on this voyage by my butler," she said. "At least then there will be some chance of everyone surviving your involvement. Omnitron, come in."

What stepped from the shadows then was something like a man, but more like an espresso machine. It had the futuristic gleam that one associates with the hood ornaments of very fast hover cars, and an air of confidence not usually seen in the lower classes, especially the artificial ones.

"Omnitron," Aunt Jabbatha said, "this is my famously worthless nephew, Werner."

"Sir." It tilted its shiny chin ever so slightly toward its shiny chest.

"You will make sure he gets on the shuttle and then onto the *Chinless*, Omnitron. If he does not fulfill his duties as I have detailed, you have my permission to twist off his ear. Ears are worth little. They can be grown on a saltine cracker these days."

The robot bowed with a whir of well-oiled gears. "As you wish, Madame." Then he lifted me up and tucked me under his arm as easily as a padded matron might hoist a small dog dressed in an embarrassing sweater, and carried me out of Aunt Jabbatha's parlor.

"Try to get things right for once," she called after me. "Don't be a weed, boy!"

I wasn't sure what a weed was—something that used to grow on the planetary surface, I suspect, before the Big Oh Dear—and so my flashing riposte was delayed until after the lift door had closed behind us.

"See here, Omnitron," I said as I surveyed my cabin. "This will never do. Old Budgie has a stateroom the size of Berkshire, but I seem to have been stowed in one of the laundry room dryers."

"I admit the room is not large, sir," said Omnitron, "but it was the best that could be done with a last minute booking—the ship was quite full. All that was available was Third Class."

The purser, who seemed to have taken against me since my first cry of "Yo ho ho! Where's my bottle of rum?" as I walked up the gangway, surveyed me with cool disdain. Considering that he had those glowing red cybernetic eyes so many people are wearing these days, it was most unappealing. "Does sir have an objection to the accommodations?" he asked.

"Oh, of course not," I replied, rapier-like. "Who could jolly well object to a stateroom the size of a face flannel? And where am I supposed to sleep?"

The purser again fixed me with his smoldering gaze. He was a small, thin man, the kind who look as though they only enjoy themselves at funerals. "Ah, but sir misunderstands. There *is* a bed. It folds down, thus." He fiddled with something on the wall and let down what I swear was a child's toy ironing board. It had a teeny tiny blanket, and a pillow that had probably been stolen from a gerbil. "I'm afraid those who wait until the last moment to book passage cannot blame the staff for the lack of choice, sir."

"No," I said under my breath, "but I can blame the staff for being unpleasant, abominable, red-eyed swine."

The purser, who had been about to leave, turned and squinted his glowing cyber eyes at me, which gave rather the impression that a couple of maraschino cherries had leaped out of a Manhattan glass and rolled into a deep ditch. "Beg pardon, sir?"

"My master merely asked for some of that pleasant Andromedan red and white wine," Omnitron cut in—quite deftly, I thought, for something that looked like a washing machine hammered into the shape of William Gladstone. This Omnitron fellow was nothing to sneeze at. "Mr. Booster likes to drink both sorts at the same time. Thank you for your help."

"Hmmmph," said the purser, and went about his business.

"Thank you, Omnitron," I said. "Considering that you are a robot, you are still a vastly superior human being to that fellow. Did you see him sizing me up? You'd think I had snuck on board in a fishing net."

"Quite, sir. A bad sort, no doubt. But now I think you had better put on your dress coat and make your way up to the Lido Deck. Your cousin and his friend will be there."

"No time for a little room service, or a swift nap? That shuttle flight took it out of me, Omnitron. I had the vacuum-hose to my mouth the whole time. Dashed bumpy."

"I'm afraid not, sir. But I understand your aunt has provided you with the wherewithal for a couple of free drinks."

"Say no more—it's Booster into the breach. Lido on, MacDuff."

The scene on deck was quite cosmopolitan, with not only all manner of Earth quality present, but the wealthy and well-fed from many other colonies and alien cultures as well. In the midst of all those unfamiliar green and blue and occasionally downright startling faces, it took me no small time to locate Cousin Budgie, but at last I spotted his generous silhouette. Budgie is a well-fed sort himself, and his cummerbund bulged like a mainsail in a stiff breeze.

"Hullo, Booster," he said as I walked cautiously across the antigravity dance floor. "What brings you out here? Didn't think this was your sort of picnic. Because it costs money and all."

I scowled as pleasantly as I could at this unneeded reminder of my current financial inconveniences, namely my continued debt-slavery to Aunt Jabbatha and the collection agents of several well-known Fleet Street touts. "Cheers, Budgie, old sprat!" I replied. "And who is this lovely young lady...?"

I almost didn't finish the sentence, because in point of fact his companion was indeed rather lovely—no, rather stunning, to be brutally precise. Black hair, raven's wing, that sort of thing, and a face like a Tanagra figurine, except less terracotta-ish, if you grasp what I mean. Clear, limpid eyes (Why do people say that anyway? Weren't those a kind of shellfish once?) and a figure that, beneath her modest netwear, would have made a tea-sipping vicar choke on his profiterole.

"This?" asked Budgie. "This lovely creature is my fiancée, Krellita Thoractia Du Palp, from the planet Cunabulum. I suppose you ought to call her Krelly, like I do." He turned to the wondrous female creature next to him. "Say hello to Wernie, Krelly, darling. He's a bit of a worn old sock, but he's good for some laughs."

She greeted me demurely. Budgie went off to find more drinks.

"And how did you meet my cousin, hey?" I asked her. "House party? The Hunstman's Ball?"

"His private cruiser crashed in the jungles of my home planet." I could hear the tiniest trace of an accent. *Ha*, I thought. *That proves she's a gold-digger. She's foreign!* "I nursed him back to health," Krellita explained, "and we became fond of each other. He is everything I ever wanted in a man. He is ideal."

I watched Budgie coming back, doing a sort of clumsy samba to avoid spilling the three Scorpio Slings he was carrying. It was hard to think of my pale, pudgy cousin as a man, let alone an ideal, but I supposed that on whatever backwater world Miss Du Palp came from, the pickings might be a bit on the slender side.

"Yes," I said, deciding to get to work. "And he's coped so brilliantly with his illness."

"Illness?"

"Oh, nothing serious. In most cases it has run its course and the victim is dead long before he reaches the homicidal insanity stage."

She gave me a startled look, but before I could elaborate (and believe me, I was prepared to elaborate—I'd spent the entire shuttle trip up to the *Chinless* thinking up things to tell her to frighten her off) Budgie reached us.

"Oof!" he said. "What a crush! Some bounder elbowed me right in the brisket, Wernie. Can you imagine that?" He turned to his fiancée. "What do you say to a little whirl around the floor, my dove? They're just starting up with the Neptunian Tango and the gravity's turned way down low, the way you like it."

"No, thank you, darling," Krelly said, "though it *does* sound terribly romantic. You dance, if you'd like. I'll watch."

He shrugged and made his way off again in search of suitably bipedal partners, which were a bit thin on the deck tonight.

"Brave, brave lad," I said, shaking my head in admiration. "He's always put such a courageous face on things. Acts just like everyone else!"

"Are you certain he has this...illness?" Krellita asked. "Because, well...we have plans." She brushed prettily. "We're going to have a family."

"Oh, I shouldn't worry about that," I said. "I'm quite certain good old Budgie will be an excellent papa, until he gets to the screaming stage."

"Screaming stage?"

"Oh, you know, when the pain of the disease becomes so great that the sufferer begins to screech continuously and tear off their own limbs and skin. Same disease took Budgie's uncle, poor old fellow. They found the old man's bloody fingertips and nails all over the National Library, but nothing else of him. Sad. Their first edition of *Burke's Peerage* was unusable afterward—they could never get the stains out."

"Oh, my!" she said, those lovely clear eyes wide. "Why didn't Budgie tell me this?"

"Oh, I'm sure he wanted to spare you the worry," I said. "Most sufferers shoot themselves long before most of the other things happen, so it seldom gets to that point. He was just looking out for your happiness."

Krellita Du Palp's eyes now narrowed, precisely like those of any young tootsie on the make who has just discovered that her golden goose is really a sitting duck. (Or something like that. To be honest, I've never really got the hang of metaphors.)

I looked up to see Budgie dancing with a long drink of champagne from the Proxima colonies. His partner was nearly eight feet tall, so he was having trouble not treading on her feet. The trotters in question were about the size of my stateroom bed—small for a bed, but perhaps a touch overlarge for a young lady.

"Poor man," I said, sipping my drink and reaching behind Krellita to the buffet table, having orbed a sumptuous, steaming ham that was almost begging to become part of Greater Boosterdom. "So brave, our Budgie, when he must already be losing control over his neuromusculature."

"Excuse me, sir." The familiar, chill tone brought me up short. It was my nemesis, the purser, his little artificial eyes glowing with *schadenfreude*. "The buffet is for First Class passengers only."

Faced with this sudden assault on my person, I decided on a dignified retreat. I gave the attractive Miss Du Palp a conspiratorial wink, then took the ham and the Scorpio Sling with me, leaving Budgie and his ladylove to their romantic destiny, into the spokes of which I hoped I had just rammed a jolly large stick.

I may have taken a bit more ham than I should have, to be honest, but I hadn't had any breakfast owing to my shuttle-impaired stomach works, and my appetite was back. Still, I could barely get the entire ham into the lift down to Third Class, and had to ask an old, limping woman to get out to make room. Such a grumpy look she gave me! I thought these cruises were supposed to make people cheerful.


"You should have seen me, Omnitron," I told him. "I was nothing short of magnificent. As soon as I mentioned Budgie's hideous illness, the young lady's attitude changed like a shot! I'll wager she can't wait to be shut of him now."

"His hideous illness, sir? As far as I know, young Lord Scallop suffers from nothing worse than a mild case of Venusian Drip, which can be easily treated these days with proper medical care..."

"I made it up! That's the genius part, Omnitron, old bucket. She'll never go near him now. Ah, I can hear her gnashing her teeth clear down here in the ship's underbelly..."

"I suspect the sound you hear is me lowering your bed," Omnitron said, folding down the tiny, handkerchief-sized platform with a squeaking, ratcheting noise like someone deboning a live rabbit.

"As I said, before some metal buffoon short-sheeted my commentary, '*I can hear her gnashing her teeth.*' Young Miss Du Palp is no doubt furious at having sunk her claws into such a sad, doomed specimen of Earth manhood when she thought she'd bagged a prize."

"You say that as though she is not of Earth herself, sir."

"I should say not! Not an earthly thing about her, except for her quite astonishing beauty and shapeliness. And her jolly nice legs. I've never run across the Du Palp family before, but I must admit they do rather sparkling work in the daughter department, her avaricious man-hunting notwithstanding."

"Did you say 'Du Palp,' sir? As in, the Cunabulum Du Palps?"

"Yes, Omnitron, I think that was her awful old planet, something like that. What of it? You have that cursed expression on your featureless face that I have already come to loathe, and your hydraulic tubes are practically rigid with disapproval."

"I'm sure you're mistaken, sir. Perhaps you should climb into bed. I will endeavour to hold it for you while you attempt it. The affair seems a bit... flexible."

Flexible, hah! "Impossible" is the word Omnitron was too craven to utilize, but I will speak the truth and shame the *Chinless*. After struggling for an hour to make myself comfortable on that slice of Melba toast they called a berth, I decamped to the floor, which although not large enough even for a proper game of blow football, let alone the nocturnal thrashing of a Booster in his prime, was still much more spacious than the Procrustean saltine I'd been given to sleep on. Thus, when somebody knocked at my stateroom door shortly after two in the AM, Earth time, I had only to crawl a few feet to find out who had so cruelly disturbed my slumbers.

"Oh, dear Mr. Booster," said Krellita Du Palp, "please don't make me stand in the corridor. Someone might see me!"

"Hmmm? Oh, right. Can't have that." Although I couldn't imagine why. As far as I knew, these cruises were like a Feydeau farce, with various coves and their hard-mouthed molls ducking in and out of each other's staterooms left and right. Still, perhaps back on Cunabulum they were a modest bunch and didn't like to be seen dashing about in their—I had to admit—somewhat spectacularly filmy nightwear. "Right ho," I said when she was inside, which necessitated me speaking almost directly to her forehead, owing to the size of the room. "Now, my dear, what can Wernie do for you? A little counseling, perhaps? Are we having second thoughts about Lord Scallop?"

"Oh, yes, Mr. Booster. Yes, you've opened my eyes! You've saved me from a hideous sham of a marriage!"

"Well, shucks, ma'am, as our American cousins like to say." I was feeling quite proud of myself. Useless, Aunt Jabbatha? Wernie Booster, useless? Way-hey! "I'm sorry I have to be the bearer of such terrible tidings, dear lady. I only wanted to spare you any unnecessary heartbreak..."

"Budgie would never survive the rigors of conjugal expression," she said. "But you, Mr. Booster—you are *perfect!* Healthy as can be, and with a fine appetite!" She leaned closer, which in those intimate confines actually caused her chin to press rather discomfortingly against my Adam's apple. "Do you care for me, Wernie? Just a little?"

I was nonplussed, as the French say, and my usually considerable aplomb was also slightly undercut by the very thick, musky-sweet scent Krellita was giving off. I could not help thinking of her shapely lower limbs and how much like springtime they had made me feel back on the Lido Deck. "Of course, I find you a very admirable woman," I began. "Sensible, too, with your unwillingness to yoke yourself to a shambling near-corpse like Cousin Budgie. But that is all I'm prepared to say at present..."

"Kiss me, you romantic fool," she said, then sort of attached her mouth to mine.

Now, I don't want you to think your humble narrator is anything less than a man of the world, but I must confess I'd never thought kissing could be quite like that, sort of...probing and...well, *biting*. At one point, as things were getting a bit too hot and heavy for my way of thinking, I actually felt something in my throat that seemed to be her tongue, except it was far too long and sort of scaly. It also seemed to be...jointed? Here, the Booster lexicon falters.

"Say, now," I squeaked, "what are you doing, Krellita? I mean, Miss Du Palp, of course, since *we hardly know each other*. I mean, my stateroom, middle of the night and all, you hardly dressed...I mean, isn't this a bit of a rum do?"

She laid a cool finger on my lips. "Oh, Wernie, you silly boy, it's all right! We'll be married soon, so there's nothing wrong with it!"

Even with the scaly, jointish, tonguelike thing no longer lapping at my uvula, I confess I choked and spluttered for a while. Do you remember how I explained that "service" was the second most feared word in the Booster dictionary? Now I can reveal that the arch-curse "married" is the Booster champion of champions, an utterance whose doomful sound turns women into grinning monsters itching to plan things, including the end of a fellow's freedom.

"M-M-Married?" I finally managed to say. "Hold on, there, dear lady. I think you have the wrong end of the stick..."

"I don't care," she said. "I'm sure it's a lovely stick, anyway. And I know I probably do things a bit differently than you—we're a bit of a backwater planet in some ways—but you'll come to relish it."

"Relish what?" I said, but she had turned away from me, not that she could go very far in that doll's house of a cabin.

"Don't look!" she said, and began to undo the straps for her gown. "Turn around! Don't be so eager, you naughty boy!"

"Eh, um, well, perhaps we should slow down for a moment and take stock of things," I said. "I mean, you're a lovely girl and all, but you see, I have a number of irons in the fire just now, and when you don't attend to them—well, you get frightfully hot irons, for one thing..."

"I knew it would be like this," she declared with the dreamy sound of a chubby schoolboy regarding a stolen éclair. "Both of us eager, panting for consummation, our breasts heaving with desire..."

"Come now," I said, and reached out to grasp her shoulder, despite its alarming nakedness, because I was thinking about shaking a little sense into her. "If anybody's breast is heaving around here, it's not mine, Miss Du Palp. No, at the moment my breast is heaveless—positively torpid."

"Don't look yet, darling," she said as she shucked off the rest of her outfit. "It's bad luck for you to see my final form before I'm ready."

I was just wondering what kind of bridal trousseau a "final form" might be, and how I could escape from a cabin as small as this one without being noticed, when she turned and I saw her final form. It was not quite what I had expected.

The skin and face and legs and complexion I had admired—in fact, pretty much everything that had pleased the Booster eye, and doubtless the Scallop eye before me—now were revealed to be mere window-dressing, on the order of an insect's chrysalis. (Or is that some kind of fancy American hover car? Let's say "cocoon" instead.) In any case, the aforementioned lovely skin cracked and peeled away in broad sheets before tumbling to the stateroom floor, discarded like a losing ticket at Epsom Downs, as Krellita Du Palp unveiled her true self in all its...well, dash it, in all its *something*. Something bad, is what I want to say, like a giant sticky spider-centipede sort of thing.

As I stared in dismay, she lifted me up as though I were a kitten—and not one of your manlier kittens either—and flung me to the floor, then stood over me on her jointed legs, dripping long ropy strings of something awful onto my face and chest.

"Oh, Wernie, to think that you, the one to warn me of Budgie's unfitness, should turn out to be my true love after all!" Krellita's compound eyes glittered with affection for Yours Truly. I was looking around for a house slipper to hit her with, but since it would have taken a slipper the size of a mail van, my search proved fruitless. "And you, Wernie, healthy, strong you, after I lay my eggs inside you, you'll provide such fine nourishment for our young when they begin to grow!" A large tubelike object rose from her abdomen, a sort of garden hosepipe made of jointed plates. The hole on the end of it coming toward me was surrounded by spiky, toothy objects that looked meant to do some kind of serious harm, and I was fairly certain that Your Humble Narrator was the intended victim.

"Here now!" I said, indignation struggling with mortal terror. "No ovipositors, please! I'm British!"

"Darling! Love me!" she cried—I think that's what she said, but her clicking, drooling mouth-parts slightly impaired her speech—and then she clutched me with all her legs. I felt the tube beginning to nudge my stomach like a pickpocket searching for Grandfather's gold watch.

"Help!" I said, quite loudly. "Help, help, help, *help*, dash it all, *somebody help!*" In fact, I said over and over (and over and over) but nobody came. The clicking and drooling increased in intensity, and the toothy probe nibbled exploringly at my tum-tum. Things looked very bad for Your Humble Etc.

"Yoo hoo!" called a strange voice from the open door of my stateroom.

The most horrible thing I had ever seen was already squatting on top of me, preparing to introduce me to the joys of involuntary fatherhood, but the weird, blobby shape in the doorway was a close second. It was lumpy and misshapen, had glowing red eyes, and was waving its limbs around in a manner only slightly less frenzied than Miss du Palp, who had the advantage of having more of them to wave.

"Hey, sweet-cheeks," the strange apparition said in a curiously metallic voice. "Why don't you lose that gink and get with a *real* man?"

"Who are you?" demanded Krellita. While she was distracted, I took the opportunity of buttoning my hired tuxedo over my exposed underpinnings.

"Just the man of your dreams, that's all." The thing in the doorway wiggled from side to side like a worm impaled on a dull fishhook. "Healthy, fat, full of protein, and anxious to settle down and raise a whole brood of larvae."

For a moment, Krellita hesitated, but then she rose off me, the joints of her legs creaking like an ancient dumbwaiter. "You do...smell good," she said. "Fatty. *Meaty.*"

"Kiss me, you fool," said the lumpy, red-eyed thing. "We were meant for each other! Leave that pale, scrawny, inbred weasel and come to me, my exoskeletal sweetheart. Let me spirit you away to a place where our love will not be disturbed by search parties or worried relatives—somewhere we can raise our young to crawl proudly toward the future!"

That did it. With a sound that was halfway between the joyous whoop of a Red Indian and the slurping noise of a toothless man finishing his soup, Krellita Du Palp leaped across the room and fastened herself to the stranger, drool flying like confetti. As the two of them fell to the passage floor outside, the door of my stateroom clicked shut and I was alone again.

Nearly half an hour later, somebody knocked on my cabin door. I didn't answer, since I had folded up the bed and was sharing the alcove in the wall with it, hoping to remain there until the *Chinless* docked, but I heard the door open and close.

"Master Wernie?" someone called.

To my great joy, I recognized the tinny tones. "Omnitron?" I managed to get the bed-cupboard open and tumbled out onto the floor. "What are you doing here? Did you see what happened? That woman was...well, she was a creature, Omnitron! A hideous, man-destroying creature."

"Yes, sir. The fairer sex can be difficult at the best of times."

"What do you mean, 'difficult'? She was going to scoop out my insides and fill them with some kind of caviar—and not the nice yummy kind, I daresay. I was going to be baby food for a very unwanted group of offspring!"

"I know, sir, which was why I took the liberty of luring Miss Du Palp away from you."

I gasped. "That was you in the doorway, then? That red-eyed thing?"

"Not exactly, sir." Omnitron had a look of great complacency on its face. At least that's what I assume it was—it's hard to tell with robots. "You see, I knew that a young woman like that would not give up a prospect like you for a lifeless array of metal components like myself. So I took the liberty of knocking the ship's purser on the head. He was sneaking around in the hallway outside trying to catch you with Miss Du Palp in your room. Then I manipulated his limbs and spoke as though I were him, to draw her away."

"You coshed the purser? Thumped him on the dome and knocked him out cold? Good lord, Omnitron, you are a hardened villain."

"I am an omnitronic butler, sir. I am programmed to respond usefully in most situations."

"Well, that explains the red eyes—those horrid, superior glowing peepers of his will haunt my dreams. Although not quite to the degree that Miss Du Palp will." I shuddered. "But the shape I saw in the doorway was quite stout, Omnitron. I recall that purser as being rather slender."

"After I had rendered him senseless, sir, I stuffed his clothing with leftover ham from your breakfast. You really took quite a bit, sir, I must say. There was enough remaining to nearly double his weight, which made him appear to be exactly the sort of mate Miss Du Palp was seeking."

"Omnitron, you are a pearl among machines. But what about when the arachnid lady finds out her liaison was begun on false if still quite meaty pretenses? What then?"

"I took an additional liberty, sir, of flushing them both out the airlock while they were engaged in their...romantic conversation. The erstwhile couple are frozen now, floating in airless space."

"Good God! Well, I can't say *she* didn't have it coming, but what about the purser? He was a nasty bit of work, true, but he was just doing his job—in an unpleasant sort of way."

"I dare say, sir, that he would prefer being frozen to the kind of fatherhood that was planned for him. I understand the young of Cunabulum are slow eaters, and it takes their victims many months to die."

"You know about those creatures?"

"I have run across references to them in my light reading, sir." Omnitron helped me to my feet and began straightening the stateroom. "I believe there was a pictorial in the Sunday *Times*. The Du Palps are an old and well-known Cunabulumian family. As soon as you told me her name, I knew you were in danger."

"Huh." I thought about it for a moment. "Well, I have definitely had a near brush today with jolly old extinction, Omnitron, and I learned two very important lessons as well."

"Yes? What are those, sir?"

"First, that matrimony is for suckers. Second, that one should always have a faithful robotic servant handy on an interplanetary trip, because in space, nobody can hear you scream."

"Oh, I rather think everybody on the ship could hear you scream, sir." Omnitron tugged loose the tiny coverlet I was still clutching in fear-cramped fingers and laid it out on the bed. "In fact, you were shrieking like a little girl. Quite piercing."

"Then, dash it, why didn't anybody help me?"

"Well, sir, after all—this is Third Class."

"I must say, Werner," said Aunt Jabbatha, "I am surprised—no, 'shocked' would be more accurate—to discover you didn't utterly botch this affair. In fact, you have almost done well. Your cousin Budgerigar is saved from a most unpleasant marriage, and you have scarcely broken anything I will have to pay for. There is the matter of several thousand credits worth of expensive Betelgeusian ham you filched, of course, which will come out of your allowance."

"Of course," I said glumly. The thing with aunts is, one does not argue if one wants to keep receiving one's allowance, even the tiny remaining fragment thereof. "Whatever you say, Auntie."

"And I think I shall leave Omnitron with you to keep you out of trouble."

Now that was a bit better. I could get used to being waited on by a stout machine like Omnitron, especially if it was going to prove useful in scraps like the one on the *Chinless*. "As you say, Auntie."

"He will in fact keep you company on your trip tomorrow to the spa on Indignation Nine."

"Beg your pardon?" Aunts have the habit of saying things that quite sneak past one's ears sometimes and don't reveal themselves in their true horror until they reach the old brainbox. "Spa? Is that meant to be a reward?" It didn't seem like my idea of the thing at all, which would have been an increase in allowance, or at least Aunt Jabbatha breaking out my late uncle's quite good brandy and offering me a snifter. "Is it at least one of those sun-and-tennis places?"

"No, you young idiot, it's a place to dry out. You're going to Indignation

Nine for the cure. You drink too much, and you are endangering your liver and kidneys. I intend to use them one day."

"Beg pardon? Did you say...use them?"

"Goodness, yes. You don't think I keep a blithering fool like you around because I like your conversation, do you? Someday I will harvest your organs and use them for myself." She frowned at the vat that contained her. "A person can grow tired of living in a jar, you know. I haven't been able to beat a servant properly in centuries. And I want to go dancing again!"

I left Aunt Jabbatha's house, accompanied by Omnitron. I was pensive with the awful twin visions of bits of the Inner Booster being removed and of my aunt cutting a rug at the Duke of Buckingham's spring do.

"Well, I can't say I'm very happy about any of this," I said. "Indignation Nine is supposed to be a famously dreadful place. They give you mineral water and rye toast and nothing more, then laugh at one's distress. I've even heard ugly rumors of..."—I lowered my voice—"...jumping jacks, Omnitron. Sit-ups! Calisthenics!"

"Buck up, sir." Omnitron leaned over and plucked a piece of lint from my lapel with one of his metal claspers. "At least you now have learned the falseness of your aunt's longtime allegations against you. That should be some comfort."

"What do you mean by that?"

"Well, sir, she has just made it very clear that, at least in the case of your kidneys and liver, she doesn't think you're a waste of human tissue after all."

I considered that for a moment. "By Jove, Omnitron," I said, "you're right."

"Of course, sir."

# Black Sunshine

FADE IN:

EXT.—PIERSON HOUSE, 1976—NIGHT
*From blackness to shadowy trees—a tangled orchard in moonlight. We move through them toward a three-story turn-of-the-century house with lights in the windows. As we track in, we hear Black Sabbath's "Iron Man" playing distantly on a stereo.*
CUT TO:

ERIC'S DREAM POV—*Micro close-up on a carpet—it's ALIVE, squirming with intricate patterns. "Iron Man" is ear-splitting now.*

> YOUNG JANICE
> Eric! Eric, talk to me!

*YOUNG ERIC'S POV swivels up from the carpet—things are dreamlike, compressed, distorted—it's an acid trip. YOUNG JANICE is so close that her face is distorted. We dimly see she is fifteen, maybe sixteen, wearing '70s clothes.*

> YOUNG JANICE
> Eric, I want to get out of here...!

*YOUNG BRENT lurches into view, looming above JANICE. He's chunky, teenage, clutching his hands against his stomach, panicky but trying to stay calm.*

> YOUNG BRENT

Shit, it's bad—Topher's freaking out for real up there.

> YOUNG JANICE

What's going on, Brent? Where's Kimmy?

> YOUNG BRENT

I don't know! I can't find her. I think...I think something bad happened! I tried to help Topher, and I...

*Just now realizing, BRENT lifts his hands away from his body and stares at them. They are smeared with blood. His eyes bug out.*

> YOUNG JANICE

Oh my God!

*Something is THUMPING on the ceiling above—something heavy thrashing around upstairs. As the POV looks upward, the ceiling suddenly becomes TRANSPARENT, a spreading puddle of translucency as though the ceiling were turning to smeared glass. A dark human shape (TOPHER) is lying on the floor of the room above, face pressed against the transparent ceiling as though it were a picture window, looking down on them. All we can make out of him is a huddled shape, distorted face, and a single staring eye.*

> TOPHER

Hey, Pierson—I seeeeee you...!

> YOUNG JANICE
> *(screaming)*

Eric!

FADE *with JANICE's cry still echoing, as we*
CUT TO:

INT.—ERIC'S MOTEL—NIGHT
*ADULT ERIC as he sits bolt upright in a motel bed, sweating.*

YOUNG JANICE
*(very faint now)*

Eric!

*ERIC PIERSON is sweaty, trembling. He's in his early forties, nice-looking, slender, but at this moment he could be twenty years older. He fumbles for a cigarette and sits smoking in the dark, as we*

ROLL CREDITS

EXT.—THE PIERSON HOUSE, NOW—MORNING
*ADULT ERIC drives down a long, dirt driveway. From atop a rise we see the house—the same house, but now sitting in a wide, empty DIRT FIELD several acres across: the orchard has been cut down. The house looks grim—peeling paint, screen door hanging halfway off. Hesitantly, he moves up the front steps and through the front door.*

INT.—HOUSE
*There's nothing Gothic or creepy about the place, it's just stripped and empty—carpets removed, no furniture, wallpaper peeling. ERIC hesitates again, then moves toward the dark stairwell. He flicks the switch—no light. He looks up the stairs, but a noise outside distracts him. A car with "Red Letter Realty" has pulled up beside his and someone is getting out.*

EXT.—HOUSE
*ERIC has returned to the dry front lawn, and stands with his back to the drive, looking up at the house. As an attractive, dark-haired woman in her late thirties approaches, he talks over his shoulder to her.*

ERIC
Things seem smaller when you see them after a

long time. I remembered this place as being so huge...

JANICE

That's funny, because I remembered you as being much shorter.

*ERIC turns, startled.*

ERIC

Janice? Janice? Oh, my God, what are you doing...
(looks at car)
Jesus. Are you the...

JANICE

The real-estate agent? Well, someone else in the office is actually handling it, but when I heard you were coming back to town to sign the sale papers, I said...
(shrugs)
Well, it seemed to make sense.

*ERIC is still staring at her.*

ERIC

You look...you look great.

JANICE

I look old. But thanks. You look okay yourself. I was sorry to hear about your grandmother.

ERIC

Well, ninety-two. We should all last so long. I thought she'd sold this years ago.

JANICE

She wasn't stupid, Eric. She was making the developers bid up the price—you can see this was the last property here. She did you a good turn.

ERIC
(*turns back to the house*)
It's hard to believe, huh? Those days seem like...like a dream.

JANICE

Not to me. I live around here, remember?

ERIC *turns at the harshness in her voice.*

ERIC

Is that bad?

JANICE

You didn't want to stay much. No, I guess it's all right. Not as exciting as Los Angeles, I'm sure.
(*she frowns, then tries to smile*)
But it's nice to send the kids off to school without firearms training.

ERIC

You...have kids?

JANICE

Callie and Jack—eight and six. But no, not at the moment. They're with their dad for the summer. We're divorced.

ERIC *is staring at the house again.*

ERIC

I was just going to visit Topher, then drive back,
but...hey, would you like to have dinner? It'd be nice
to catch up.

JANICE

You're...going to visit Topher?

ERIC

Thought I should. You want to come along?

JANICE

(shakes her head; then:)
You haven't seen him lately. It's bad.

ERIC

(shrugs)
Yeah, that's what they told me. So, dinner. What
do you say?

JANICE

I don't think it's a good idea, Eric.

ERIC

Just talk. Catch up. I...really feel like I need to.

JANICE

You don't want to catch up, Eric. It's better to leave
things alone.

ERIC

C'mon...Jan-Jan

JANICE *looks at him for a long moment, both touched and irritated by the use
of the name. She rolls her eyes like a schoolgirl.*

JANICE

Asshole.

FADE TO:

EXT.—LAS LOMAS CONVALESCENT HOSPITAL—DAY

*It's a quiet, decent place. ERIC pulls into the parking lot.*

INT.—HOSPITAL

*ERIC walks down the hallway, past various geriatrics in wheelchairs and one young man twisted with palsy. As ERIC's gaze sweeps across the young man's face, a voice speaks behind him.*

OLD WOMAN

Stop! Stop!

*He turns. A scowling OLD WOMAN in a wheelchair is following him.*

OLD WOMAN

It's all a mistake! Call my mother!

*ERIC walks on a little faster than before.*

CUT TO:

INT.—HOSPITAL LOUNGE

*The room is filled with old people on benches, in chairs, mostly staring into space. ERIC is talking with a NURSE in the lounge doorway. She points toward the corner. As ERIC approaches, looking around, he doesn't see TOPHER until the last moment—then a look of SHOCK runs across his face.*

FLASH CUT TO:

*TOPHER as a teenager in 1976, handsome, blond, surfer-ish, a shit-eating grin on his face as he lounges on a couch.*

TOPHER

Eric, my man! Have I got something for you...

CUT TO:

*TOPHER NOW, in his wheelchair.*
*He is startlingly grotesque, hairless and hunched, but his SKIN is the worst part—a crusty brown SHELL over his whole body, as though he's covered with dried mud. He sits as stiff as if paralyzed. Two pale blue eyes peer out of the masklike face.*

ERIC

(trying to cover his shock)

Topher, man. Long time. Long time... I'm sorry I haven't been to see you in a while. Life, man, it's just...you know.

*A horrible silence. TOPHER peers outward, not even looking at ERIC.*

ERIC (cont.)

I never...I never stop being sorry, man. It was just so screwed up. You...we never thought...

NURSE

(appearing over his shoulder)

Is everything all right?

*ERIC suddenly gets up and lurches toward the door.*

CLOSE-UP: *TOPHER'S FACE, staring at nothing.*

*In the doorway, the NURSE nods understandingly.*

NURSE

It's very disturbing if you haven't seen it before.

ERIC
(still in shock)
It's been years...


NURSE
It's come on very badly lately. Nobody knows what
it is. It's flexible at the joints, though, when he
moves. When we move him, that is—he doesn't do
anything himself, doesn't talk... The skin tissue is
unusual—hard and brittle, like...what is it insects
make? A chrysalis?
(she looks at ERIC)
I'm sorry, am I upsetting you? Is he a relative?


ERIC
(shaking his head)
High school friend...


FADE TO:


EXT.—RURAL ROAD—DAY, MINUTES LATER
ERIC is driving, face troubled. He fumbles for a tape and pushes it into the
player. Something contemporary begins to fill the car, as we
CUT TO:


INT.—HOSPITAL—SAME TIME
CLOSE-UP on TOPHER's strange face. The eyes blink for the first time,
slow-motion, as we
CUT TO:


INT.—REAL-ESTATE OFFICE—SAME TIME
JANICE, phone against her ear, is looking for something on top of her desk,
holding a styrofoam cup of coffee in her hand.


JANICE

...I think they're looking for something a bit less pricey...

*She looks at the coffee, which is suddenly black as ink. There is black on her hand, too, and smeared up her arm. She drops the black liquid to the floor, but her desk is covered in black smears too, and it's all over her legs and skirt and chair. She screams and leaps up, rubbing frantically at herself, as we*
CUT TO:

TOPHER'S EYES: *Another SLOW BLINK*

INT.—ERIC'S CAR
*The contemporary music abruptly twists sideways into the drum-and-screams intro of the Stones' "Sympathy for the Devil." Eric stares at the tape player, starts to pop the tape, then hears:*

TOPHER
Hook a right, man—time we got back to your place.

*The high-school TOPHER is sitting in the passenger seat, grinning, thumb pointing down a side road. ERIC gasps and hits the brakes. The car fishtails to a stop on the side of the road. ERIC stares. The passenger seat is EMPTY. The music is back to normal.*
CUT TO:

INT.—REAL ESTATE OFFICE
*JANICE is standing up, perfectly clean, her desk clean too, everything fine but for the coffee she spilled on the floor. All her co-workers are STARING at her, as we*
CUT TO:

EXT.—GAS STATION—MINUTES LATER
*ERIC has pulled his car into a small service station. The CASHIER, a fifty-something skinny guy with a beard and ponytail, wanders out. ERIC gets out and leans against the car, stunned.*

CASHIER

It's self-serve. Hey, you feel all right?

ERIC

Yeah, I guess so.

CASHIER

We got a bathroom if you need to puke or something.

ERIC

No, I...I think I just...had a flashback.

CASHIER
(chortles)

I know about that shit, man. Between acid and that Post Traumatic Stress shit, I've had so many of them things I prolly spend more time in the old days than I do in the right-now...

ERIC *is looking back over the fields and through the trees, as we* DISSOLVE TO:

INT.—RESTAURANT—NIGHT
ERIC *and* JANICE *eating dinner in an upscale Mexican restaurant. She has dolled up a bit, but has a sweater over her shoulders as though unwilling to relax too much. Neither is eating very heartily.*

ERIC

...Had no idea. Oh my God, he looks like...like...

JANICE

Like a monster. I know.

ERIC
It really got to me. I kind of freaked out on the
ride back.

JANICE *looks troubled, but also angry.*

JANICE
Yeah. Tension and guilt will do that to you.

ERIC
Are you saying I should feel guilty, Janice? I do. Of
course I do. But it's not all my fault.

JANICE
You sure left town like you thought it was.

*She has been fidgeting with her silverware. She waves a waiter over.*

JANICE *(cont.)*
Could you please give me a clean fork, if it's not too
much to ask? This fork is dirty. It's disgusting.

*The waiter leaves. ERIC looks at her. She stares defiantly back.*

JANICE *(cont.)*
Well, you did, didn't you?

ERIC
What did you want me to do? I had a scholarship
that fall, remember? Did you want me not to go to
UCLA?

JANICE
To become a journalist and save the world.

ERIC

To become a journalist, yeah, even if I didn't know
it then. Should I have just stayed?

JANICE

Of course not. Then you would have had to break
up with me face-to-face.

ERIC

C'mon—it was as much your idea as mine, wasn't
it?

JANICE

Maybe. But I didn't get to leave. I had to go to that
high school for two years. How do you think that
felt? To have people pointing at me, whispering
about me...?

ERIC

If you want me to say I'm sorry, Janice, I will. I'm
sorry.
          (He toys with his food.)
Didn't you have anyone else to talk to? What
about Brent?

JANICE

Oh, sure, Brent. I hardly saw him. He got all
weird—started reading like Tibetan Buddhism
and stuff.

ERIC

Brent? Reading books?

JANICE

He's a lot different, Eric. You'd hardly know him.

He's done really well, actually. He lost a lot of
weight, married some ex-model, owned his own
advertising agency in Los Angeles for a while, then
sold out and moved back here...

ERIC
Advertising agency? Oh, shit, he wasn't the Zenger
in Zenger-Kimball, was he? That's too weird.

JANICE
Like I said, you wouldn't recognize him...

DISSOLVE TO:

INT.—BRENT'S HOUSE—SAME TIME
*The ADULT BRENT ZENGER looks fit and successful—nice haircut, buff
body, expensive casual clothes. His wife TRACY and daughter JOANIE look
up from the couch where they're watching television. BRENT heads for the
closet to hang up his coat.*

BRENT
The man is home.

TRACY
Hi.

JOANIE
Hi, Daddy. The class hamster had babies.

BRENT
I'd love to hear about it after I get myself one little,
much-deserved drink.

TRACY
You're home late.

**BRENT**

Dinner with a client...

*He reaches the closet and throws open the door, starts to hang up his coat, then sees there's a light of some kind at the back of the closet. BRENT is surprised. He pushes through the coat hangers and discovers a door on the back of the closet, where clearly none has ever been before. He steps through it and into an EXACT DUPLICATE of the living room he's just left.*

**BRENT**

What the hell...?

**TRACY**
*(looking up in alarm)*
Who are you? What are you doing in here?

**JOANIE**

Mommy? Mommy!

**BRENT**

What are you talking about...?

**TRACY**
*(pulling JOANIE backward toward the phone)*
I don't know what you think you're doing, but I'm calling the police. Don't move!

**JOANIE**
*(crying)*
Who is that man, Mommy?

*Terrified, stunned, BRENT takes a stumbling step backward and falls into the closet. After a confused moment, he fights his way out of darkness again.*

TRACY

Brent? What on earth are you doing? Do you need some help?

JOANIE

Daddy's tangled up in the coats!

CLOSE UP—BRENT, *pale and shaken, as we*
DISSOLVE TO:

EXT.—RESTAURANT PARKING LOT—NIGHT
*JANICE and ERIC are walking through the lot. She has her sweater pulled tight around her shoulders.*

ERIC

...And she put all my stuff in boxes and put them out on the sidewalk with—you know those label guns? With a label on each one reading "property of shit head." Which is how I became single again.
        (*a beat*)
Hey, I thought you would have enjoyed hearing about my hopeless love life.

JANICE

Oh, Eric, I never wished you bad luck. Not really.
        (*a beat*)
I'm sorry if...if I wasn't very good company tonight. I told you this was a poor idea.

ERIC

I said I'm sorry about everything, Janice. I really am, I...I was just scared of the whole thing. You, life, what happened...

*They have stopped beside his car.*

JANICE

I accept the apology. I did stupid things too. Let's just say goodnight and maybe we can be friends again. That would be something, wouldn't it? After all this time?

ERIC

It sure would.

*He reaches out and takes her hand, holding it awkwardly for a moment—he's trying to find a way to pull her closer but she's quietly resisting. Abruptly he drops her hand and walks to his car.*

JANICE

Eric?

ERIC

Hang on a second.

*He fumbles around, then pops a tape into the player and leaves the door open as he walks back. The quiet intro to Traffic's "Low Spark of High Heeled Boys" begins to play.*

JANICE

I know that.

ERIC

Of course you do. This is now officially middle-aged-people's music.

*He suddenly takes her hand again, then pulls her toward him.*

ERIC *(cont.)*

Remember slow dancing?

> JANICE
>
> The only kind you could do. A casualty of the Disco
> Invasion is what you were. C'mon, Eric, stop.

> ERIC
>
> Just a dance. Better than arguing. Come on.

*JANICE allows herself to be drawn slowly into a dance.*

> JANICE
>
> You do know you're going back to your motel alone,
> don't you?

> ERIC
>
> All the more reason to be quiet and let me enjoy
> this...

*They circle across the parking lot, under the lights. A foursome walks past them and makes joking comments, but sweetly—it's a nice moment.*
SLOW DISSOLVE TO:

EXT.—PIERSON HOUSE, 1976—NIGHT
*Another quiet song rises up, supplanting Traffic's—it's Roxy Music's "In Every Dream Home a Heartache." Five people are sitting on the roof of the house. It's a summer evening, last rays of sunset just vanishing, and the lights of other houses are far on the other side of the orchard.*

*Five teenagers are sitting along the edge of the roof, passing a joint. YOUNG ERIC and YOUNG JANICE are pressed close. Chunky YOUNG BRENT, wearing cutoffs and deck shoes, is dangling his feet over the edge and taking his turn with the joint. KIMMY, a small girl with glasses, a hooded sweatshirt, and overalls, sits a yard or so from him but close to YOUNG JANICE. TOPHER sits against the chimney, swigging from a bottle of Bacardi.*

YOUNG ERIC

Last night of summer.

YOUNG JANICE

Shut up. You'll ruin it.

YOUNG BRENT
(*inhaling deeply*)

Nothing could ruin it but running out of dope. I love this song. Manzanera rocks so bad on this solo that it isn't funny.

YOUNG ERIC

The last night of the last summer we're all in high school together. The night summer vacation dies forever.

TOPHER
(*reaching down to take the joint*)

Oh, shit. Poetry alert!

*Everybody laughs.*

YOUNG ERIC

Okay, I'll just shut up.

YOUNG JANICE

No, baby, you're so sweet when you talk. But just be quiet for a little while, okay?

*She presses in against his side. TOPHER passes the joint to KIMMY. After a hit, she starts to cough. JANICE leans over to slap her back.*

YOUNG JANICE (*cont.*)

Kimmy, just take little hits! You always do that.

KIMMY
(raspy, almost unable to talk)
At least I didn't throw up. This time.


TOPHER
Erky. Throw me a cigarette, man.


ERIC *tosses up his pack.* TOPHER *takes one and lights it.*


KIMMY
How long are your grandparents gone, Eric?


YOUNG ERIC
Weeks. Months. Years.


YOUNG BRENT
(laughing)
Erky is high.


YOUNG JANICE
They missed their plane. They were supposed to be
back today.


*The Roxy Music song has been playing under all this, and it's building to a
climax now.* YOUNG TOPHER *stands up and begins playing air-guitar,
using the rum bottle as the guitar neck. He sings along with the song being
played.*


YOUNG ERIC
Yeah, and if you get too fucked up and put a
foot through my grandparents' roof, it'll be my
fucking heartache, all right. Topher, what are you
doing?

YOUNG BRENT
Topher's higher than Erky.

YOUNG JANICE
Topher, be careful...

*The climax of the song comes. TOPHER strides down to the edge of the roof and braces himself, serenading the orchard and surrounding town. He begins to sing, quiet but getting louder, then bellowing the final line about blowing his mind..*

*As the guitar solo comes wailing in, TOPHER staggers for a moment on the edge of the roof, air-strumming the bottle. Abruptly, he pitches over the edge and vanishes. After a stunned second:*

YOUNG ERIC
Shit!

KIMMY
(*almost crying*)
Is he hurt? Is he hurt?

YOUNG ERIC
Topher, man? You all right?

YOUNG TOPHER
(*weakly; offscreen*)
It was all great, except the last little bit. But I think
I spilled some of my Bacardi.

YOUNG BRENT
(*relieved*)
You are such an asshole, man!

YOUNG ERIC

Are you sure you're okay?

*As ERIC begins climbing down from the roof, TOPHER suddenly sits up.*

YOUNG TOPHER

Shit!
                    *(fumbles in pockets)*
If those fuckers get lost...
                    *(finds what he's looking for)*
Ah. Far out.

YOUNG ERIC

Don't do shit like that, man.

YOUNG TOPHER

I fucking thought I smashed these or something.

YOUNG ERIC

Smashed what?

YOUNG TOPHER

Let's go in, man, put on some more tunes—I'll
show you. It's a surprise...

*As Roxy Music plays out, we*
DISSOLVE TO:

EXT.—ERIC'S MOTEL—NIGHT
*Just to establish the transition, we see the outside of a mid-grade side-of-the-road motel. We move in on ERIC's room.*

INT.—ERIC'S MOTEL—NIGHT
*ADULT ERIC is sleeping. We move in on his face, lips moving a little, hear his voice in a dreaming whisper:*

ERIC

Topher, don't...

CUT TO:

*Quick FLASH of TOPHER's distorted current face coming out of shadow, as though it were in ERIC's room.*

*ERIC wakes up, gasping, but there's nothing in the room but a little light from the streetlights leaking through the curtain. ERIC lets his head fall back, then we hear a faint noise. ERIC sits up: he hears it. It's someone CRYING.*

*Looking really disturbed, ERIC glances at the digital clock, which reads 3:17. We hear the crying a little louder—a woman's voice, a hopeless, quiet weeping. ERIC stands up by the bed, turning his head slowly, locating the source of the sound. It's more upsetting to him than us, because he RECOGNIZES it.*

*ERIC moves slowly across the dark room toward the bathroom door, which is closed. He slowly leans his head against the door and we hear the crying louder. He looks terrified. The crying gets louder.*

ERIC

K-K-Ki...Kimmy?

*The crying continues, a little more frightened and miserable now.*

ERIC

Kimmy, is...is that you?

KIMMY
*(tiny, whispery voice)*

I'm so scared.

*ERIC, hands shaking violently, tries the door. It's locked.*

ERIC

Kimmy, let me in.

KIMMY

I'm...scared. Eric, where is everyone? What's happening?

*Something THUMPS, as though someone has just climbed into the bathtub. The thumping gets louder—something very strange is happening in the bathroom.*

ERIC

Kimmy? Kimmy!

*Her weeping has changed to sounds of panicked grunts, like someone fighting for their life or being raped.*

KIMMY

Why...why can't...I...see? You told me...you told me I could see...everything!

*On "everything," the door finally pops open in ERIC's hand. He throws on the light. The bathroom is EMPTY. He staggers back, looks wildly at the clock. It reads 3:18, as we CUT TO:*

INT.—HOSPITAL—NIGHT, SAME TIME

*We see TOPHER's strange head on a pillow, eyes open, staring straight up into the darkness. A light from outside is making tree-branch shadows flail on the walls and across his expressionless face, but he is utterly, utterly still.*
CUT TO:

INT.—JANICE'S KITCHEN—NIGHT

*ADULT JANICE is in her dressing gown, hugging herself against a chill, stumbling a little as though just awakened. There's streetlight coming through the blinds and a bathroom light in the hall. She takes a glass and fills it from a dispenser bottle of water by the refrigerator, then drinks it, as we*

CUT TO:

CLOSE UP: RIM OF GLASS
*There's an ANT on the glass, feelers waving.*
*JANICE makes an "urp" of shock and jerks the glass away from her mouth,*
*then slams it down in the sink. A moment later she snatches it up again,*
*plunges it under the faucet and washes the ANT down the drain. She looks,*
*and there are a few ANTS on the dispenser bottle as well. A little less*
*surprised now, but just as unhappy, she starts to lift the bottle into the sink,*
*then snatches her hand back. There are more than a couple of ants—at least a*
*dozen are running along the counter and in a line to the refrigerator door. She*
*takes a napkin and flicks them off the handle, then pulls open the refrigerator,*
*spilling out the light.*
CUT TO:

INTERIOR OF REFRIGERATOR
*There are MILLIONS of ANTS in the refrigerator—a boiling black mass that*
*tumbles out the door and all over the linoleum. JANICE leaps back, shrieking*
*and shrieking and shrieking as we go to BLACK and then, when the screams*
*have faded, DISSOLVE TO:*

INT.—MOTEL COFFEE SHOP—MORNING
*ADULT JANICE and ADULT ERIC are having coffee. They both look like*
*hell—they clearly haven't slept.*

ERIC

I...I've been having bad dreams for a few weeks
now. About...that night. That's one of the reasons
I decided to come back. I thought, y'know, seeing
the place again...

JANICE

But not me. Just the place.

ERIC

I didn't think you'd WANT to see me. Stop playing
games. You've been having them too, haven't you?

                    JANICE
Yeah. But it wasn't bad at first. Just a couple of
nightmares, and I used to have those all the
time. But...things have started happening. In the
daytime.

                    ERIC
Me too. Bad. Bad stuff.

                    JANICE
But why? It's too weird, Eric. It doesn't make sense.
I'm scared I'm going crazy.

                    ERIC
I don't think so—not both of us at the same time.
                  (he stands up)
Well, as long as I'm back in town, I guess it's time to
go see another old friend...

DISSOLVE TO:

EXT.—BRENT'S HOUSE—HALF AN HOUR LATER
*The house is big, nice, with two SUVs in the driveway. ERIC and JANICE
are on the front porch.*

                    JANICE
We could have called first...

                    ERIC
If he's really Zenger-Kimball, I don't trust ad guys
on the phone.

JANICE

He's still Brent!

ERIC

Yeah. Whatever that means after twenty-five years.

*The door opens. BRENT ZENGER doesn't look good. In fact, he looks worse than ERIC and JANICE: it's early in the morning and he has a drink in his hand and a sour, sick expression on his face.*

BRENT

Hey, Janice. Pierson. Long time.

ERIC

You don't seem surprised to see us.

*BRENT shrugs and turns, waving for them to follow him. He leads them across the entry into the large living room. The television is playing and there's a Bacardi bottle on top of it, half-full.*

BRENT

Drink?

ERIC

A bit early.

BRENT

Tracy and Joanie are out at the park.
(looks at Eric)
My wife and kid. Sit down.

ERIC

Like I said, Brent, you don't look surprised to see us.

BRENT

Not feeling very surprised today, I guess. Watching
Jenny Jones'll do that to you—kind of burns the
surprise glands right out.

ERIC

Me and Janice—we've been having some weird
dreams. Ring any bells?

BRENT

Yeah, and it's nice to see you, too, Pierson. It HAS
been a long time. I'm doing well, thanks for asking.

JANICE

Neither of us has had much sleep, Brent. Eric
doesn't mean to be rude.

BRENT

That's pretty good, Pierson. Back after twenty years
and already she's sticking up for you again.
(he looks around)
Do you think there's too much white in this room?
Tracy kind of bugged out on the all-white thing.

ERIC

Have you been to see Topher?

BRENT

I saw him. Once. That was enough.

JANICE

He's gotten a lot worse.

BRENT

No shit.

ERIC
(*angry*)
Look—enough! Brent, man, I'm sorry I haven't been around. You could have called me too, for that matter. But the fact is that we went different ways.

BRENT
Yeah. It happens.

ERIC
So let's cut the bullshit, okay? I knew you in the fucking third grade, man. Being a grown-up sucks, cool, we'll all agree. Now let's get down to business. There's something really strange going on. Janice and I have been having hallucinations, all about that night. THAT night. Nothing else. How about you?

BRENT
I don't really want to spend a lot of time thinking about that shit.

ERIC
It doesn't feel like we have much choice.
(*a beat*)
It's happening to you, too, isn't it? How long?

BRENT
I don't know what you're talking about.

ERIC
Don't give me that, man, I know you. How long? Weeks?

BRENT
(*after a pause*)
Yeah. For a while. But it goes away sometimes.

ERIC
Maybe it did, but now it's getting worse. We have to do something.

BRENT
(*laughs*)
Oh, yeah? What's that? Write a little Sunday magazine section piece? "High School Nightmare Reunions"? Or maybe call the cops? The dream police? What the fuck do you think we can do about it, Erky?

ERIC
It's something to do with Topher. I could feel it when I saw him. There's something...alive in there. Angry.

JANICE
That doesn't make any sense.

ERIC
None of this does—but it's happening. We have to go see him. All of us. If this is something to do with...that stuff...that stuff he took...

BRENT
Talk to him? You really have turned into liberal dickhead, Pierson, just like I always thought you would. What are we going to say? "If that's you fucking with our minds, Topher, could you please stop?" You must be joking.

ERIC

He was our friend...

BRENT

And look at him now! You think talking to that... thing is going to change anything? Is it going to change the past? Is it going to make up for what happened to him, to...to Kimmy?

*Shockingly, BRENT suddenly bursts into tears—he's had quite a lot to drink.*

BRENT *(cont.)*

Kimmy. Oh, man, poor Kimmy... Shit!

JANICE

It's okay, Brent. It wasn't your fault, either...

BRENT

Okay? It fucking well is not. And if you want to go talk to that...that thing...go ahead. But don't expect me to come with you. I wouldn't go within a mile of that freak.

ERIC

That doesn't make...

BRENT

Just get out. Get out of here before my wife comes home. I used to tell her about what great friends I had. Don't fuck it up for me.

JANICE

Brent, come on...

> BRENT
> (*shouting*)
> Get out of my damned house!

CUT TO:

INT.—ERIC'S CAR—MINUTES LATER
*They are driving out of BRENT's nice neighborhood.*

> ERIC
> That went well, didn't it?

> JANICE
> He's terrified. What's going on?

> ERIC
> Guess what. I'm terrified too...

DISSOLVE TO:

INT.—HOSPITAL—AN HOUR LATER
*JANICE and ERIC are talking to an ADMINISTRATOR at the main desk,
a lady in her fifties or early sixties.*

> ADMINISTRATOR
> I don't quite understand what you're asking, sir.
> Mr. Holland's records are private, but I can assure
> you he's been getting the best possible care.

> ERIC
> Who DOES have access to his records? His father's
> dead—he must have a legal guardian.

> ADMINISTRATOR
> He has an aunt in Northern California. But I'm not

sure I should be discussing any of this with you. He's been a patient with us for almost thirteen years now. I recognize Mrs. Moorehead, but I don't think I've even seen you before.

ERIC
(to JANICE)
Mrs. Moorehead?

JANICE
(to ADMINISTRATOR)
That's fine, thanks. We were mainly wondering about whether there had been any...changes. To his condition.

ADMINISTRATOR
Only the skin problem, which seems to be getting worse.

ERIC
But what did they say when they sent him here...?

JANICE pulls him away.

ERIC (cont.)
He was in a government psychiatric hospital— under security. I still have the clippings. Would they really just let him go?

JANICE
(a little angry)
This isn't some big investigative report, Eric. Topher hasn't spoken or moved in years. His dad went to court and asked to have him sent here, so he'd be closer to home.

ERIC
(disgusted)
His old man must have been happy Topher couldn't
get into trouble any more.

The OLD WOMAN ERIC has seen earlier rolls out in front of them, then
paces them until they stop in front of TOPHER's door.

OLD WOMAN
(eyes wide)
You going in there?

JANICE
We're going to see a friend.

OLD WOMAN
(grabbing ERIC's arm)
You tell my mother I been good. Tell her I never
went in there.

As they open the door, she rolls herself backward down the hall.

OLD WOMAN (cont.)
That's where the devil lives...

The door swings open. It's a small room, but with TOPHER at the far end it
seems very large. He is sitting in his wheelchair by the bed, staring at nothing.
ERIC and JANICE hesitate, then JANICE at last moves forward and sits on
the bed. ERIC picks up a chair and puts himself on the other side of TOPHER.

JANICE
Eric and I are here to see you, Topher. We've been
thinking about you a lot.

ERIC

Yeah. A lot.


JANICE

We've been having...bad dreams. About that night.
We thought...you might be having bad dreams too.


*ERIC looks at her, a little surprised; this is an unexpected approach. He
struggles to find the wavelength.*


ERIC

We...want to help you. God, man, we're so sorry
that this happened to you. To all of us.


*TOPHER is rigid as a statue, staring past them.*


ERIC *(cont.)*

But it isn't anybody's fault. It just...happened.


*JANICE hesitates, then reaches out and takes TOPHER's hand. It's a brave
act—we can sense how weird it must feel.*


JANICE

I haven't slept well in months, Topher. You know
I've tried to help you, come visit you. How can I
do that if I'm scared all the time? If I can't get any
sleep?


ERIC

We were all friends, remember? Before that...that
bad night. We're still your friends. We...we miss
you.
*(after a long moment, he touches TOPHER's other hand.)*
Please, man. Please.

*The strange tableau falls silent, two people holding hands with a rigid monstrosity, as we*
DISSOLVE TO:

EXT.—BRENT'S HOUSE—SAME TIME
*ADULT BRENT is loading things into his SUV. It looks like he's getting the family ready for a camping vacation, but not a happy one: he's very blank and silent, even though his wife TRACY is standing at the front door, talking to him.*

> TRACY
>
> Brent? What are you doing? Are we going some-
> where?

*He continues to load the SUV, not answering.*

> TRACY (*cont.*)
>
> Whatever it is you're doing, we're not going
> anywhere until you talk to me. What's going on?
> It's like I don't even know who you are anymore...!

*BRENT slows and then stops in the middle of the driveway like a toy winding down. He puts his hands over his face, shoulders shaking.*

> TRACY
>
> Brent? Brent, you're scaring me...

INT.—ERIC'S CAR—LATE AFTERNOON
*They are driving along a tree-lined road. Both look troubled.*

> ERIC
>
> ...I mean, what was that all about? Are we saying
> that it's Topher who's making us see these things?
> There are a lot of better explanations, Janice.
> Janice?

JANICE shakes her head, too tired to talk about it. We close on JANICE's face, her eyes closed, thinking, hand on head like she's got a migraine coming on. The sound of The Doors' "Riders on the Storm" comes up slowly, filling the car.

> JANICE
> I don't want to hear any music, Eric. Could you turn the tape off?

> ERIC
> (sounding strange)
> It's not the tape player.

> JANICE
> (opens eyes)
> Then turn off the fucking radio! My head hurts.

> ERIC
> I didn't turn it on. It's not on.

As they both stare at the dark radio dial and the music grows louder, something suddenly appears for an instant in front of the car—a dark shape. JANICE and ERIC both shout in terror and ERIC jams on the brakes, sending the car squealing and sliding. Something THUMPS against the car as they screech to a halt, halfway across the road.

> JANICE
> We hit somebody! We hit somebody!

ERIC is sitting stunned in his seat, trying to get his breath, when something large and dark lands on the windshield. For a moment there's a dim glimpse of YOUNG TOPHER's face, distorted against the glass, then he bursts into roaring FLAMES which surround the car.

TOPHER
(screaming with laughter in the flames)
I see you! I see you!

An instant later the FLAMES vanish. Everything is NORMAL, the car still skewed across the empty road, but no sign of anything else. ERIC turns to JANICE, bloodless, shocked. She's just as devastated.

JANICE
Oh, my God, Eric, what's happening to us...?

We pull back slowly from the pair of them, back until we see the car in the middle of the country road, back and back, as we
DISSOLVE TO:

EXT.—HOSPITAL—NIGHT
The wind is blowing the trees, hard. Except for a light in the front lobby, the hospital windows are all dark. The wind gets stronger, the tree-shadows flailing along the walls.

INT.—BRENT'S HOUSE—SAME TIME
BRENT is sitting cross-legged on the floor in front of the television. The sound is off. As we pan around we see that he has a bottle and glass on the rug in front of him. The glass is upside-down. BRENT has arranged five BULLETS in a little circle on the bottom of the glass, and is holding the sixth in his hand, looking at it. A gun is lying on the carpet next to his leg.

INT.—JANICE'S HOUSE—SAME TIME
JANICE and ERIC have finished a meal of take-out food. JANICE is washing the few dishes while ERIC wanders around in the kitchen/dining room. We can hear the wind getting LOUD outside. He picks up a picture of JANICE'S CHILDREN and looks at it.

JANICE

I'm glad you're here. I don't think I could have faced spending the night here by myself.

ERIC

I felt the same about the motel. So...tell me about your marriage. Was he a good guy?

JANICE

Terry? I don't know. He's an engineer. Not the most talkative guy in the world. I thought I could make it work. It seemed like a good idea at the time...

ERIC

What went wrong?

JANICE

Nothing, really. But nothing went right after a while, either. Another guy I cared more about than he cared about me.
(turns, drying her hands)
But it's different when a marriage goes off the tracks and you have kids. It's...there's still something that worked. I love my children. I miss them so much.

ERIC

I can't seem to get a handle on it. You married. Children.

JANICE

It's been a quarter of a century, Pierson. You haven't exactly stayed in touch.

ERIC

All I've been doing since I came back here is saying I'm sorry, and it doesn't seem to be working on anyone. But I am sorry, Janice, especially about the way I treated you. Shit, I didn't know what was going on—I was numb, crazy. I was a kid! We were all kids. I just wanted it all to go away.

*JANICE sits down on the couch. ERIC joins her.*

### JANICE

I used to call you. You never called back. It was horrible, having to keep leaving messages with those guys in your dorm—I could just hear them thinking, "Oh, no, it's that pathetic hometown chick that Pierson dropped..."

### ERIC

It wasn't like that...

### JANICE

But you know what the worst thing was? Do you remember that stupid song about the telephone? It was playing every time I turned the radio on that fall.

*JANICE blinks angrily, fighting tears.*

### ERIC

I never liked Electric Light Orchestra, anyway. Brent really hated 'em. Said they'd gone downhill after Roy Wood left the group.

### JANICE

Boys. You can talk about guitar solos, but anything else just paralyzes you, doesn't it?

### ERIC

Look, for years there wasn't a fucking day that went by when I didn't think about how things went so wrong—with you and me, that night...everything. Over and over. Thinking about how if I'd only done this thing different or that thing different...

JANICE
(*after a pause*)
What are we going to do, Eric? I'm frightened.

ERIC *shakes his head, then moves closer to her and puts his arm around her. She relaxes into his chest.*

ERIC
I have no idea at all. I'm scared shitless myself. But this feels good. It's the first thing that's felt that way for a while.
(*a beat*)
I haven't really been able to make it work with anyone. Scared I never will. Sometimes it feels like I'm getting paid back for being a shit to you, back then.

JANICE *lifts her face to look at him. She has a tear on her cheek. ERIC gently wipes it away with his finger. After a moment, he touches her cheek again, letting his hand stay. She leans forward and they kiss. What starts out careful and tentative begins to turn passionate—JANICE is crying as they kiss, almost climbing onto his lap. Then she pulls away.*

JANICE
No. No, it's not right.

ERIC
If you want...

JANICE

After all these years, I don't know what I want. But you don't know me any more, Eric. I'm not the same person, and neither are you. We can't just fall into bed. We'd be...I don't know, fucking our past, not each other.

ERIC

Seems like it's our past that's fucking us. In more ways than one.

JANICE *slowly moves back against his chest.*

JANICE

You're still pretty funny, you know? Too bad it's true.
                    (*after a moment*)
I was so scared.

ERIC

It's been a weird day all around.

JANICE

No! Back then. That night. I was acting cool because I hated you guys treating me like a wimpy girl, but I didn't really want to take that stuff...

DISSOLVE TO:

INT.—PIERSON HOUSE, 1976—NIGHT
CLOSE ON: BRENT'S PALM
YOUNG BRENT *is shaking a little bit of something out of a pill bottle onto the cotton wadding in his hand. As we pull back, we see that everyone is sitting in a circle on the living room floor, except TOPHER who is lying on the couch with his feet up.*

YOUNG BRENT

Four-way windowpane. Decks are cleared. Ready
to beam up, Mr. Spock.

KIMMY
(nervously)
I thought acid came in, like, a sugar cube.

YOUNG BRENT

That was in the old days. This is the latest and greatest. Come on, you don't know who your friends
really are until you trip with them—right, Erky?

YOUNG ERIC
(singing)
"Oh I wish I was an Oscar Mayer wiener..."

YOUNG BRENT

Five hits. Kimmy, put a record on so we don't have
to listen to fucking Pierson.

YOUNG ERIC
(finishing)
"Everyone would be in love with me!"

YOUNG JANICE

You wish.

KIMMY

What should I put on?

YOUNG BRENT

I don't know. You got anything decent, Pierson?

You got Yes? *Fragile* would be pretty bitchin'.

### KIMMY
Here's a Yes album, I think. It's hard to read the writing.

*As she's putting it on, YOUNG TOPHER swings his legs down from the couch back and sits looking over the others as the acoustic intro of "And You and I" begins. JANICE and KIMMY are both clearly nervous.*

### YOUNG JANICE
They're so tiny! How long is this going to last?

### YOUNG BRENT
A while. I wish I could have got Stringer to get me this stuff earlier—it's amazing to go, like, to the park. The grass looks alive.

### YOUNG ERIC
The grass is alive.

### YOUNG BRENT
You know what I mean.
(*to Kimmy*)
But wait 'til you see the stars. They look just...far out.

### YOUNG ERIC
They are far out.

*Everyone laughs, even BRENT.*

### YOUNG BRENT
(*in a bad Brooklyn accent*)
Quit bustin' my balls, Pierson.

(holds out the acid; normal voice:)
Okay, boys and girls. Come and get it!

YOUNG TOPHER
Slow down, Zenger. I wanna show you guys something.

YOUNG BRENT
Fuck, Holland, this shit doesn't even come on for an hour. Let's just take it and then you can show us.

YOUNG TOPHER
(enjoying his mystery)
No, you're definitely gonna wanta see this first.

There's a pause: TOPHER's clearly waiting to be asked.

YOUNG ERIC
Okay, what is it?

TOPHER extends his hand, in a fist, palmside down, then turns it over and uncurls his fingers to reveal five shiny BLACK PILLS.

YOUNG BRENT
What the fuck are those?

YOUNG TOPHER
The. Fucking. Best. High. Ever.

YOUNG BRENT
Looks like speed, man. Black beauties.

YOUNG TOPHER
Oh, no, my little Bent Zengerdenger. This is shit

you've never seen. Ain't nobody ever seen this. This...is Black Sunshine.

### YOUNG ERIC

Topher, what exactly the hell are you talking about?

*TOPHER slides from the couch onto the floor, takes a theatrical swig from the rum bottle, enjoying everyone's attention. Just to piss them off, he takes an elaborate time lighting a cigarette, too.*

### YOUNG BRENT

Come on. Jesus!

### YOUNG JANICE

Ooh, the mystery man.

### YOUNG TOPHER

Okay, you know the lab? The place my old man works?

### YOUNG BRENT

Where you have a job pushing a broom on Saturday mornings?

### YOUNG TOPHER
*(unfazed)*

Yeah. That lab. Well, Castillo the fuckin' head janitor had to go home because he got sick—he was, like, green—and he left me the keys to lock up. Man, normally he'd rather leave me alone with his fuckin' daughter than even let me touch 'em, but he was in bad shape, pukin' his lungs out all over the restroom...

### YOUNG ERIC

You have a gift for storytelling, amigo.

### YOUNG TOPHER
I do, don't I? So anyway, I thought it might be a good time to check out the drug refrigerator, the one that's always locked with this big old fuckin' lock? Just in case they had some like pharmaceutical quality coke lying around, or some shit like that.

### KIMMY
Topher! You could go to jail.

### YOUNG TOPHER
Not unless I was stupid enough to get caught. So I'm checking it out, and they've got a little glass jar of these babies in the back, in some kind of a plastic envelope, with all these yellow warning stickers. The name was fucked up—Dee-oh-noxy-somefucking or other—but right there on the label it says, "hallucinogen." You know what that means, right, Pierson? 'Cause you're so smart and shit in English?

### YOUNG ERIC
You stole some drugs you don't know anything about, except they said "hallucinogen"? You're crazy, Topher.

### YOUNG TOPHER
(*suddenly angry*)
Don't fucking talk to me like you're my dad or something, Pierson. I'm not stupid. I had the keys, remember, like to the files and stuff? I went and looked in the folders, checked it out. It's an

experimental drug they're working on for some government project, and it's basically just like acid, except cleaner, 'cause there's a couple of different electrons or some chemistry shit like that.

### YOUNG BRENT

Fuckin A. Experimental acid? For the government? What kind of shit is that?

### YOUNG ERIC

And you just walked off with 'em? Like they're not going to notice.

### YOUNG TOPHER

Cool out, man. I found some other pills that looked just like 'em—some kinda water-retention shit. So if they give 'em out to somebody for an experiment they won't get high, they'll just get...whatever. Bloated.
            *(cackles)*
And the scientist guys'll just say it's like "a nonstandard reaction to the medication." I hear my dad talk about this stuff.
            *(brightly)*
So, whaddaya say? Let's get high!

### YOUNG JANICE
*(incredulous)*
Huh? You don't think we're going to take those, do you?

### KIMMY

I think maybe I should go home.

### YOUNG BRENT

No! No, don't, Kimmy. It's cool. We're just going to take acid—Topher's only playing around.

### YOUNG TOPHER
I ain't fuckin' playin' around, Zenger. This is fuckin' straight up. What, are you all pussies? No offense, ladies.

### YOUNG ERIC
Just cool out, Topher. It was pretty amazing you did that, but we're not going to take something no one's ever heard about. What is this "Black Sunshine" shit, anyway? They give their drugs names like that?

### YOUNG TOPHER
I made it up. Pretty bitchin', huh? I made a copy of Castillo's key too. If this shit is half as good as I think it is, I'm gonna creep half the next batch and sell it for ten bucks a hit. Send some to Ozzy and the boys and get a backstage pass forever. Come on, Pierson—it'll be far fucking out!

ERIC *shakes his head grimly.* BRENT *has already begun giving out his* WINDOWPANE ACID *to the girls.*

### YOUNG BRENT
Just forget it, Holland. Come on, you'll blow the mood. We're just getting to the good part of this song.

BRENT *puts his own portion on his tongue, then hands the rest to* ERIC; *as* ERIC *takes his, the girls look at each other.*

### YOUNG JANICE

We're just going to take half.

*They break one hit of acid in half and each take part, KIMMY having trouble swallowing. ERIC turns and offers the last squares of WINDOWPANE on his fingertip to TOPHER.*

> ### YOUNG TOPHER
> I can't fuckin' believe you guys. The last night of summer. Fuckin' lightweights! What have you got to lose, Erky? You ain't even staying around this asshole town.

*He holds the five black pills in his hands and stares at them, then stares at ERIC's proffered acid. BRENT has his eyes closed, swaying to the music—one hand is against KIMMY's leg, which she's trying to ignore. TOPHER looks them all over, then abruptly THROWS the five pills up in the air.*

CLOSE ON: BLACK PILLS, TUMBLING

*As they come down, TOPHER lets them fall into his mouth like candy. It's hard to tell whether they all make it in—at least one bounces away—but from the way TOPHER holds his mouth closed, he's clearly got some.*

> ### ERIC
> *(genuinely startled)*
> Fuck, man, what are you doing...?

> ### JANICE
> Topher? You're joking, right? Spit them out!

*TOPHER swallows elaborately, then grins.*

> ### YOUNG TOPHER
> Party time...!

DISSOLVE TO:

INT.—JANICE'S HOUSE—MIDNIGHT
ADULT ERIC and ADULT JANICE have fallen asleep on the couch, curled together. Shadows are moving across their faces—it's windy outside. JANICE is twitching. ERIC is murmuring in his sleep, small, unintelligible sounds of fear.

INT.—BRENT'S HOUSE—SAME TIME
ADULT BRENT is lying face down on the rug with the bottle of rum tipped over beside him, wind moaning in the chimney. At first we think he might be dead, but as we move closer we see the sixth BULLET is still gripped in his fingertips.

INT.—CONVALESCENT HOSPITAL—SAME TIME
TOPHER'S POV: We are looking down a long hospital corridor, from TOPHER'S POV—it's his odd SHADOW we see on the wall beside us. The wind is loud now, wailing. As the shadow passes across the open doors of the patients' rooms, we hear some of them cry out loudly in nightmares. We see others flail in their beds. The shadow passes the nursing station where the DUTY NURSE is sleeping as though she's been poleaxed; as the shadow crosses her she flinches and whimpers. A few more steps and our POV reaches the hospital's front doors, which FLY OPEN so hard the glass shatters. The sound of the wind is a ROAR now. POV pauses for a moment, looking out on the dark and the trees.

We are now behind the dark humanoid SHAPE, which moves out the doors, out of our view. The doors swing back, as if the force that held them open has released them. A few more shards of glass tinkle. The winds are still fierce.

Our viewpoint turns, moving back down the hall much faster than we came the other way, past the sleeping nurse, past a few patients wandering in the hall, lost and weeping, to TOPHER's room.

On the bed is the hardened shell of TOPHER'S DISCARDED SKIN, a

*horrible relic, clearly empty now, lying cracked open, broken into several pieces on the white sheets.*
SLOW DISSOLVE TO:

INT.—JANICE'S HOUSE—MORNING
CLOSE ON ADULT ERIC'S FACE: *He's sleeping, still fully dressed on the couch. JANICE comes into the room in a bathrobe, toweling her hair. She stands over him, a look of troubled fondness on her face, then lays her hand on his cheek for a long moment before sliding it down to his shoulder and gently shaking him.*

> JANICE
> Wake up, Rip Van Winkle. The power's off. I used most of the not-very-hot water on a quick shower, so you have a choice—a cup of lukewarm water to wash with, or a cup of lukewarm water to make instant coffee with.

> ERIC
> *(groaning)*
> An embarrassment of riches. Jesus, give me the coffee, please.
> *(a beat)*
> It was nice. Holding you last night.

> JANICE
> Oh, shit! It's Saturday, isn't it? I have to call the kids about when they're coming in so I can pick them up. Where's my watch?
> *(she examines it)*
> After ten. Damn.

> ERIC
> When are they due back?

> JANICE

Tomorrow. School starts on Monday.
> (*she picks up the phone*)

Oh, damn, damn, damn, the phone's out too. I
knew I should have gotten a cell phone.

> ERIC

Use mine. Shit, dead battery. Okay, we'll drive
into town. Maybe stop somewhere and get some
actually hot coffee, hmmm?

> JANICE
> (*a sudden thought*)

Eric, how can I let them come back to...to this stuff?
To their mother having some kind of breakdown,
complete with screaming daytime nightmares?

> ERIC

I think the parenting magazines always say, "Tell
them the truth."
> (*a beat*)

But speaking as a journalist, I doubt the writers
have ever had this particular problem to deal with.

> JANICE

Speaking as non-journalist and parent...thanks a lot.
CUT TO:

## INT./EXT.—DRIVING THROUGH TOWN—MORNING

*The storm damage is pretty extensive—trees down in the road, some power
poles and phone poles tipped over. Many stores have plywood or plastic
sheeting in place of windows and people are sweeping up the sidewalks. There's
no power anywhere, including the traffic lights. ERIC stops at an intersection
where a COP is directing traffic.*

> ERIC
>
> Hey, Officer, do you know if any of the pay phones are working?

> COP
>
> Not right around here. Besides the wind, we must have had a little electrical storm or something— there's a lot of stuff on the fritz besides just phone lines. Screwing up our radios, too. And some of the power poles actually caught fire.

*JANICE and ERIC for the first time look at each other, a dawning idea that something is not completely ordinary here. ERIC pulls out of the line of cars so he can continue talking to the officer.*

> ERIC
>
> So...so where would the nearest working phones be?

> COP
>
> You'd practically have to get to the county line, I think, other side of the hills. PacBell's got crews out though. They should have the service on in a couple of hours. Power might take a little longer...

CUT TO:

INT./EXT.—DRIVING—MINUTES LATER
*There are repair crews out along the road. ERIC and JANICE are behind an ambulance and firetruck, which turn down a side road.*

> ERIC
> (slowing car)
>
> That's...

> JANICE

They're going to the convalescent hospital. Have to
be. It's the only thing down there.

ERIC *pulls the car around and follows the ambulance, as we*
CUT TO:

EXT.—HOSPITAL—MINUTES LATER
*The front grounds of Las Lomas Convalescent Hospital are a surreal sight.*
*Many of the windows are broken out, and a tree has crashed down on the*
*front of the building, smashing the roof and damaging one of the walls. Several*
*of the patients are wandering around the grounds, many still in nightgowns.*
*Police and fire people are trying to clear some of them out of the driveway so the*
*firetruck and ambulance can get in.*

ERIC *and* JANICE *park the car and walk across the front lawn. Some of the*
*patients are just wandering. Others seem frightened or dreamy, but all turn to*
STARE *fixedly at* ERIC *and* JANICE *as they walk past.*

*The* ADMINISTRATOR *is standing next to the fallen tree, talking to one of*
*the police officers while the ambulance paramedics roll a stretcher in through the*
*ruined doors. The* ADMINISTRATOR *looks up in surprise as* ERIC *and*
JANICE *approach.*

> ADMINISTRATOR
> Mrs. Moorehead? Did someone...? I mean, how
> could anyone have called you when the phones are
> out...?

> JANICE
> Called me? Why would anyone call me?

> ADMINISTRATOR
> (flustered)
> Oh. I just thought...because of your friend, Mr.
> Holland.

(*her look grows sharper*)
If no one called you, how did you know?

CUT TO:


INT.—HOSPITAL—MINUTES LATER
*ERIC and JANICE are walking fast down the hallway, across leaves and other debris which have blown in through the broken doors and windows. The NURSE is walking with them, talking fast and nervously.*


NURSE

He's the only one...it's a miracle more didn't wander away—it was terrible! Some of them were so frightened they hid under the beds and we missed them when we did the count this morning.


JANICE

But you said he couldn't move—that he couldn't even get into a wheelchair by himself!


NURSE

It's so strange—I've never heard of anything like it. In a way, it's a kind of miracle...oh, but I hope he's all right! Poor Mr. Holland. Poor, poor Mr. Holland...


*The OLD WOMAN that ERIC had met previously is standing in the hall, wearing a jacket over her nightgown. As they push through the door of TOPHER'S ROOM she calls after them:*


OLD WOMAN

He's gone home! I heard him when I was sleeping!
Tell Mama I'm all right, 'cause he's gone home!


*TOPHER's empty "shell" is still lying on the bed. JANICE muffles a noise of fear and disgust behind her hand. After a moment, ERIC steps forward and*

*hesitantly touches it. He lifts the masklike skin of the face, staring at the hollow eyeholes. It breaks apart in his hand, as we*
DISSOLVE TO:

EXT.—BRENT'S HOUSE—LATER IN THE MORNING
*ERIC and JANICE are walking up BRENT's walkway. There's only one SUV in the driveway now.*

> JANICE
> He can't be more than a few hundred yards
> from there, Eric. He's crippled! He's been mostly
> bedridden for years!

> ERIC
> A chrysalis—that's what the nurse said the first
> time I saw him. Like a cocoon. And now he's
> hatched.

*ERIC knocks at BRENT's door.*

> ERIC *(cont.)*
> You don't think all that's a coincidence, do you? The
> power failures, all that shit, and Topher just sheds
> his skin and walks away? After all these years?

> JANICE
> What are you saying? That he did it, somehow? I
> thought you were supposed to be the rationalist.

> ERIC
> When the facts themselves are irrational, you still
> have to work with them. Just think about it for a
> second. Think! What night is it tonight?

*JANICE stares at him in incomprehension as the door opens. BRENT is standing there clutching his hand, with blood on his arms and shirt. He looks numb and half-dead. JANICE and ERIC gasp.*

> BRENT

I was wondering when you'd show up.
> *(their expression finally penetrates; he looks down at the blood)*
Oh. I broke a glass. Guess you might as well come in.

*He turns as if he couldn't care less and walks inside. After a moment, ERIC and JANICE follow him.*

INT.—BRENT'S HOUSE—HALF AN HOUR LATER
*BRENT is pretty drunk. He's sitting on the couch with his head in his hands while ERIC and JANICE make coffee on a camping stove they've set up on the counter.*

> BRENT

I sent Tracy and Joanie away. Tracy didn't want to go, but I think she thought I was going to get violent or something... Joanie wanted to take all her dolls.
> *(fighting tears)*
Oh, God, I sent them away...!

*ERIC pours a cup of coffee for himself, sips it and burns his tongue. He blows and sips it again gratefully while JANICE takes a cup to BRENT.*

> BRENT *(cont.)*

I should have gone with them. I don't want to be here. It's all going to hell.

> ERIC

Shut up and get some coffee into you. Jesus, Brent, do you always drink like this?

BRENT
(*indignantly*)
What? Are you going to tell me everything's normal?
That it's fucking inappropriate to be drinking in
the morning? You think I should just sit here sober
waiting for that...thing to come kill me?

JANICE
(*sharply*)
You knew he got out of the hospital?

*BRENT looks up with such SHOCK in his eyes that he clearly did not. His hands begin trembling so badly that coffee spatters the rug.*

BRENT
(*looking down at the mess*)
Jesus. Jesus, look at that.

ERIC
Give it to me.

*He sets the cup on the table in front of BRENT. As ERIC stares at haggard, shivering BRENT, his face softens.*

ERIC (*cont.*)
You didn't know he'd gotten out of the hospital?

BRENT
Christ, no. But I had dreams...

JANICE
We all had dreams. But he's a sick man, catatonic—a
cripple!

BRENT

He's coming for us. He wants...he's angry. Because of...of what we did.

JANICE

But that doesn't make any sense! We were his friends! And why now, after all these years?

ERIC

Maybe because he had to get ready. Like a caterpillar who had to wait until he could become a butterfly. He was just waiting all that time, changing inside, growing into...something else.
(turns to JANICE)
You know what tonight is, don't you? Don't you? Why are your kids coming back tomorrow?

JANICE

Oh, shit, I never called them. What do you mean, why are they coming back? Because they have to be back for school...
(it finally hits her)
Oh. Oh, God, tonight is...

ERIC

Yeah. The last Saturday night of the summer.

They look at each other across the sunlit living room of a nice, ordinary house, as we DISSOLVE TO:

INT.—BRENT'S HOUSE—HOURS LATER

The living room is beginning to look a bit like a cage. A house of cards has fallen over on the coffee table. BRENT and ERIC are smoking. BRENT has sobered a bit—he just looks hellishly depressed. JANICE is clearing up in a sort of obsessive way, straightening things on shelves, etc.

ERIC

Leave it alone. It's okay.

JANICE

It's driving me crazy. All this mess... It's something
to do, for God's sake. What are we waiting for?

ERIC

The power to come back on. The phone to start
working. A monster who used to be our friend to
knock on the front door. Who knows?

JANICE

If you really think this is going to happen, why
don't we just leave? Let's just get in the car and go!

BRENT

Won't do any good...

ERIC

For once I agree with Zenger. What if the engine
just happens to die while we're driving down some
back road somewhere? There we'll be, out in the
woods somewhere, stuck, no walls, no locked
doors...

JANICE

It just seems...it just seems so stupid. All of it. This
is stuff that happened years ago! What's it doing
screwing things up now? I just want it all to go
away so I can have my kids and my life back.

ERIC

There has to be some kind of sense to this. He was

in that psychiatric hospital for years. What did they find? What the hell was in those pills?

BRENT
(*shaking his head*)
Doesn't matter now.

ERIC
But it does! Was it some kind of psychic warfare experiment? Some kind of biological modification thing? The CIA, a bunch of other government groups were working on all kinds of crazy shit in the Seventies. What did Topher get his hands on?

*JANICE has finished nervously clearing the living room. She wanders into the hall and through the open bathroom door. We can still hear ERIC's voice.*

ERIC (*cont.*)
For a while, about ten years ago, I thought I might write an article about it—I even started researching. Nobody wanted to say a fucking word—total blackout. It was definitely something big. But I just couldn't go through with it, you know, dragging all that stuff back out again...?

*JANICE is staring at herself in the mirror, hands on the sink. ERIC's voice has become a faint murmur. As she stares, the radio beside the bath begins to play Cat Stevens' "Moonshadow." She stares at it in shock. When she looks back at the mirror, it's her own YOUNGER FACE looking back. At first she is terrified, but the impulse to look at this lost version is irresistible. As she lifts her hand to touch her own adult face, the YOUNG JANICE image mirrors her.*
CUT TO:

EXT.—PIERSON HOUSE, 1976—NIGHT

# BLACK SUNSHINE

*It's dark now, and YOUNG ERIC and YOUNG JANICE are sitting on the front porch overlooking the orchard. "Moonshadow" is wafting out the front door. There are stars in the sky and crickets chirping. JANICE is looking into the mirror of her compact, her hand in the same position we last saw it.*

### YOUNG ERIC
*(amused)*

What are you doing?

### YOUNG JANICE

You know Carly Heener? She said that when she did acid, she knew when she was tripping because she looked in the mirror and her face was melting.

### YOUNG ERIC

Carly Heener's brain was already melted. Cool out, it won't even hit for half an hour or so. You're just high from all that weed.
*(a beat)*
Man, Zenger must have a serious crush on Kimmy. He's actually in there listening to Cat Stevens with her. Like the Pope sitting down to have breakfast with Satan.

### YOUNG JANICE
*(laughing, high)*

You're so funny, Eric. But if you guys all think Cat Stevens is so bad, how come you have one of his records? Busted!

### YOUNG ERIC

I think my cousin must have left it or something.

### YOUNG JANICE

Yeah, sure.

*(looks at him fondly, then frowns)*
You know, you're kind of sweating a lot.

### YOUNG ERIC
I think it might be coming on a little.

### YOUNG JANICE
Do you think Topher will be all right? Where is he, anyway?

### YOUNG ERIC
Out running through the trees, probably. Yeah, he'll be fine. I saw him drink gasoline out of a jug once. He thought it was white wine. Crazy fucker's invincible. Besides, I bet he's bullshitting anyway. His dad would beat the shit out of him if he got caught ripping that place off. I bet it's just speed, or some psilocybin he bought off Ricky Caffaro or something...

JANICE *nestles against* ERIC, *looking out at the orchard. "Moonshadow" ends and is replaced by Peter Frampton's "Baby I Love Your Way."* ERIC *laughs.*

### YOUNG ERIC
Man, Zenger's really got it bad.
*(shouts toward the door)*
Put on some decent music, will you?

### YOUNG JANICE
I never noticed how close the trees are to the house. They look...I don't know. Like they're surrounding the place.

### YOUNG ERIC

They are surrounding the place.

YOUNG JANICE
You already did that joke. But don't you think they're weird? Like they're reaching...

YOUNG ERIC
Ssshhh. You're just starting to come on. It's fine. It's all fine.

*He puts his arm around her. After a moment, he starts to kiss her neck, then her mouth. She tries to respond, but when his hand moves up to her breast she pulls away.*

YOUNG JANICE
Don't...

YOUNG ERIC
It's okay.

YOUNG JANICE
It's not okay. I feel weird. Like...like I've got a battery on my tongue. I don't think I like this.

YOUNG ERIC
Shit. You only took half a hit.
(*he sits up*)
I'm leaving in like a week, you know.

YOUNG JANICE
(*quietly*)
I know.

YOUNG ERIC
And, I don't know, since I'm going to be in LA, and

we'll only be able to see each other on weekends...I
don't know, maybe we should start thinking about...
about...

*There is a loud CLATTER from just overhead, then something large and
dark DROPS down from the roof above them and lands with a SLAM on the
porch, making ERIC and JANICE shout and jump in shock. It's TOPHER,
very wired and grinning. He's got his shirt off and tied around his waist. He
looks like a wild man.*

### TOPHER

Take me to your leader!
     *(cocks an ear to music)*
What is that queer shit?
     *(shouts)*
Zengerdenger! Put on some Zep or some Sabbath
or I'll kick your ass into next year!
     *(he leans over ERIC and JANICE)*
Man, I'm so fucking thirsty—let's make a run for
brews. C'mon, Erky, you drive.

### YOUNG ERIC

I'm not driving, man. The acid's just starting to
come on.

### TOPHER

Then we'll walk. C'mon. Janice, make your fuckin'
boyfriend get off his ass. Come on, come on!

### YOUNG JANICE

Why do we need beer?

### TOPHER

Why do we need beer? Why do we need anything?
Why do we need fucking music? Why do we need

dope? Because life is shit and I'm so fucking high
I can't believe it!
> (he laughs and shadow-punches the air,
> circling ERIC and JANICE like a dog
> excited about going for a walk)

Party time!

TOPHER *throws back his head and howls like a wolf, a rising, hoarse note that turns into ERIC yelling:*

> ADULT ERIC

Janice! Janice!

*As we*
DISSOLVE TO:

INT.—BRENT'S HOUSE—EVENING
*ADULT JANICE is staring at the mirror, at her own grown-up face. She looks at her hand on the counter. There's an ANT crawling on it. JANICE gasps and flails until she brushes it off. ADULT ERIC appears in the bathroom doorway, obviously upset. The house is dark, but there's light behind him from (as we'll find out) a camping lantern in the living room.*

> ERIC

Where have you been?

> JANICE
> (near tears)

You were going to break up with me, you bastard!
Before any of that other stuff even happened!

> ERIC

What are you talking about?

> JANICE

We were sitting on the porch, and you were just about to tell me we should break up...

ERIC

I have no idea what you're talking about, Janice. Where the hell have you been? I've been looking for you for half an hour all over the house. I've been screaming your name! I was worried to death!

JANICE

I've been right here...
                    (*a beat*)
Half an hour?

ERIC

Brent's not doing too well. Where were you?

JANICE *suddenly grabs him.*

JANICE

Oh my God. I am going crazy.
                    (*looks around*)
It's dark!

ERIC

Yes, it damn well is. That's why I've been looking all over for you—I didn't know what happened. Where were you?

JANICE

Back there. Back there, Eric.

BRENT *stumbles into the hallway, haggard, haunted.*

BRENT

(*even more overwhelmed than ERIC and JANICE*)
Can't get away. He's in our heads! We're fucked.


ERIC
Come on, pull yourself together.


BRENT
You think I'm useless, don't you? But I know how
to end this.
(*he produces his GUN*)
It's easy. One bullet in Topher Holland's brain and
everything's over...


ERIC
Jesus, Brent, put that thing away! That's all we need,
you pulling some cowboy shit like that.


JANICE
Why is this happening to us? He was our friend!


BRENT
You have no idea how hard I worked to make a life
for myself. Worked damn hard. It was a nice life,
too. I just wanted to forget...


*BRENT pauses; then, as if he has really noticed ERIC and JANICE for the
first time, he looks at them sorrowfully.*


BRENT (*cont.*)
I'm sorry. I'm so sorry. It's all my fault. I...


*He turns and staggers out of the hallway. A moment later a CRASH startles
ERIC and JANICE. They run to the living room. BRENT has knocked over
the coffee table.*

ERIC

Jesus, you almost busted the lantern...!
(realizes BRENT is staring in horror at the front door)
Brent, what's...

As JANICE comes up beside him, the three of them standing close together
in the middle of the living room, the DOORKNOB of the front door turns a
little, clicks, turns again. They stare at it, frozen. After a moment, the door
clicks and slowly swings open... BRENT makes little panting noises of terror.
JANICE and ERIC grab for each other's hands.

The door is all the way open. The street outside is dark. The doorway is EMPTY.

ERIC
(hoarsely)

Who...?

He picks up a broken table-leg and the lantern and slowly moves toward the
open door. JANICE grabs a heavy vase and moves up beside him. BRENT
is on his knees on the floor behind them. They reach the doorway and peer
out. Empty, dark street. ERIC cautiously extends the lantern, taking a step
outside, looking, looking...

ERIC

There's no one here...

ERIC glances down. A symbol written in FLAMES on the porch—a crude
drawing of an EYE, surrounded by rays like the sun—is flickering out. As it
disappears, the PHONE rings, making them all JUMP in shock. It takes a
second for the import to reach them.

JANICE
(excited, relieved)

The phones! The phones are working!

*The cordless phone is in the table-wreckage near BRENT, but he doesn't move. JANICE picks it up and listens for a second. Her eyes widen, her jaw drops. She turns like an accident victim in shock and hands the phone to ERIC.*

JANICE

It's for you. It's...it's Kimmy.

KIMMY
*(on phone; as if from
a great distance)*
Help me...! I'm lost, and it's so dark! Come home,
Eric! Come home...!

*ERIC is pale and half-dead-looking as the phone drops from his hand. He looks at JANICE, then at weeping BRENT. He and JANICE turn to stare at the open door.*
DISSOLVE TO:

EXT.—STREETS—MINUTES LATER
*The ADULT versions of ERIC, JANICE, and BRENT walk down the dark, deserted suburban streets like they're going to their own execution. All the houses are lightless and look deserted.*

ERIC

I told you the car wasn't going to start. It's not going
to work that way—none of it.

JANICE

We could wait until tomorrow and call the police!
He's an escaped patient! This isn't just us having
some hallucination—he's real!

ERIC

You think that's going to happen?

333

JANICE

It makes more sense than walking into your grandmother's deserted house, looking for him. The lights
have to come back on some time...the phones...

ERIC

Let's find out.

*ERIC suddenly steps out of the road and walks across a lawn toward one of the
houses. He stops in front of the door and pounds on it.*

ERIC

Hello? Can you help us, please? It's an emergency.
(*no answer; he knocks louder*)
You don't have to open the door, just talk to us.

JANICE

Eric, you're acting crazy...

ERIC

Am I?

*He vaults over the hedge to the next yard and begins pounding on that door,
too. No answer.*

ERIC

Help! Nuclear war! Invasion of wild pigs! Call the
police! Call the National Guard!

*He picks up a porch chair, heaves it over his head, then SMASHES it through
the picture window.*

JANICE

Stop it! Why are you doing this!

ERIC

Because there's nobody there, Janice! No-fucking-body! Look at the windows—no candles, nothing. People in the real world have batteries, Janice. They have radios and flashlights. They still go out and walk their dogs, even when there's a blackout.

*ERIC reaches for a chunk of the windowsill and pulls it away. It comes off like it's rotten and CRUMBLES into dust in his hands. He pushes his hand through the wall and another section breaks away and dissolves into powder.*

ERIC *(cont.)*

He's playing with us. Don't you remember that night, when we were walking on this same road?

JANICE

Stop it. You're making it worse.

ERIC

Do you remember what I said? He remembers. He's pulled us back into it—it's all happening again, but twisted up...

*As ERIC speaks,*
SLOW DISSOLVE:

EXT: STREET – 1976

*The street is still dark, but only because it's a quiet neighborhood, late at night. There are a few lights in the windows, streetlights, the glow of a television through curtains. YOUNG JANICE and YOUNG TOPHER are walking with YOUNG ERIC, who has stopped in the middle of the street, clearly beginning to feel the acid. JANICE turns and starts back toward him.*

YOUNG JANICE

Eric? What're you doing?
>           (quietly, now she's close)
Would you come on? Topher's making me nervous.

*ERIC lets himself be led. As they catch up to TOPHER, ERIC is clearly disoriented.*

### YOUNG ERIC

Is it...this year? In all the houses?

### YOUNG JANICE

What are you talking about?

### YOUNG ERIC

I thought...for a minute I thought... I mean, how do we know it's still now?

### TOPHER

Oh, he's coming on real good.

### YOUNG ERIC

No, really. I mean, we don't know. Time could have just...stopped. For us, I mean. And like everyone else just went on. So in all those houses, it could be twenty years later, but we're still stuck in this one night, forever. Like we were ghosts.

### YOUNG JANICE

Don't say things like that. You're giving me the creeps.

*TOPHER is swigging from a beer, even more full of manic energy. He's carrying the rest of the two six-packs in a bag.*

### TOPHER

Twenty years there ain't gonna be no town here—
'cause one of these days I'm gonna burn the fucking
place down. Maybe I'll do it tonight.

(*turns to ERIC*)

You want another beer? It'll cut the harsh on that
buzz.

YOUNG ERIC

No. I don't think so. Not now.

YOUNG JANICE

I feel really strange, Eric. I wish you hadn't said
that. I feel...empty.

TOPHER

(*oblivious*)

I told you we could pimp some brews up at the One
Stop, no problem, man. It's 'cause we had a chick
along, just like I told you. Those older guys, they always want to look cool when there's a chick around.

YOUNG JANICE

I can see my hand moving—look. It's all blurry.

TOPHER

You got tracers, baby! It's coming on!

YOUNG ERIC

(*forcing himself back to reality*)

How 'bout you, Topher—you okay, man?

TOPHER

(*a flash of suspicion*)

Why? You think I'm acting weird? You're just
paranoid—you always get paranoid, Pierson. I'm

fucking great. Black Sunshine, bay-bee! I'm so big
I'm gonna blow up like a balloon!

### YOUNG JANICE
I hope Kimmy's all right. We should have made her
come with us. She's really nervous about all this...

### TOPHER
Zenger's sniffin' after her. Boy is workin' hard,
workin' hard.

### YOUNG JANICE
(suddenly)
I probably will still be here in twenty years. This
fucking dead town.
(she is suddenly very emotional)
You'll go off to college and you'll be some famous
guy, and I'll see you on television, and I'll still be
working in that coffee shop, refilling the catchup
bottles.

ERIC is lost in thought, silent, plodding along.

### TOPHER
Yeah, you'll be sixty years old, wearin' that fucking
little skirt. "Hi, my name is Janice, happy to serve
you!"

### YOUNG JANICE
Like you'll be doing anything different, Topher. At
least I'll have a job, which is more than you'll have
when they find out you were ripping off the lab.

### TOPHER
Man, I'll be so far out of here. Once I bag fuckin'

high school, I'm gone, and my dad can fuck himself. I'll join the fuckin' Air Force, be a pilot. I'll be all over the world, checkin' out the señoritas, all that shit.

*TOPHER's voice is getting strangely loud and off-key. He's even twitching a bit. ERIC is staring at him.*

### TOPHER *(cont.)*
I'll be so fuckin' high you won't even be able to see me. You and Pierson and all the others, you'll be pretending you're my friends, but you'll be on the ground, living in this dick town, on the ground, round and round on the ground...

### YOUNG JANICE
*(angry)*
Shut up, Topher. You aren't going to do shit. Your old man's going to throw you out and you'll wind up hangin' around on the benches at Tyner Park like all the other losers...

### TOPHER
*(suddenly screams)*
Fuck you, bitch!

*TOPHER is suddenly shaking with rage, eyes rolling. ERIC, startled out of his reverie, takes a step forward.*

### YOUNG ERIC
Hey, man, cool out...

### TOPHER
Keep your woman in line, man! She can't talk to me like that...!

YOUNG JANICE

You can't talk to me like that...

TOPHER

(screaming again)

I ain't stupid! I ain't fucking stupid! I'll fucking show you!

TOPHER *turns and runs away down the street. ERIC looks at JANICE in worried irritation, as if to say it's her fault, then starts after him. They have reached the end of the wooded street that leads to the orchard and the Pierson House. TOPHER stops under the last streetlight before the orchard, huddled. ERIC approaches him slowly.*

YOUNG ERIC

Topher? Topher, man, just take it easy...

*As ERIC is reaching to put a hand on his shoulder, TOPHER looks up, grimacing in MISERY. His features appear for a moment to RIPPLE, like something powerful is shifting below the skin. As he shrieks at ERIC, the streetlight above them EXPLODES in a shower of glass.*

TOPHER

Leave me alone!

*ERIC reels back, shielding himself from falling glass, as TOPHER flees into the orchard and we*
CUT TO:

EXT.—STREET—SAME TIME, BUT THE PRESENT

*ADULT ERIC is clutching the same streetlight, unbroken now but also unlit. ADULT JANICE is beside him, crying, staring out across the empty lot where the orchard was, while ADULT BRENT simply stares.*

JANICE

I don't want to go there. I don't care if this is all real
or not. I don't want to go there.

LONG SHOT: PIERSON HOUSE, NOW
*Over her shoulder, we see the dark house in the empty field.*

BRENT
*(almost like talking in his sleep)*
He wants it back. He wants it back...

ERIC

I don't think we can run away from this, Jan-Jan.

JANICE

My kids. I'll never get back to them—never see my
kids again. Callie...Jack...

ERIC

I don't want to go either. But I think the only way
out is...there.

*He takes an awkward step toward the field. He reaches back for JANICE's
hand. She looks at him, miserable but sobered. She reaches out as if to touch
his hand, but lets her hand drop again, as we*
DISSOLVE TO:

EXT.—ORCHARD—1976
*YOUNG ERIC and YOUNG JANICE are holding hands, deep in the trees
of the orchard. The branches are so close that they block everything except thin
moonlight.*

YOUNG JANICE
He...he was acting like he was crazy. Really crazy.
I'm scared and I want to go home, Eric. Can you

just take me home? I want this all to stop.

> YOUNG ERIC
> We can't leave Topher like that. We have to find
> him—he's freaking.

> YOUNG JANICE
> What about me, Eric?

*ERIC shakes his head—a choice he does not want to be forced to make. Suddenly, something RATTLES the trees nearby. ERIC and JANICE freeze, startled. Whatever it is, it's making a strange MOANING sound and it's coming closer. JANICE presses into ERIC as they wait, helplessly. The sound gets louder, then an instant later YOUNG BRENT blunders through the trees and almost runs into them.*

> YOUNG ERIC
> Brent! Damn, man, you scared me to death. Have
> you seen...?

*He suddenly realizes BRENT has tears on his cheeks.*

> YOUNG ERIC (cont.)
> Oh, shit, what's up? Are you all right...?

*BRENT pushes him aside.*

> YOUNG BRENT
> Fuck off, Pierson. Leave me alone.

> YOUNG JANICE
> Where's Kimmy? Brent, where's Kimmy?

> YOUNG BRENT
> (stopping for a moment)

Your friend is a bitch, Janice. A total bitch.

*His face screws up with anger and hurt and he blunders away.*

> YOUNG ERIC
> Jesus, what's going on around here...?

*He stops as JANICE pulls away from him and heads toward the house.*

> YOUNG ERIC (*cont.*)
> Janice! Where are you going...?

> YOUNG JANICE
> I have to find Kimmy!

*He tries to follow her, but stumbles on something and falls. He gets up, calling JANICE's name.*
DISSOLVE TO:

EXT.—THE DIRT FIELD, NOW—NIGHT
*ADULT ERIC is in the middle of the empty field. There is nothing in front of him but the dark, empty house several hundred yards away. He is ALONE.*

> ERIC
> Janice? Brent?

CUT TO:

EXT.—THE DIRT FIELD, NOW—NIGHT
ADULT JANICE, SAME SITUATION
*She's alone, nothing but her and the house.*

> JANICE
> Eric? Where are you?

CUT TO:

EXT.—THE DIRT FIELD, NOW—NIGHT
ADULT BRENT, SAME SITUATION
BRENT *is standing in the same field, also alone. As he stares at the house, light begins to GLOW in the windows—not sudden, like a light switch, but like something smoldering into life. The first spooky piano notes of David Bowie's "Time" begin to waft across the field of dirt. BRENT slumps to his knees facing the house like a man awaiting execution, as we*
SLOW DISSOLVE TO:

EXT.—ORCHARD, THEN—NIGHT
*The David Bowie song is playing, but a little more muffled, as YOUNG ERIC makes his way through the trees, which seem very tangled and dense. He stumbles into an open clearing and sees TOPHER sitting cross-legged, eyes closed, at the base of a tree.*

YOUNG ERIC
Topher! Man, you okay?

TOPHER's *eyes open very slowly. He looks at ERIC with an expression almost of amusement.*

TOPHER
Erky. Give me a smoke, man.

ERIC *fumbles out a cigarette and hands it to him.*

YOUNG ERIC
This is all crazy, man. I think I'm starting to peak...

*As he's talking, TOPHER lights it simply by touching the tip of his finger to the end of the cigarette. ERIC stares, open-mouthed.*

TOPHER

Zenger tried to get himself some. He touched little
Kimmy's tit and she smacked him.

YOUNG ERIC
Did he tell you that?

TOPHER
I saw it.

YOUNG ERIC
You were with us.

TOPHER
(imperturbable)
I saw it. I can see your old lady right now. She and
Kimmy're having an argument because she wants
to go home and Kimmy doesn't. Kimmy's kind of
digging the high.

YOUNG ERIC
What are you talking about? You can't see them
from here.

TOPHER
I can see everything, man. I can see my fucking
dad watching television in the living room at our
house, drinking a fucking beer and squeezing his
dick. Everything. I can see the, like, radio waves
between the stars—they look like black rainbows.
(he stands and lets his head fall back)
You don't know what I can do. I can see the worms
in the ground under your feet, these little silver
strings crisscrossing...
(lets his head loll forward until he's
looking at ERIC; grins)

I can even see inside your head, Pierson. You've been thinking all night about some little blonde chick you met at Bader's party who said she was going to UCLA in the fall—thinking about how she slipped you some tongue when you went out with her to get smokes...

*TOPHER's laugh is a cackle. ERIC takes a stumbling step backward. TOPHER opens his eyes wider—the pupils are so dilated that there are no irises, only BLACK HOLES in the middle of the white.*

### TOPHER

Don't run away, Erky. It's all starting to happen now—I can feel it. I'm getting so big that I'm not going to need my body soon. I'll be flying, man, flying...

*TOPHER actually begins to FLOAT up from the ground until he is hovering at least a foot in the air, head thrown back, laughing. ERIC turns and runs, as we* CUT TO:

EXT.—PIERSON HOUSE, 1976—MINUTES LATER
*YOUNG ERIC stands on the front porch, gasping for breath: he's run all the way. He braces his hands on his knees. David Bowie is still playing inside.*

### YOUNG ERIC
*(to himself; a terrified mantra)*
Too high. Just peaking, that's all. Cool out, man. Cool out.

*Shakily, he stands and opens the door—the music comes rolling out. YOUNG BRENT is crouched beside the stereo system, records all over the floor, feverishly looking for something.*

### YOUNG ERIC

Where's Janice?

BRENT *shakes his head; he's too busy.*

> ### YOUNG BRENT
> Gotta change the music—too many edges. You got some Floyd, don't you? Reverse the flow, you know what I mean? *Dark Side of the Moon?* No, no, too much electricity. The new one, the new one, the new one. *Wish You Were Here,* yeah, that'd close up the holes.
> > *(he looks up at ERIC,*
> > *eyes wild, face flushed)*
> Where's your Floyd, Pierson? You have *Wish You Were Here,* don't you? Don't you?

> ### YOUNG ERIC
> Take it easy, dude.

> ### YOUNG BRENT
> There's fucking electricity, man! It's leaking all over the place! I gotta put something on...!

> ### YOUNG ERIC
> Uh...I think I've got some Crosby, Stills, and Nash...

> ### YOUNG BRENT
> Perfect!
> > *(he returns to pawing frantically through*
> > *the records, not really looking at any of them)*
> Crosby, Nash, Stills, still crazy, Crazy Horse, Young, young gifted and black, Black Mariah, Blackmore, Richie Blackmore, Black Oak, blackout, Black Sabbath...
> > *(he pauses for a moment, startled)*

No. No!
    *(returns to his pawing and gibberish)*
Nash, Stills, steel, steal your face, Steely Dan,
Steeleye Span, Stealer's Wheel, wheels, wild, child,
chill, still, Stills, Nash, Crosby, Nash...

*ERIC is looking for JANICE. The living room is a mess. So is the kitchen, even worse. Someone has started to make a pot of Spaghetti-Os on the stove, but stopped partway through, leaving tomato sauce splashed on the counter. Someone has finger-painted a crude EYE on the counter with the tomato sauce—the eye with sun's rays we've seen on BRENT's doorstep—and a few ants are crawling around it.*

*As ERIC reaches the stairs leading upstairs, BRENT has put on a "mellower" record—King Crimson's* Court of the Crimson King. *ERIC hesitates, then moves up into the shadowed staircase. As he reaches the landing, he pauses.*

### YOUNG ERIC

Janice?

*He looks up and down the hall, then moves toward the only closed door—for a moment the hallway STRETCHES, so that it seems a VERY LONG WAY. He takes another step and his hand closes on the doorknob and the door swings open.*

*It's his grandparent's BEDROOM—fussy, tidy. The only light is from a small bedside lamp with a heavy shade, so the room is shadowy. A FIGURE is seated on the bed, back to him, very still. ERIC, clearly nervous, begins to walk around. It's KIMMY, head down as though she's asleep sitting up, her hair covering her face. As ERIC nervously reaches his hand toward her, she lifts her face, eyes wide.*

### KIMMY

Eric! I thought you were Janice.
    *(she smiles)*

Not Janice-Janice, of course, but this Janice.

YOUNG ERIC

Where is she?

KIMMY

I don't know. She's mad at me because I want to stay. Maybe she went home. If she has a home here, I mean—do you think everyone has one here, just like in real life?

ERIC *shakes his head in confusion and sits beside her.*

YOUNG ERIC

This is such a weird night...

KIMMY

I think it's nice you're in my dream.

YOUNG ERIC

Huh?

KIMMY

Because I thought about it happening like this, and then it happened, so that's how I know I'm dreaming.

YOUNG ERIC

You're not dreaming, Kimmy. You're just tripping.

KIMMY

Maybe you dreamed it, too. Maybe you just went to sleep, and now you're dreaming the same dream as me. That's okay. It means no one can get in except us.

YOUNG ERIC

Like ghosts...


KIMMY

Yes. Like we're ghosts, maybe. I never knew that there were so many places outside the world, Eric. I never thought there was any place I could really talk to you.


*She turns to him, very intent.*


KIMMY *(cont.)*

I could never say this to you in real life, but since this is a dream it doesn't matter—I'm just talking to myself. I've been in love with you since ninth grade, Eric. Since we were in that Social Studies class together and did that project. When Janice started to go out with you, it hurt so much...
     *(smiling but teary-eyed)*
And I just thought, I can never say it, she's my best friend. But now you and I are dreaming the same dream.


*ERIC, overwhelmed, just stares.*


KIMMY *(cont.)*

You'll never know how much I wished this could happen for real. I used to imagine that we met at a party, and that you didn't know Janice, and that we...
     *(she turns her head away; when she turns back,*
          *her expression is almost feverish)*
Sometimes I think about that at night, when I'm in bed, and I...I touch myself.

> YOUNG ERIC
Jesus, Kimmy, I...

*She leans over and puts her finger against his lips.*

> KIMMY
Ssshhh. I know—it doesn't matter. I never understood that before, but I do now. Because there are
places like this where we can be together—where
we were always together.
> *(she giggles)*
I wonder if I'm asleep now? Lying on the floor, and
you guys are trying to wake me up...

*KIMMY takes off her glasses.*

> KIMMY *(cont.)*
I want to learn everything, do everything. I probably
won't even remember this when I stop dreaming,
but...

*She suddenly leans forward and kisses him. ERIC, still stunned, almost pulls
back, but the intensity of her kiss is compelling and he is drawn into it. After
a moment they roll over onto the bed. A couple of times ERIC starts to draw
away, more from overload than moral resistance, but KIMMY is uninhib-
itedly PASSIONATE—kissing and even licking his face and neck, climbing
onto him, slithering her body over his with abandon. The kissing grows more
intense; both of them have their hands in each other's shirts and pants—ERIC
has begun pulling KIMMY's pants down over her hips when he suddenly
hears JANICE's voice loud in the hall just outside the door.*

> YOUNG JANICE
No, I don't know where the Led Zeppelin is, Brent.
You've got the records all over the place, how am I
supposed to know?

*Startled, ERIC slides away from KIMMY and onto the floor with a painful thump, almost tipping over the lamp table. He begins zipping himself up. KIMMY shows no such guilt, still deep in her "dream."*

### KIMMY
Eric...? What are you doing?

*ERIC hurriedly finishes, then gets his hand on the door just as JANICE starts to open it. For a moment they stand face-to-face.*

### YOUNG JANICE
What...?

### YOUNG ERIC
(*blustering*)
Where have you been?

### YOUNG JANICE
What do you mean, where have I been? You're really sweating again.

### YOUNG ERIC
I'm high, Janice. I'm tripping. But I was...I was worried about you.
> (*he begins to move toward the stairs,*
> *leading her away from the bedroom.*)
Topher's acting crazy. Completely crazy. It's fucking with my mind. Do you think he really took all those pills?

### YOUNG JANICE
I don't want to think about him. Maybe I should just go home—I don't feel very good. Besides, my mom didn't answer the phone, so I couldn't tell

her I was staying at Kimmy's. She'll be pissed if she comes back and I'm not there.

YOUNG ERIC

What are you talking about? You already called her. Jesus, Janice, you call her again and she'll know you're high.

YOUNG JANICE

I called her already? Really?
(looks distraught)
Is that 'cause I'm tripping? I don't like this stuff, Eric. I want to come down.

ERIC puts an arm around her, leads her back downstairs.

YOUNG ERIC

I think there's some of that sinsemilla left. We should have a couple of hits, mellow us out...

As they reach the bottom of the stairs, BRENT suddenly lurches into view, holding a monstrous pile of records; some are slipping out of their jackets onto the floor, but he doesn't even notice.

YOUNG BRENT

I figured it out. It's okay. It's all handled.

YOUNG JANICE

What are you talking about?

YOUNG BRENT

See, I was thinking, "Stairway to Heaven," but that's so obvious, but Jimmy Page used to play in the Yardbirds, just like Clapton, and Clapton was in Blind Faith. And "Yardbird" means "prisoner," see?

YOUNG ERIC
You need to calm down, man.


YOUNG BRENT
No, no, you're not thinking. You remember that
Blind Faith song, "Sea of Joy"? Get how it connects?
Because "Sea" is not only "Sea" like "ocean," but it's
"C" like "Clapton" and also "Crimson," right? *Court
of the Crimson King,* and that's the devil, right, the
devil's court—that's hell. So how do you get out
of hell, that's the Stairway to Heaven. Blind Faith.
So it's also "C" like "see"—seeing. With your eyes.
You have to just...close your eyes, and you'll get
out. We'll all get out, someday, even...even if it takes
a thousand years.
            (*a long pause; BRENT looks haunted*)
Don't you get it?


*Before ERIC or JANICE can answer, the FRONT DOOR swings open.
TOPHER stands framed in it, feet wide apart, head down, face obscured by
dangling hair. When he looks up, we see that his face is streaked with dirt and
scratches and his eyes are wild and lost.*


TOPHER
It's...getting too big...


*He staggers forward, raising his hand to his friends. He looks so deranged that
ERIC, JANICE, and BRENT all step back from him.*


TOPHER (*cont.*)
            (*a moment of focus; a cracked smile*)
Hey, Erky, check it out.


*He sings the old Oscar Meyer hot dog jingle, ending with the bit about everyone being in love with him. He suddenly stumbles and falls to his knees in front of them, head back, this time the eyes rolled up until only the whites show.*

> TOPHER *(cont.)*
> *(almost whispering)*

Help me...

DISSOLVE TO:

EXT.—PIERSON HOUSE, NOW—NIGHT
*ADULT ERIC stands by himself on the front porch of the house. He looks around. There's no one in sight, no lights but the strong glow of a full moon. The house itself is dark, too, and everything is dead silent. ERIC takes a breath, opens the front door, and steps through. He is tensed, but moonlight streaming through the windows shows the house is stripped, EMPTY.*

*Coming up from silence, slowly, is T. Rex's "Bang a Gong." As ERIC hears it, he shudders and turns to locate the sound of the noise, and as he turns the MUSIC and LIGHT and MOVEMENT all EXPLODE simultaneously. "Bang a Gong" is playing earsplittingly loud, and the room is suddenly the LIVING ROOM, CIRCA 1976. But this time, the ADULT ERIC is right in the middle, a witness to everything, including the younger version of himself.*

*ADULT ERIC stands in the middle of the floor, blinking, astonished, as TOPHER collapses to the floor and YOUNG ERIC, YOUNG BRENT, and YOUNG JANICE stand staring.*

> YOUNG ERIC
> Oh, man, why did you take that shit?

*As he bends over TOPHER, who is shaking violently, JANICE grabs at YOUNG ERIC's arm.*

> YOUNG JANICE

We have to call an ambulance.

YOUNG BRENT

No fucking way. The cops will be all over this place!

YOUNG JANICE

He might be dying!

YOUNG ERIC

Topher? Can you hear me, man? You're just tripping.

YOUNG JANICE

We have to get him to a doctor!

YOUNG ERIC

Topher?

*TOPHER looks up, ragged and pale, but suddenly smiling.*

TOPHER

Tripping? You wish, man. I'm...I'm becoming.

YOUNG ERIC

Let me help you...

*He reaches down to pull TOPHER to his feet, but TOPHER simply shrugs
and is three feet to one side. He has MOVED INSTANTANOUSLY, like
a jump-cut. YOUNG ERIC is holding empty air. He is stunned, and looks
up at the others. YOUNG JANICE is blankly terrified. YOUNG BRENT
suddenly turns away, scuttling toward the stereo.*

YOUNG BRENT

I definitely gotta put something else on...

*He takes off T. Rex with a jagged scratch and begins scrambling among the albums scattered all over the floor.*

*ADULT ERIC has been watching this. Now he takes a step forward toward his younger self, reaching out as if to take himself in his own arms, but ADULT ERIC's hand passes right through YOUNG ERIC, who is still staring after TOPHER.*

### YOUNG ERIC

What...what's going on?

### TOPHER

Don't touch me, Erky. You can't stop it.

### YOUNG JANICE

Topher, you're scaring me...

*She cautiously reaches toward him, as though he might be hot to the touch, but TOPHER is suddenly GONE again, having moved instantaneously to the base of the stairway leading upstairs.*

### ADULT ERIC
*(shouts)*

Just get out of the house!
   *(no one can hear him; his face crumples in misery)*
Get Kimmy...

### YOUNG BRENT

Topher, man, I couldn't find the Sabbath, but check
this out! You love this! You love this, man!

*The choppy opening licks of Jimi Hendrix's "Voodoo Chile (Slight Return)" come out of the speakers.*

### YOUNG BRENT *(cont.)*

Just sit down and listen to Jimi, man.

TOPHER
(*a big grin*)
Listen to him? I'm talking to him, bro! I'm talking
to all the dead people...

*TOPHER turns and makes his way up the stairs into the darkness.*

YOUNG ERIC
It's the acid. I didn't see it. It's the acid. It's the acid...

YOUNG JANICE
What are we going to do? We have to call an
ambulance, the police, something...
(*sudden realization*)
Where's Kimmy?

*ADULT ERIC turns to YOUNG JANICE, who cannot see or hear him.
Tears are in his eyes.*

ADULT ERIC
I'm sorry, Jan-Jan. Oh, God, I'm so sorry. It was all
my fault.

*YOUNG ERIC looks up at the mention of KIMMY. A look of guilt flashes
across his face.*

YOUNG ERIC
Kimmy's fine. She's fine. I think...she went out
walking. Yeah, she's out in front.

YOUNG JANICE
I can't stand this! I feel like things are crawling all
over me. Eric, what are we going to do about Topher?

ADULT ERIC

I'm so, so sorry...

YOUNG ERIC

It's okay. We're all tripping—we're just high, having
a bit of a freak-out. Stay with me. Stay with me.
It'll be okay.

YOUNG JANICE
(*wanting to believe*)
You think so? Will you put your arms around me?
I'm really scared.

*YOUNG ERIC wraps his arms around her and they stand swaying in the
middle of the living room. ADULT ERIC slowly reaches his hand out to the
two of them, then lets it drop, as we*
SLOW DISSOLVE TO:

INT.—PIERSON HOUSE, NOW—NIGHT, SAME TIME
*ADULT JANICE stands in a darkened, deserted hallway of the present-day
house, moonlight coming in through the windows. A few objects remain after
the house was emptied and some windblown leaves lie on the floors. After a
moment, she hears a sniffling sound—someone CRYING. Frightened, she
makes her way slowly down the hallway, listening, until she stops in front of one
of the doors. She opens that door, but instead of a room, there's ANOTHER
HALLWAY—incredibly long, equally dark, with a huddled shape sitting at
the far end. The crying is louder.*

JANICE

K-Kimmy?

KIMMY

You never came back for me.

*JANICE is suddenly near tears. Music rises quietly—ELO's "Telephone."*

> JANICE
>
> I...I didn't know...

> KIMMY
>
> You followed Eric like you were his dog. He was so much more important to you than me—your best friend...!

*JANICE moves toward her but the hallway does not seem to get any shorter. KIMMY is still far away, her back to JANICE, face hidden.*

> JANICE
>
> I didn't know any better. He was my boyfriend... Oh, Kimmy, that was twenty-five years ago!

> KIMMY
> *(a cracked laugh)*
> Not for me. For me it's still happening. For me, it's always happening...

> JANICE
>
> I'm so sorry!

*The distance suddenly telescopes—JANICE is right on top of KIMMY. She reaches out to touch her.*

> JANICE
>
> Kimmy? Can I do anything...anything to make it better?

*KIMMY turns, except it isn't KIMMY, it's YOUNG JANICE, but still with KIMMY's voice. YOUNG JANICE lifts BLOODY HANDS.*

### YOUNG JANICE/KIMMY
You betrayed me...!

*ADULT JANICE screams; it echoes down the long corridor, twisting, growing fainter as we follow it around many twists and turns, until it fades back into the music of Hendrix, still playing somewhere. ADULT BRENT is standing in a corridor of his own, an Escher-like impossibility of stairs and weird angles. He turns, bewildered. A little SMOKE drifts along the passageway.*

*BRENT is frightened and clearly lost. He takes a step, then another. A shadow falls on the wall across from him, and he turns with eyes wide. A dark figure steps from an open door—it's the ADULT ERIC.*

### ERIC
Brent? That you?

### BRENT
Oh my God. Oh my God. I've been in here for hours—where did you go? Where's Janice?

### ERIC
I don't know. Everything's...strange.

### BRENT
We have to get out of here. We should never have come. He's going to...

### ERIC
There must be some kind of sense to it, like Janice said. A reason. We were his friends,...!

### BRENT
No! He's crazy. It wasn't anybody's fault—things just went wrong.

ERIC

Really? I thought you said it was all your fault.

BRENT

Let's just get out of here.

ERIC

No, you distinctly said it was your fault. In fact, you were going to say that you betrayed him, weren't you?

BRENT

What...what are you talking about?

ERIC

Come on...Brent. You know what betrayal is, don't you?

ERIC *steps closer, resting his hands on* BRENT's *shoulders.* BRENT *is struggling, but he can't get away.*

ERIC

"You don't know who your friends really are until you trip with them..." Remember that? Remember?

BRENT
(*struggling*)

Let go of me!

ERIC's *face is beginning to change—to harden and grow brittle.* BRENT *struggles harder, but it's like being held by a statue.* ERIC's *face grows completely rigid, like* TOPHER'S SHELL. *Then it cracks, and falls away, to reveal* TOPHER *beneath.*

> TOPHER
> *(big grin)*
> It's all about the Court of the Crimson King, Brent.
> And hell has a special place saved for traitors...

*BRENT's clothes start to smolder where TOPHER is holding them. BRENT shrieks and flails and at last breaks away, falling backward.*

> TOPHER
> Wait! There's still the big finale...

*TOPHER reaches up and PEELS AWAY his face, revealing YOUNG BRENT'S FACE underneath. ADULT BRENT doesn't stay to watch—he drags himself to his feet, running down the distorted corridor, shrieking and crying, as we*
CUT TO:

INT.—LIVING ROOM—THEN AND NOW
*ADULT ERIC is miserably watching his YOUNG ERIC self combing through the carpet of the living room floor while YOUNG JANICE watches him, worried. No music is playing.*

> YOUNG JANICE
> Eric? Eric, what are you doing?

> YOUNG ERIC
> He's faking. He has to be faking. He couldn't have
> taken all of those pills...

*YOUNG BRENT looks up from his records.*

> YOUNG BRENT
> Hey, where's Kimmy?

> ADULT ERIC

(*a hopeless whisper*)
Just tell them...


YOUNG ERIC
(*hurriedly*)
Outside! She went for a walk!


BRENT *rises and heads for the front door. He pauses in the open doorway.*


YOUNG BRENT

The moon! It's fucking huge—like a big eye!


As *he goes out,* YOUNG ERIC *is still on his hands and knees, running his fingers through the carpet, searching.*


YOUNG ERIC

It's all bullshit. It has to be! We're just too high.


YOUNG JANICE

What are you talking about?


YOUNG ERIC

(*looks up, desperate-eyed*)
It's not real. We're all just tripping. Topher's trying
to freak us out. He just pretended to catch those
pills, but they're here somewhere. I'll find them.
That'll prove it.


*He goes back to his relentless combing of the carpet, crawling with his face practically down against the fibers.* YOUNG BRENT *comes back in and walks past them, then heads up the stairs.* ADULT ERIC *looks after him, then closes his eyes.*


YOUNG JANICE *doesn't know what to do. She looks up at the stairway, then toward the front door. She watches* YOUNG ERIC *for a moment, then sits back, hugging herself and looking very frightened. ADULT ERIC moves toward her, and although she can't see him, he kneels in front of her.*

ERIC
You were right. Oh, God, I was a fucking idiot, a terrified kid, trying to talk myself into thinking everything made sense.
(*a beat*)
And now I'm just a ghost and you can't hear me...

*For a moment YOUNG JANICE almost does seems to hear him: she tilts her head, as though searching for a tiny sound. Abruptly, the stereo comes on full-blast—"Iron Man," by Black Sabbath—and she jerks her head back around to stare at it. There's no one nearby: it has turned on by itself.*

*We begin to experience the first scene over again, but this time from ADULT ERIC's viewpoint.*

YOUNG JANICE
Eric! Eric, talk to me!

*YOUNG ERIC looks up blearily from the carpet.*

YOUNG JANICE
Eric, I want to get out of here right now...!

*YOUNG BRENT, staggers down the stairs, clutching his hands against his stomach, panicky but trying to stay calm.*

YOUNG BRENT
Shit, it's bad—Topher's freaking out for real up there.

YOUNG JANICE
Where's Kimmy, Brent? What's going on?

YOUNG BRENT

I don't know! I can't find her. I think...I think
something bad happened! I...

*As if finally realizing something, BRENT lifts his hands away from his body
and stares at them. They are covered in blood, smeared to the elbows. His eyes
bug out.*

YOUNG JANICE

Oh my God!

*YOUNG ERIC stares at BRENT, then looks up at the ceiling. He SEES
something no one else can see, and cowers back in horror, gasping in panic,
covering his face.*

YOUNG JANICE

Eric! Eric, what's going on? Stop that!

*YOUNG BRENT has just noticed the music playing.*

YOUNG BRENT

Why is this on? Who put on Sabbath? I hid the
Sabbath!

YOUNG JANICE

*(panicked, overwhelmed)*

It just...came on. Why do you have blood on you?

YOUNG BRENT

No, no, no! It's all wrong! It'll fuck everything up!

*YOUNG BRENT runs to the stereo and starts trying to turn it off, but can't
make the buttons work. Blood is smearing on the stereo knobs. He takes out
the record and throws it on the floor, but "Iron Man" keeps on playing. He*

*picks the record up and breaks it. He's crying. The music keeps on playing. Something begins thumping on the ceiling—weird sounds, like there's a large animal thrashing around up there.*

> YOUNG JANICE
> *(suddenly certain)*
> Oh, no. Kimmy's up there. With him.
> *(to YOUNG ERIC)*
> She's up there.

*YOUNG ERIC shakes his head, but it's not a denial.*

> YOUNG ERIC
> *(gesturing frantically at carpet)*
> He didn't take all the pills. They're around here somewhere. It's okay! Everything's going to be okay...!

*An even stranger NOISE comes through the roof, a long muffled shriek. The three teenagers look up. For a moment none of them move or speak, although the music continues loud.*

> YOUNG JANICE
> I'm going to get her.

*She reaches the stairs, then turns to the two boys. She's clearly terrified, but trying to be brave.*

> YOUNG JANICE
> Well? Are you coming with me?

> YOUNG ERIC
> Everything will be all right.

> YOUNG BRENT

(*dropping the bits of shattered record*)
No. It won't.

YOUNG JANICE *waits until* YOUNG ERIC *drags himself off the carpet and stands.* ADULT ERIC *leaps to the stairs and tries to block the way with his body.*

ADULT ERIC
Don't go up there! Don't...!

*But he's insubstantial—they walk* THROUGH HIM, *as we*
DISSOLVE TO:

INT.—STAIRS, THEN—MOMENTS LATER
*We've dropped back into the shaky, distorted perspective from the beginning of the film, more or less* YOUNG ERIC'S POV. YOUNG JANICE *leads,* YOUNG ERIC *and* YOUNG BRENT *right behind. We can still hear the music, but it seems odd, underwater.*

*Everything upstairs is very trippy—angles seem strange. The hall lights are* FLICKERING *between bright and dim. It makes for an eerie, almost "strobe-light" effect.*

YOUNG JANICE
Kimmy! Kimmy, where are you?

YOUNG ERIC
Where's...where's Topher?

YOUNG BRENT
I don't know. He was here a minute ago—man, he was acting so strange... I think he cut himself or something...

*The corridor is distorted, the walls so narrow that it seems they might crush the viewer. YOUNG ERIC looks down to the far end, sees the door to his GRANDMOTHER'S ROOM—the place he left KIMMY. He turns like a sleepwalker and moves toward it. We follow right up to the door, feel him hesitate, then push it open.*

*Inside, there's only the one light of the bedside lamp, flickering, making a little humming noise as though you can HEAR the ELECTRICTY. The bed is empty now, the sheets disarranged, smeared. On the wall over the head of the bed is the EYE WITH SUN RAYS, drawn crudely in smeared dark liquid, still wet.*

*There's a brighter light coming from under the bedroom door. ERIC moves toward it slowly. He stands in front of it and we hear a strange muffled THUMPING noise, and also heavy breathing and moans, like someone quietly reaching orgasm. ERIC pushes the door and it swings open. There's something in the tub, moving clumsily, hidden from us by the shower curtain.*

YOUNG ERIC

Kimmy...?

*YOUNG JANICE is stuck behind YOUNG BRENT, and cannot see properly. She makes a face as something CRAWLS over her foot. She looks down blankly and sees that she's standing in a couple of dozen ANTS. She shudders and takes a step back, trying to brush them off.*

YOUNG ERIC (cont.)

Is that you, Kimmy?

*He pulls the shower curtain aside and we see that KIMMY is huddled on her hands and knees, face pressed against the wall, partially hidden by the curtain. She's breathing in a very jerky way, and her voice is very thin.*

KIMMY

Eric? I'm...scared. It's dark, Eric. But Topher's... going to help me to see...like he does. Could you turn off the water? I'm getting all...wet.

YOUNG JANICE
(*still behind* BRENT, *trying to get over the ants and past him*)
Kimmy? Are you okay?

*YOUNG ERIC reaches out to KIMMY and she turns. Her eyes are GONE—only RAGGED BLACK SOCKETS—and her face and shirt are soaked in blood. The wall where she's been leaning is smeared with blood and the bathtub is full of it—she's kneeling in it.*

*YOUNG ERIC and YOUNG BRENT both scream and reel back, knocking YOUNG JANICE over, tumbling in a panic on top of her, which prevents her from seeing.*

YOUNG JANICE
Kimmy! Kimmy? Eric, what's wrong?

YOUNG ERIC
Don't look! Don't look!

*Scrambling away from the bathroom, he tries to pull YOUNG JANICE with him, but she's fighting him, crying, trying to get to KIMMY. She manages to grab the doorframe of the bathroom and pull herself crawling onto the tiles. As she turns away from fighting with ERIC, she sees (with her face at floor-level) a black knot of ANTS, boiling, swarming over some small object lying on the tiles just a few inches from her nose. It's a bloody EYE—one of KIMMY's eyes.*

*The POV SWINGS CRAZILY as she flails backward, retching and shrieking, tangling with YOUNG ERIC and YOUNG BRENT as they try to rise. They tumble back into the bedroom, sprawling on the floor. The lights are still flickering slowly on and off, and in a moment of shadow we see that there's a LARGE DARK SHADOW on the ceiling—like a stain, but more complicated.*

*As the lights flicker up again, the shadow opens its EYES—it's TOPHER,* stretched on the ceiling as though it were the floor. A trail of BLOODY HAND-PRINTS leads up the wall and across the ceiling to where he is.

> TOPHER
>
> Seen enough?

The three terror-stricken teenagers crush themselves into the corner of the bedroom, staring as TOPHER crawls back across the ceiling and down the wall like a spider, until he reaches the floor and stands at the center of the room, blood-smeared arms held wide.

> TOPHER (cont.)
>
> It's almost done now. I can fucking feel it happening—I don't need this body anymore, don't need any of this...

> YOUNG JANICE
> (a ragged screech)
> What did you do to Kimmy...?

> TOPHER
>
> I helped her. Helped her to see...all the way...to the end...

TOPHER suddenly convulses—not just a twitch, but something that physically distorts his ENTIRE BODY. He SCREAMS—a whistling shriek of agony.

> TOPHER (cont.)
> Oh God! Oh God! Oh God!

He is thrashing now, his body BULGING and TWISTING. STEAM begins to rise from his skin, leaking from his mouth and nostrils, and his gasps and screams become even more tortured. The three teenagers are all weeping in terror, fighting to force themselves even farther back into the corner. TOPHER is between them and the door.

>                    TOPHER (*cont.*)
> Oh, fuck, it hurts! Help me! It hurts it hurts it
> hurts! I don't want to be...inside this...any more...
> Ah! Ah!

*TOPHER suddenly staggers forward, his face seeming to MELT from within, little ripples of flame lifting from the skin. He grabs YOUNG BRENT, who shrieks and struggles. YOUNG ERIC and YOUNG JANICE do not try to help him, but only fight to get further away, clawing at each other. TOPHER pulls YOUNG BRENT close so that their faces are only inches apart, wreathed in steam, and shrieks at him.*

>                    TOPHER (*cont.*)
> Get me out of here! Fuuuuuck! Make it stop!

*The biggest convulsion of all, a moment in which TOPHER seems almost to turn INSIDE-OUT, and YOUNG BRENT is flung away, slamming against the bedroom wall. TOPHER falls onto the floor, writhing like a smashed snake, making awful gargling noises. YOUNG BRENT slowly climbs to his feet, stumbling and gasping, then staggers out the bedroom door.*

>                    TOPHER (*cont.*)
>       (*his voice is different now, weak and ragged*)
>
> Stop! Come back! It's...this is all wrong...

*YOUNG ERIC and YOUNG JANICE struggle onto their feet and sprint for the bedroom door. TOPHER's twitching has slowed—he raises a quivering hand after them.*

>                    TOPHER (*cont.*)
> Come...back! Eric! J-Janice! Don't...leave me...
> Don't leave me...

*We are on YOUNG ERIC and YOUNG JANICE as they hurtle down the stairs in a distortion of sound and vision. YOUNG BRENT is already gone, the front door swinging, and they CRASH through it after him, still screaming into the darkness, screaming, SCREAMING...*

*As the door swings back and clicks shut (we see it from the inside) the screaming abruptly STOPS.*

*We are in the empty, current LIVING ROOM with ADULT ERIC, ADULT JANICE, and ADULT BRENT. They turn in unison from the front door and look at the entrance to the stairway. There is a long, grim silence.*

> JANICE
> *(a ragged whisper)*
> We should have taken Kimmy...

> ERIC
> We were afraid...

> JANICE
> We left her there to bleed to death.

> BRENT
> *(staring at them)*
> Who are you?

> ERIC
> What?

> BRENT
> Who are you? Is it you again, another trick? Do we
> have to do this all over again?
> *(he begins to cry)*
> I've been here for years. There's nothing left you can
> do to me...

JANICE

Brent, it's us. We're here. It's really us.


ERIC

(*to nobody in particular*)

You know what we need to do, don't you?


BRENT

But how do I know that?


ERIC

We need to go upstairs.


*JANICE closes her eyes, not arguing, knowing it's true.*


BRENT

Upstairs? We can't!

(*whispers*)

He's up there.


ERIC

(*to JANICE*)

I tried to make it all go away. I was wrong. I lied to you about Kimmy, because...she and I were making out, getting it on, and...and I was feeling like everything would fall apart if you found out.


JANICE

(*startled*)

Oh, God, Eric, really?


ERIC

But I lied and it killed her.

*JANICE hesitates, trying to decide what she feels. At last:*

> ### JANICE
> You can't change the past. You can't let it haunt
> you. We all wish we'd done things...differently.

*Without quite realizing it, they both look at BRENT, but he will not meet their eyes.*

> ### ERIC
> We should have called someone—the police, an
> ambulance. Instead of just leaving Topher there all
> night, turning into...whatever it was.
> > *(a sudden, nasty thought)*
> Whatever it is.

> ### BRENT
> He hates us. We betrayed him.

> ### JANICE
> We didn't know any better.

*She looks at ERIC, then holds out her hand, which he takes. As if they've had a silent conversation, they both move toward the STAIRS, then, with only the smallest hesitation, they mount up into the shadows. BRENT stares after them for a moment.*

> ### BRENT
> > *(quietly)*
> Don't leave me here.

*He stands for a moment, then—with an expression of great hopelessness—he pulls the GUN out of his pocket and starts up the steps after them.*

BACK WITH ERIC AND JANICE:

*The stairway is impossibly long, as distorted as some of the earlier hallucinations. They climb silently, clutching each other's hands. A little MIST or STEAM drifts down from the doorway at the top and eddies past them down the stairs.*

*They finally reach the door at the top and look into the upper hallway. It's DISTORTED like 1976, with mist along the wood floor, but empty like "now." A few leaves rustle beneath their feet, blown in through the broken window at the end of the hall. Silently, ERIC and JANICE step up and begin to walk down the hall. A small cracked voice begins to sing the Oscar Meyer hot dog jingle again, close by.*

*As ERIC and JANICE reach the bedroom door, it swings open. The empty bedroom has EXPANDED—it seems dozens of yards across. At the far end, a pale shape—TOPHER REBORN—sits in front of the wall in low mist, head sunken on his chest. The EYE WITH SUN RAYS is scrawled on the wall above his head in dried blood. TOPHER finishes the jingle with the line about there soon being nothing left of him.*

*He lifts his head. He is VERY PALE all over, without any hair, his skin raw and clammy, like some sea creature that has been pulled from a shell. His eyes are all BLACK.*

> TOPHER (*cont.*)
> Hi, Erky. Hi, Jan-Jan.

*JANICE tries to say something, but TOPHER lifts his hand and her mouth works without sound. ERIC takes a step toward him, but TOPHER lifts his other hand and ERIC and JANICE are both frozen in place.*

> TOPHER
> Ssshhhhh. It's time for you to be quiet.

*A strange SHIFT in perspective and TOPHER is suddenly right in front of them, still sitting cross-legged.*

TOPHER (*cont.*)

I spent a long time being quiet, while I changed. It was like being buried alive. Helpless in the dark—screaming but no one could hear me. Twenty-five years. Twenty-five years, screaming! Think about that.

(*he reaches out and touches
JANICE's face, then ERIC's*)

I thought of lots of ways to make you suffer for leaving me. Oh, I lay there a long time in the dark, trapped in that body, thinking about it. What I would do to you. When I had finished...changing.

TOPHER *stands. He has no genitals, no nipples, no fingernails or toenails. Music begins to play—Roxy Music again, "In Every Dream Home a Heart-ache," slow and building.*

TOPHER (*cont.*)

I thought I might...melt you. Or turn you inside out. Or maybe just let you experience what happened to me—a quarter of a century locked inside yourselves—but that all seemed so...obvious. And after a while, I began to really think...

BRENT *suddenly appears in the doorway—staggering, panting for breath.*

BRENT

Leave them alone!

TOPHER

Hey, I was wondering when you'd show up!

BRENT

Fuck you! You know it's not them you want. You know it!

TOPHER

Do I? It's funny how you think you know things about your friends, isn't it?

BRENT *suddenly levels the gun and shoots, five times in rapid succession, screaming as he does so.*

BRENT

Fuck you! Fuck you!

*When the smoke clears, the REBORN TOPHER is still standing there, unharmed but for five little puckered holes across his pale body. He smiles and looks down at the bloodless wounds. They close up.*

TOPHER

Did you really think you were in a place where that would work? This all belongs to me—don't you know that? This is all my dream, and this time I'm taking you along.

BRENT *sobs and lifts the gun.*

BRENT

There's one bullet left...

TOPHER

Go ahead. What was it you said? "One bullet in Topher Holland's brain and everything's over"?

BRENT *slams the gun against his own head and pulls the trigger. Nothing. A moment later the gun crumbles into dust in his hand.*

TOPHER

You didn't think it would be that easy, did you?

*He turns to ERIC and JANICE; they tumble to the floor, moving again.*

> TOPHER *(cont.)*
> I never finished my story. See, I spent a long
> time—years—thinking about what to do to you.
> But then, slowly—oh, I had a lot of time—I came
> to understand that there are levels of betrayal.
> Many levels. And you were scared and young, just
> like I was.
> > *(a beat)*
> But there are some betrayals that can't be forgiven.
> > *(he turns to BRENT)*
> Right, Topher? Come here.

*BRENT (as we've been thinking of him) sways and crumples to the floor.
TOPHER (as we've been thinking of him) points, and BRENT begins to
crawl toward him, despite himself. TOPHER's skin is giving off faint curls of
smoke now. The music is growing more insistent as it builds toward its slow
climax.*

> TOPHER
> You ran, and ran, and ran, didn't you? But you
> never really got away.

> BRENT
> *(weeping, fighting, crawling)*
> No, please! I didn't mean to...!

> TOPHER
> But you did it, and that's all that matters. Aban-
> doned this body like rats off a burning ship. Pushed
> me out of my own, so I had nowhere to go.
> > *(a beat)*
> Black Sunshine. We'll never know quite what that

shit was, will we? The answer is probably buried in some government file forever. But it was sure something strange, something...bad. But no one asked you to take those pills, Topher. It was your own stupid idea. So why didn't you live with it, you selfish bastard?

*(He leans down toward*
*crawling BRENT/TOPHER)*

You wanted to get out of this body bad, didn't you? What you did to Kimmy, all the other crazy shit—none of that bothered you. But when the pain came, then you wanted out. And you got out. Jumped right into my body, didn't you, Topher? And I had nowhere to go but this ruined, mutating shell. You took my body, didn't you? You took my whole life!

BRENT/TOPHER *has now arrived weeping at* TOPHER/BRENT's *feet.*

### BRENT/TOPHER
I'm sorry! I'm so sorry!

### TOPHER/BRENT
Sometimes it's too late for "sorry." Twenty-five years... Yeah, I'd say it was too late.

ERIC *struggles to his feet.*

### ERIC
*(to TOPHER)*
Brent...? It's you?

### TOPHER/BRENT
He took my body just like a thief. Tried to make

it his own, like repainting a stolen car. But it's over
now, Holland, isn't it...?

*TOPHER/BRENT pulls BRENT/TOPHER up off the ground and into his*
*arms. The smoke is rising in earnest now, the first flames beginning to flicker*
*from TOPHER/BRENT's skin. BRENT/TOPHER is screeching and*
*fighting, in pain, but can't escape.*

> JANICE
> Don't! Oh, God, don't...!

> ERIC
> Brent, we'll help you...!

*TOPHER/BRENT shakes his pale head. As the Roxy Music song comes up*
*louder, he leans close to BRENT/TOPHER, close as a lover, and stares into*
*his eyes. BRENT/TOPHER struggles even harder, like an animal in a trap,*
*but it's no use.*

> TOPHER/BRENT
> (*to ERIC*)
> No, there's no help now—only loose ends. Only
> circles being closed. Sometimes the future can't
> begin...until you kill your past...

*Fire and smoke are leaking out of TOPHER/BRENT's mouth as he turns*
*back to BRENT/TOPHER.*

> TOPHER/BRENT
> And now I want back all the things you took. The
> things that would have been mine...

*The smoke and light is leaking from BRENT/TOPHER's mouth, nose, and*
*eyes now, being INHALED by TOPHER/BRENT.*

TOPHER/BRENT (*cont.*)

A life...you got to live a life...but it should have been
mine...

BRENT/TOPHER
(*shrieking in terror*)

No...no...!

TOPHER/BRENT

We got married, didn't we...and we even had a
child! Ah, she's beautiful...

BRENT/TOPHER

No! Not them! Tracy, Joanie! Give it back!

TOPHER/BRENT
(*gently*)

No, it's you who have to give it back now, Topher.
Everything you stole. But don't worry—it's only for
a moment...

BRENT/TOPHER *is fighting, struggling, but his life and memories are
leaking out of him, being devoured by TOPHER/BRENT—the real BRENT.
The music comes up—Roxy Music, swelling...*

TOPHER/BRENT

So many things that should have been mine. My
memories, my future. Stolen. All you left me was
the past. All you left me was that night.
(*a beat*)
Remember this song, Topher? It used to be one of
your favorites...
(*sings, almost a whisper*)
"Inflatable dolly—dee-luxe and dee-lightful. I blew
up your body...but you blew my mind!"

*As the guitar solo wails in, the flames suddenly become an INFERNO—a wall of fire. We see the two figures writhing within it, hear BRENT/ TOPHER's shrieks grow more and more SHRILL, then descend into bubbling GASPS as the figures in the flames slowly MELT TOGETHER...*

*A moment later, there is NOTHING: TOPHER and BRENT and the painted EYE on the wall are gone. The music is gone. ERIC and JANICE are huddled together in the deserted empty bedroom, with dawn light filtering through the cracked windowpane.*

*Silently, and as carefully as if they've both been badly bruised, they walk down the stairs, which look quite normal now. They make their way across the bare living room and out onto the front porch, where they stand for a moment, looking out across the empty dirt lot in the early morning light, to the trees and town beyond.*

JANICE

What happens now?

ERIC

The future.

JANICE

Brent...Topher...whoever he was. He has a wife, a daughter. What are we going to tell them?

ERIC
*(shrugs)*

The truth? Or some part of it?

*(a beat)*

Maybe not.

*Without looking, they reach out and find each other's hands, then walk down the porch steps and out into the field that once was an orchard. We pull back, watching two small figures walk slowly, holding hands, across the empty field. Pink Floyd's "Wish You Were Here" comes up, sweet and sad.*

ROLL CREDITS.

THE END.

# And Ministers of Grace

T he seed whispers, sings, offers, instructs.

    *A wise man of the homeworld once said, "Human beings can alter their lives by altering their attitudes of mind." Everything is possible for a committed man or woman. The universe is in our reach.*

    *Visit the Orgasmium—now open 24 hours. We take Senior Credits. The Orgasmium—where YOU come first!*

    *Your body temperature is normal. Your stress levels are normal, tending toward higher than normal. If this trend continues, you are recommended to see a physician.*

    *I'm almost alive! And I'm your perfect companion—I'm entirely portable. I want to love you. Come try me. Trade my personality with friends. Join the fun!*

    *Comb properties now available. Consult your local environment node. Brand new multi-family and single-family dwellings, low down payment with government entry loans...!*

    *Commodity prices are up slightly on the Sackler Index at this hour, despite a morning of sluggish trading. The prime minister will detail her plans to reinvigorate the economy in her speech to Parliament...*

    *A wise woman of the homeworld once said, "Keep your face to the sunshine and you cannot see the shadow."*

His name is Lamentation Kane and he is a Guardian of Covenant—a holy assassin. His masters have placed a seed of blasphemy in his head. It itches like unredeemed sin and fills his skull with foul pagan noise.

    The faces of his fellow travelers on the landing shuttle are bored and vacuous. How can these infidels live with this constant murmur in their heads? How can they survive and stay sane with the constant pinpoint flashing of attention signals at the edge of vision, the raw, sharp pulse of a world bristling and burbling with information?

It is like being stuck in a hive of insects, Kane thinks—insects doing their best to imitate human existence without understanding it. He longs for the sweet, singular voice of Spirit, soothing as cool water on inflamed skin. Always before, no matter the terrors of his mission, that voice has been with him, soothing him, reminding him of his holy purpose. All his life, Spirit has been with him. All his life until now.

*Humble yourselves therefore under the strong hand of God, so that He may raise you up in due time.*

Sweet and gentle like spring rain. Unlike this unending drizzle of filth, each word Spirit has ever spoken has been precious, bright like silver.

*Cast all your burdens on Him, for He cares for you. Be in control of yourself and alert. Your enemy, the devil, prowls around like a roaring lion, looking for someone to devour.*

Those were the last words Spirit spoke to him before the military scientists silenced the Word of God and replaced it with the endless, godless prattle of the infidel world, Archimedes.

For the good of all mankind, they assured him: Lamentation Kane must sin again so that one day all men would be free to worship God. Besides, the elders pointed out, what was there for him to fear? If he succeeds and escapes Archimedes the pagan seed will be removed and Spirit will speak in his thoughts again. If he does not escape—well, Kane will hear the true voice of God at the foot of His mighty throne. *Well done, my good and faithful servant...*

*Beginning descent. Please return to pods,* the pagan voices chirp in his head, prickling like nettles. *Thank you for traveling with us. Put all food and packaging in the receptacle and close it. This is your last chance to purchase duty-free drugs and alcohol. Cabin temperature is 20 degrees centigrade. Pull the harness snug. Beginning descent. Cabin pressure stable. Lander will detach in twenty seconds. Ten seconds. Nine seconds. Eight seconds...*

It never ends, and each godless word burns, prickles, itches.

Who needs to know so much about nothing?

———

A child of one of the Christian cooperative farms on Covenant's flat and empty plains, he was brought to New Jerusalem as a candidate for the elite Guardian unit. When he saw for the first time the white towers and golden domes of his planet's greatest city, Kane had been certain that Heaven would look just that way. Now, as Hellas City rises up to meet him, capitol of great Archimedes and stronghold of his people's enemies, it is bigger than even his grandest, most exaggerated memories of New Jerusalem—an immense sprawl with no visible ending, a lumpy white and gray and green patchwork of complex structures and orderly parks and lacy polyceramic web skyscrapers that bend gently in the cloudy upper skies like an oceanic kelp forest. The scale is astounding. For the first time ever in his life, Lamentation Kane has a moment of doubt—not in the rightness of his cause, but in the certainty of its victory.

But he reminds himself of what the Lord told Joshua: *Behold I have given into thy hands Jericho, and the king thereof, and all the valiant men...*

*Have you had a Creemy Crunch today?* It blares through his thoughts like a klaxon. *You want it! You need it! Available at any food outlet. Creemy Crunch makes cream crunchy! Don't be a bitch, Mom! Snag me a CC—or three!*

*The devil owns the Kingdom of Earth.* A favorite saying of one of his favorite teachers. *But even from his high throne he cannot see the City of Heaven.*

*Now with a subdermal glow-tattoo in every package! Just squeeze it in under the skin—and start shining!*

*Lord Jesus, protect me in this dark place and give me strength to do your work once more,* Kane prays. *I serve You. I serve Covenant.*

It never stops, and only gets more strident after the lander touches down and they are ushered through the locks into the port complex. *Remember the wise words, air quality is in the low thirties on the Teng Fuo scale today, first time visitors to Archimedes go here, returning go there, where to stand, what to say, what to have ready.* Restaurants, news feeds, information for transportation services, overnight accommodations, immigration law, emergency services, yammer yammer yammer until Kane wants to scream.

He stares at the smug citizens of Archimedes around him and loathes every one of them. How can they walk and smile and talk to each other with this Babel in their heads, without God in their hearts?

*Left. Follow the green tiles. Left. Follow the green tiles.* They aren't even people, they can't be—just crude imitations. And the variety of voices with which the seed bedevils him! High-pitched, low-pitched, fast and persuasive, moderately slow and persuasive, adult voices, children's voices, accents of a dozen sorts, most of which he can't even identify and can barely understand. His blessed Spirit is one voice and one voice only and he longs for her desperately. He always thinks of Spirit as "her," although it could just as easily be the calm, sweet voice of a male child. It doesn't matter. Nothing as crass as earthly sexual distinctions matter, any more than with God's holy angels. Spirit has been his constant companion since childhood, his advisor, his inseparable friend. But now he has a pagan seed in his brain and he may never hear her blessed voice again.

*I will never leave thee, nor forsake thee.* That's what Spirit told him the night he was baptized, the night she first spoke to him. Six years old. *I will never leave thee, nor forsake thee.*

He cannot think of that. He will not think of anything that might undermine his courage for the mission, of course, but there is a greater danger: some types of thoughts, if strong enough, can trigger the port's security E-Grams, which can perceive certain telltale patterns, especially if they are repeated.

*A wise man of the homeworld once said, "Man is the measure of all things..."* The foreign seed doesn't want him thinking of anything else, anyway.

*Have you considered living in Holyoake Harbor?* another voice asks, cutting through the first. *Only a twenty-minute commute to the business district, but a different world of ease and comfort.*

*...And of things which are not, that they are not,* the first voice finishes, swimming back to the top. *Another wise fellow made the case more directly: "The world holds two classes of men—intelligent men without religion, and religious men without intelligence."*

Kane almost shivers despite the climate controls. *Blur your thoughts,* he reminds himself. He does his best to let the chatter of voices and the swirl of passing faces numb and stupefy him, making himself a beast instead of a man, the better to hide from God's enemies.


He passes the various mechanical sentries and the first two human guard posts as easily as he hoped he would—his military brethren have prepared his disguise well. He is in line at the final human checkpoint when he catches a glimpse of her, or at least he thinks it must be her—a small, brown-skinned woman sagging between two heavily armored port security guards who clutch her elbows in a parody of assistance. For a moment their eyes meet and her dark stare is frank before she hangs her head again in a convincing imitation of shame. The words from the briefing wash up in his head through the fog of Archimedean voices—*Martyrdom Sister*—but he does his best to blur them again just as quickly. He can't imagine any word that will set off the E-Grams as quickly as "Martyrdom."

The final guard post is more difficult, as it is meant to be. The sentry, almost faceless behind an array of enhanced light scanners and lenses, does not like to see Arjuna on Kane's itinerary, his last port of call before Archimedes. Arjuna is not a treaty world for either Archimedes or Covenant, although both hope to make it so, and is not officially policed by either side.

The official runs one of his scanners over Kane's itinerary again. "Can you tell me why you stopped at Arjuna, Citizen McNally?"

Kane repeats the story of staying there with his cousin who works in the mining industry. Arjuna is rich with platinum and other minerals, another reason both sides want it. At the moment, though, neither the Rationalists of Archimedes or the Abramites of Covenant can get any traction there: the majority of Arjuna's settlers, colonists originally from the homeworld's Indian subcontinent, are comfortable with both sides—a fact that makes both Archimedes and Covenant quite uncomfortable indeed.

The guard post official doesn't seem entirely happy with Lamentation Kane's explanation and is beginning to investigate the false personality a little more closely. Kane wonders how much longer until the window of distraction is opened. He turns casually, looking up and down the transparent u-glass cells along the far wall until he locates the one in which the brown-skinned woman is being questioned. Is she a Muslim? A Copt? Or perhaps something entirely different—there are Australian Aboriginal Jews on Covenant, remnants of the Lost Tribes movement back on the homeworld. But whoever or whatever she is doesn't matter, he reminds himself: she is a sister in God and she has volunteered to sacrifice herself for the sake of the mission—*his* mission.

She turns for a moment and their eyes meet again through the warping glass. She has acne scars on her cheeks but she's pretty, surprisingly young to be given such a task. He wonders what her name is. When he returns— if he returns—he will go to the Great Tabernacle in New Jerusalem and light a candle for her.

Brown eyes. She seems sad as she looks at him before turning back to the guards. Could that be true? The Martyrs are the most privileged of all during their time in the training center. And she must know she will be looking on the face of God Himself very soon. How can she not be joyful? Does she fear the pain of giving up her earthly body?

As the sentry in front of him seems to stare out at nothing, reading the information that marches across his vision, Lamentation Kane opens his mouth to say something—to make small-talk the way a real returning citizen of Archimedes would after a long time abroad, a citizen guilty of nothing worse than maybe having watched a few religious broadcasts on Arjuna—when he sees movement out of the corner of his eye. Inside the u-glass holding cell the young, brown-skinned woman lifts her arms. One of the armored guards lurches back from the table, half-falling, the other reaches out his gloved hand as though to restrain her, but his face has the hopeless, slack expression of a man who sees his own death. A moment later bluish flames run up her arms, blackening the sleeves of her loose dress, and then she vanishes in a flare of magnesium white light.

People are shrieking and diving away from the glass wall, which is now spiderwebbed with cracks. The light burns and flickers and the insides of the walls blacken with a crust of what Kane guesses must be human fat turning to ash.

A human explosion—nanobiotic thermal flare—that partially failed. That will be their conclusion. But of course, the architects of Kane's mission didn't want an actual explosion. They want a distraction.

The sentry in the guard post polarizes the windows and locks up his booth. Before hurrying off to help the emergency personnel fight the blaze that is already leaking clouds of black smoke into the concourse, he thrusts Kane's itinerary into his hand and waves him through, then locks off the transit point.

Lamentation Kane would be happy to move on, even if he were the innocent traveler he pretends to be. The smoke is terrible, with the disturbing, sweet smell of cooked meat.

What had her last expression been like? It is hard to remember anything except those endlessly deep, dark eyes. Had that been a little smile or is he trying to convince himself? And if it had been fear, why should that be surprising? Even the saints must have feared to burn to death.

*Yea, though I walk through the valley of the shadow of death, I will fear no evil...*

*Welcome back to Hellas, Citizen McNally!* a voice in his head proclaims, and then the other voices swim up beneath it, a crowd, a buzz, an itch.

He does his best not to stare as the cab hurtles across the metroscape, but he cannot help being impressed by the sheer size of Archimedes' first city. It is one thing to be told how many millions live there and to try to understand that it is several times the size of New Jerusalem, but another entirely to see the hordes of people crowding the sidewalks and skyways. Covenant's population is mostly dispersed on pastoral settlements like the one on which Kane was raised, agrarian cooperatives that, as his teachers explained to him, keep God's children close to the earth that nurtures them. Sometimes it is hard to realize that the deep, reddish soil he had spent his childhood digging and turning and nurturing was not the same soil as the Bible described. Once he even asked a teacher why, if God made Earth, the People of the Book had left it behind.

"God made all the worlds to be earth for His children," the woman explained. "Just as He made all the lands of the old Earth, then gave them to different folk to have for their homes. But He always kept the sweetest lands, the lands of milk and honey, for the children of Abraham, and that's why when we left earth He gave us Covenant."

As he thinks about it now Kane feels a surge of warmth and loneliness commingled. It's true that the hardest thing to do for love is to give up the beloved. At this moment, he misses Covenant so badly it is all he can do not to cry out. It is astounding in one as experienced as himself. *God's warriors don't sigh*, he tells himself sternly. *They make others sigh instead. They bring lamentation to God's enemies. Lamentation.*

He exits the cab some distance from the safehouse and walks the rest of the way, floating in smells both familiar and exotic. He rounds the neighborhood twice to make sure he is not followed, then enters the flatblock, takes the slow but quiet elevator up to the eighteenth floor, and lets himself in with the key code. It looks like any other Covenant safehouse on any of the other colony worlds, cupboards well stocked with nourishment and medical supplies, little in the way of furniture but a bed and a single chair and a small table. These are not places of rest and relaxation, these are way stations on the road to Jericho.

It is time for him to change.

Kane fills the bathtub with water. He finds the chemical ice, activates a dozen packs, and tosses them in. Then he goes to the kitchen and locates the necessary mineral and chemical supplements. He pours enough water into the mixture to make himself a thick, bitter milkshake, and drinks it down while he waits for the water in the tub to cool. When the temperature has dropped far enough he strips naked and climbs in.

"You see, Kane," one of the military scientists had explained, "we've reached a point where we can't smuggle even a small hand-weapon onto Archimedes, let alone something useful, and they regulate their own citizens' possession of weapons so thoroughly that we cannot chance trying to obtain one there. So we have gone another direction. We have created Guardians—human weapons. That is what you are, praise the Lord. It started in your childhood. That's why you've always been different from your peers—faster, stronger, smarter. But we've come to the limit of what we can do with genetics and training. We need to give you what you need to make yourself into the true instrument of God's justice. May He bless this and all our endeavors in His name. Amen."

"Amen," the Spirit in his head told him. "You are now going to fall asleep."

"Amen," said Lamentation Kane.

And then they gave him the first injection.

When he woke up that first time he was sore, but nowhere near as sore as he was the first time he activated the nanobiotes or "notes" as the scientists liked to call them. When the notes went to work, it was like a terrible sunburn on the outside and the inside both, and like being pounded with a roundball bat for at least an hour, and like lying in the road while a good-sized squadron of full-dress Holy Warriors marched over him.

In other words, it hurt.

Now, in the safehouse, he closes his eyes, turns down the babble of the Archimedes seed as far as it will let him, and begins to work.

It is easier now than it used to be, certainly easier than that terrible first time when he was so clumsy that he almost tore his own muscles loose from tendon and bone.

He doesn't just *flex*, he thinks about where the muscles are that would flex if he wanted to flex them, then how he would just begin to move them if he were going to move them extremely slowly, and with that first thought comes the little tug of the cells unraveling their connections and re-knitting in different, more useful configurations, slow as a plant reaching toward the sun. Even with all this delicacy, his temperature rises and his muscles spasm and cramp, but not like the first time. That was like being born—no, like being judged and found wanting, as though the very meat of his earthly body was trying to tear itself free, as though devils pierced his joints with hot iron pitchforks. Agony.

Had the sister felt something like this at the end? Was there any way to open the door to God's house without terrible, holy pain? She had brown eyes. He thinks they were sad. Had she been frightened? Why would Jesus let her be frightened, when even He had cried out on the cross?

*I praise You, Lord,* Lamentation Kane tells the pain. *This is Your way of reminding me to pay attention. I am Your servant, and I am proud to put on Your holy armor.*


It takes him at least two hours to finish changing at the best of times. Tonight, with the fatigue of his journey and long entry process and the curiously troubling effect of the woman's martyrdom tugging at his thoughts, it takes him over three.

Kane gets out of the tub shivering, most of the heat dispersed and his skin almost blue-white with cold. Before wrapping the towel around himself he looks at the results of all his work. It's hard to see any differences except for a certain broadness to his chest that was not there before, but he runs his fingers along the hard shell of his stomach and the sheath of gristle that now protects his windpipe and is satisfied. The thickening beneath the skin will not stop high-speed projectiles from close up, but they should help shed the energy of any more distant shot and will allow him to take a bullet or two from nearer and still manage to do his job. Trellises of springy cartilage strengthen his ankles and wrists. His muscles are augmented, his lungs and circulation improved mightily. He is a Guardian, and with every movement he can feel the holy modifications that have been given to him. Beneath the appearance of normality he is strong as Goliath, scaly and supple as a serpent.

He is starving, of course. The cupboards are full of powdered nutritional supplement drinks. He adds water and ice from the kitchen unit, mixes the first one up and downs it in a long swallow. He drinks five before he begins to feel full.

Kane props himself up on the bed—things are still sliding and grinding a little inside him, the last work of change just finishing—and turns the wall on. The images jump into life and the seed in his head speaks for them. He wills his way past sports and fashion and drama, all the unimportant gibberish with which these creatures fill their empty hours, until he finds a stream of current events. Because it is Archimedes, hive of Rationalist pagans, even the news is corrupted with filth, gossip, and whoremongering, but he manages to squint his way through the offending material to find a report on what the New Hellas authorities are calling a failed terrorist explosion at the port. A picture of the Martyrdom Sister flashes onto the screen—taken from her travel documents, obviously, anything personal in her face well hidden by her training—but seeing her again gives him a strange jolt, as though the notes that tune his body have suddenly begun one last, forgotten operation.

*Nefise Erim*, they call her. Not her real name, that's almost certain, any more than Keenan McNally is his. *Outcast*, that's her true name. *Scorned*—that could be her name too, as it could be his. Scorned by the unbelievers, scorned by the smug, faithless creatures who, like Christ's ancient tormentors, fear the word of God so much they try to ban Him from their lives, from their entire planet! But God can't be banned, not as long as one human heart remains alive to His voice. As long as the Covenant system survives, Kane knows, God will wield his mighty sword and the unbelievers will learn real fear.

*Oh, please, Lord, grant that I may serve you well. Give us victory over our enemies. Help us to punish those who would deny You.*

And just as he lifts this silent prayer, he sees *her* face on the screen. Not his sister in martyrdom, with her wide, deep eyes and dark skin. No, it is her—the devil's mistress, Keeta Januari, Prime Minister of Archimedes.

His target.

Januari is herself rather dark skinned, he cannot help noticing. It is disconcerting. He has seen her before, of course, her image replayed before him dozens upon dozens of times, but this is the first time he has noticed a shade to her skin that is darker than any mere suntan, a hint of something else in her background beside the pale, Scandinavian forebears so obvious in her bone structure. It is as if the martyred sister Nefise has somehow suffused everything, even his target. Or is it that the dead woman has somehow crept into his thoughts so deeply that he is witnessing her everywhere?

*If you can see it, you can eat it!* He has mostly learned to ignore the horrifying chatter in his head, but sometimes it still reaches up and slaps his thoughts away. *Barnstorm Buffet! We don't care if they have to roll you out the door afterward—you'll get your money's worth!*

It doesn't matter what he sees in the prime minister, or thinks he sees. A shade lighter or darker means nothing. If the devil's work out here among the stars has a face, it is the handsome, narrow-chinned visage of Keeta Januari, leader of the Rationalists. And if God ever wanted someone dead, she is that person.


She won't be his first: Kane has sent eighteen souls to judgement already.

Eleven of them were pagan spies or dangerous rabble-rousers on Covenant. One of those was the leader of a crypto-rationalist cult in the Crescent— the death was a favor to the Islamic partners in Covenant's ruling coalition, Kane found out later. Politics. He doesn't know how he feels about that, although he knows the late Doctor Hamoud was a doubter and a liar and had been corrupting good Muslims. Still...politics.

Five were infiltrators among the Holy Warriors of Covenant, his people's army. Most of these had half-expected to be discovered, and several of them had resisted desperately.

The last two were a politician and his wife on the unaffiliated world of Arjuna, important Rationalist sympathizers. At his masters' bidding Kane made it look like a robbery gone wrong instead of an assassination: this was not the time to make the Lord's hand obvious in Arjuna's affairs. Still, there were rumors and accusations across Arjuna's public networks. The gossipers and speculators had even given the unknown murderer a nickname—the Angel of Death.

Dr. Prishrahan and his wife had fought him. Neither of them had wanted to die. Kane had let them resist even though he could have killed them both in a moment. It gave credence to the robbery scenario. But he hadn't enjoyed it. Neither had the Prishrahans, of course.

*He will avenge the blood of His servants, and will render vengeance to His adversaries,* Spirit reminded him when he had finished with the doctor and his wife, and he understood. Kane's duty is not to judge. He is not one of the flock, but closer to the wolves he destroys. Lamentation Kane is God's executioner.

He is now cold enough from his long submersion that he puts on clothes. He is still tender in his joints as well. He goes out onto the balcony, high in the canyons of flatblocks pinpricked with illuminated windows, thousands upon thousands of squares of light. The immensity of the place still unnerves him a little. It's strange to think that what is happening behind one little lighted window in this immensity of sparkling urban night is going to rock this massive world to its foundations.

It is hard to remember the prayers as he should. Ordinarily Spirit is there with the words before he has a moment to feel lonely. *"I will not leave you comfortless: I will come to you."*

But he does not feel comforted at this moment. He is alone.

*"Looking for love?"* The voice in his head whispers this time, throaty and exciting. A bright twinkle of coordinates flicker at the edge of his vision. *"I'm looking for you...and you can have me almost nothing..."*

He closes his eyes tight against the immensity of the pagan city.

*Fear thou not; for I am with thee: be not dismayed; for I am thy God.*


He walks to the auditorium just to see the place where the prime minister will speak. He does not approach very closely. It looms against the grid of light, a vast rectangle like an axe head smashed into the central plaza of Hellas City. He does not linger.

As he slides through the crowds it is hard not to look at the people around him as though he has already accomplished his task. What would they think if they knew who he was? Would they shrink back from the terror of the Lord God's wrath? Or would a deed of such power and piety speak to them even through their fears?

*I am ablaze with the light of the Lord,* he wants to tell them. *I have let God make me His instrument—I am full of glory!* But he says nothing, of course, only walks amid the multitudes with his heart grown silent and turned inward.

Kane eats in a restaurant. The food is so over-spiced as to be tasteless, and he yearns for the simple meals of the farm on which he was raised. Even military manna is better than this! The customers twitter and laugh just like the Archimedes seeds in their heads, as if it is that babbling obscenity that has programmed them instead of the other way around. How these people surrounded themselves with distraction and glare and noise to obscure the emptiness of their souls!

He goes to a place where women dance. It is strange to watch them, because they smile and smile and they are all as beautiful and naked as a dark dream, but they seem to him like damned souls, doomed to act out this empty farce of love and attraction throughout eternity. He cannot get the thought of martyred Nefise Erim out of his head. At last he chooses one of the women—she does not look much like the martyred one, but she is darker than the others—and lets her lead him to her room behind the place where they dance. She feels the hardened tissues beneath his skin and tells him he is very muscular. He empties himself inside her and then, afterward, she asks him why he is crying. He tells her she is mistaken. When she asks again he slaps her. Although he holds back his strength he still knocks her off the bed. The room adds a small surcharge to his bill.

He lets her go back to her work. She is an innocent, of sorts: she has been listening to the godless voices in her head all her life and knows nothing else. No wonder she dances like a damned thing.

Kane is soiled now as he walks the streets again, but his great deed will wipe the taint from him as it always does. He is a Guardian of Covenant, and soon he will be annealed by holy fire.


His masters want the deed done while the crowd is gathered to see the prime minister, and so the question seems simple: before or after? He thinks at first that he will do it when she arrives, as she steps from the car and is hurried into the corridor leading to the great hall. That seems safest. After she has spoken it will be much more difficult, with her security fully deployed and the hall's own security acting with them. Still, the more he thinks about it the more he feels sure that it must be inside the hall. Only a few thousand would be gathered there to see her speak, but millions more will be watching on the screens surrounding the massive building. If he strikes quickly his deed will be witnessed by this whole world—and other worlds, too.

Surely God wants it that way. Surely He wants the unbeliever destroyed in full view of the public waiting to be instructed.

Kane does not have time or resources to counterfeit permission to be in the building—the politicians and hall security will be checked and rechecked, and will be in place long before Prime Minister Januari arrives. Which means that the only people allowed to enter without going through careful screening will be the prime minister's own party. That is a possibility, but he will need help with it.

Making contact with local assets is usually a bad sign—it means something has gone wrong with the original plan—but Kane knows that with a task this important he cannot afford to be superstitious. He leaves a signal in the established place. The local assets come to the safehouse after sunset. When he opens the door he finds two men, one young and one old, both disconcertingly ordinary-looking, the kind of men who might come to tow your car or fumigate your flat. The middle-aged one introduces himself as Heinrich Sartorius, his companion just as Carl. Sartorius motions Kane not to speak while Carl sweeps the room with a small object about the size of a toothbrush.

"Clear," the youth announces. He is bony and homely, but he moves with a certain grace, especially while using his hands.

"Praise the Lord," Sartorius says. "And blessings on you, brother. What can we do to help you with Christ's work?"

"Are you really the one from Arjuna?" young Carl asks suddenly.

"Quiet, boy. This is serious." Sartorius turns back to Kane with an expectant look on his face. "He's a good lad. It's just—that meant a lot to the community, what happened there on Arjuna."

Kane ignores this. He is wary of the Death Angel nonsense. "I need to know what the prime minister's security detail wears. Details. And I want the layout of the auditorium, with a focus on air and water ducts."

The older man frowns. "They'll have that all checked out, won't they?"

"I'm sure. Can you get it for me without attracting attention?"

"'Course." Sartorius nods. "Carl'll find it for you right now. He's a whiz. Ain't that right, boy?" The man turns back to Kane. "We're not backward, you know. The unbelievers always say it's because we're backward, but Carl here was up near the top of his class in mathematics. We just kept Jesus in our hearts when the rest of these people gave Him up, that's the difference."

"Praise Him," says Carl, already working the safehouse wall, images flooding past so quickly that even with his augmented vision Kane can barely make out a tenth of them.

"Yes, *praise* Him," Sartorius agrees, nodding his head as though there has been a long and occasionally heated discussion about how best to deal with Jesus.

Kane is beginning to feel the ache in his joints again, which usually means he needs more protein. He heads for the small kitchen to fix himself another nutrition drink. "Can I get you two anything?" he asks.

"We're good," says the older man. "Just happy doing the Lord's work."

*They make too much noise*, he decides. Not that most people would have heard them, but Kane isn't most people.

*I am the sword of the Lord*, he tells himself silently. He can scarcely hear himself think it over the murmur of the Archimedes seed, which although turned down low is still spouting meteorological information, news, tags of philosophy and other trivia like a madman on a street corner. Below the spot where Kane hangs, the three men of the go-suited security detail communicate among themselves with hand-signs as they investigate the place where he has entered the building. He has altered the evidence of his incursion to look like someone has tried and failed to get into the auditorium through the intake duct.

The guards seem to draw the desired conclusion: after another flurry of hand-signals, and presumably after relaying the all-clear to the other half of the security squad, who are doubtless inspecting the outside of the same intake duct, the three turn and begin to walk back up the steep conduit, the flow of air making their movements unstable, headlamps splashing unpredictably over the walls. But Kane is waiting above them like a spider, in the shadows of a high place where the massive conduit bends around one of the building's pillars, his hardened fingertips dug into the concrete, his augmented muscles tensed and locked. He waits until all three pass below him, then drops down silently behind them and crushes the throat of the last man so he can't alert the others. He then snaps the guard's neck and tosses the body over his shoulder, then scrambles back up the walls into the place he has prepared, a hammock of canvas much the same color as the inside of the duct. In a matter of seconds he strips the body, praying fervently that the other two will not have noticed that their comrade is missing. He pulls on the man's go-suit, which is still warm, then leaves the guard's body in the hammock and springs down to the ground just as the second guard realizes there is no one behind him.

As the man turns toward him Kane sees his lips moving behind the face shield and knows the guard must be talking to him by seed. The imposture is broken, or will be in a moment. Can he pretend his own communications machinery is malfunctioning? Not if these guards are any good. If they work for the prime minister of Archimedes, they probably are. He has a moment before the news is broadcast to all the other security people in the building.

Kane strides forward making nonsensical hand-signs. The other guard's eyes widen: he does not recognize either the signs or the face behind the polymer shield. Kane shatters the man's neck with a two-handed strike even as the guard struggles to pull his side arm. Then Kane leaps at the last guard just as he turns.

Except it isn't a he. It's a woman and she's fast. She actually has her gun out of the holster before he kills her.

He has only moments, he knows: the guards will have a regular check-in to their squad leader. He sprints for the side-shaft that should take him to the area above the ceiling of the main hall.

Women as leaders. Women as soldiers. Women dancing naked in public before strangers. Is there anything these Archimedeans will not do to debase the daughters of Eve? Force them all into whoredom, as the Babylonians did?

The massive space above the ceiling is full of riggers and technicians and heavily armed guards. A dozen of those, at least. Most of them are sharpshooters keeping an eye on the crowd through the scopes on their high-powered guns, which is lucky. Some of them might not even see him until he's on his way down.

Two of the heavily armored troopers turn as he steps out into the open. He is being queried for identification, but even if they think he is one of their own they will not let him get more than a few yards across the floor. He throws his hands in the air and takes a few casual steps toward them, shaking his head and pointing at his helmet. Then he leaps forward, praying they do not understand how quickly he can move.

He covers the twenty yards or so in just a little more than a second. To confound their surprise, he does not attack but dives past the two who have already seen him and the third just turning to find out what the conversation is about. He reaches the edge of the flies and launches himself out into space, tucked and spinning to make himself a more difficult target. Still, he feels a high-speed projectile hit his leg and penetrate a little way, slowed by the guard's go-suit and stopped by his own hardened flesh.

He lands so hard that the stolen guard helmet pops off his head and bounces away. The first screams and shouts of surprise are beginning to rise from the crowd of parliamentarians, but Kane can hardly hear them. The shock of his fifty-foot fall swirls through the enhanced cartilage of his knees and ankles and wrists, painful but manageable. His heart is beating so fast it almost buzzes, and he is so accelerated that the noise of the audience seemed like the sound of something completely inhuman, the deep scrape of a glacier, the tectonic rumbling of a mountain's roots. Two more bullets snap into the floor beside him, chips of concrete and fragments of carpet spinning slowly in the air, hovering like ashes in a fiery updraft. The woman at the lectern turns toward him in molasses-time and it is indeed her, Keeta Januari, the Whore of Babylon. As he reaches toward her he can see the individual muscles of her face react—eyebrows pulled up, forehead wrinkling, surprised...but not frightened.

How can that be?

He is already leaping toward her, curving the fingers of each hand into hardened claws for the killing strike. A fraction of a second to cross the space between them as bullets snap by from above and either side, the noise scything past a long instant later, *wow, wow, wow.* Time hanging, disconnected from history. God's hand. He *is* God's hand, and this is what it must feel like to be in the presence of God Himself, this shimmering, endless, bright NOW...

And then pain explodes through him and sets his nerves on fire and everything goes suddenly and irrevocably

black.


Lamentation Kane wakes in a white room, the light from everywhere and nowhere. He is being watched, of course. Soon, the torture will begin.

"*Beloved, think it not strange concerning the fiery trial which is to try* you, *as though some strange thing happened unto you...*" Those were the holy words Spirit whispered to him when he lay badly wounded in the hospital after capturing the last of the Holy Warrior infiltrators, another augmented soldier like himself, a bigger, stronger man who almost killed him before Kane managed to put a stiffened finger through his eyeball into his brain. Spirit recited the words to him again and again during his recuperation: "*But rejoice, inasmuch as ye are partakers of Christ's sufferings; that, when his glory...when his glory....*"

To his horror, he cannot remember the rest of the passage from Peter.

He cannot help thinking of the martyred young woman who gave her life so that he could fail so utterly. He will see her soon. Will he be able to meet her eye? Is there shame in Heaven?

*I will be strong,* Kane promises her shade, *no matter what they do to me.*

One of the cell's walls turns from white to transparent. The room beyond is full of people, most of them in military uniforms or white medical smocks. Only two wear civilian clothing, a pale man and...her. Keeta Januari.

"You may throw yourself against the glass if you want." Her voice seems to come out of the air on all sides. "It is very, very thick and very, very strong."

He only stares. He will not make himself a beast, struggling to escape while they laugh. These people are the ones who think themselves related to animals. Animals! Kane knows that the Lord God has given his people dominion.

"Over all the beasts and fowls of the earth," he says out loud.

"So," says Prime Minister Januari. "So, this is the Angel of Death."

"That is not my name."

"We know your name, Kane. We have been watching you since you reached Archimedes."

A lie, surely. They would never have let him get so close.

She narrows her eyes. "I would have expected an angel to look more... angelic."

"I'm no angel, as you almost found out."

"Ah, if you're not, then you must be one of the ministers of grace." She sees the look on his face. "How sad. I forgot that Shakespeare was banned by your mullahs. 'Angels and ministers of grace defend us!' From *Macbeth*. It proceeds a murder."

"We Christians do not have mullahs," he says as evenly as he can. He does not care about the rest of the nonsense she speaks. "Those are the people of the Crescent, our brothers of the Book."

She laughed. "I thought you would be smarter than the rest of your sort, Kane, but you parrot the same nonsense. Do you know that only a few generations back your 'brothers' as you call them set off a thermonuclear device, trying to kill your grandparents and the rest of the Christian and Zionist 'brothers'?"

"In the early days, before the Covenant, there was confusion." Everyone knew the story. Did she think to shame him with old history, ancient quotations, banned playwrights from the wicked old days of Earth? If so, then both of them had underestimated each other as adversaries.

Of course, at the moment she did hold a somewhat better position.

"So, then, not an angel but a minister. But you don't pray to be protected from death, but to be able to cause it."

"I do the Lord's will."

"Bullshit, to use a venerable old term. You are a murderer many times over, Kane. You tried to murder me." But Januari does not look at him as though at an enemy. Nor is there kindness in her gaze, either. She looks at him as though he is a poisonous insect in a jar—an object to be careful with, yes, but mostly a thing to be studied. "What shall we do with you?"

"Kill me. If you have any of the humanity you claim, you will release me and send me to Heaven. But I know you will torture me."

She raises an eyebrow. "Why would we do that?"

"For information. Our nations are at war, even though the politicians have not yet admitted it to their peoples. You know it, woman. I know it. Everyone in this room knows it."

Keeta Januari smiles. "You will get no argument from me or anyone here about the state of affairs between Archimedes and the Covenant system. But why would we torture you for information we already have? We are not barbarians. We are not primitives—like some others. We do not force our citizens to worship savage old myths..."

"You force them to be silent! You punish those who would worship the

God of their fathers. You have persecuted the People of the Book wherever you have found them!"

"We have kept our planet free from the mania of religious warfare and extremism. We have never interfered in the choices of Covenant."

"You have tried to keep us from gaining converts."

The prime minister shakes her head. "Gaining converts? Trying to hijack entire cultures, you mean. Stealing the right of colonies to be free of Earth's old tribal ghosts. We are the same people that let your predecessors worship the way they wished to—we fought to protect their freedom, and were repaid when they tried to force their beliefs on us at gunpoint." Her laugh is harsh. "'Christian tolerance'—two words that do not belong together no matter how often they've been coupled. And we all know what your Islamists and Zionists brothers are like. Even if you destroy all of the Archimedean alliance and every single one of us unbelievers, you'll only find yourself fighting your allies instead. The madness won't stop until the last living psychopath winds up all alone on a hill of ashes, shouting praise to his god."

Kane feels his anger rising and closes his mouth. He suffuses his blood with calming chemicals. It confuses him, arguing with her. She is a woman and she should give comfort, but she is speaking only lies—cruel, dangerous lies. This is what happens when the natural order of things is upset. "You are a devil. I will speak to you no more. Do whatever it is you're going to do."

"Here's another bit of Shakespeare," she says. "If your masters hadn't banned him, you could have quoted it at me. '*But man, proud man, dressed in a little brief authority, most ignorant of what he's most assured*'—that's nicely put, isn't it? '*His glassy essence, like an angry ape, plays such fantastic tricks before high heaven as make the angels weep.*'" She puts her hands together in a gesture disturbingly reminiscent of prayer. He cannot turn away from her gaze. "So—what *are* we going to do with you? We could execute you quietly, of course. A polite fiction—died from injuries sustained in the arrest—and no one would make too much fuss."

The man behind her clears his throat. "Madame Prime Minster, I respectfully suggest we take this conversation elsewhere. The doctors are waiting to see the prisoner..."

"Shut up, Healy." She turns to look at Kane again, really look, her blue eyes sharp as scalpels. She is older than the Martyrdom Sister by a good twenty years, and despite the dark tint her skin is much paler, but somehow, for a dizzying second, they are the same.

*Why do you allow me to become confused, Lord, between the murderer and the martyr?*

"Kane comma Lamentation," she says. "Quite a name. Is that your enemies lamenting, or is it you, crying out helplessly before the power of your God?" She holds up her hand. "Don't bother to answer. In parts of the Covenant system you're a hero, you know—a sort of superhero. Were you aware of that? Or have you been traveling too much?"

He does his best to ignore her. He knows he will be lied to, manipulated, that the psychological torments will be more subtle and more important than the physical torture. The only thing he does not understand is: Why her—why the prime minister herself? Surely he isn't so important. The fact that she stands in front of him at this moment instead of in front of God is, after all, a demonstration that he is a failure.

As if in answer to this thought, a voice murmurs in the back of his skull, *"Arjuna's Angel of Death captured in attempt on PM Januari."* Another inquires, *"Have you smelled yourself lately? Even members of parliament can lose freshness—just ask one!"* Even here, in the heart of the beast, the voices in his head will not be silenced.

"We need to study you," the prime minister says at last. "We haven't caught a Guardian-class agent before—not one of the new ones, like you. We didn't know if we could do it—the scrambler field was only recently developed." She smiles again, a quick icy flash like a first glimpse of snow in high mountains. "It wouldn't have meant anything if you'd succeeded, you know. There are at least a dozen more in my party who can take my place and keep this system safe against you and your masters. But I made good bait—and you leaped into the trap. Now we're going to find out what makes you such a nasty instrument, little Death Angel."

He hopes that now the charade is over they will at least shut off the seed in his head. Instead, they leave it in place but disable his controls so that he can't affect it at all. Children's voices sing to him about the value of starting each day with a healthy breakfast and he grinds his teeth. The mad chorus yammers and sings to him nonstop. The pagan seed shows him pictures he does not want to see, gives him information about which he does not care, and always, always, it denies that Kane's God exists.

The Archimedeans claim they have no death penalty. Is this what they do instead? Drive their prisoners to suicide?

If so, he will not do their work for them. He has internal resources they cannot disable without killing him and he was prepared to survive torture of a more obvious sort—why not this? He dilutes the waves of despair that wash through him at night when the lights go out and he is alone with the idiot babble of their idiot planet.

No, Kane will not do their job for him. He will not murder himself. But it gives him an idea.

If he had done it in his cell they might have been more suspicious, but when his heart stops in the course of a rather invasive procedure to learn how the note biotech has grown into his nervous system, they are caught by surprise.

"It must be a failsafe!" one of the doctors cries. Kane hears him as though from a great distance—already his higher systems are shutting down. "Some kind of auto-destruct!"

"Maybe it's just cardiac arrest..." says another, but it's only a whisper and he is falling down a long tunnel. He almost thinks he can hear Spirit calling after him...

*And God shall wipe away all tears from their eyes; and there shall be no more death, neither sorrow, nor crying, neither shall there be any more pain: for the former things are passed away.*

His heart starts pumping again twenty minutes later. The doctors, unaware of the sophistication of his autonomic control, are trying to shock his system back to life. Kane hoped he would be down longer and that they would give him up for dead but that was overly optimistic: instead he has to roll off the table, naked but for trailing wires and tubes, and kill the startled guards before they can draw their weapons. He must also break the neck of one of the doctors who has been trying to save him but now makes the mistake of attacking him. Even after he leaves the rest of the terrified medical staff cowering on the emergency room floor and escapes the surgical wing, he is still in a prison.

*"Tired of the same old atmosphere? Holyoake Harbor, the little village under the bubble—we make our own air and it's guaranteed fresh!"*

His internal modifications are healing the surgical damage as quickly as possible but he is staggering, starved of nutrients and burning energy at brushfire speed. God has given him this chance and he must not fail, but if he does not replenish his reserves he *will* fail.

Kane drops down from an overhead air duct into a hallway and kills a two-man patrol team. He tears the uniform off one of them and then, with stiffened, clawlike fingers, pulls gobbets of meat off the man's bones and swallows them. The blood is salty and hot. His stomach convulses at what he is doing—the old, terrible sin—but he forces himself to chew and swallow. He has no choice.

*Addiction a problem? Not with a NeoBlood transfusion! We also feature the finest life-tested and artificial organs...*

He can tell by the sputtering messages on the guards' communicators that the security personnel are spreading out from the main guardroom. They seem to have an idea of where he has been and where he now is. When he has finished his terrible meal he leaves the residue on the floor of the closet and then makes his way toward the central security office, leaving red footprints behind him. He looks, he feels sure, like a demon from the deepest floors of Hell.

The guards make the mistake of coming out of their hardened room, thinking numbers and weaponry are on their side. Kane takes several bullet wounds but they have nothing as terrible as the scrambling device which captured him in the first place and he moves through his enemies like a whirlwind, snapping out blows of such strength that one guard's head is knocked from his shoulders and tumbles down the hall.

Once he has waded through the bodies into the main communication room, he throws open as many of the prison cells as he can and turns on the escape and fire alarms, which howl like the damned. He waits until the chaos is ripe, then pulls on a guard's uniform and heads for the exercise yard. He hurries through the shrieking, bloody confusion of the yard, then climbs over the three sets of razor-wire fencing. Several bullets smack into his hardened flesh, burning like hot rivets. A beam weapon scythes across the last fence with a hiss and pop of snapping wire, but Kane has already dropped to the ground outside.

He can run about fifty miles an hour under most circumstances, but fueled with adrenaline he can go almost half again that fast for short bursts. The only problem is that he is traveling over open, wild ground and has to watch for obstacles—even he can badly injure an ankle at this speed because he cannot armor his joints too much without losing flexibility. Also, he is so exhausted and empty even after consuming the guard's flesh that black spots caper in front of his eyes: he will not be able to keep up this pace very long.

*Here are some wise words from an ancient statesman to consider: "You can do what you have to do, and sometimes you can do it even better than you think you can."*

*Kids, all parents can make mistakes. How about yours? Report religious paraphernalia or overly superstitious behavior on your local Freedom Council tip node...*

*Your body temperature is far above normal. Your stress levels are far above normal. We recommend you see a physician immediately.*

Yes, Kane thinks. *I believe I'll do just that.*

He finds an empty house within five miles of the prison and breaks in. He eats everything he can find, including several pounds of frozen meat, which helps him compensate for a little of the heat he is generating. He then rummages through the upstairs bedrooms until he finds some new clothes to wear, scrubs off the blood that marks him out, and leaves.

He finds another place some miles away to hide for the night. The residents are home—he even hears them listening to news of his escape, although it is a grossly inaccurate version that concentrates breathlessly on his cannibalism and his terrifying nickname. He lays curled in a box in their attic like a mummy, nearly comatose. When they leave in the morning, so does Kane, reshaping the bones of his face and withdrawing color from his hair. The pagan seed still chirps in his head. Every few minutes it reminds him to keep an eye open for himself, but not to approach himself, because he is undoubtedly very, very dangerous.

———————

"Didn't know anything about it." Sartorius looks worriedly up and down the road to make sure they are alone, as if Kane hadn't already done that better, faster, and more carefully long before the two locals had arrived at the rendezvous. "What can I say? We didn't have any idea they had that scrambler thing. Of course we would have let you know if we'd heard."

"I need a doctor—somebody you'd trust with your life, because I'll be trusting him with mine."

"Cannibal Christian," says young Carl in an awed voice. "That's what they're calling you now."

"That's crap." He is not ashamed because he was doing God's will, but he does not want to be reminded, either.

"Or the Angel of Death, they still like that one, too. Either way, they're sure talking about you."


The doctor is a woman too, a decade or so past her child-bearing years. They wake her up in her small cottage on the edge of a blighted park that looks like it was manufacturing space before a halfway attempt to redeem it. She has alcohol on her breath and her hands shake, but her eyes, although a little bloodshot, are intelligent and alert.

"Don't bore me with your story and I won't bore you with mine," she says when Carl begins to introduce them. A moment later her pupils dilate. "Hang on—I already know yours. You're the Angel everyone's talking about."

"Some people call him the Cannibal Christian," says young Carl helpfully.

"Are you a believer?" Kane asks her.

"I'm too flawed to be anything else. Who else but Jesus would keep forgiving me?"

She lays him out on a bed sheet on her kitchen table. He waves away both the anesthetic inhaler and the bottle of liquor.

"They won't work on me unless I let them, and I can't afford to let them work. I have to stay alert. Now please, cut that godless thing out of my head. Do you have a Spirit you can put in?"

"Beg pardon?" She straightens up, the scalpel already bloody from the incision he is doing his best to ignore.

"What do you call it here? My kind of seed, a seed of Covenant. So I can hear the voice of Spirit again..."

As if to protest its own pending removal, the Archimedes seed abruptly fills his skull with a crackle of interference.

A bad sign, Kane thinks. He must be overworking his internal systems. When he finishes here he'll need several days rest before he decides what to do next.

"Sorry," he tells the doctor. "I didn't hear you. What did you say?"

She shrugs. "I said I'd have to see what I have. One of your people died on this very table a few years ago, I'm sad to say, despite everything I did to save him. I think I kept his communication seed." She waves her hand a little, as though such things happen or fail to happen every day. "Who knows? I'll have a look."

He cannot let himself hope too much. Even if she has it, what are the odds that it will work, and even more unlikely, that it will work here on Archimedes? There are booster stations on all the other colony worlds like Arjuna where the Word is allowed to compete freely with the lies of the Godless.

The latest crackle in his head resolves into a calm, sweetly reasonable voice. ...*No less a philosopher than Aristotle himself said, "Men create gods after their own image, not only with regard to their form, but with regard to their mode of life."*

Kane forces himself to open his eyes. The room is blurry, the doctor a faint shadowy shape bending over him. Something sharp probes in his neck.

"There it is," she says. "It's going to hurt a bit coming out. What's your name? Your real name?"

"Lamentation."

"Ah." She doesn't smile, at least he doesn't think she does—it's hard for him to make out her features—but she sounds amused. "'*She weepeth sore in the night, and her tears are on her cheeks: among all her lovers she hath none to comfort her: all her friends have dealt treacherously with her, they are become her enemies.*' That's Jerusalem they're talking about," the doctor adds. "The original one."

"Book of Lamentations," he says quietly. The pain is so fierce that it's all he can do not to reach up and grab the hand that holds the probing, insupportable instrument. At times like this, when he most needs to restrain himself, he can most clearly feel his strength. If he were to lose control and loose that unfettered power, he feels that he could blaze like one of the stellar torches in heaven's great vault, that he could destroy an entire world.

"Hey," says a voice in the darkness beyond the pool of light on the kitchen table—young Carl. "Hey. Something's going on."

"What are you talking about?" demands Sartorius. A moment later the window explodes in a shower of sparkling glass and the room fills with smoke.

Not smoke, gas. Kane springs off the table, accidentally knocking the doctor back against the wall. He gulps in enough breath to last him a quarter of an hour and flares the tissues of his pharynx to seal his air passages. If it's a nerve gas there is nothing much he can do, though—too much skin exposed.

In the corner the doctor struggles to her feet, emerging from the billows on the floor with her mouth wide and working but nothing coming out. It isn't just her. Carl and Sartorius are holding their breath as they shove furniture against the door as a makeshift barricade. The bigger, older man already has a gun in his hand. Why is it so quiet outside? What are they doing out there?

The answer comes with a stuttering roar. Small arms fire suddenly fills the kitchen wall with holes. The doctor throws up her hands and begins a terrible jig, as though she is being stitched by an invisible sewing machine. When she falls to the ground it is in pieces.

Young Carl stretches motionless on the floor in a pool of his own spreading blood and brains. Sartorius is still standing unsteadily, but red bubbles through his clothing in several places.

Kane is on the ground—he has dropped without realizing it. He does not stop to consider near-certainty of failure, but instead springs to the ceiling and digs his fingers in long enough to smash his way through with the other hand, then hunkers in the crawlspace until the first team of troopers come in to check the damage, flashlights darting through the fog of gas fumes. How did they find him so quickly? More importantly, what have they brought to use against him?

Speed is his best weapon. He climbs out through the vent. He has to widen it, and the splintering brings a fusillade from below. When he reaches the roof dozens of shots crack past him and two actually hit him, one in the arm and one in the back, these from the parked security vehicles where the rest of the invasion team are waiting for the first wave to signal them inside. The shock waves travel through him so that he shakes like a wet dog. A moment later, as he suspected, they deploy the scrambler. This time, though, he is ready: he saturates his neurons with calcium to deaden the electromagnetic surge, and although his own brain activity ceases for a moment and he drops bonelessly across the roofcrest, there is no damage. A few seconds later he is up again. Their best weapon spent, the soldiers have three seconds to shoot at a dark figure scrambling with incredible speed along the roofline, then Lamentation Kane jumps down into the hot tracery of their fire, sprints forward and leaps off the hood of their own vehicle and over them before they can change firing positions.

He can't make it to full speed this time—not enough rest and not enough refueling—but he can go fast enough that he has vanished into the Hellas city sewers by time the strike team can re-mobilize.

The Archimedes seed, which has been telling his enemies exactly where he is, lies behind him now, wrapped in bloody gauze somewhere in the ruins of the doctor's kitchen. Keeta Januari and her Rationalists will learn much about the ability of the Covenant scientists to manufacture imitations of Archimedes technology, but they will not learn anything more about Kane. Not from the seed. He is free of it now.

He emerges almost a full day later from a pumping station on the outskirts of one of Hellas City's suburbs, but now he is a different Kane entirely, a Kane never before seen. Although the doctor removed the Archimedes seed, she had no time to locate, let alone implant, a Spirit device in its place: for the first time in as long as he can remember his thoughts are entirely his own, his head empty of any other voices.

The solitude is terrifying.

He makes his way up into the hills west of the great city, hiding in the daytime, moving cautiously by night because so many of the rural residents have elaborate security systems or animals who can smell Kane even before he can smell them. At last he finds an untended property. He could break in easily, but instead extrudes one of his fingernails and hardens it to pick the lock. He wants to minimize his presence whenever possible—he needs time to think, to plan. The ceiling has been lifted off his world and he is confused.

For safety's sake, he spends the first two days exploring his new hiding place only at night, with the lights out and his pupils dilated so far that even the sudden appearance of a white piece of paper in front of him is painful. From what he can tell, the small, modern house belongs to a man traveling for a month on the eastern side of the continent. The owner has been gone only a week, which gives Kane ample time to rest and think about what he is going to do next.

The first thing he has to get used to is the silence in his head. All his life since he was a tiny, unknowing child, Spirit has spoken to him. Now he cannot hear her calm, inspiring voice. The godless prattle of Archimedes is silenced, too. There is nothing and no one to share Kane's thoughts.

He cries that first night as he cried in the whore's room, like a lost child. He is a ghost. He is no longer human. He has lost his inner guide, he has botched his mission, he has failed his God and his people. He has eaten the flesh of his own kind, and for nothing.

Lamentation Kane is alone with his great sin.


He moves on before the owner of the house returns. He knows he could kill the man and stay for many more months, but it seems time to do things differently, although Kane can't say precisely why. He can't even say for certain what things he is going to do. He still owes God the death of Prime Minister Januari, but something seems to have changed inside him and he is in no hurry to fulfill that promise. The silence in his head, at first so frightening, has begun to seem something more. Holy, perhaps, but certainly different than anything he has experienced before, as though every moment is a waking dream.

No, it is more like waking up from a dream. But what kind of dream has he escaped, a good one or a bad one? And what will replace it?

Even without Spirit's prompting, he remembers Christ's words: *You shall know the truth, and the truth shall set you free.* In his new inner silence, the ancient promise seems to have many meanings. Does Kane really want the truth? Could he stand to be truly free?

Before he leaves the house he takes the owner's second-best camping equipment, the things the man left behind. Kane will live in the wild areas in the highest parts of the hills for as long as seems right. He will think. It is possible that he will leave Lamentation Kane there behind him when he comes out again. He may leave the Angel of Death behind as well.

What will remain? And who will such a new sort of creature serve? The angels, the devils...or just itself?

Kane will be interested to find out.

**Tad Williams** is an internationally bestselling fantasy and science fiction author whose work includes *Tailchaser's Song*, *The War of the Flowers*, and the *Memory, Sorrow, and Thorn*; *Shadowmarch*; and *Otherland* series. He is also the author of a miniseries called *The Next*, published by DC Comics. *Tailchaser's Song* is currently being adapted as a CG-animated feature film from Animetropolis and International Digital Artists. His recent projects include the Bobby Dollar series and the Ordinary Farm Adventures (co-written with Deborah Beale). Before finding success as an author, Williams held numerous odd jobs, including insurance salesman, radio host, laying tiles, and several years in a rock band called Idiot. He lives in Soquel, California, with (his co-conspirator) author and editor Deborah Beale, two children, and a menagerie of high-energy beasts.